CAT'S CRADLE

THE GOLDEN TWINE

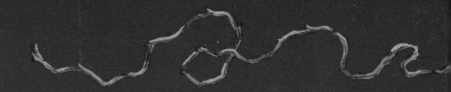

CAT'S CRADLE

THE GOLDEN TWINE

JO RIOUX

:01

First Second
NEW YORK

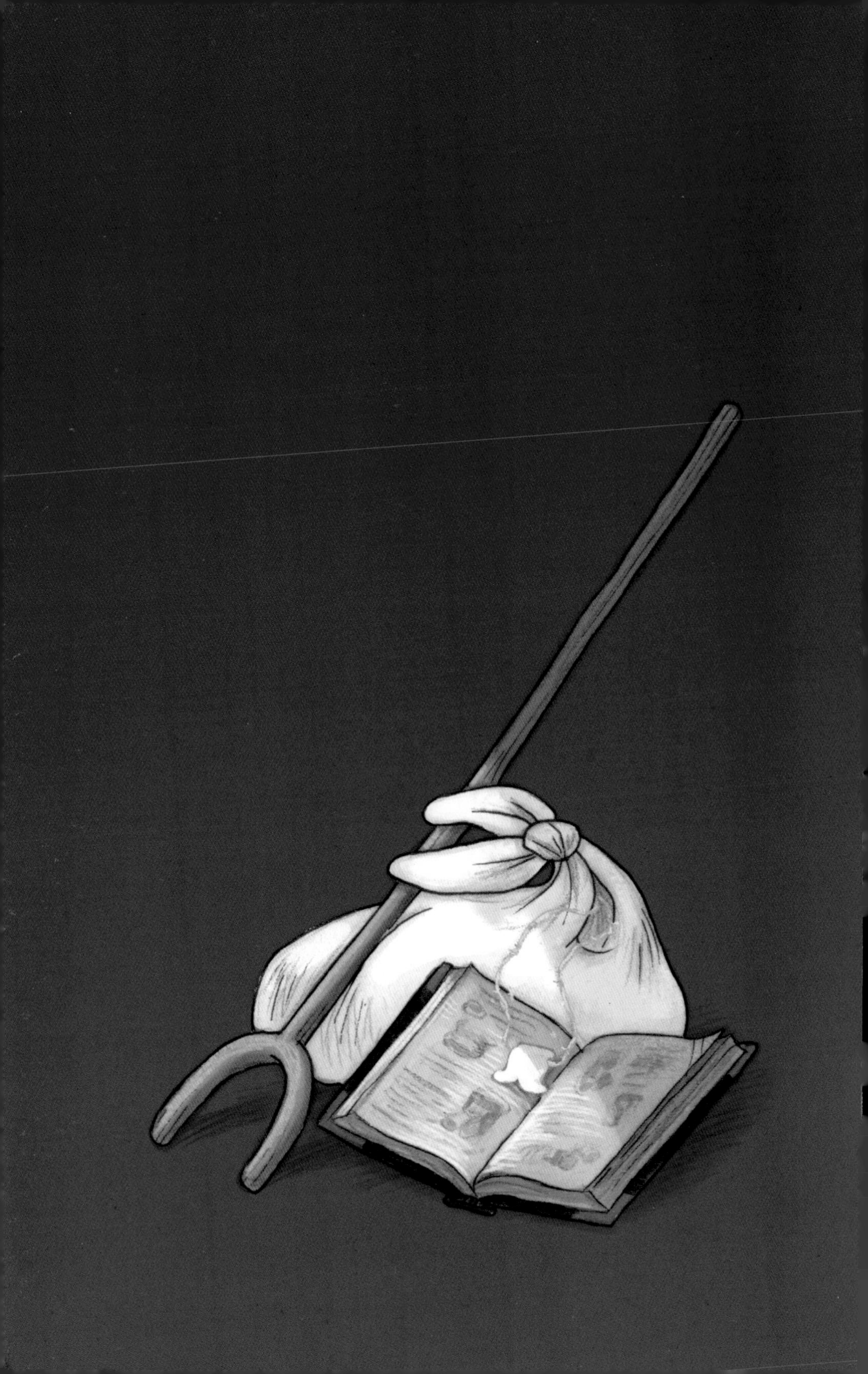

TO KEITH,
FOR ALWAYS BELIEVING IN ME

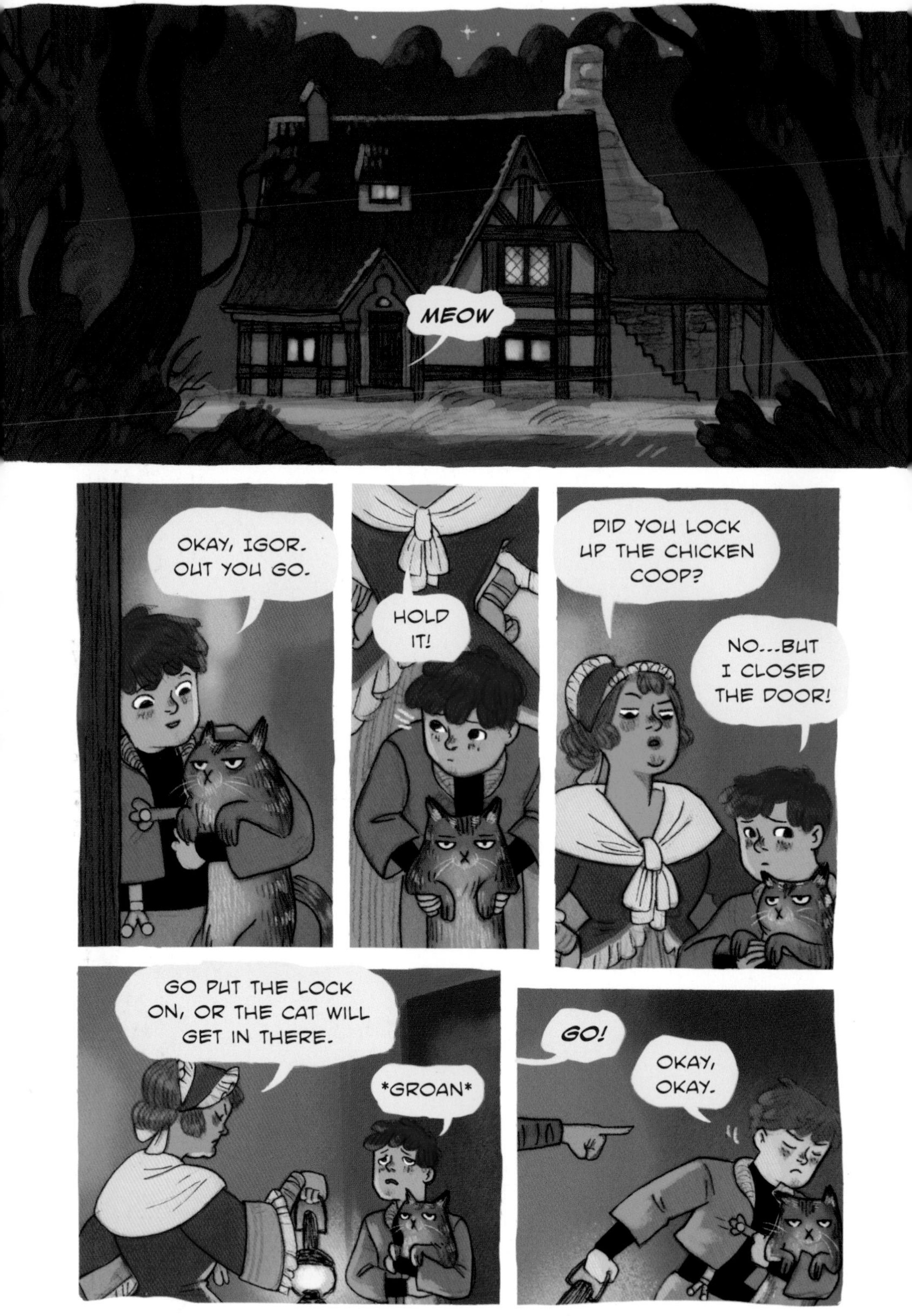
MEOW
OKAY, IGOR. OUT YOU GO.
HOLD IT!
DID YOU LOCK UP THE CHICKEN COOP?
NO...BUT I CLOSED THE DOOR!
GO PUT THE LOCK ON, OR THE CAT WILL GET IN THERE.
GROAN
GO!
OKAY, OKAY.

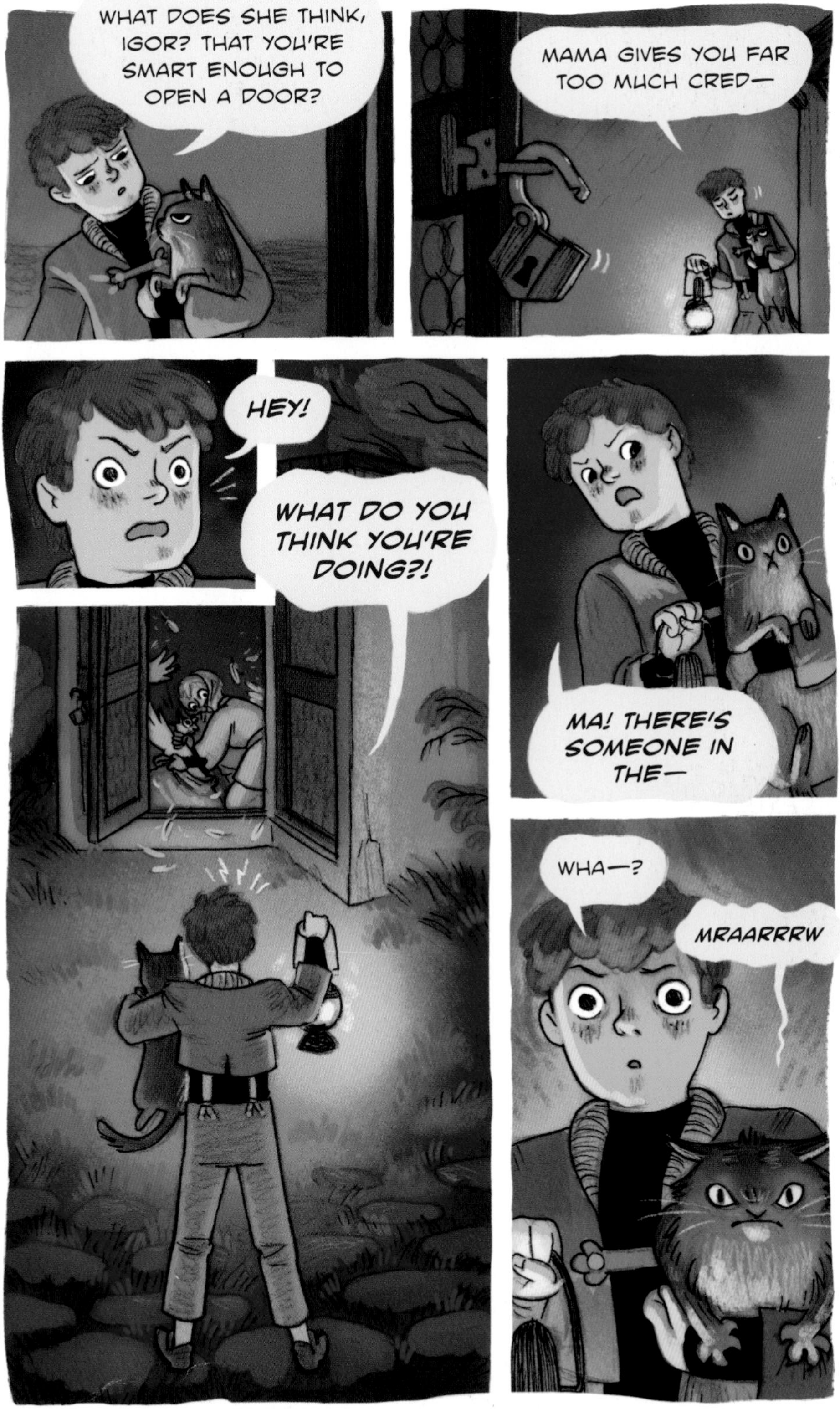
WHAT DOES SHE THINK, IGOR? THAT YOU'RE SMART ENOUGH TO OPEN A DOOR?
MAMA GIVES YOU FAR TOO MUCH CRED—
HEY!
WHAT DO YOU THINK YOU'RE DOING?!
MA! THERE'S SOMEONE IN THE—
WHA—?
MRAARRRW

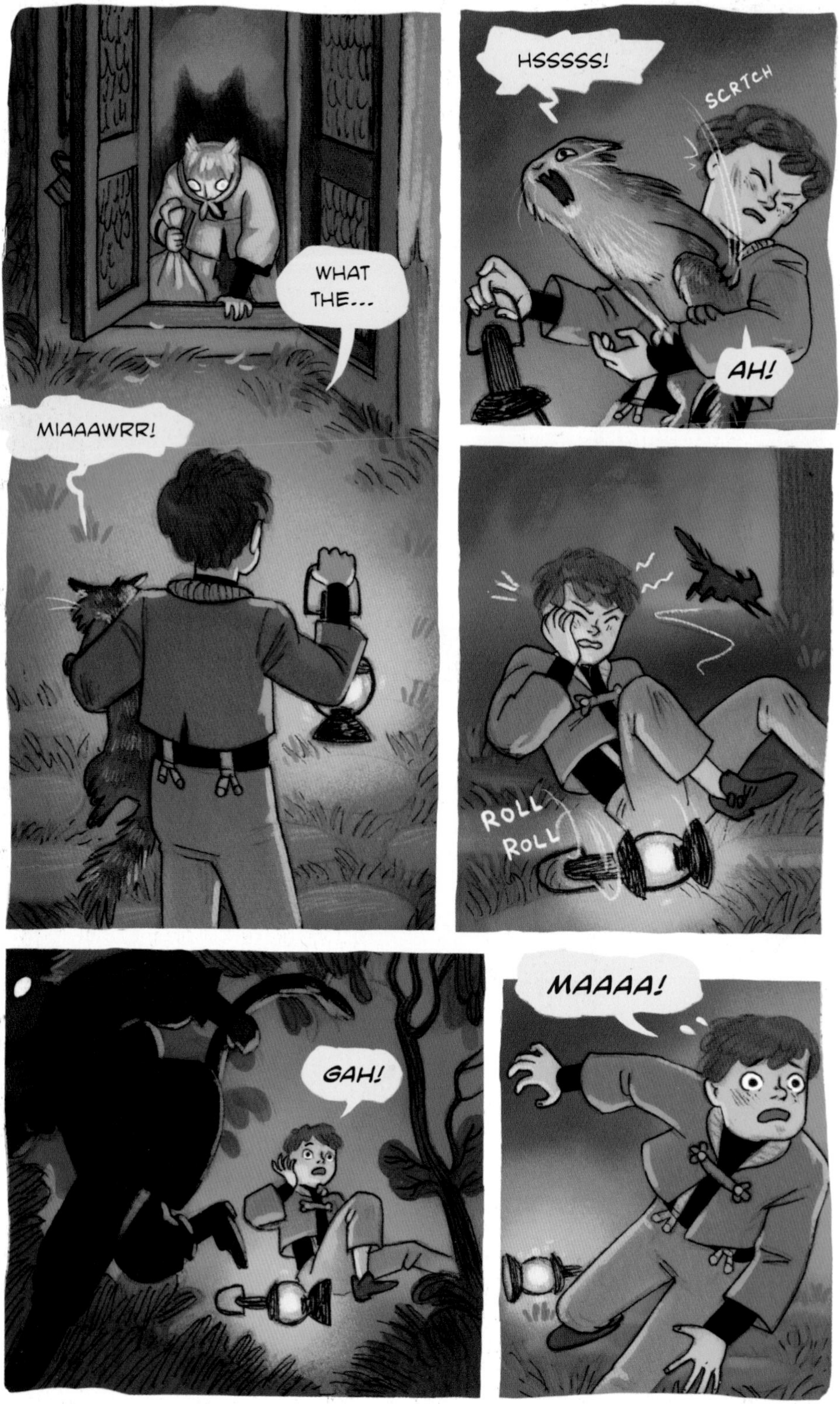
WHAT THE...
MIAAAWRR!
HSSSSS!
SCRTCH
AH!
ROLL
ROLL
GAH!
MAAAA!

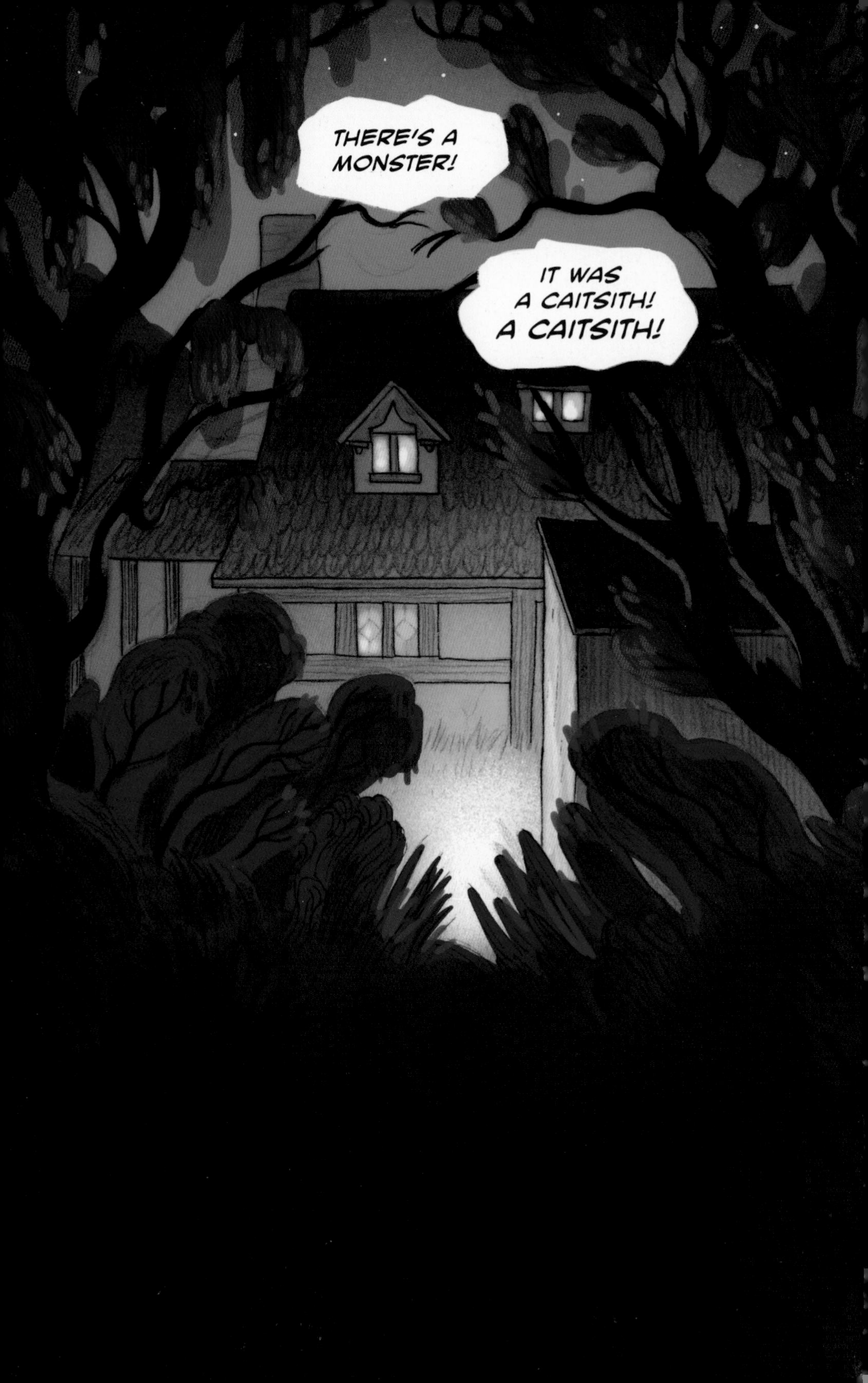
THERE'S A MONSTER!
IT WAS A CAITSITH! A CAITSITH!

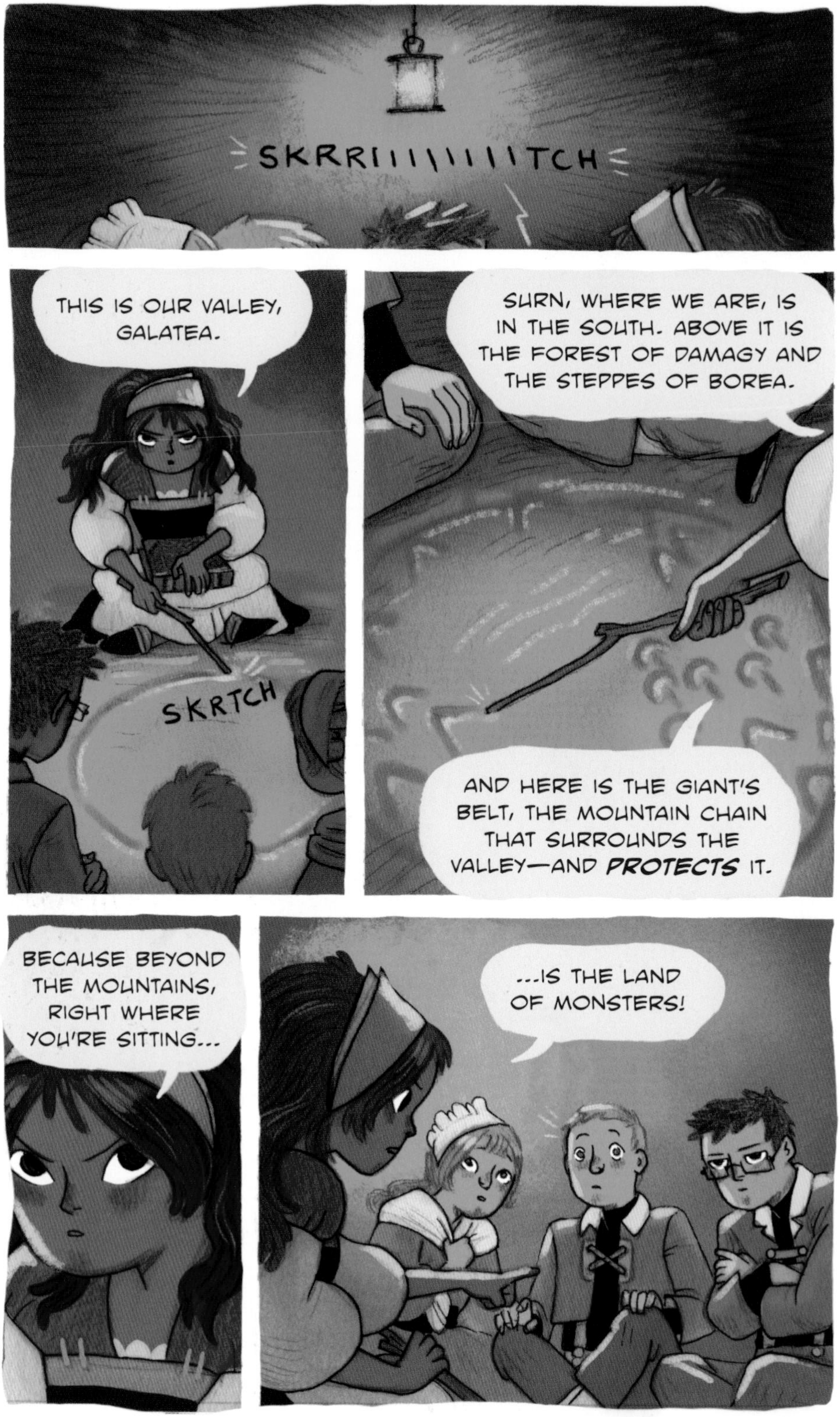
SKRRIIIIIIIIIITCH
THIS IS OUR VALLEY, GALATEA.
SKRTCH
SURN, WHERE WE ARE, IS IN THE SOUTH. ABOVE IT IS THE FOREST OF DAMAGY AND THE STEPPES OF BOREA.
AND HERE IS THE GIANT'S BELT, THE MOUNTAIN CHAIN THAT SURROUNDS THE VALLEY—AND ***PROTECTS*** IT.
BECAUSE BEYOND THE MOUNTAINS, RIGHT WHERE YOU'RE SITTING...
...IS THE LAND OF MONSTERS!

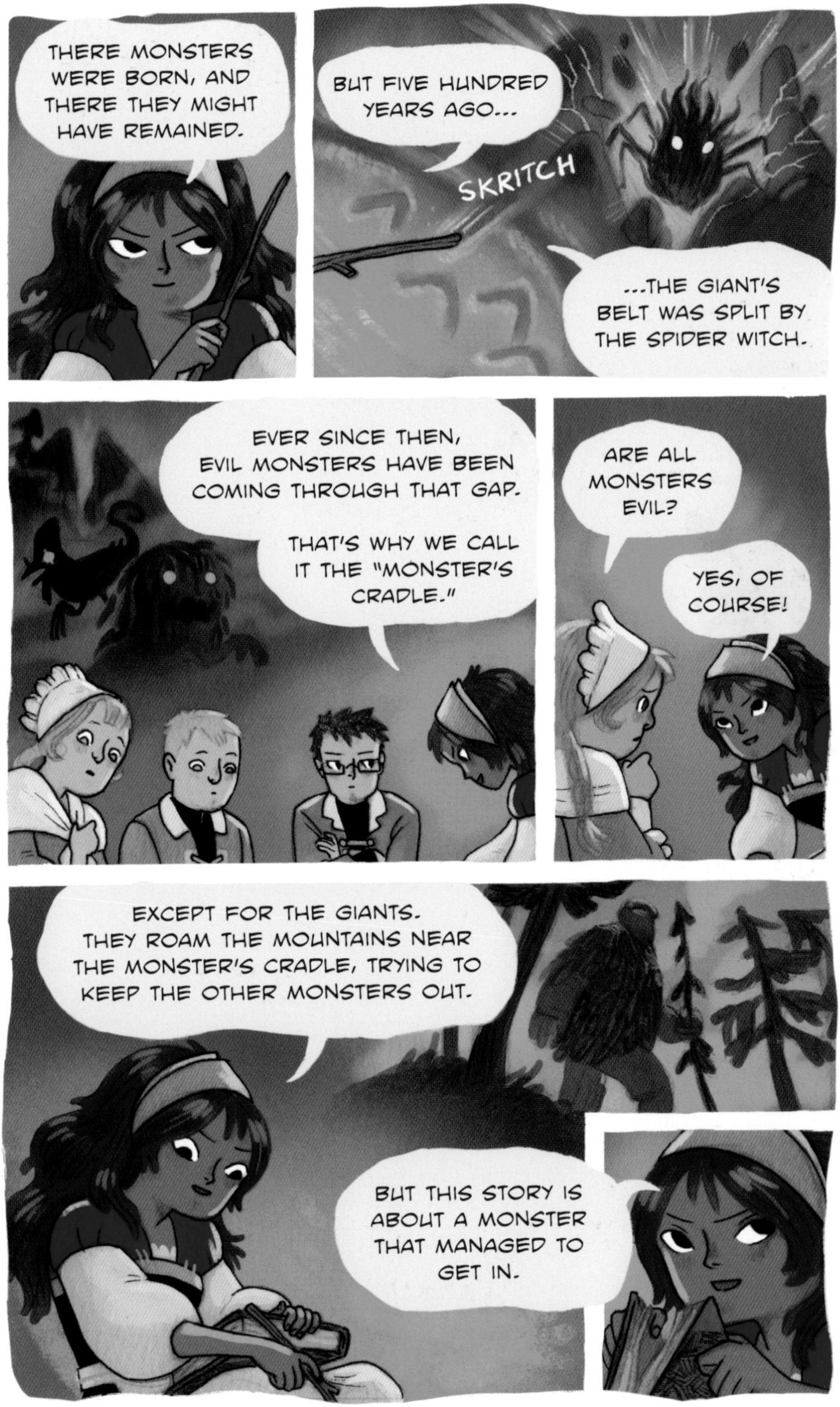
THERE MONSTERS WERE BORN, AND THERE THEY MIGHT HAVE REMAINED.
BUT FIVE HUNDRED YEARS AGO...
SKRITCH
...THE GIANT'S BELT WAS SPLIT BY THE SPIDER WITCH.
EVER SINCE THEN, EVIL MONSTERS HAVE BEEN COMING THROUGH THAT GAP.
THAT'S WHY WE CALL IT THE "MONSTER'S CRADLE."
ARE ALL MONSTERS EVIL?
YES, OF COURSE!
EXCEPT FOR THE GIANTS. THEY ROAM THE MOUNTAINS NEAR THE MONSTER'S CRADLE, TRYING TO KEEP THE OTHER MONSTERS OUT.
BUT THIS STORY IS ABOUT A MONSTER THAT MANAGED TO GET IN.

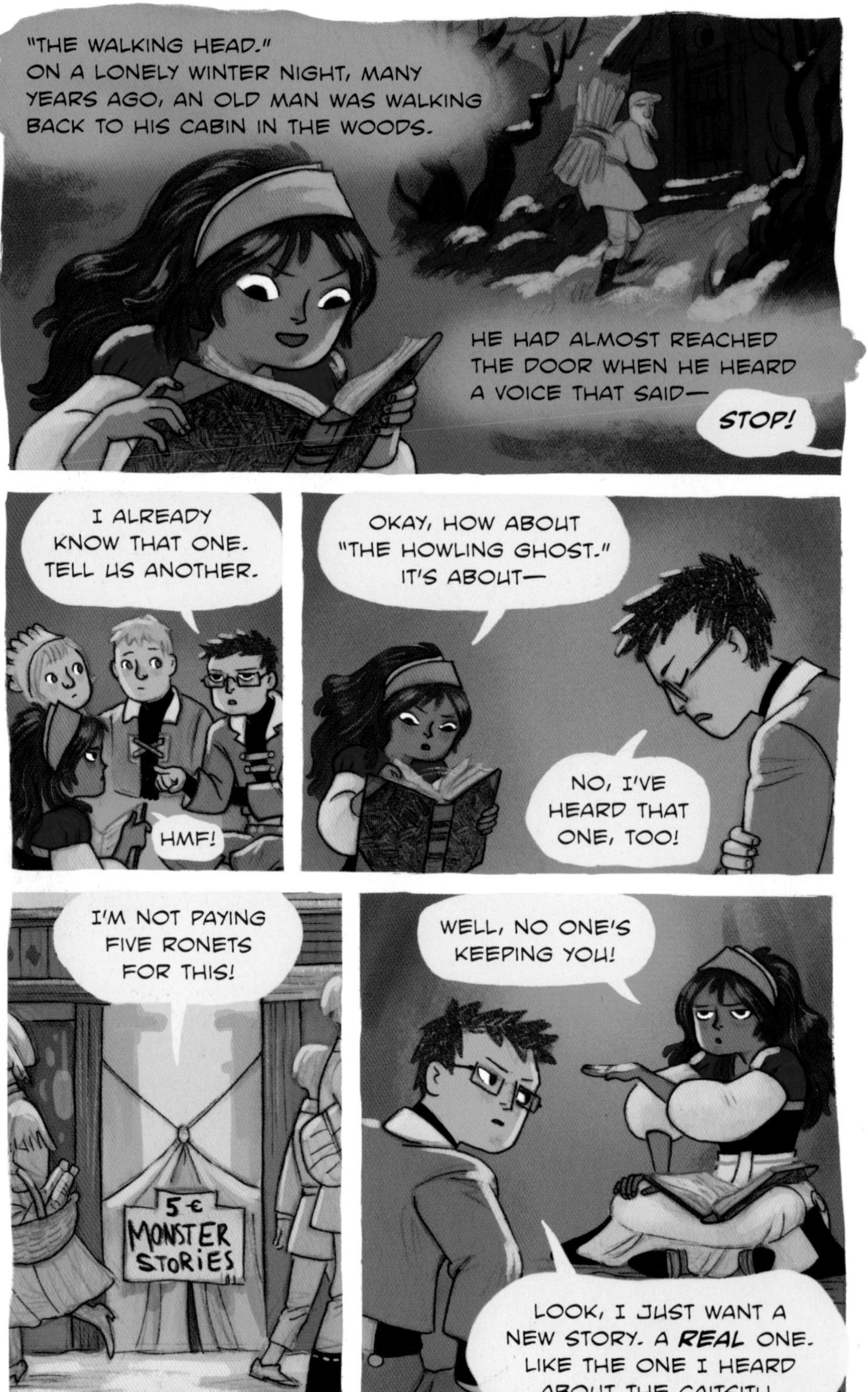
"THE WALKING HEAD."
ON A LONELY WINTER NIGHT, MANY YEARS AGO, AN OLD MAN WAS WALKING BACK TO HIS CABIN IN THE WOODS.
HE HAD ALMOST REACHED THE DOOR WHEN HE HEARD A VOICE THAT SAID—
STOP!
I ALREADY KNOW THAT ONE. TELL US ANOTHER.
HMF!
OKAY, HOW ABOUT "THE HOWLING GHOST." IT'S ABOUT—
NO, I'VE HEARD THAT ONE, TOO!
I'M NOT PAYING FIVE RONETS FOR THIS!
5 €
MONSTER STORIES
WELL, NO ONE'S KEEPING YOU!
LOOK, I JUST WANT A NEW STORY. A **REAL** ONE. LIKE THE ONE I HEARD ABOUT THE CAITSITH.

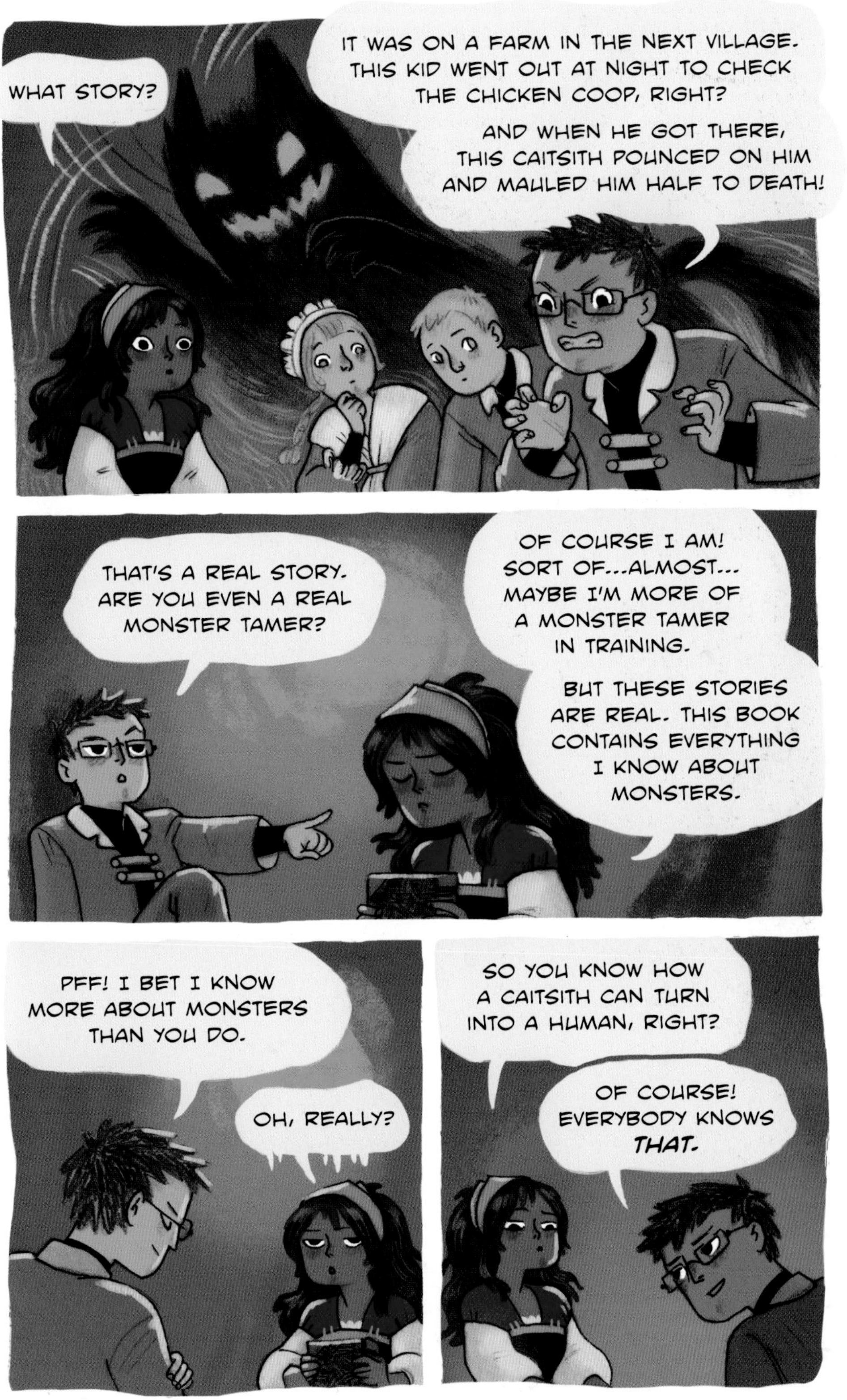
WHAT STORY?
IT WAS ON A FARM IN THE NEXT VILLAGE. THIS KID WENT OUT AT NIGHT TO CHECK THE CHICKEN COOP, RIGHT?
AND WHEN HE GOT THERE, THIS CAITSITH POUNCED ON HIM AND MAULED HIM HALF TO DEATH!
THAT'S A REAL STORY. ARE YOU EVEN A REAL MONSTER TAMER?
OF COURSE I AM! SORT OF...ALMOST... MAYBE I'M MORE OF A MONSTER TAMER IN TRAINING.
BUT THESE STORIES ARE REAL. THIS BOOK CONTAINS EVERYTHING I KNOW ABOUT MONSTERS.
PFF! I BET I KNOW MORE ABOUT MONSTERS THAN YOU DO.
OH, REALLY?
SO YOU KNOW HOW A CAITSITH CAN TURN INTO A HUMAN, RIGHT?
OF COURSE! EVERYBODY KNOWS *THAT*.

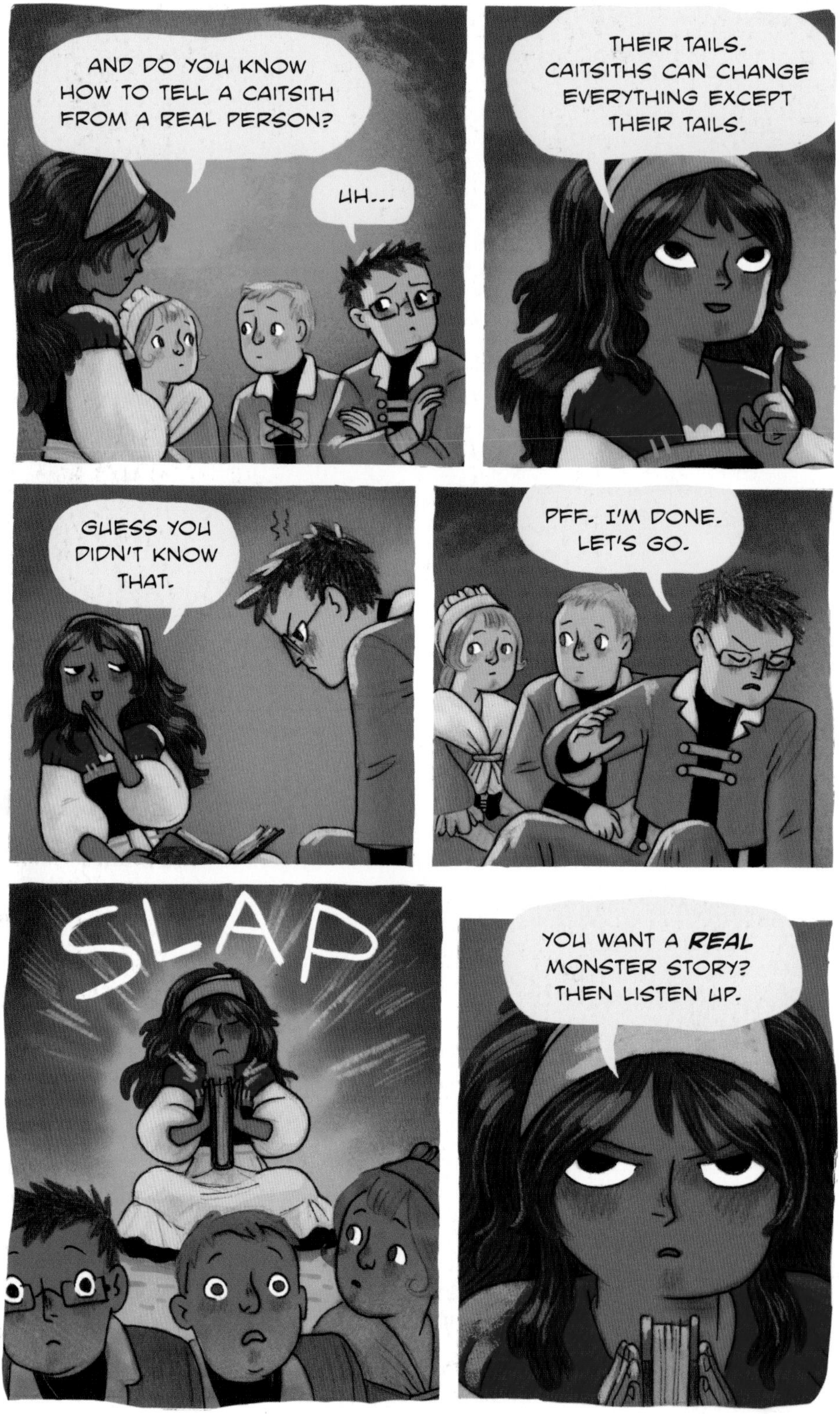
AND DO YOU KNOW HOW TO TELL A CAITSITH FROM A REAL PERSON?
UH...
THEIR TAILS. CAITSITHS CAN CHANGE EVERYTHING EXCEPT THEIR TAILS.
GUESS YOU DIDN'T KNOW THAT.
PFF. I'M DONE. LET'S GO.
SLAP
YOU WANT A ***REAL*** MONSTER STORY? THEN LISTEN UP.

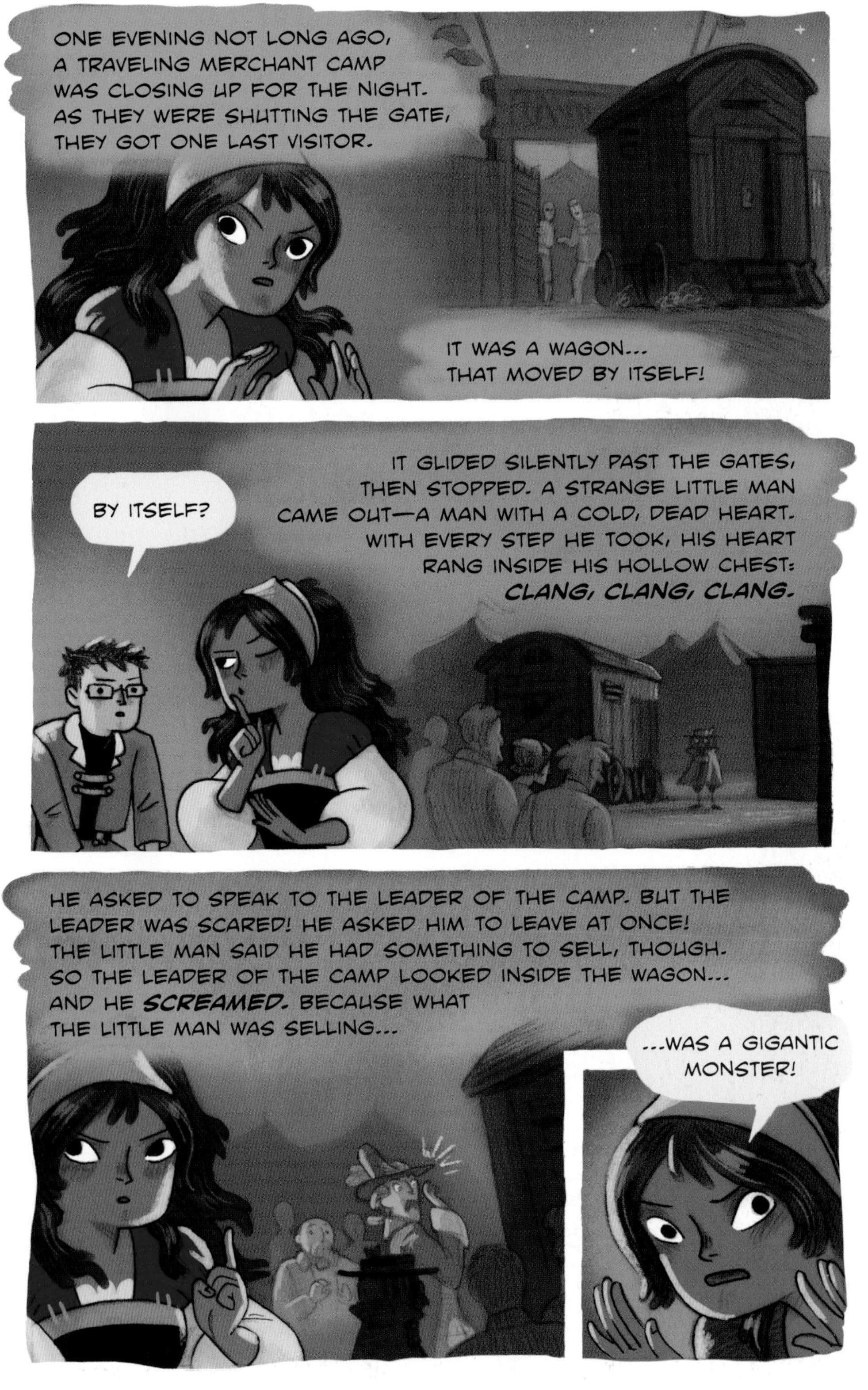
ONE EVENING NOT LONG AGO, A TRAVELING MERCHANT CAMP WAS CLOSING UP FOR THE NIGHT. AS THEY WERE SHUTTING THE GATE, THEY GOT ONE LAST VISITOR.
IT WAS A WAGON... THAT MOVED BY ITSELF!
BY ITSELF?
IT GLIDED SILENTLY PAST THE GATES, THEN STOPPED. A STRANGE LITTLE MAN CAME OUT—A MAN WITH A COLD, DEAD HEART. WITH EVERY STEP HE TOOK, HIS HEART RANG INSIDE HIS HOLLOW CHEST: *CLANG, CLANG, CLANG.*
HE ASKED TO SPEAK TO THE LEADER OF THE CAMP. BUT THE LEADER WAS SCARED! HE ASKED HIM TO LEAVE AT ONCE! THE LITTLE MAN SAID HE HAD SOMETHING TO SELL, THOUGH. SO THE LEADER OF THE CAMP LOOKED INSIDE THE WAGON... AND HE *SCREAMED.* BECAUSE WHAT THE LITTLE MAN WAS SELLING...
...WAS A GIGANTIC MONSTER!

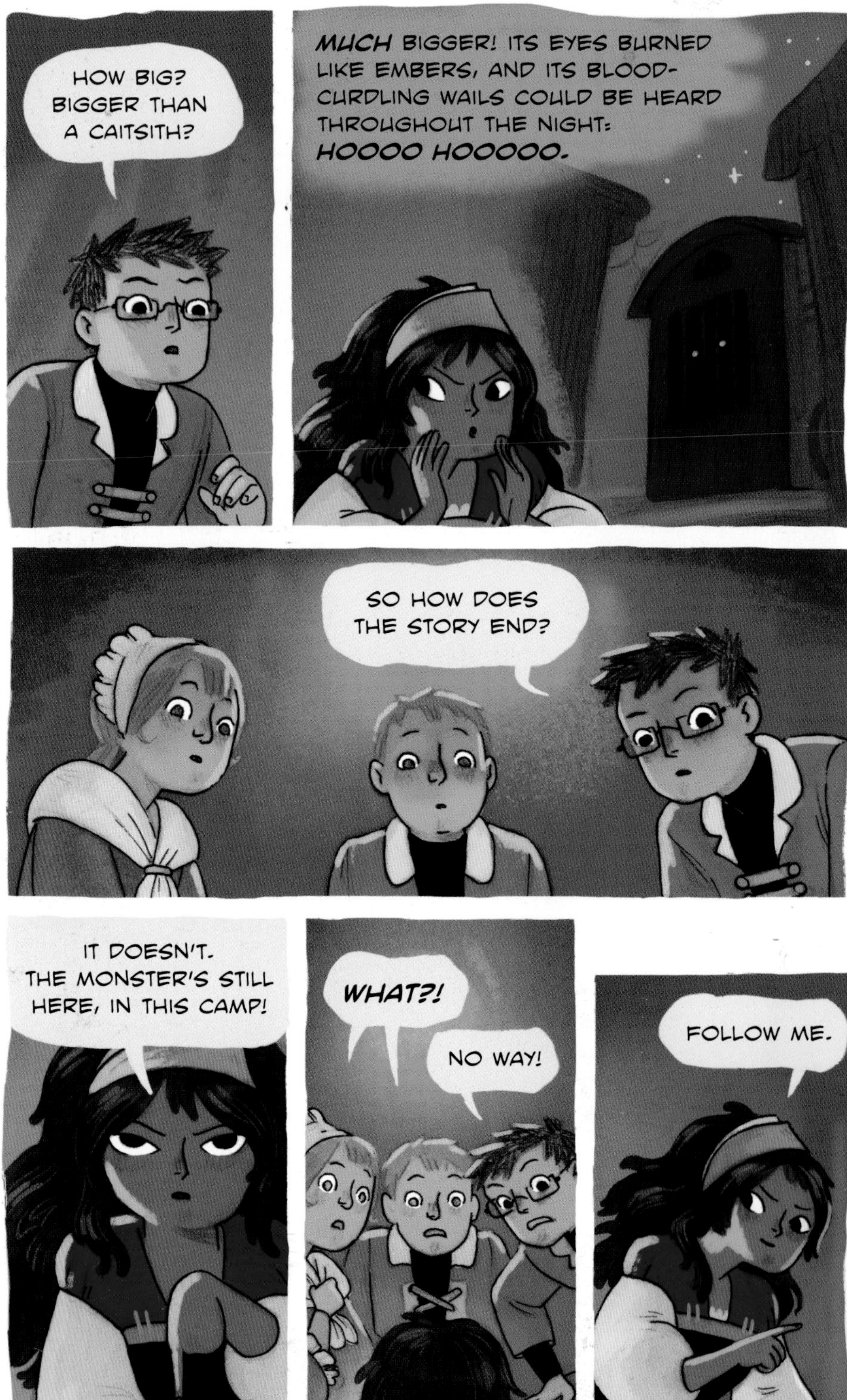
HOW BIG? BIGGER THAN A CAITSITH?
MUCH BIGGER! ITS EYES BURNED LIKE EMBERS, AND ITS BLOOD-CURDLING WAILS COULD BE HEARD THROUGHOUT THE NIGHT: HOOOO HOOOOO.
SO HOW DOES THE STORY END?
IT DOESN'T. THE MONSTER'S STILL HERE, IN THIS CAMP!
WHAT?!
NO WAY!
FOLLOW ME.

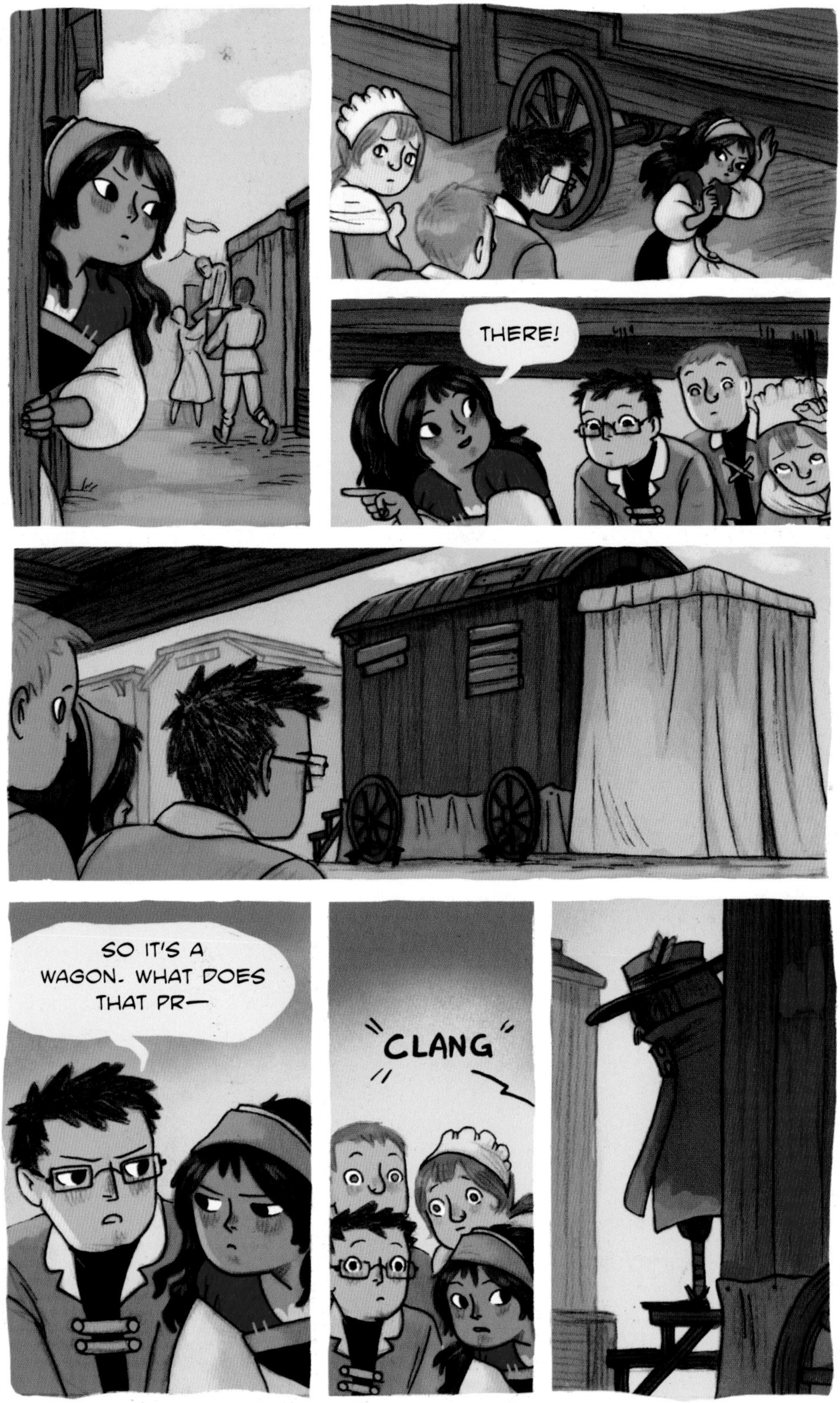
THERE!
SO IT'S A WAGON. WHAT DOES THAT PR—
CLANG

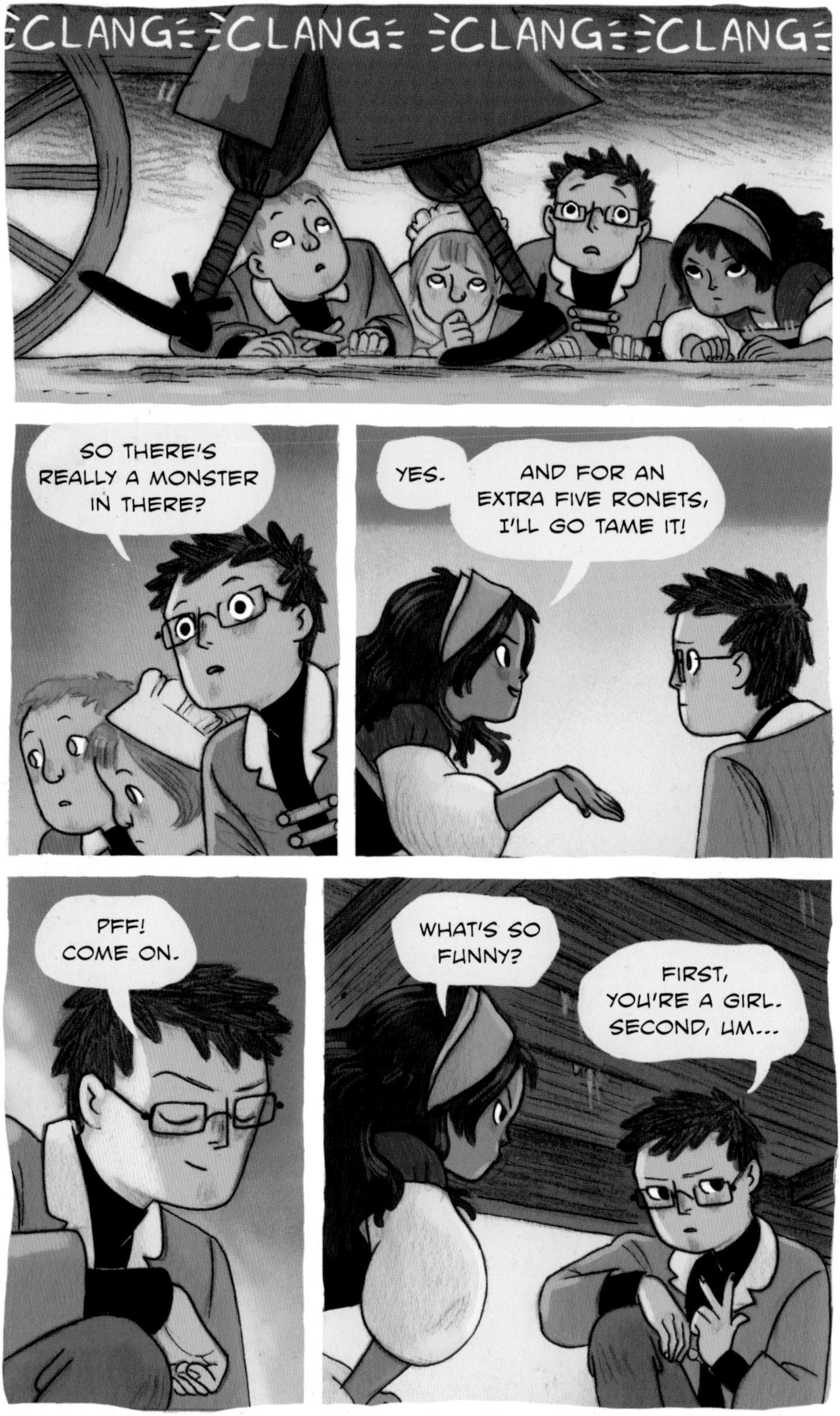
CLANG CLANG CLANG CLANG
SO THERE'S REALLY A MONSTER IN THERE?
YES.
AND FOR AN EXTRA FIVE RONETS, I'LL GO TAME IT!
PFF! COME ON.
WHAT'S SO FUNNY?
FIRST, YOU'RE A GIRL. SECOND, UM...

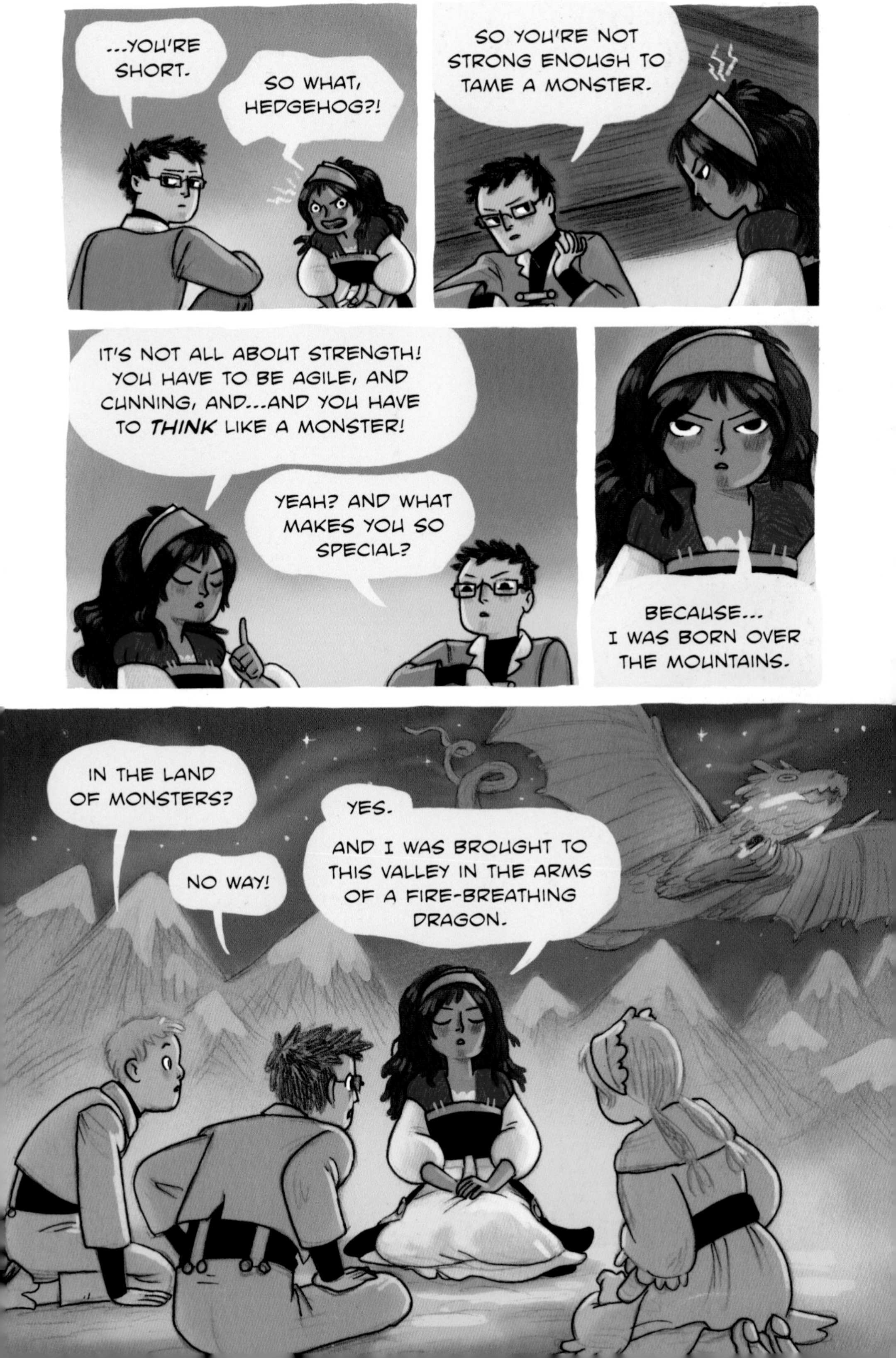
...YOU'RE SHORT.
SO WHAT, HEDGEHOG?!
SO YOU'RE NOT STRONG ENOUGH TO TAME A MONSTER.
IT'S NOT ALL ABOUT STRENGTH! YOU HAVE TO BE AGILE, AND CUNNING, AND...AND YOU HAVE TO *THINK* LIKE A MONSTER!
YEAH? AND WHAT MAKES YOU SO SPECIAL?
BECAUSE... I WAS BORN OVER THE MOUNTAINS.
IN THE LAND OF MONSTERS?
NO WAY!
YES.
AND I WAS BROUGHT TO THIS VALLEY IN THE ARMS OF A FIRE-BREATHING DRAGON.

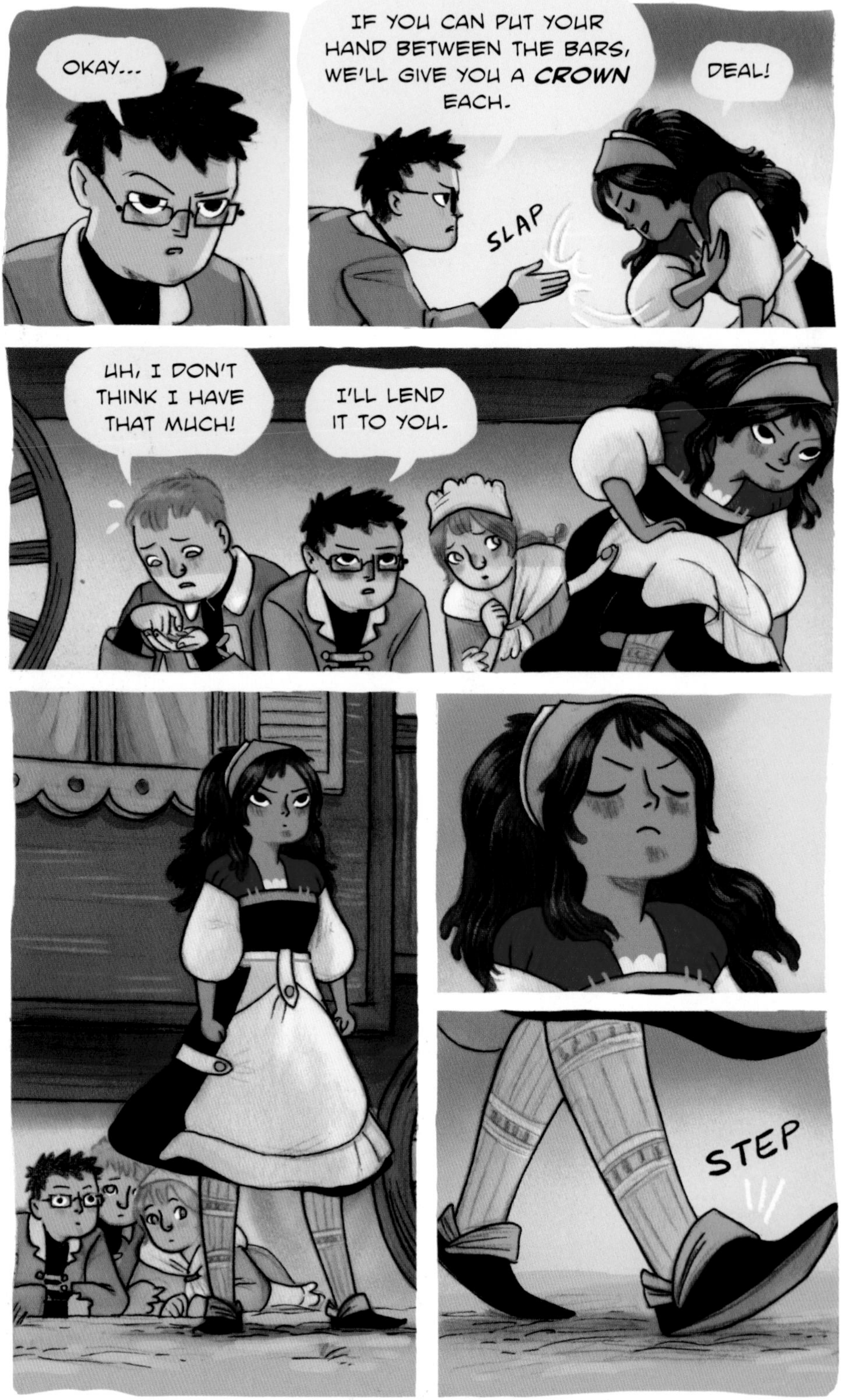
OKAY...
IF YOU CAN PUT YOUR HAND BETWEEN THE BARS, WE'LL GIVE YOU A **CROWN** EACH.
DEAL!
SLAP
UH, I DON'T THINK I HAVE THAT MUCH!
I'LL LEND IT TO YOU.
STEP

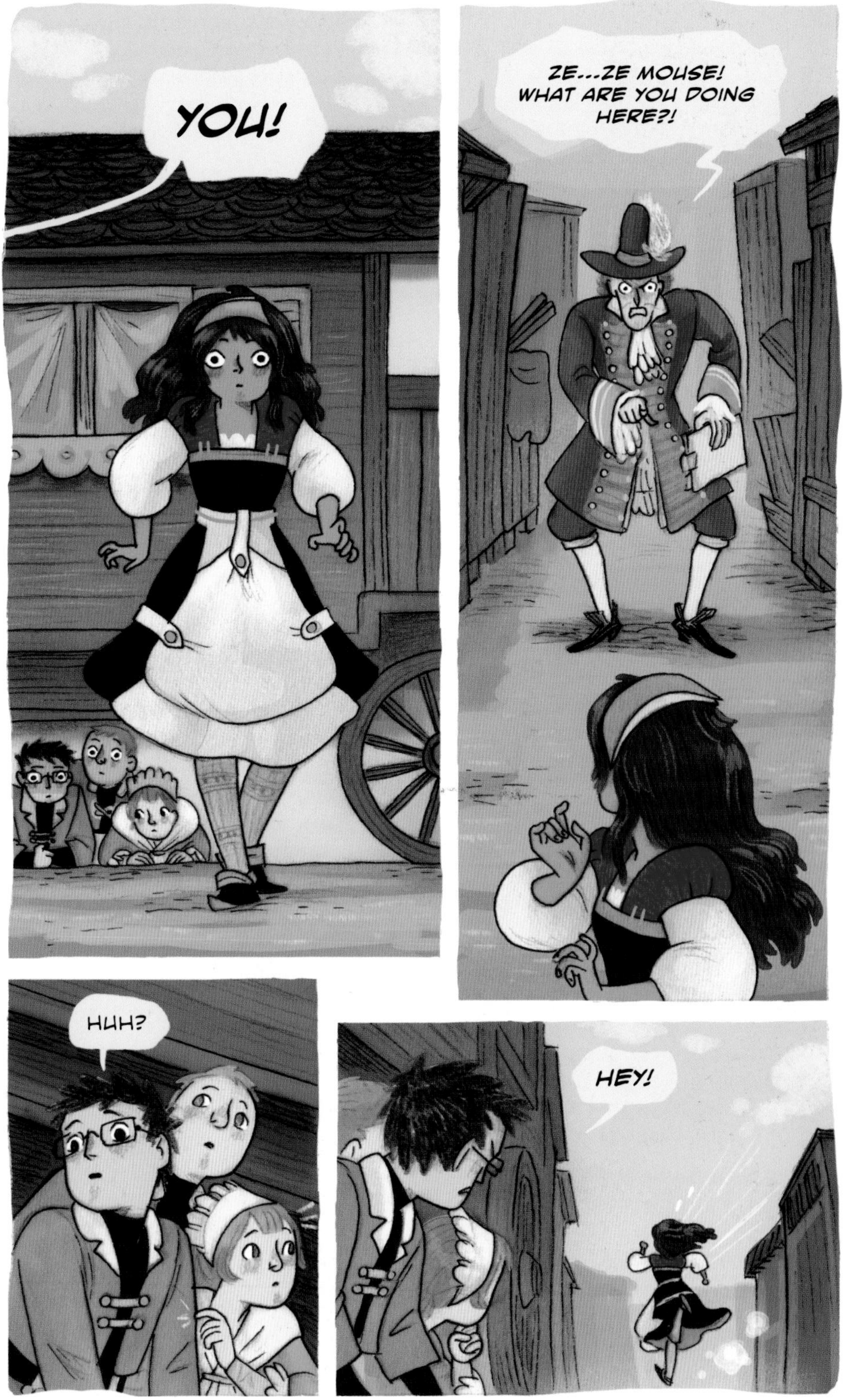
YOU!
ZE...ZE MOUSE! WHAT ARE YOU DOING HERE?!
HUH?
HEY!

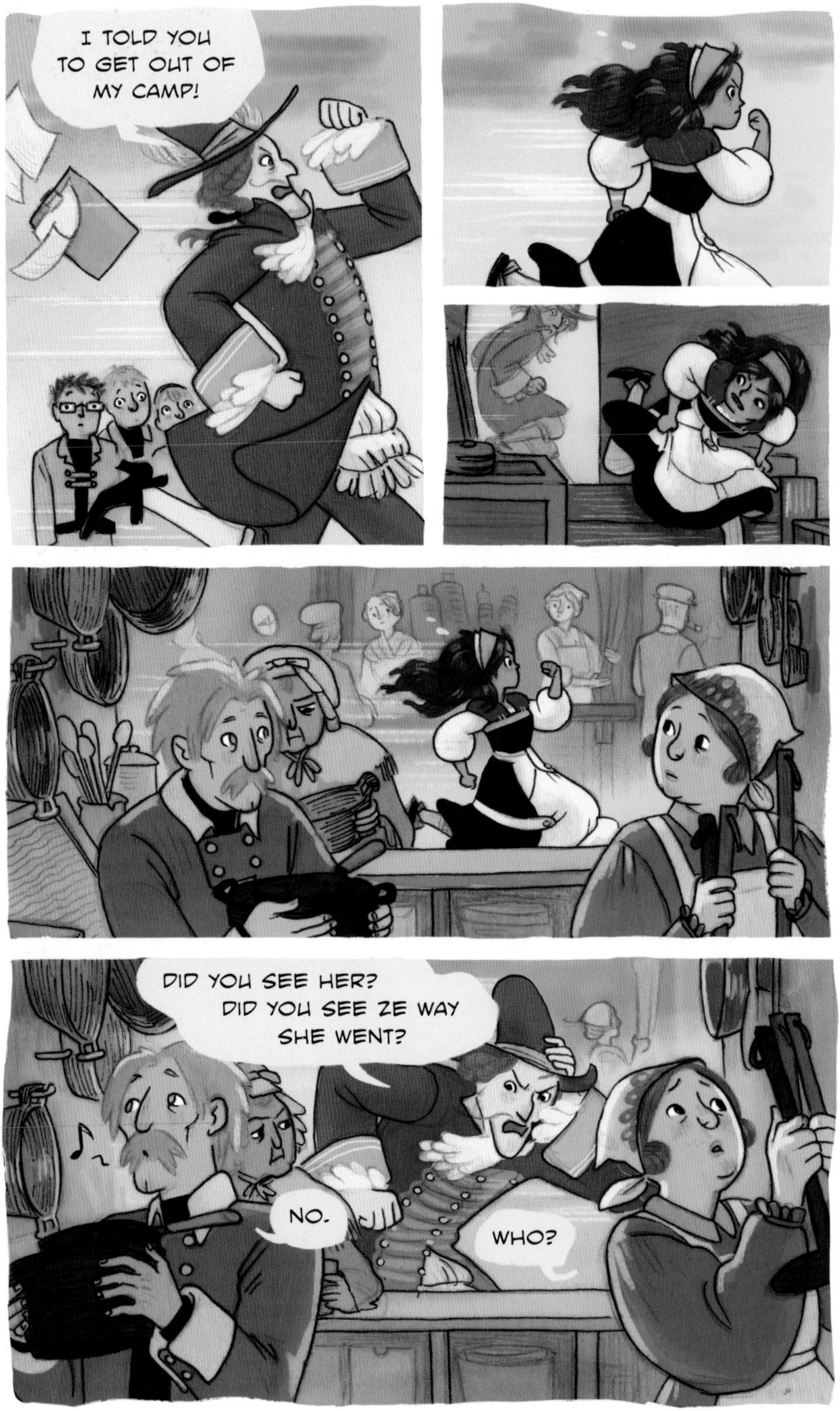
I TOLD YOU TO GET OUT OF MY CAMP!
DID YOU SEE HER? DID YOU SEE ZE WAY SHE WENT?
NO.
WHO?

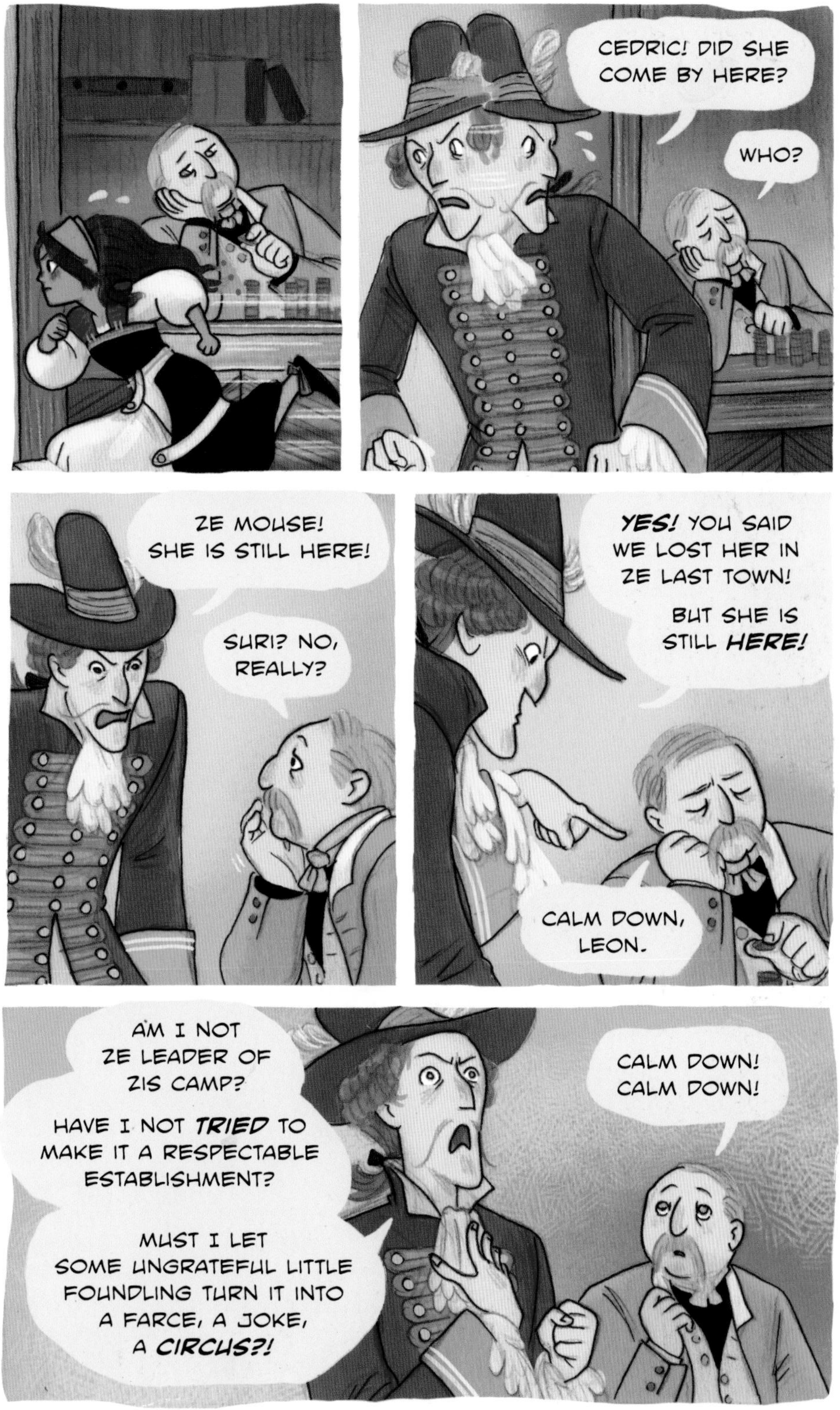
CEDRIC! DID SHE COME BY HERE?
WHO?
ZE MOUSE! SHE IS STILL HERE!
SURI? NO, REALLY?
YES! YOU SAID WE LOST HER IN ZE LAST TOWN!
BUT SHE IS STILL HERE!
CALM DOWN, LEON.
AM I NOT ZE LEADER OF ZIS CAMP?
HAVE I NOT TRIED TO MAKE IT A RESPECTABLE ESTABLISHMENT?
MUST I LET SOME UNGRATEFUL LITTLE FOUNDLING TURN IT INTO A FARCE, A JOKE, A CIRCUS?!
CALM DOWN! CALM DOWN!

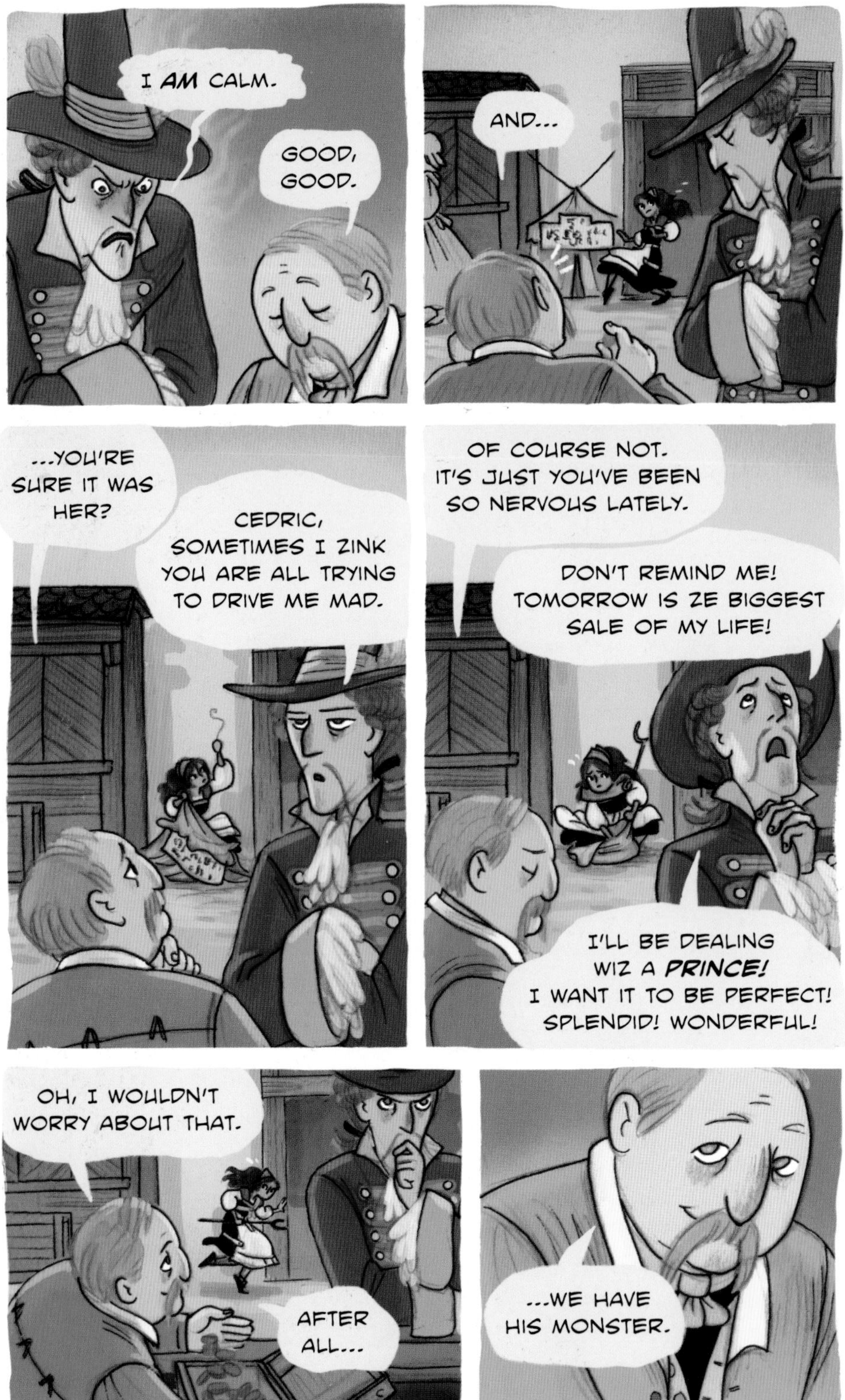
I AM CALM.
GOOD, GOOD.
AND...
...YOU'RE SURE IT WAS HER?
CEDRIC, SOMETIMES I ZINK YOU ARE ALL TRYING TO DRIVE ME MAD.
OF COURSE NOT. IT'S JUST YOU'VE BEEN SO NERVOUS LATELY.
DON'T REMIND ME! TOMORROW IS ZE BIGGEST SALE OF MY LIFE!
I'LL BE DEALING WIZ A PRINCE! I WANT IT TO BE PERFECT! SPLENDID! WONDERFUL!
OH, I WOULDN'T WORRY ABOUT THAT.
AFTER ALL...
...WE HAVE HIS MONSTER.

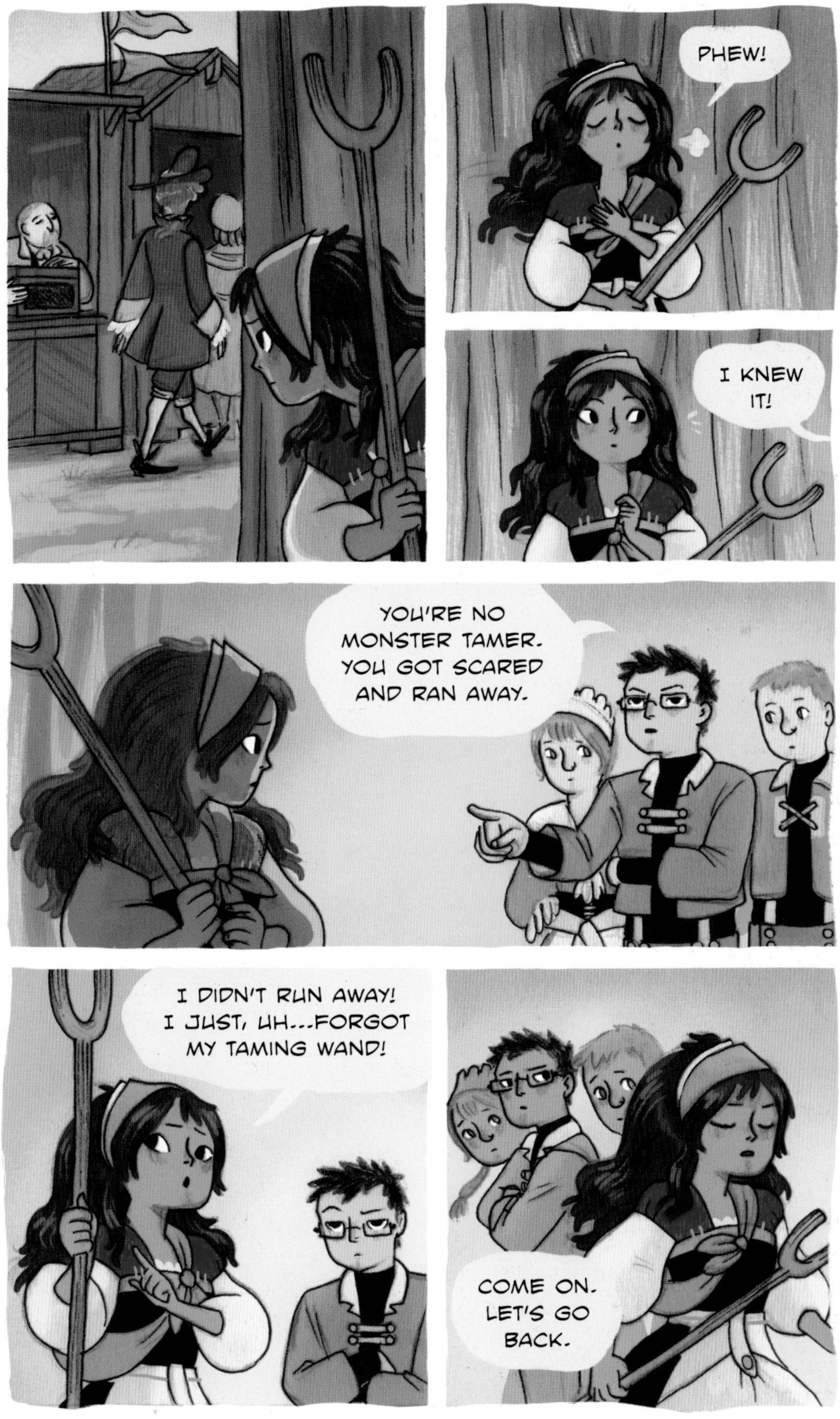
PHEW!
I KNEW IT!
YOU'RE NO MONSTER TAMER. YOU GOT SCARED AND RAN AWAY.
I DIDN'T RUN AWAY! I JUST, UH...FORGOT MY TAMING WAND!
COME ON. LET'S GO BACK.

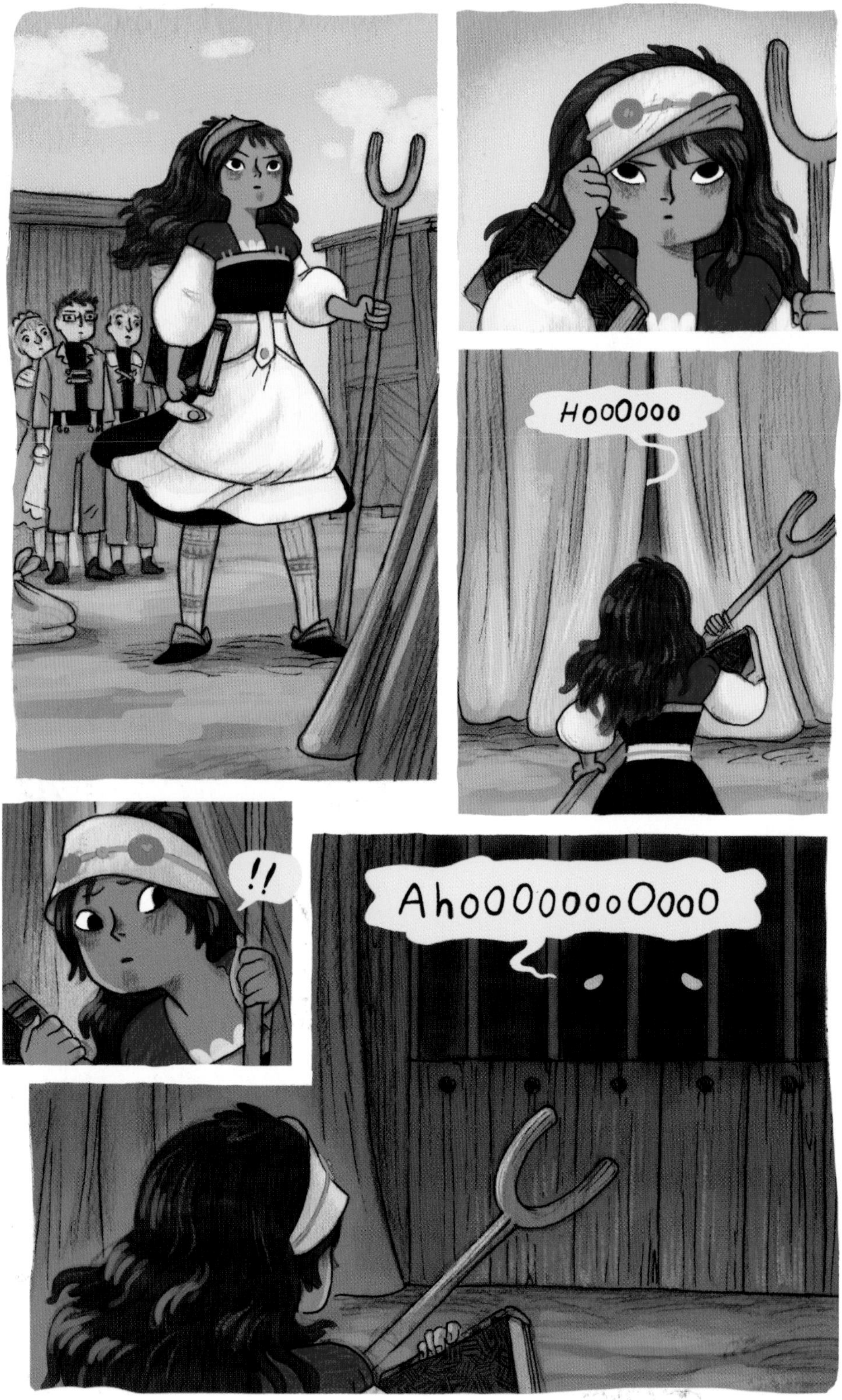
HoOOooo
!!
AhoOOOoooOooO

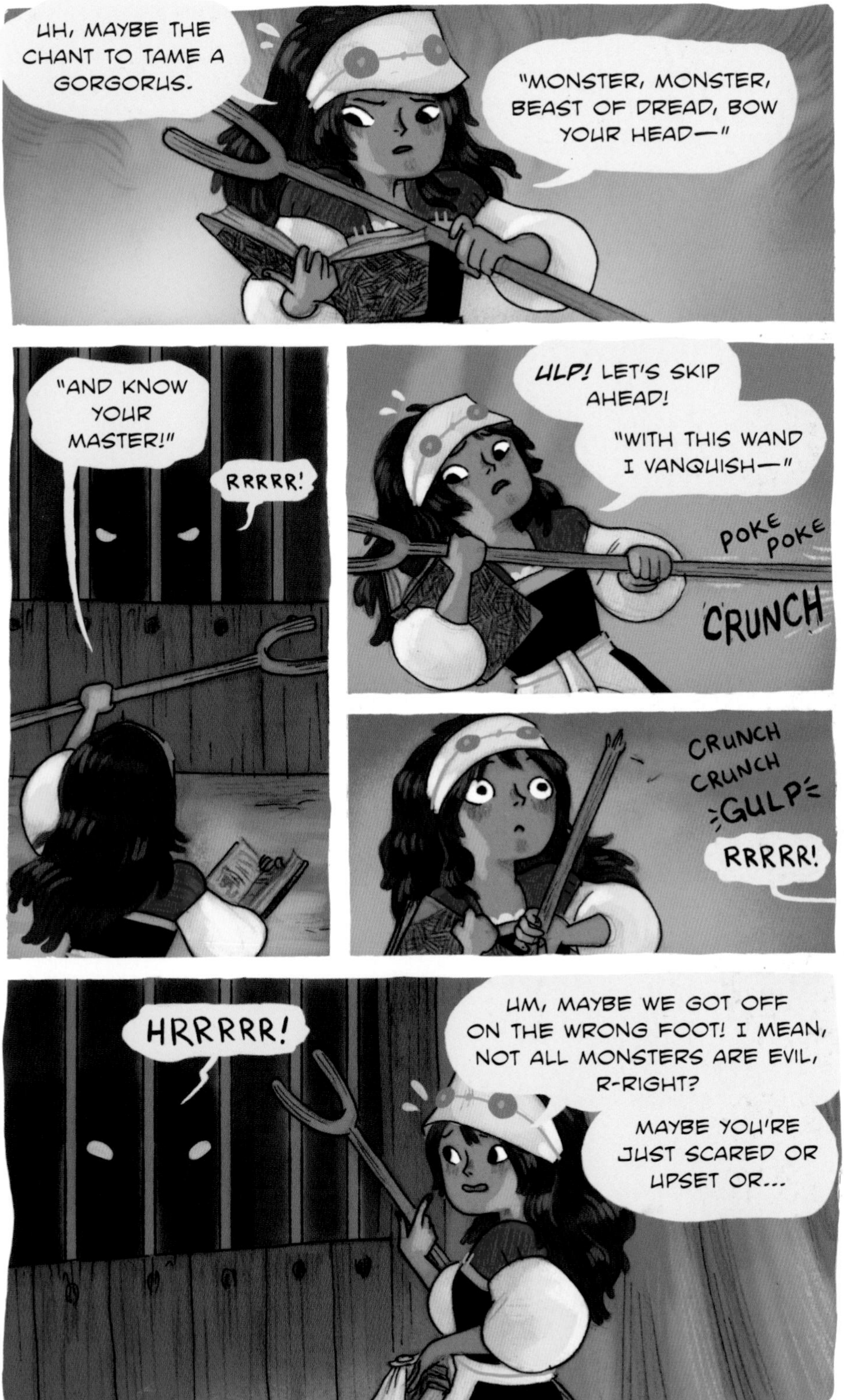
UH, MAYBE THE CHANT TO TAME A GORGORUS.
"MONSTER, MONSTER, BEAST OF DREAD, BOW YOUR HEAD—"
"AND KNOW YOUR MASTER!"
RRRRR!
ULP! LET'S SKIP AHEAD!
"WITH THIS WAND I VANQUISH—"
POKE POKE
CRUNCH
CRUNCH CRUNCH GULP
RRRRR!
HRRRRR!
UM, MAYBE WE GOT OFF ON THE WRONG FOOT! I MEAN, NOT ALL MONSTERS ARE EVIL, R-RIGHT?
MAYBE YOU'RE JUST SCARED OR UPSET OR...

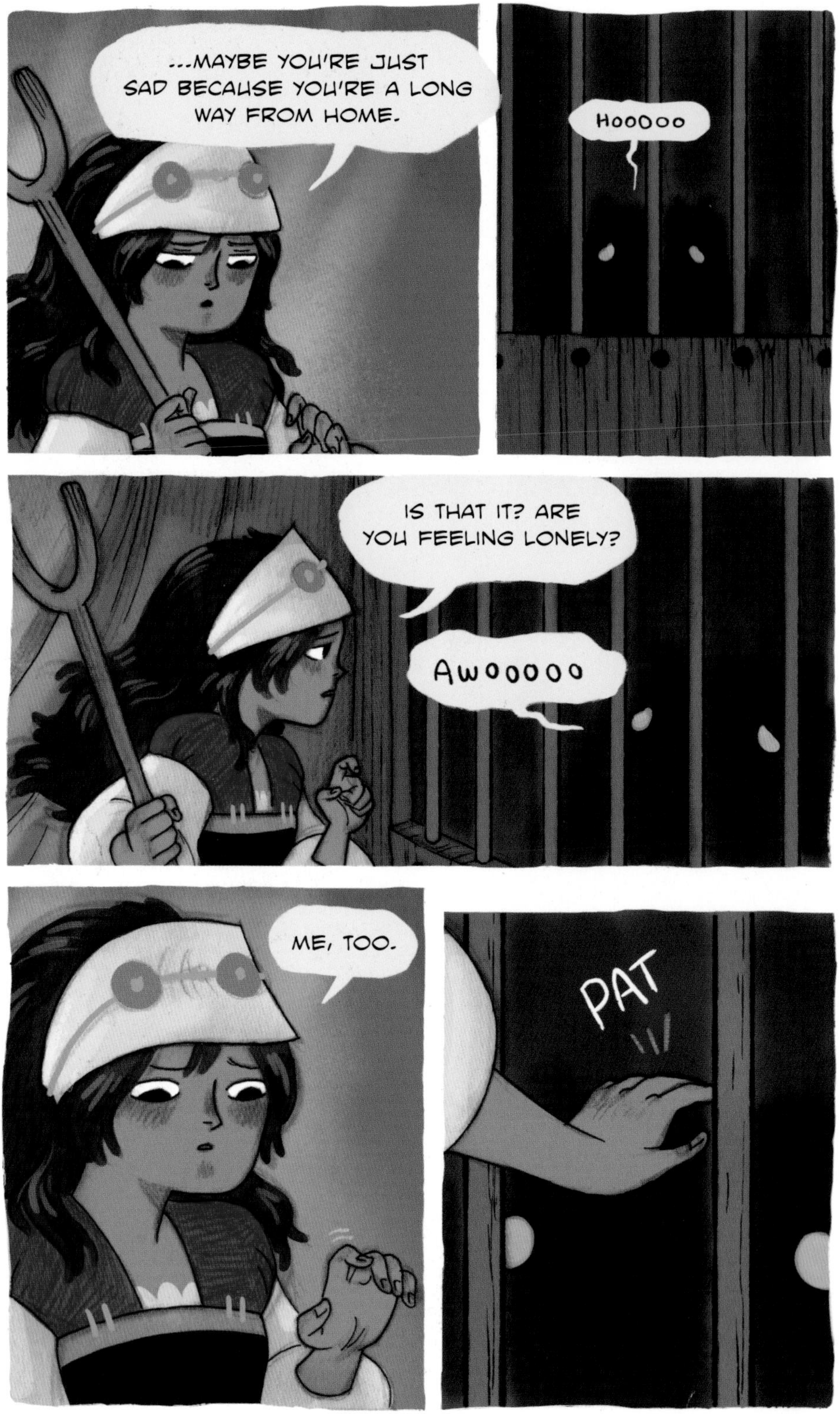
...MAYBE YOU'RE JUST SAD BECAUSE YOU'RE A LONG WAY FROM HOME.
HOOOOO
IS THAT IT? ARE YOU FEELING LONELY?
AWOOOOO
ME, TOO.
PAT

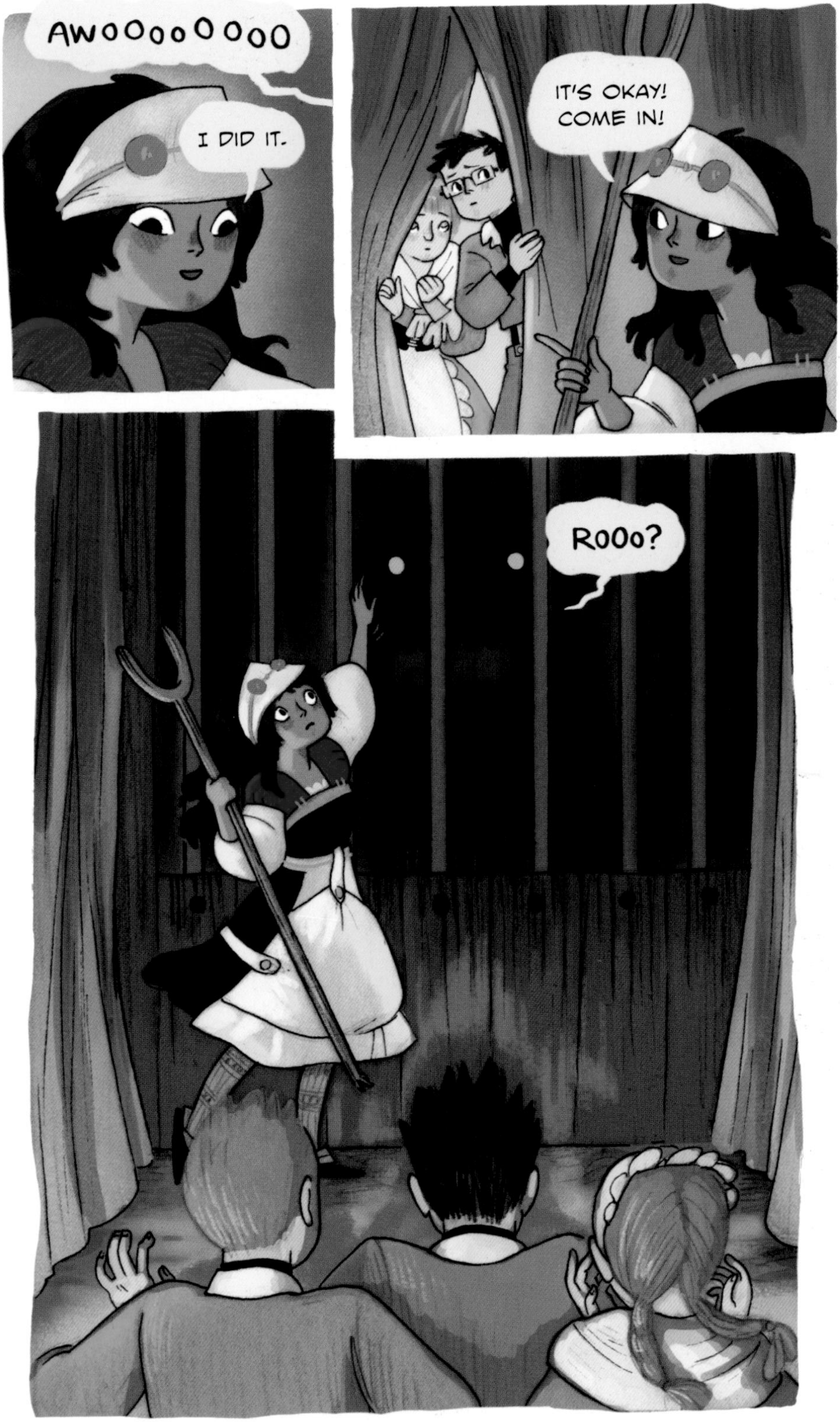
AWOOooOOOO
I DID IT.
IT'S OKAY! COME IN!
ROOo?

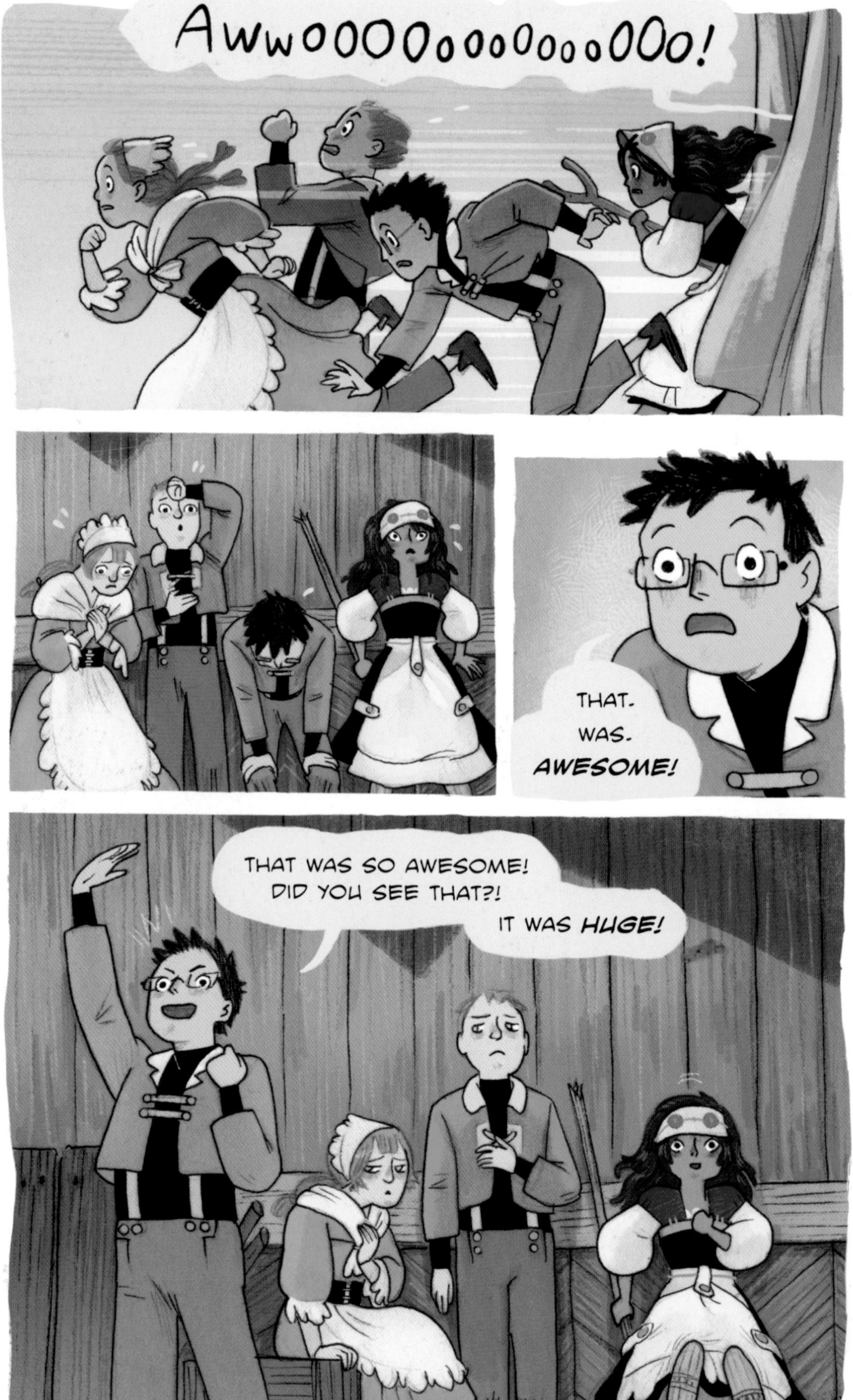
Awwoooooooooooooo!
THAT. WAS. AWESOME!
THAT WAS SO AWESOME! DID YOU SEE THAT?!
IT WAS HUGE!

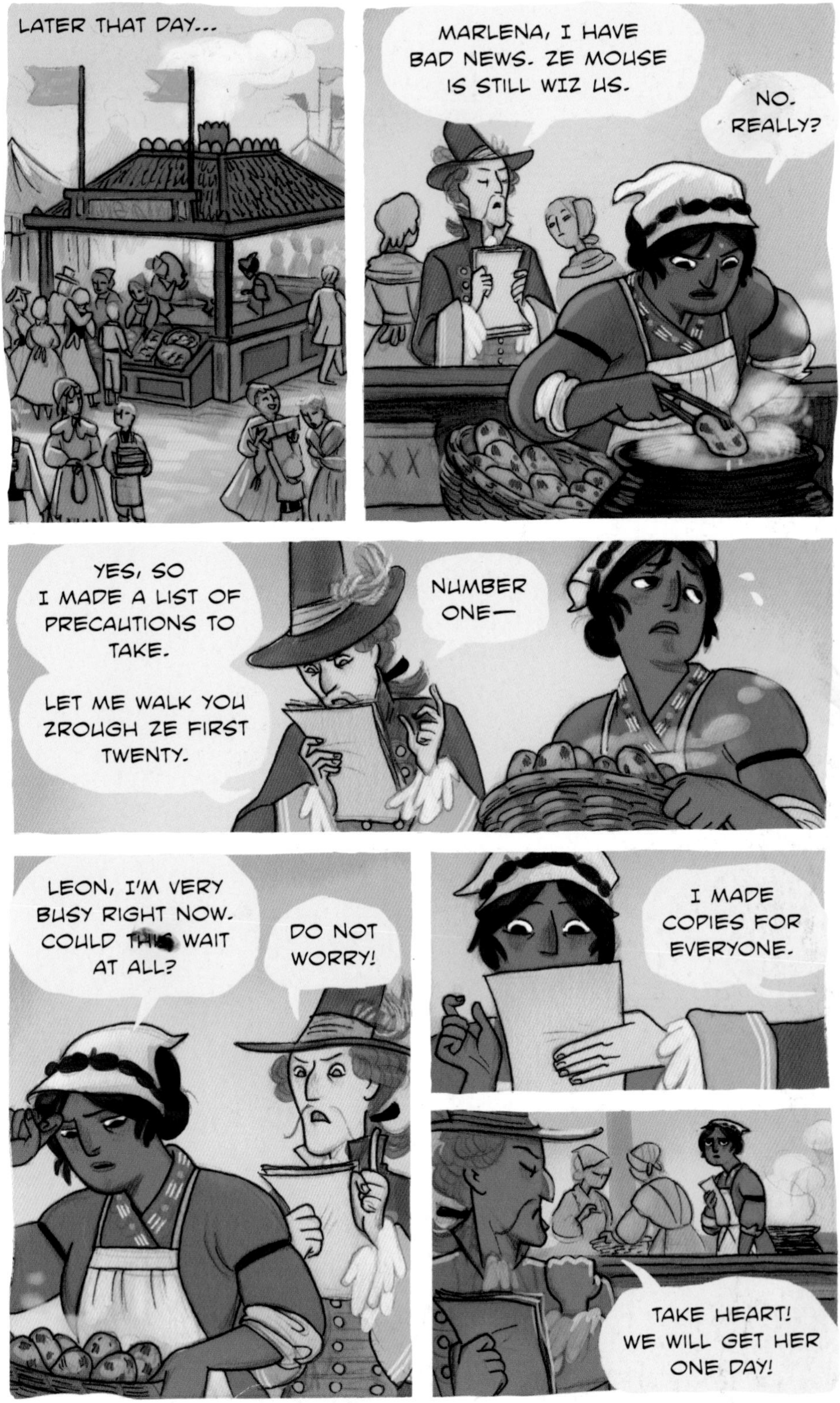
LATER THAT DAY...
MARLENA, I HAVE BAD NEWS. ZE MOUSE IS STILL WIZ US.
NO. REALLY?
YES, SO I MADE A LIST OF PRECAUTIONS TO TAKE.
LET ME WALK YOU ZROUGH ZE FIRST TWENTY.
NUMBER ONE—
LEON, I'M VERY BUSY RIGHT NOW. COULD THIS WAIT AT ALL?
DO NOT WORRY!
I MADE COPIES FOR EVERYONE.
TAKE HEART! WE WILL GET HER ONE DAY!

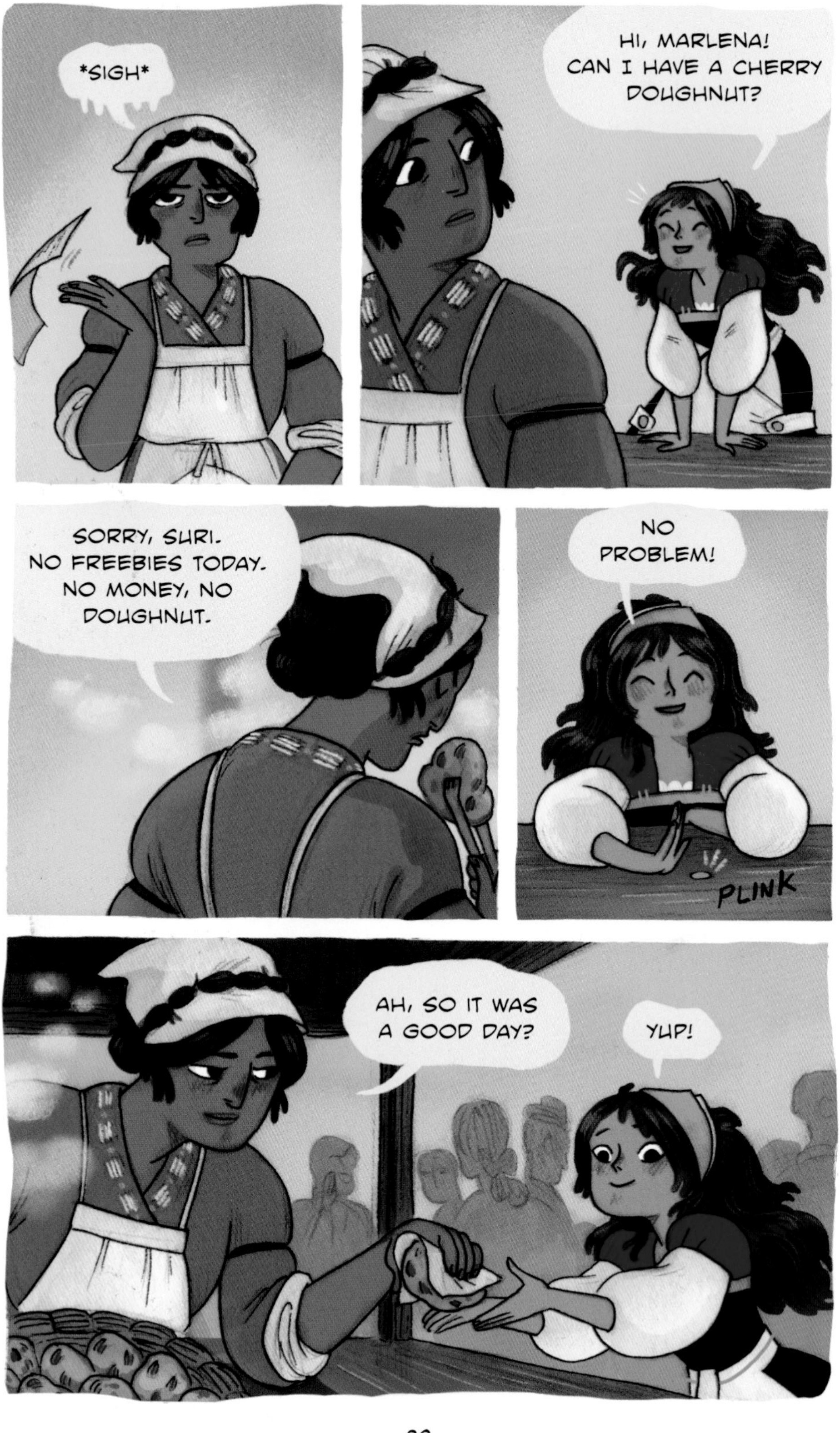
SIGH
HI, MARLENA! CAN I HAVE A CHERRY DOUGHNUT?
SORRY, SURI. NO FREEBIES TODAY. NO MONEY, NO DOUGHNUT.
NO PROBLEM!
PLINK
AH, SO IT WAS A GOOD DAY?
YUP!

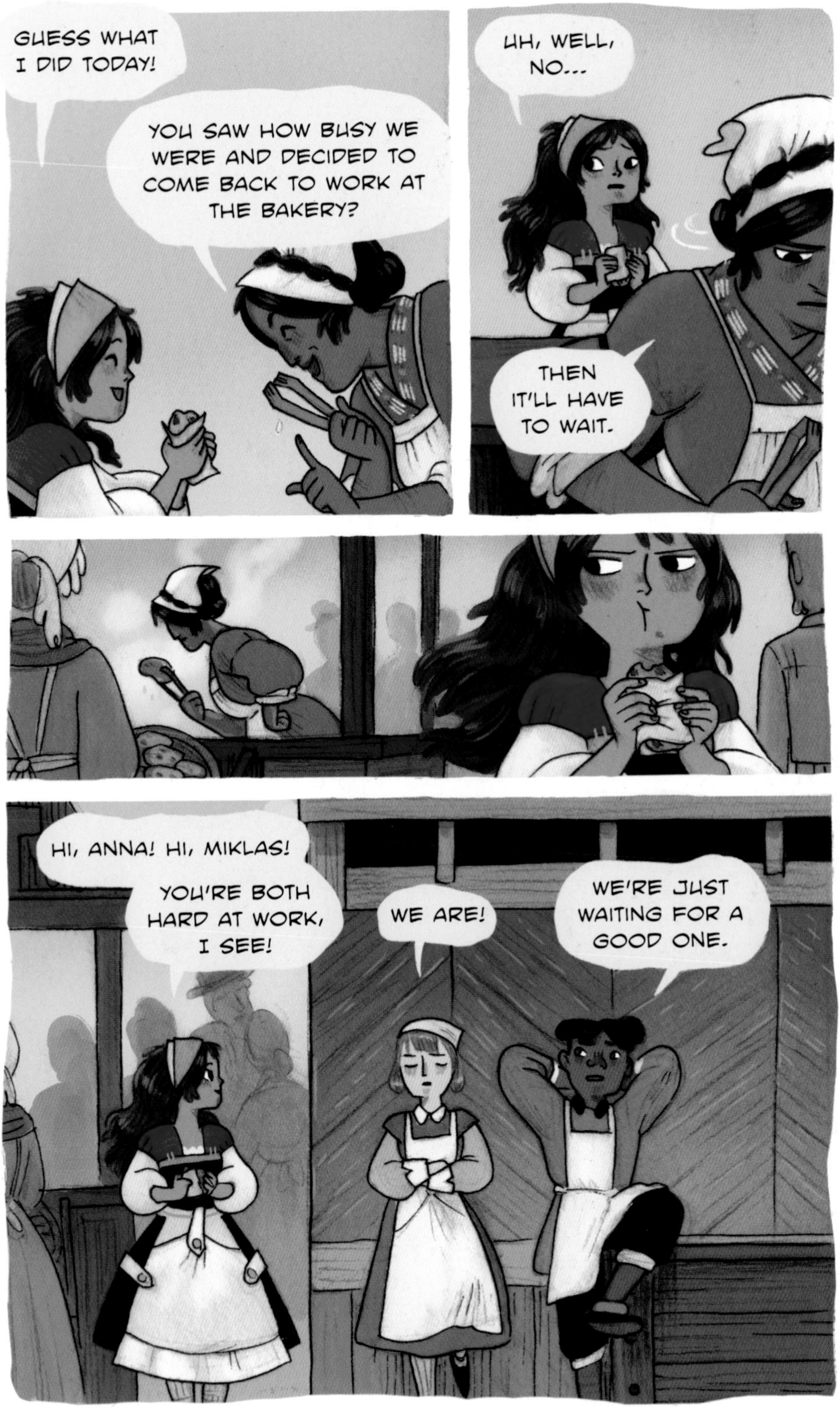
GUESS WHAT I DID TODAY!
YOU SAW HOW BUSY WE WERE AND DECIDED TO COME BACK TO WORK AT THE BAKERY?
UH, WELL, NO...
THEN IT'LL HAVE TO WAIT.
HI, ANNA! HI, MIKLAS!
YOU'RE BOTH HARD AT WORK, I SEE!
WE ARE!
WE'RE JUST WAITING FOR A GOOD ONE.

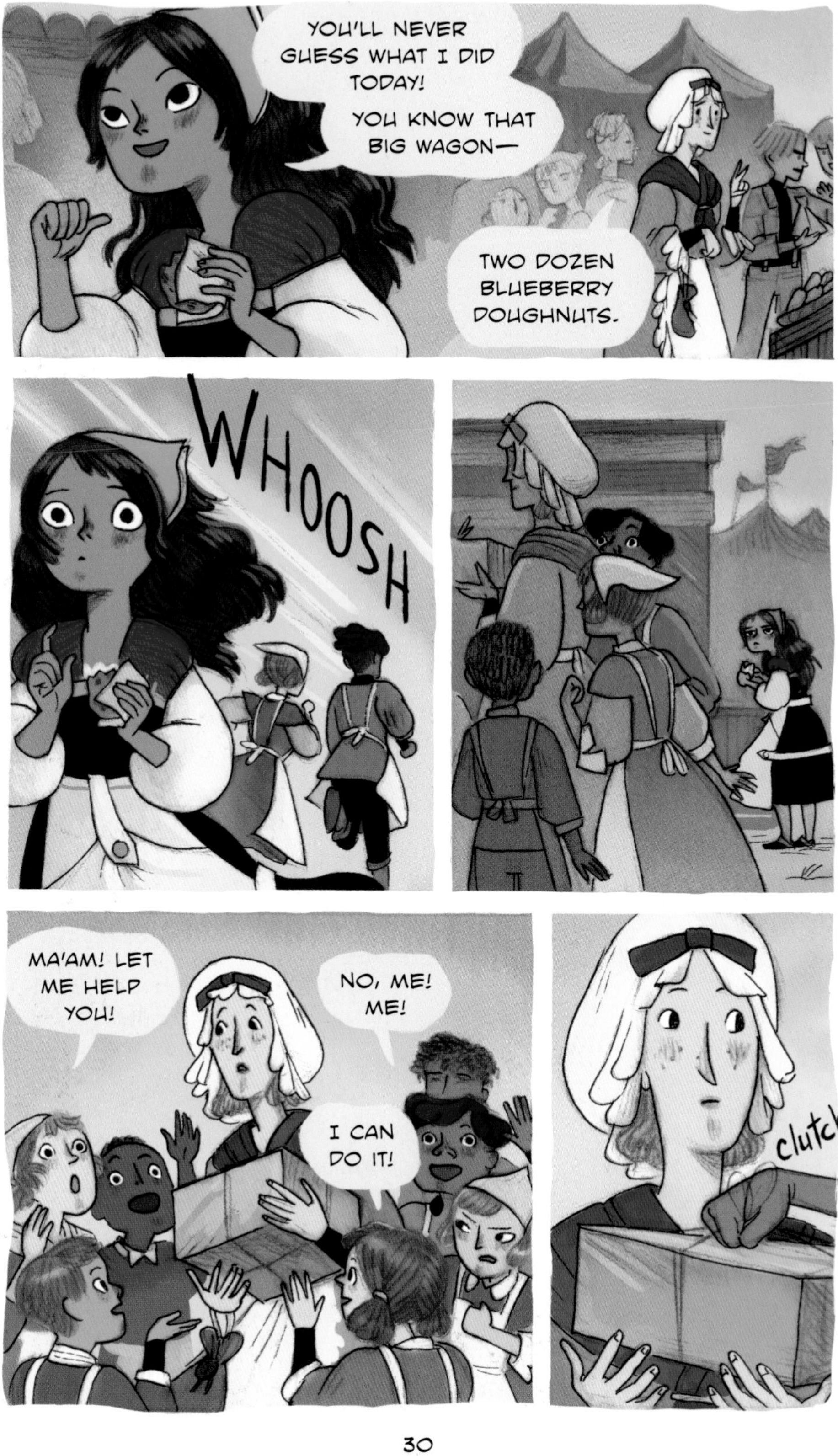
YOU'LL NEVER GUESS WHAT I DID TODAY!
YOU KNOW THAT BIG WAGON—
TWO DOZEN BLUEBERRY DOUGHNUTS.
WHOOSH
MA'AM! LET ME HELP YOU!
NO, ME! ME!
I CAN DO IT!
clutch

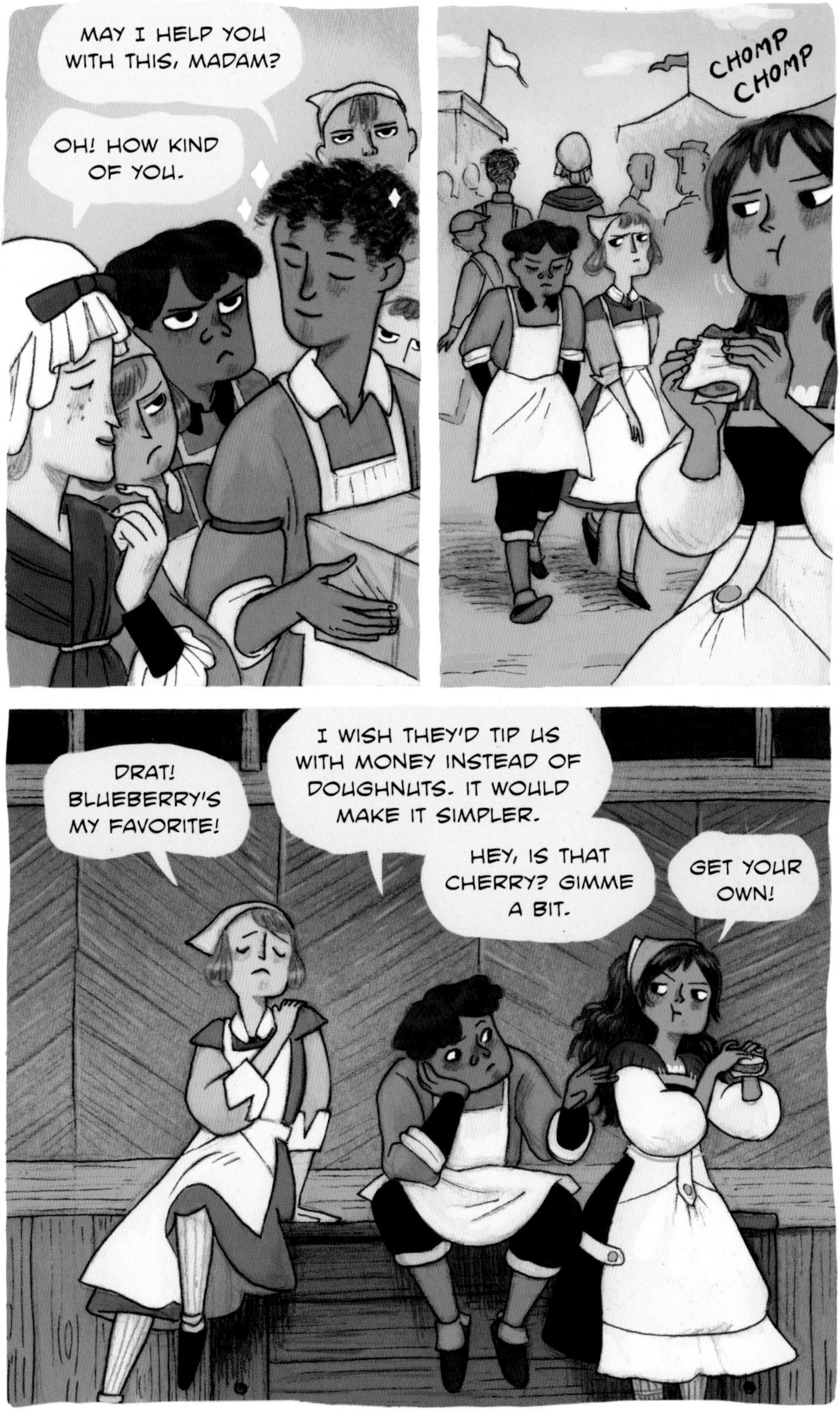
MAY I HELP YOU WITH THIS, MADAM?
OH! HOW KIND OF YOU.
CHOMP CHOMP
DRAT! BLUEBERRY'S MY FAVORITE!
I WISH THEY'D TIP US WITH MONEY INSTEAD OF DOUGHNUTS. IT WOULD MAKE IT SIMPLER.
HEY, IS THAT CHERRY? GIMME A BIT.
GET YOUR OWN!

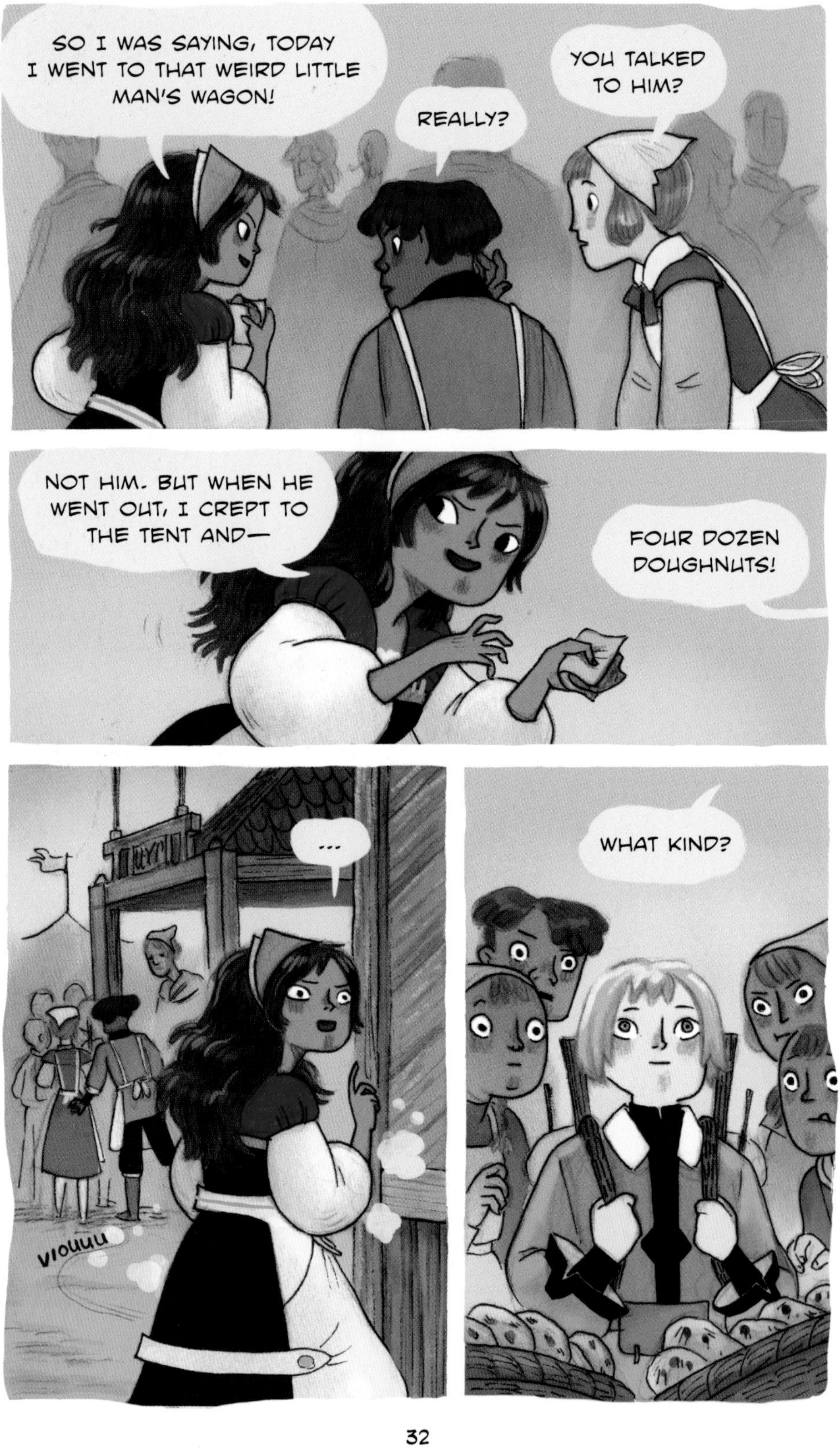
SO I WAS SAYING, TODAY I WENT TO THAT WEIRD LITTLE MAN'S WAGON!
REALLY?
YOU TALKED TO HIM?
NOT HIM. BUT WHEN HE WENT OUT, I CREPT TO THE TENT AND—
FOUR DOZEN DOUGHNUTS!
...
VIOUUU
WHAT KIND?

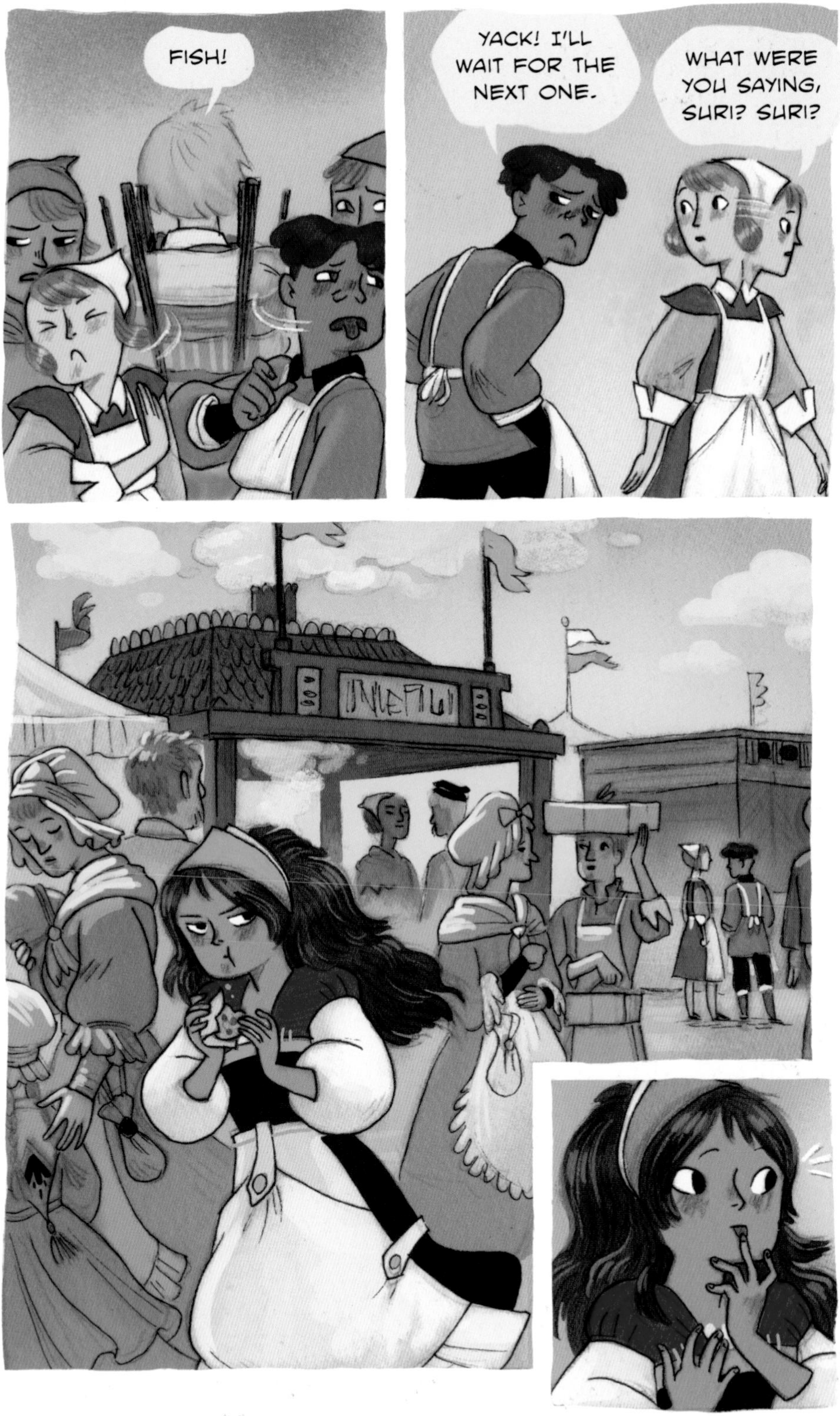
FISH!
YACK! I'LL WAIT FOR THE NEXT ONE.
WHAT WERE YOU SAYING, SURI? SURI?

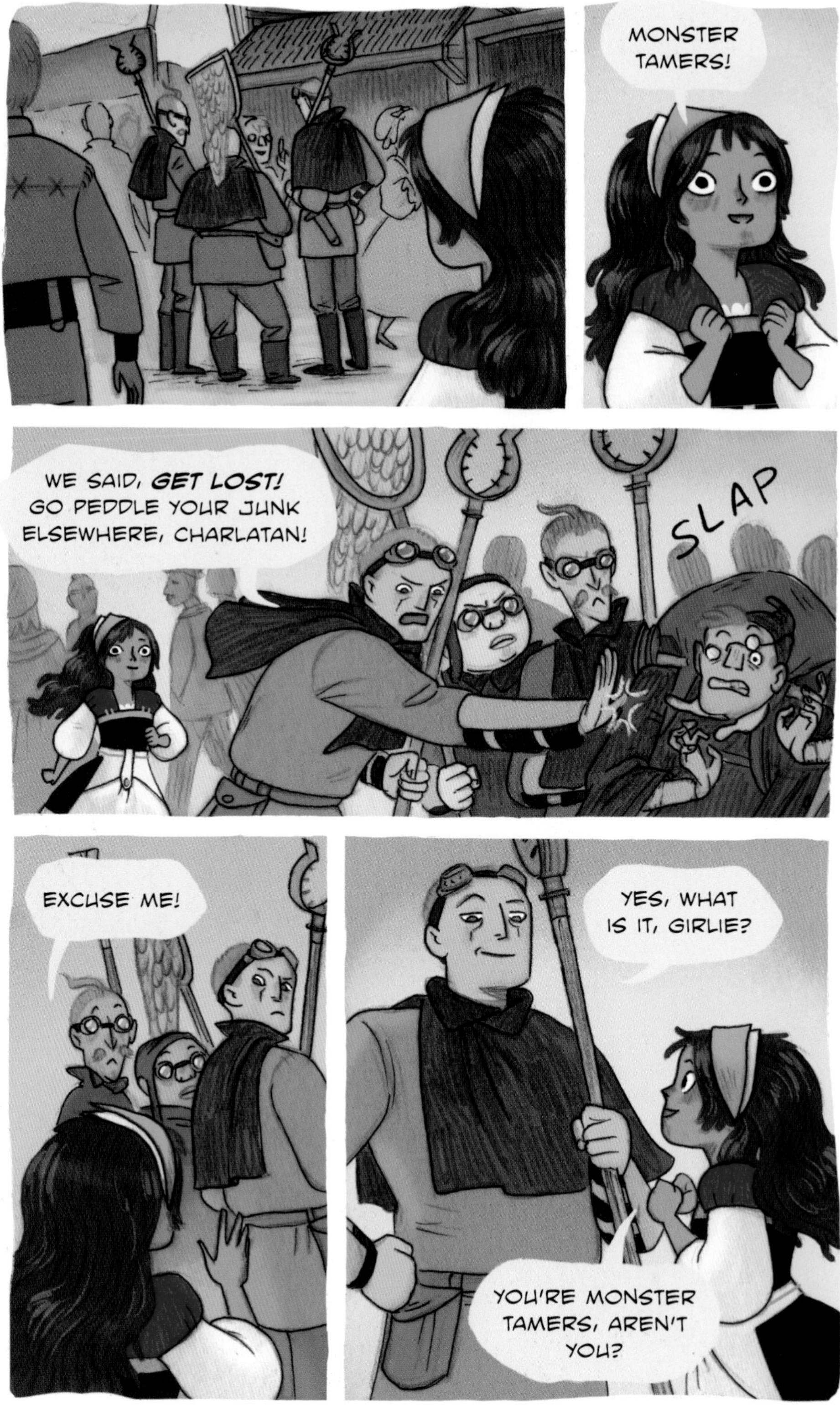
MONSTER TAMERS!
WE SAID, **GET LOST!** GO PEDDLE YOUR JUNK ELSEWHERE, CHARLATAN!
SLAP
EXCUSE ME!
YES, WHAT IS IT, GIRLIE?
YOU'RE MONSTER TAMERS, AREN'T YOU?

THAT'S RIGHT! THE PRINCE IS PAYING BIG FOR MONSTERS CAPTURED ALIVE. WE'RE HERE TO CATCH THE CAITSITH.

I HAVE SO MANY QUESTIONS! I DON'T KNOW WHERE TO START!

HAHA! *I* DO!

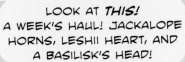

LOOK AT *THIS!* A WEEK'S HAUL! JACKALOPE HORNS, LESHII HEART, AND A BASILISK'S HEAD!

IS THAT ALL OF IT?

"IS THAT—" YOU *BRAT!*

TSH! WHAT DO YOU KNOW, ANYWAY?

I KNOW THAT LESHII ARE HARMLESS IF YOU JUST TRIM THEIR HEADS ONCE A YEAR.

AND THAT SINCE THAT BASILISK DOESN'T HAVE A WATTLE, IT WAS ALREADY PETRIFYING WHEN YOU CAUGHT IT!

35

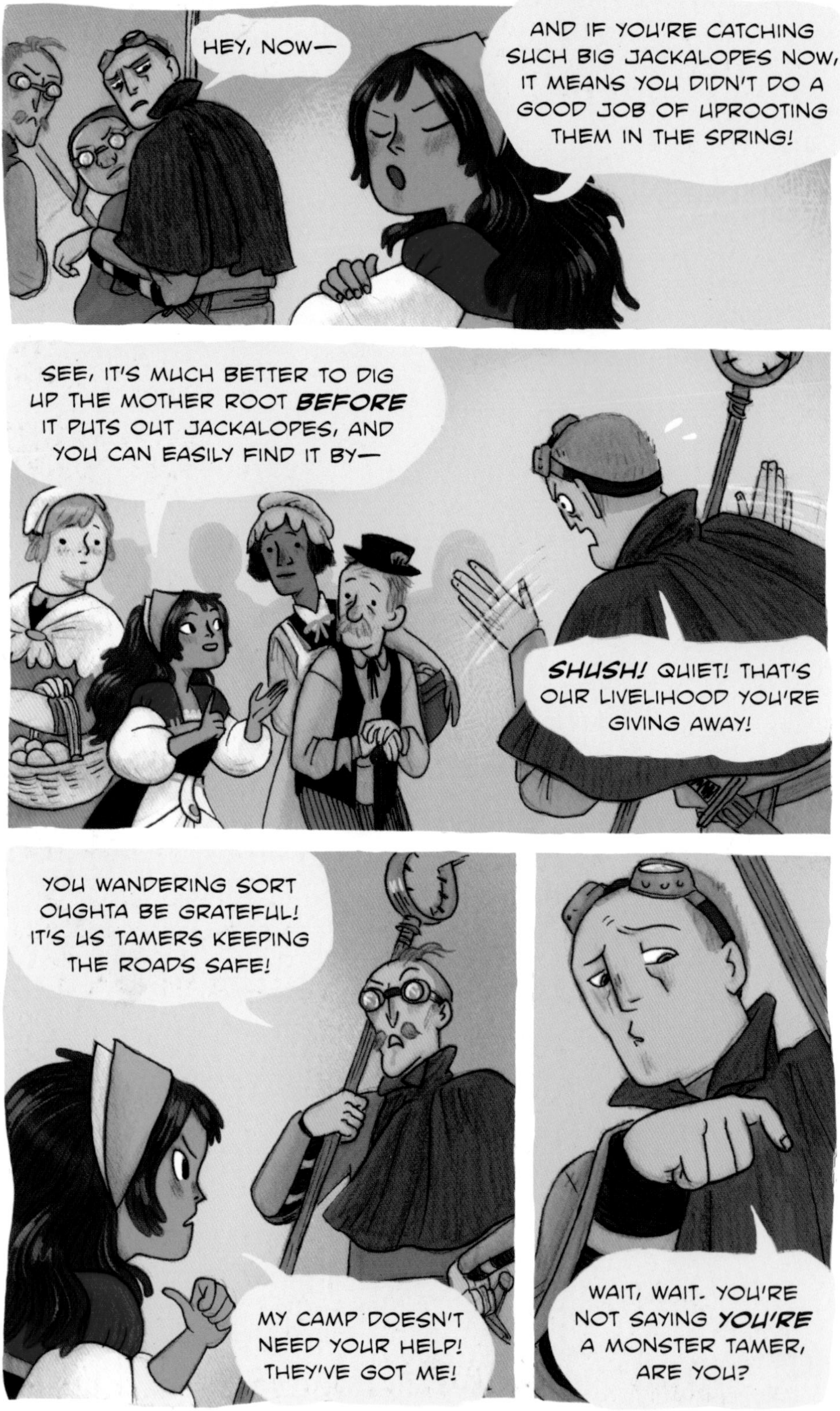
HEY, NOW—
AND IF YOU'RE CATCHING SUCH BIG JACKALOPES NOW, IT MEANS YOU DIDN'T DO A GOOD JOB OF UPROOTING THEM IN THE SPRING!
SEE, IT'S MUCH BETTER TO DIG UP THE MOTHER ROOT BEFORE IT PUTS OUT JACKALOPES, AND YOU CAN EASILY FIND IT BY—
SHUSH! QUIET! THAT'S OUR LIVELIHOOD YOU'RE GIVING AWAY!
YOU WANDERING SORT OUGHTA BE GRATEFUL! IT'S US TAMERS KEEPING THE ROADS SAFE!
MY CAMP DOESN'T NEED YOUR HELP! THEY'VE GOT ME!
WAIT, WAIT. YOU'RE NOT SAYING YOU'RE A MONSTER TAMER, ARE YOU?

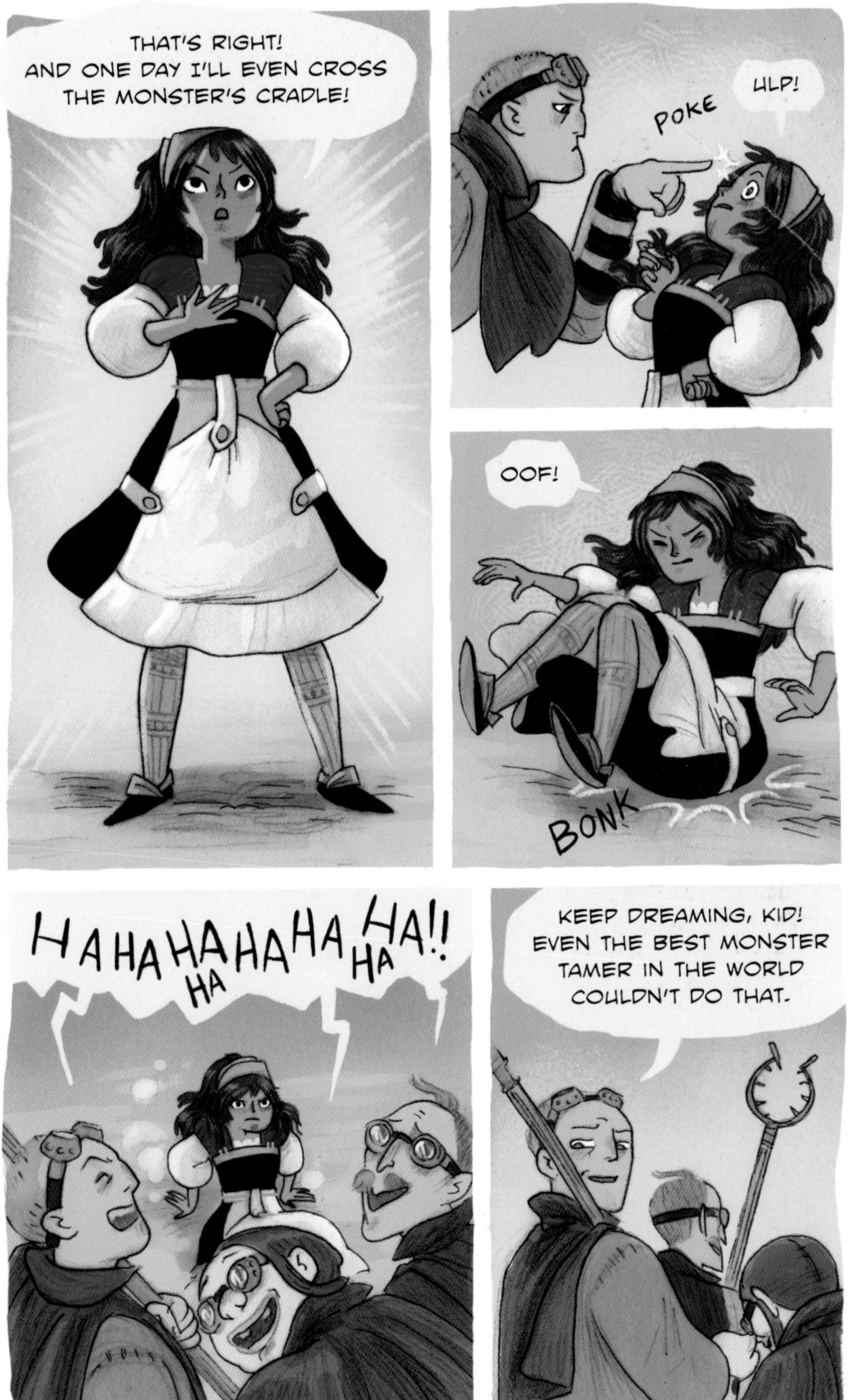
THAT'S RIGHT!
AND ONE DAY I'LL EVEN CROSS THE MONSTER'S CRADLE!
POKE
ULP!
OOF!
BONK
HAHAHAHAHAHAHAHAHA!!
KEEP DREAMING, KID! EVEN THE BEST MONSTER TAMER IN THE WORLD COULDN'T DO THAT.

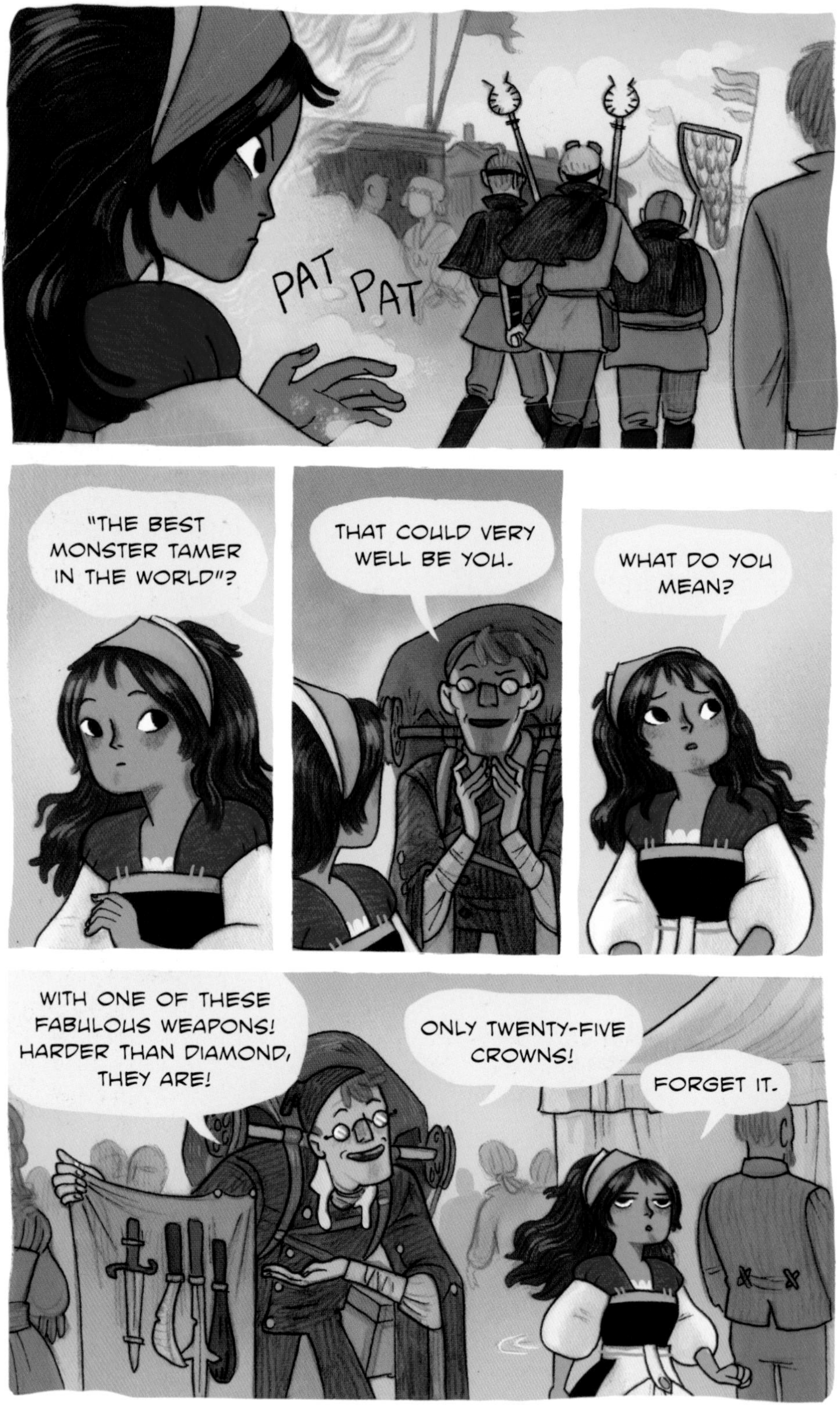
PAT PAT
"THE BEST MONSTER TAMER IN THE WORLD"?
THAT COULD VERY WELL BE YOU.
WHAT DO YOU MEAN?
WITH ONE OF THESE FABULOUS WEAPONS! HARDER THAN DIAMOND, THEY ARE!
ONLY TWENTY-FIVE CROWNS!
FORGET IT.

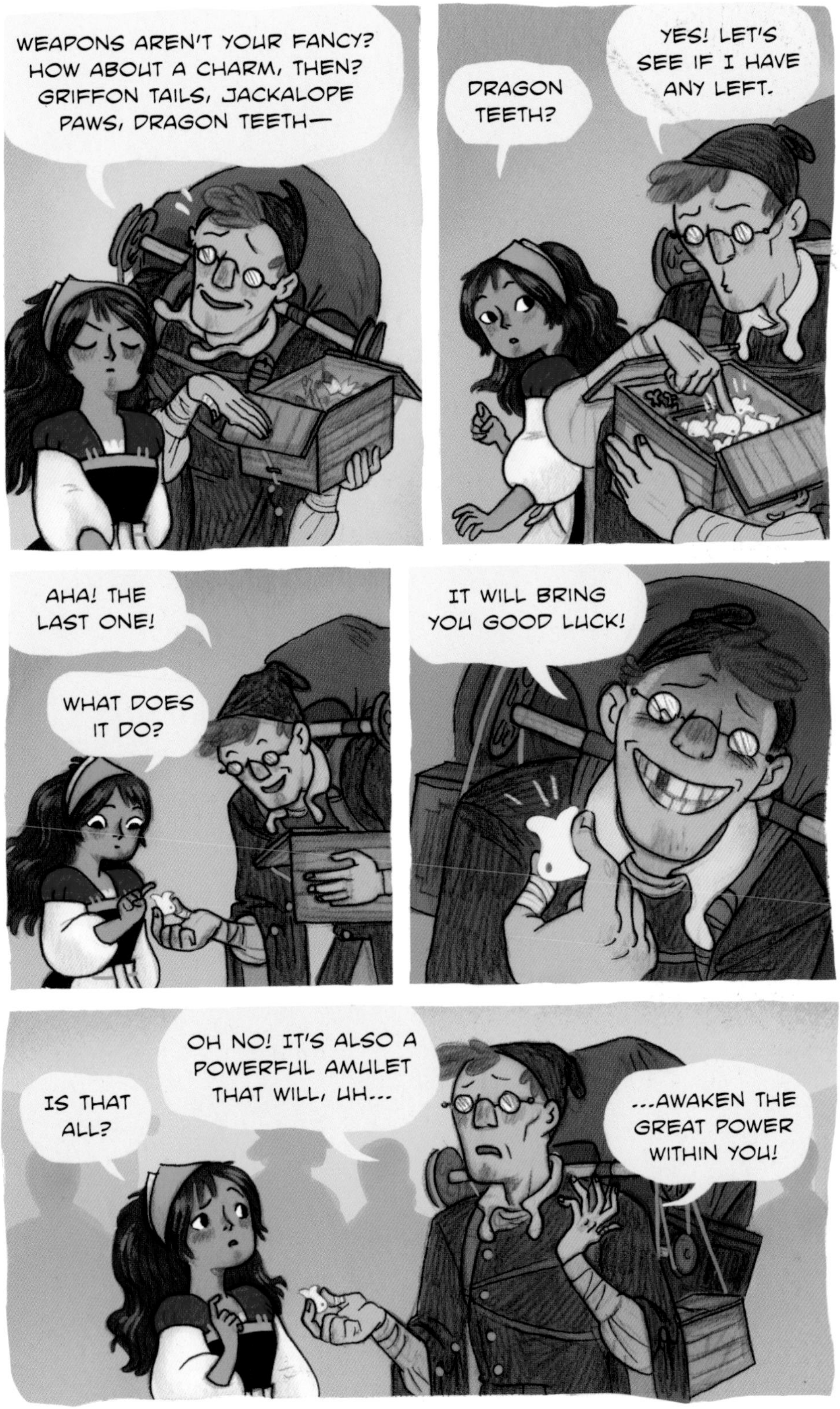
WEAPONS AREN'T YOUR FANCY? HOW ABOUT A CHARM, THEN? GRIFFON TAILS, JACKALOPE PAWS, DRAGON TEETH—
DRAGON TEETH?
YES! LET'S SEE IF I HAVE ANY LEFT.
AHA! THE LAST ONE!
WHAT DOES IT DO?
IT WILL BRING YOU GOOD LUCK!
IS THAT ALL?
OH NO! IT'S ALSO A POWERFUL AMULET THAT WILL, UH...
...AWAKEN THE GREAT POWER WITHIN YOU!

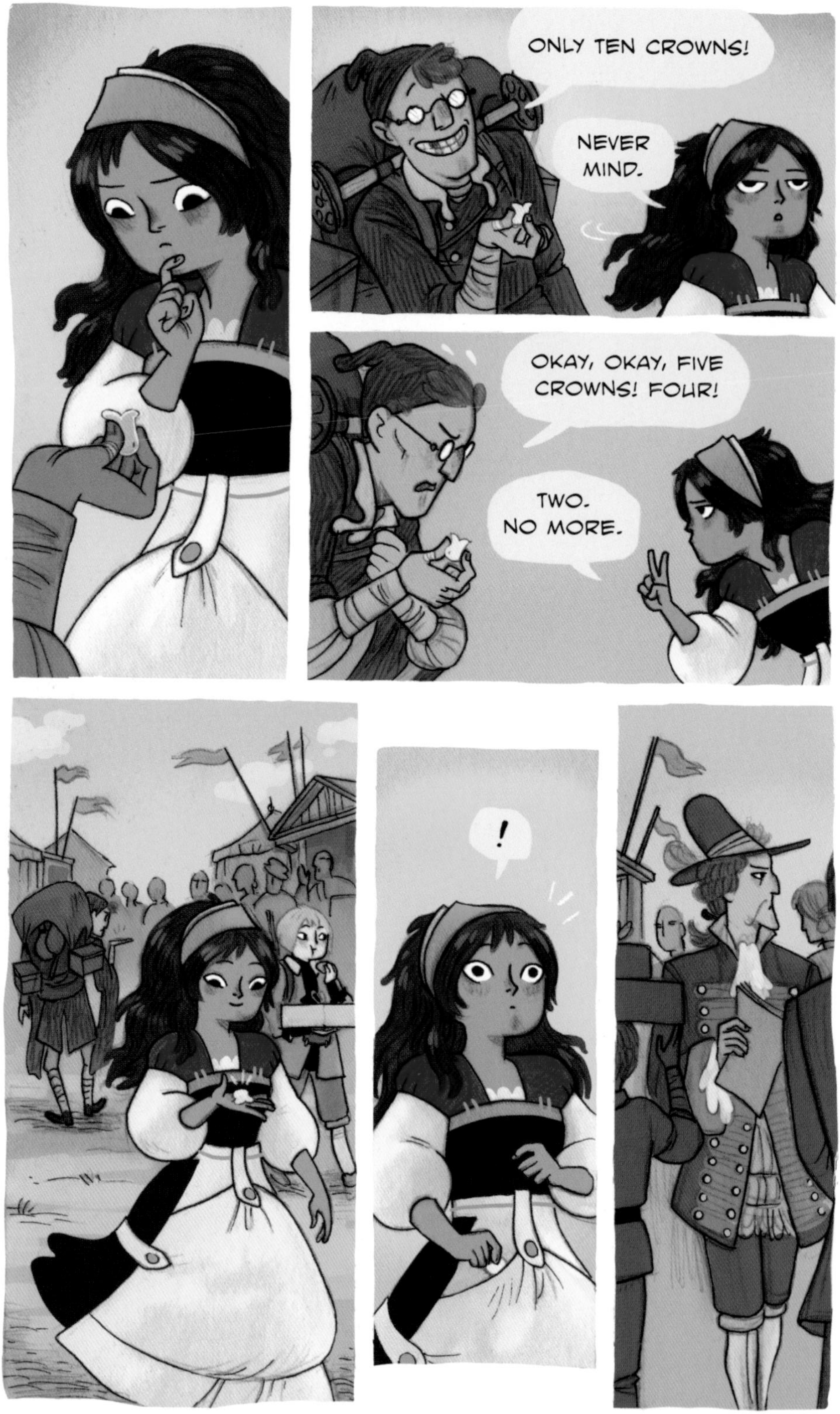
ONLY TEN CROWNS!
NEVER MIND.
OKAY, OKAY, FIVE CROWNS! FOUR!
TWO. NO MORE.
!

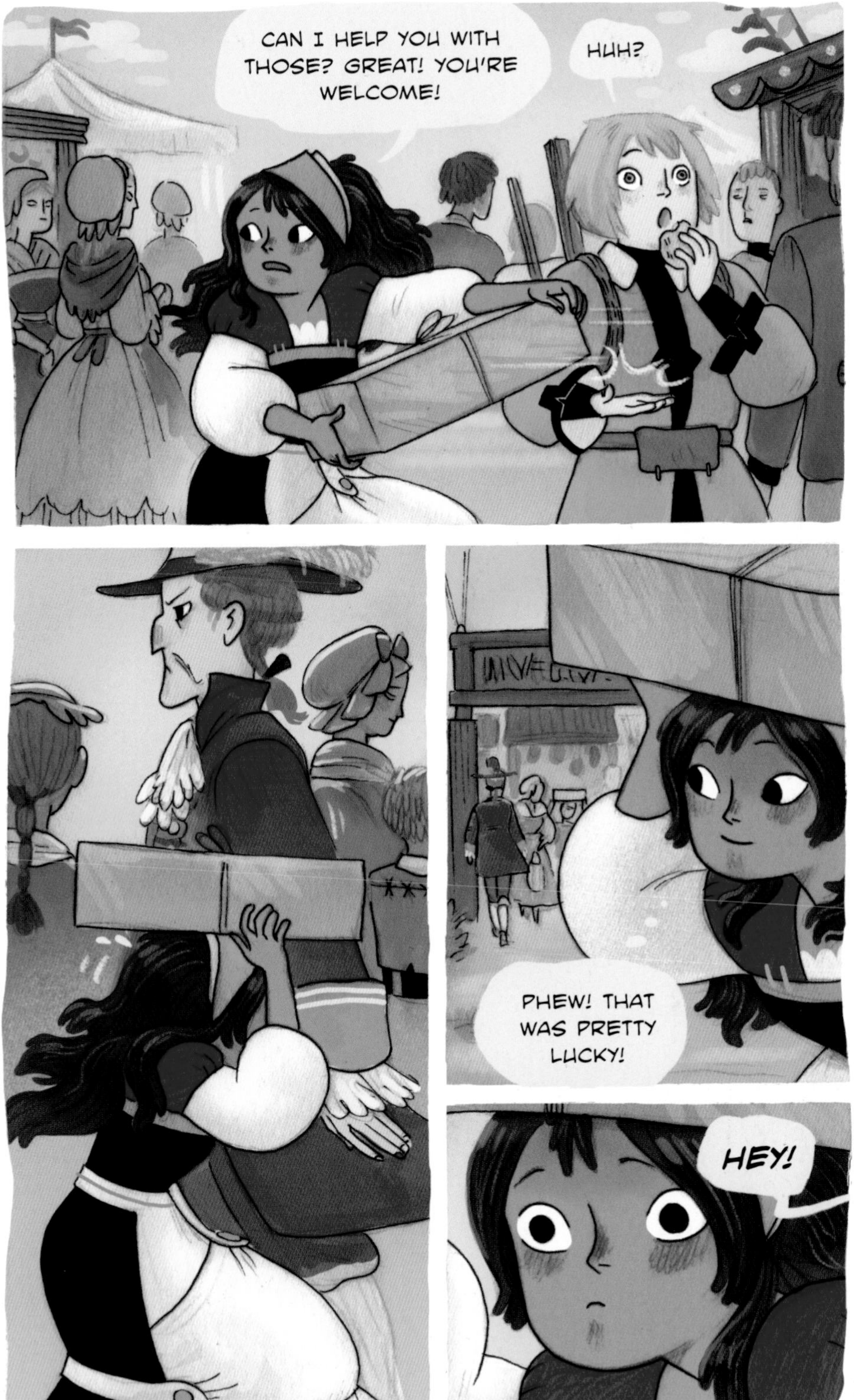
CAN I HELP YOU WITH THOSE? GREAT! YOU'RE WELCOME!
HUH?
PHEW! THAT WAS PRETTY LUCKY!
HEY!

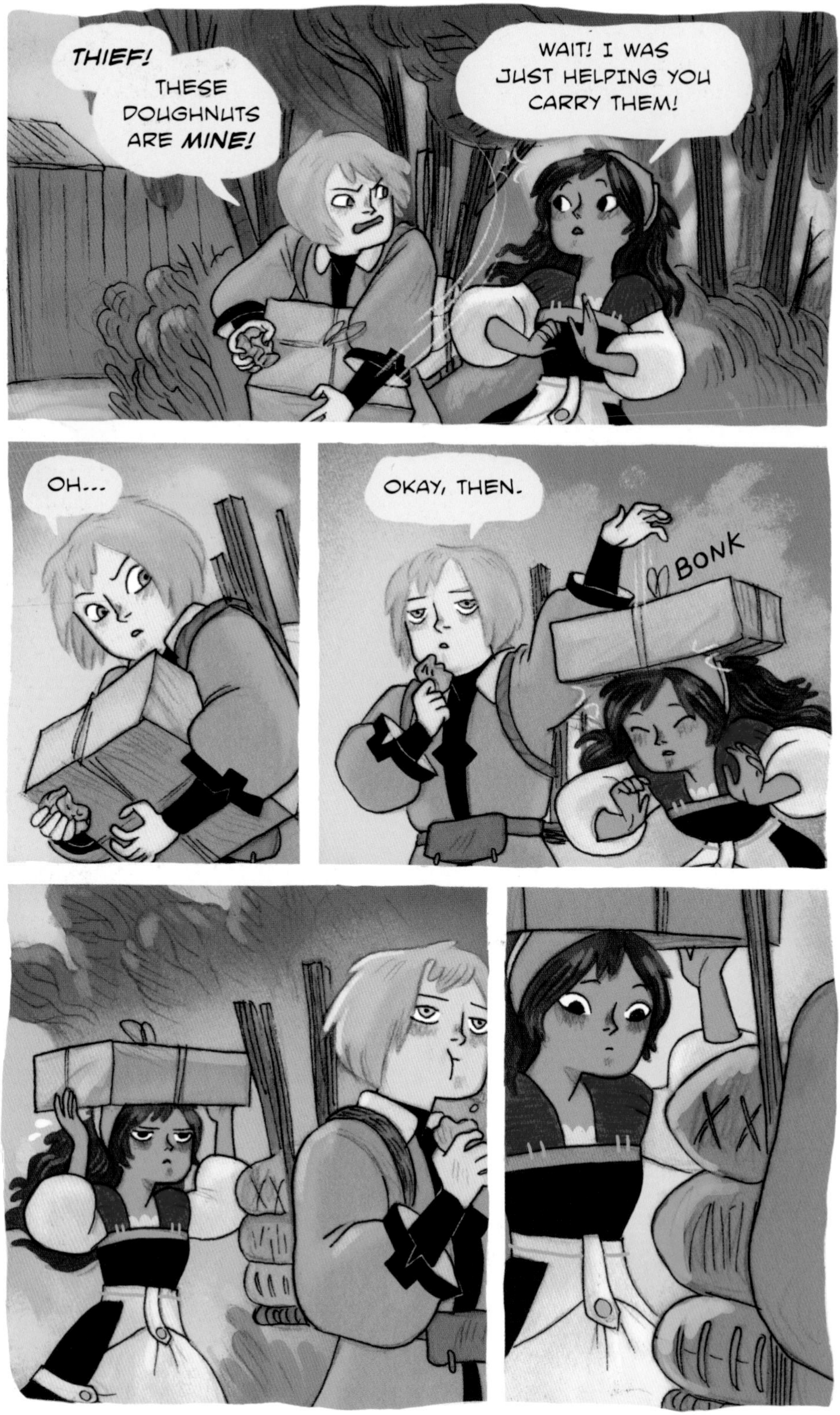
THIEF! THESE DOUGHNUTS ARE MINE!
WAIT! I WAS JUST HELPING YOU CARRY THEM!
OH...
OKAY, THEN.
BONK

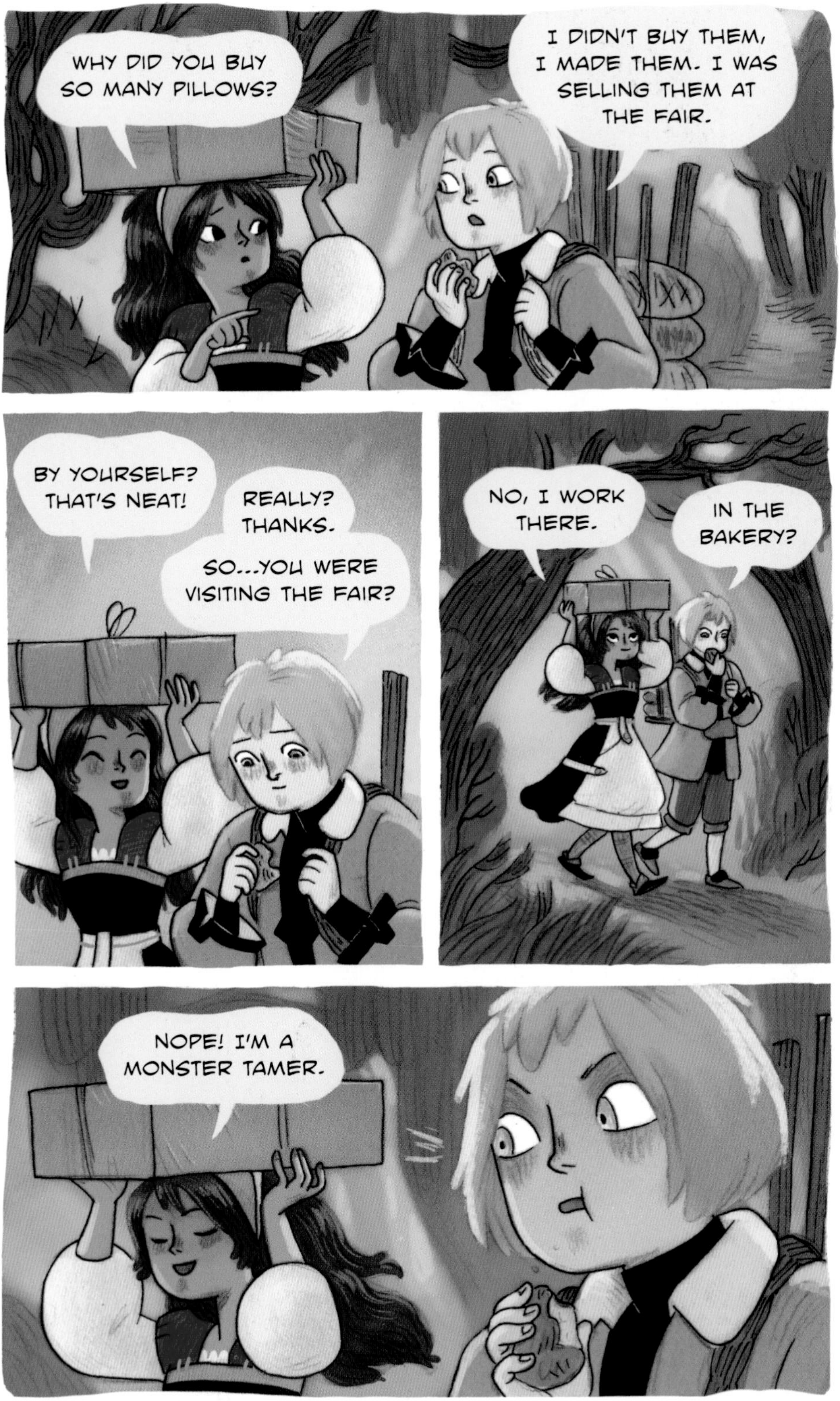
WHY DID YOU BUY SO MANY PILLOWS?
I DIDN'T BUY THEM, I MADE THEM. I WAS SELLING THEM AT THE FAIR.
BY YOURSELF? THAT'S NEAT!
REALLY? THANKS.
SO...YOU WERE VISITING THE FAIR?
NO, I WORK THERE.
IN THE BAKERY?
NOPE! I'M A MONSTER TAMER.

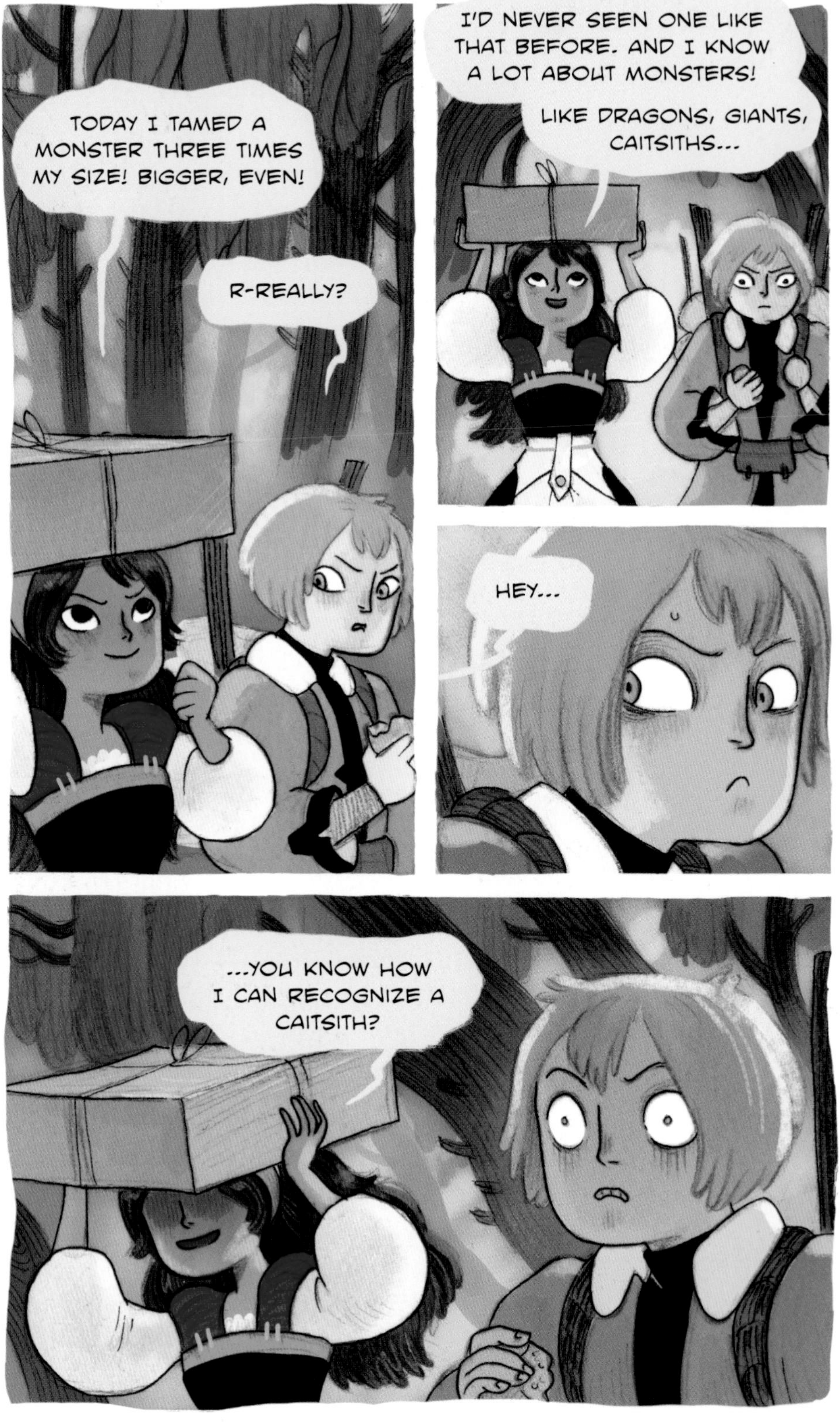

TODAY I TAMED A MONSTER THREE TIMES MY SIZE! BIGGER, EVEN!
R-REALLY?
I'D NEVER SEEN ONE LIKE THAT BEFORE. AND I KNOW A LOT ABOUT MONSTERS!
LIKE DRAGONS, GIANTS, CAITSITHS...
HEY...
...YOU KNOW HOW I CAN RECOGNIZE A CAITSITH?

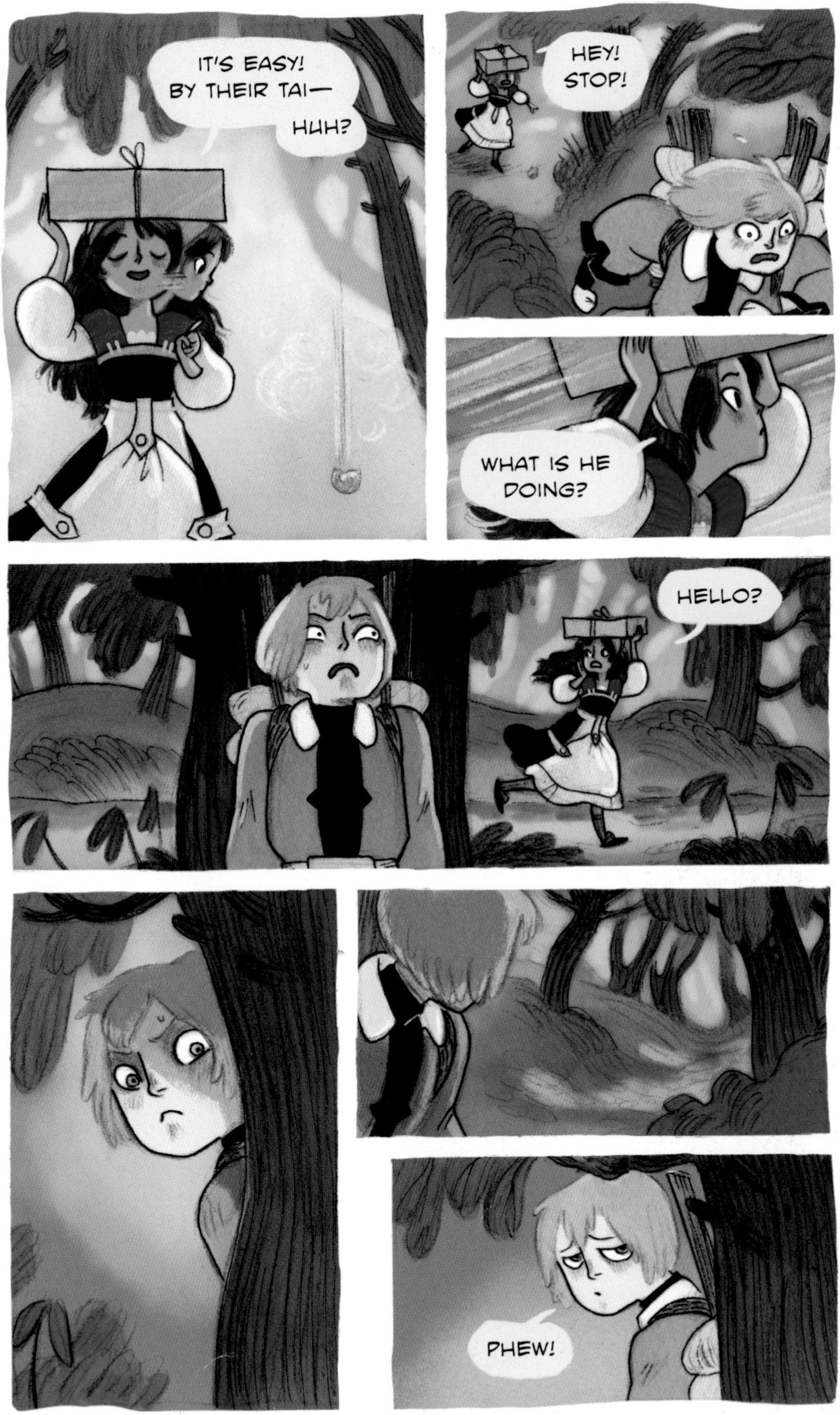
IT'S EASY! BY THEIR TAI—
HUH?
HEY! STOP!
WHAT IS HE DOING?
HELLO?
PHEW!

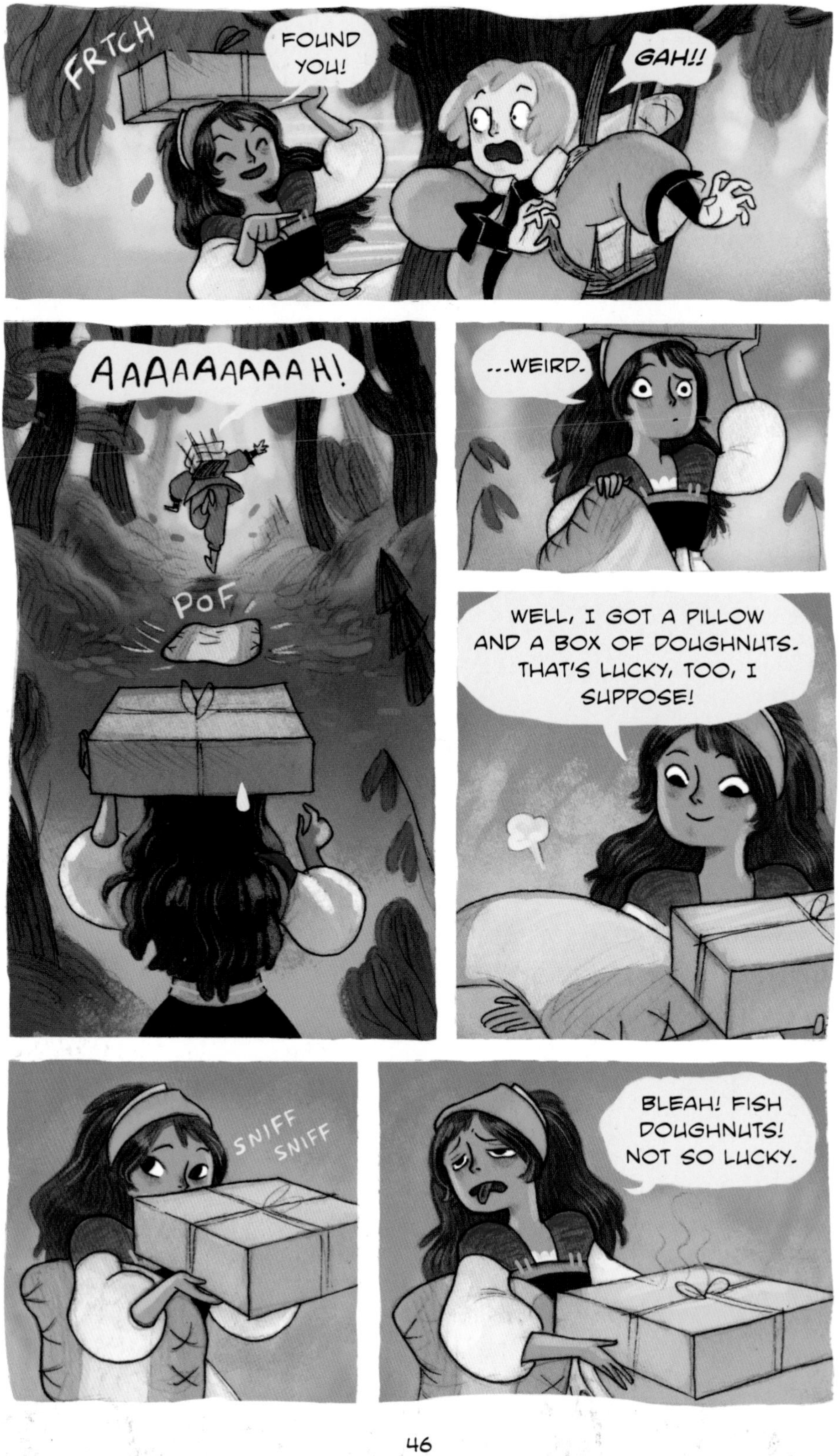
FRTCH
FOUND YOU!
GAH!!
AAAAAAAAAH!
POF
...WEIRD.
WELL, I GOT A PILLOW AND A BOX OF DOUGHNUTS. THAT'S LUCKY, TOO, I SUPPOSE!
SNIFF SNIFF
BLEAH! FISH DOUGHNUTS! NOT SO LUCKY.

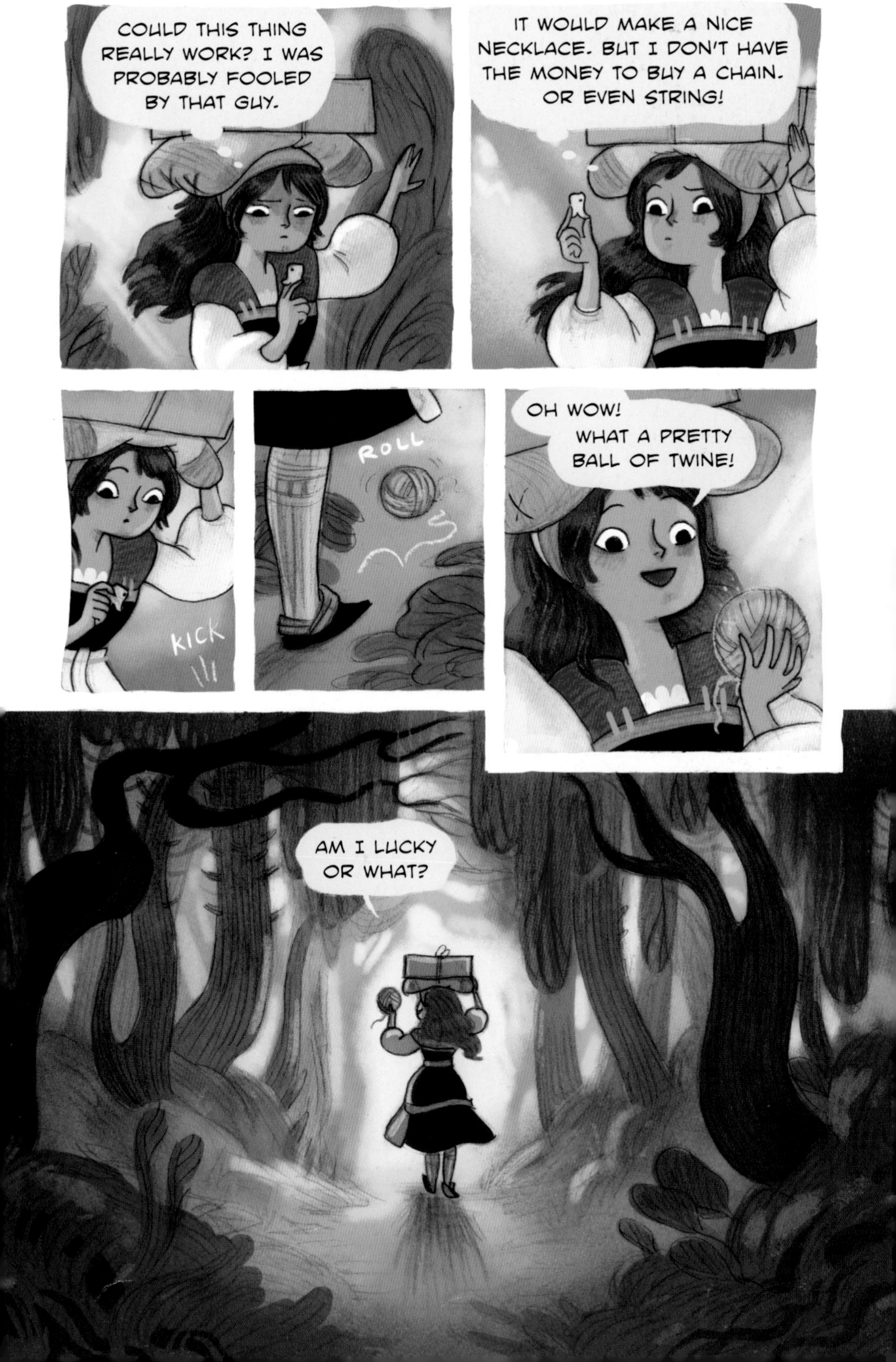
COULD THIS THING REALLY WORK? I WAS PROBABLY FOOLED BY THAT GUY.
IT WOULD MAKE A NICE NECKLACE. BUT I DON'T HAVE THE MONEY TO BUY A CHAIN. OR EVEN STRING!
KICK
ROLL
OH WOW! WHAT A PRETTY BALL OF TWINE!
AM I LUCKY OR WHAT?

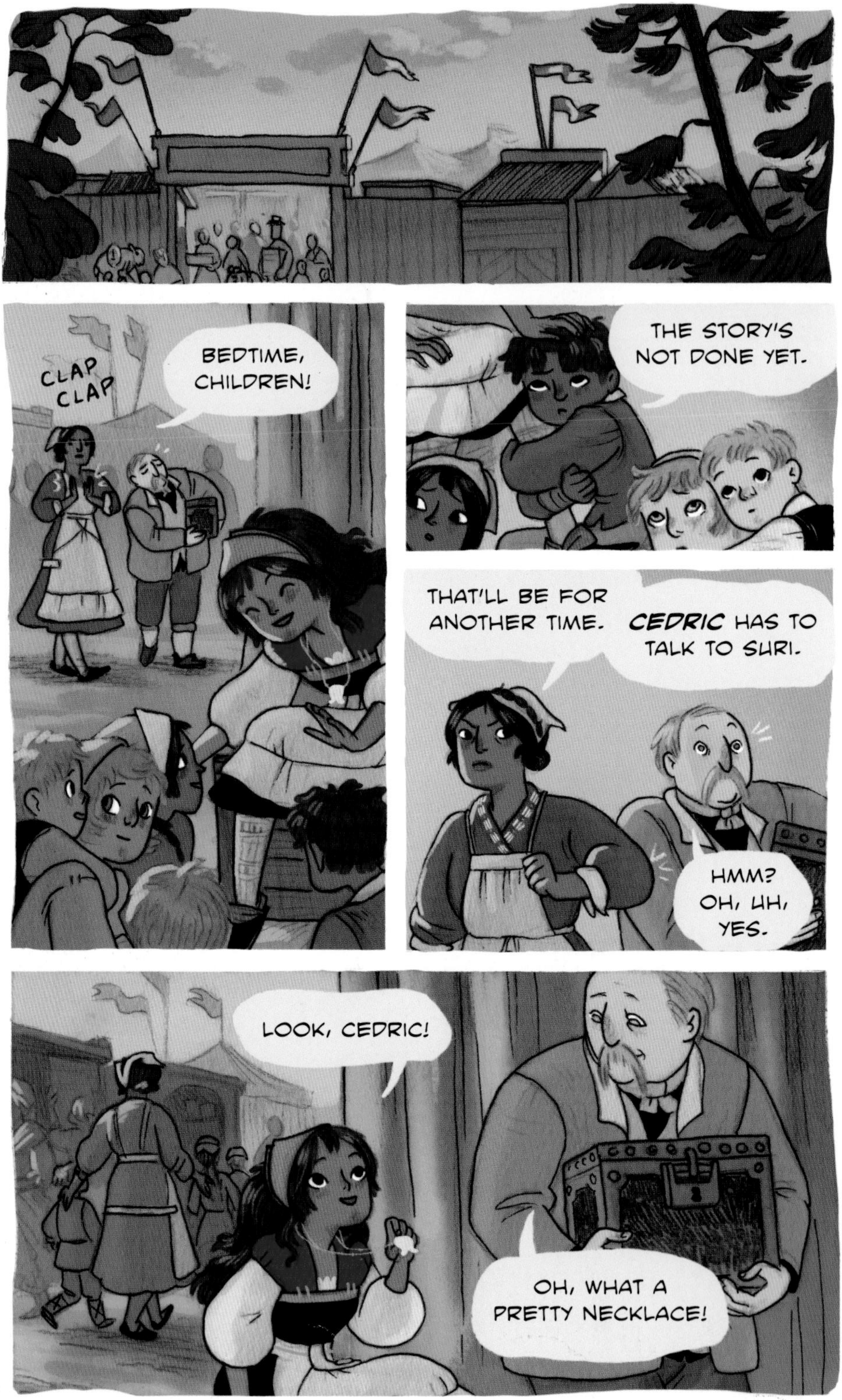
CLAP
CLAP
BEDTIME, CHILDREN!
THE STORY'S NOT DONE YET.
THAT'LL BE FOR ANOTHER TIME.
CEDRIC HAS TO TALK TO SURI.
HMM? OH, UH, YES.
LOOK, CEDRIC!
OH, WHAT A PRETTY NECKLACE!

IT'S A DRAGON TOOTH. IT'S SUPPOSED TO BE A POWERFUL AMULET THAT CAN—

MMHMM.

GRR. YOU'RE NOT LISTENING!

SIGH

SURI... HOW LONG DO YOU THINK YOU CAN OUTRUN LEON?

WELL, IF I'VE HAD BREAKFAST, AND I'M WEARING MY GOOD SHOES...

NO, THAT'S NOT WHAT I MEANT!

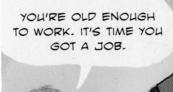

YOU'RE OLD ENOUGH TO WORK. IT'S TIME YOU GOT A JOB.

I HAVE A JOB!

I MEAN A **REAL** JOB. THIS IDEA OF BEING A MONSTER TAMER, IT'S... NOT REALISTIC!

AND ALL BECAUSE OF A DREAM YOU HAD WHEN YOU WERE LITTLE...

IT WASN'T A DREAM!

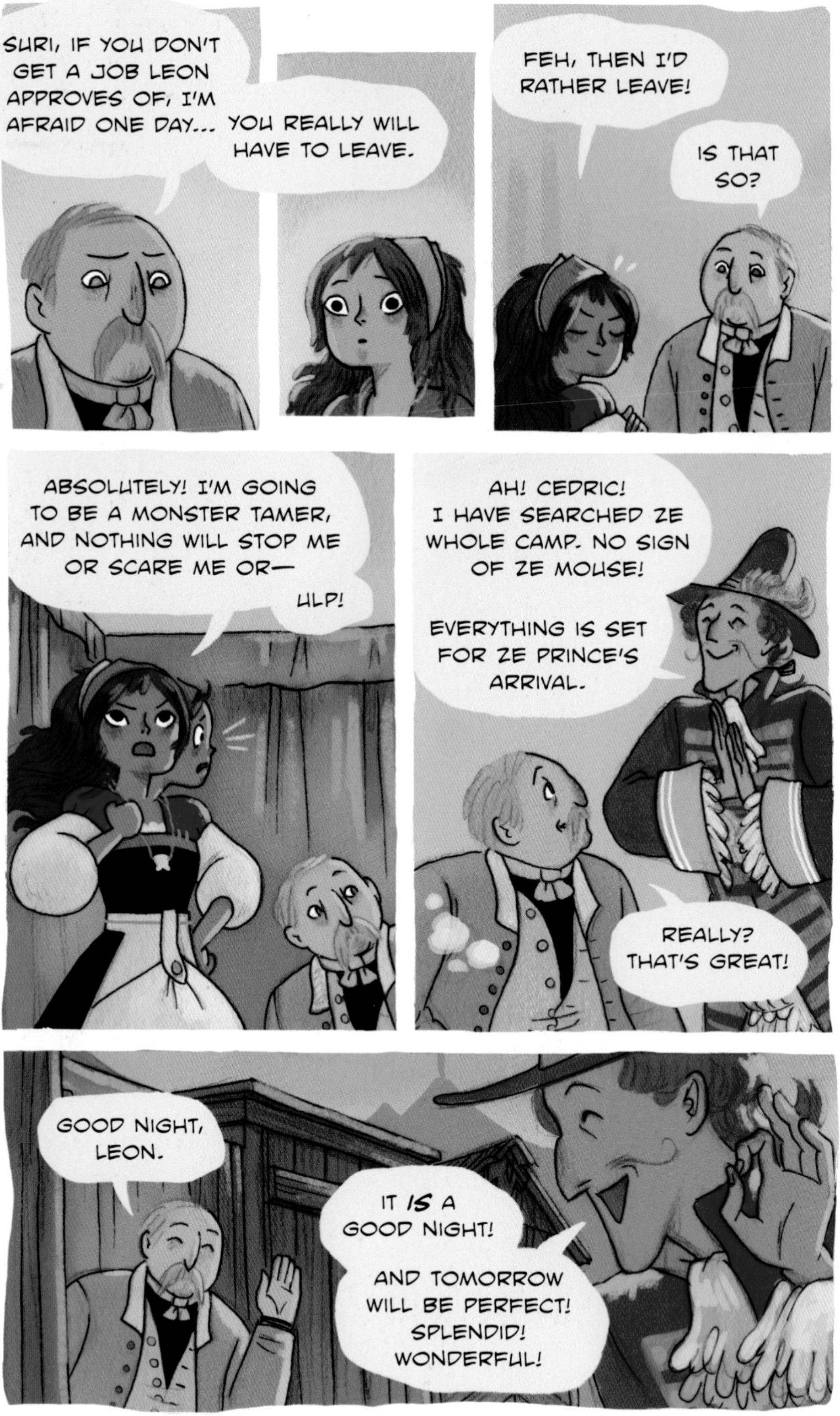
SURI, IF YOU DON'T GET A JOB LEON APPROVES OF, I'M AFRAID ONE DAY...
YOU REALLY WILL HAVE TO LEAVE.
FEH, THEN I'D RATHER LEAVE!
IS THAT SO?
ABSOLUTELY! I'M GOING TO BE A MONSTER TAMER, AND NOTHING WILL STOP ME OR SCARE ME OR—
ULP!
AH! CEDRIC! I HAVE SEARCHED ZE WHOLE CAMP. NO SIGN OF ZE MOUSE!
EVERYTHING IS SET FOR ZE PRINCE'S ARRIVAL.
REALLY? THAT'S GREAT!
GOOD NIGHT, LEON.
IT *IS* A GOOD NIGHT!
AND TOMORROW WILL BE PERFECT! SPLENDID! WONDERFUL!

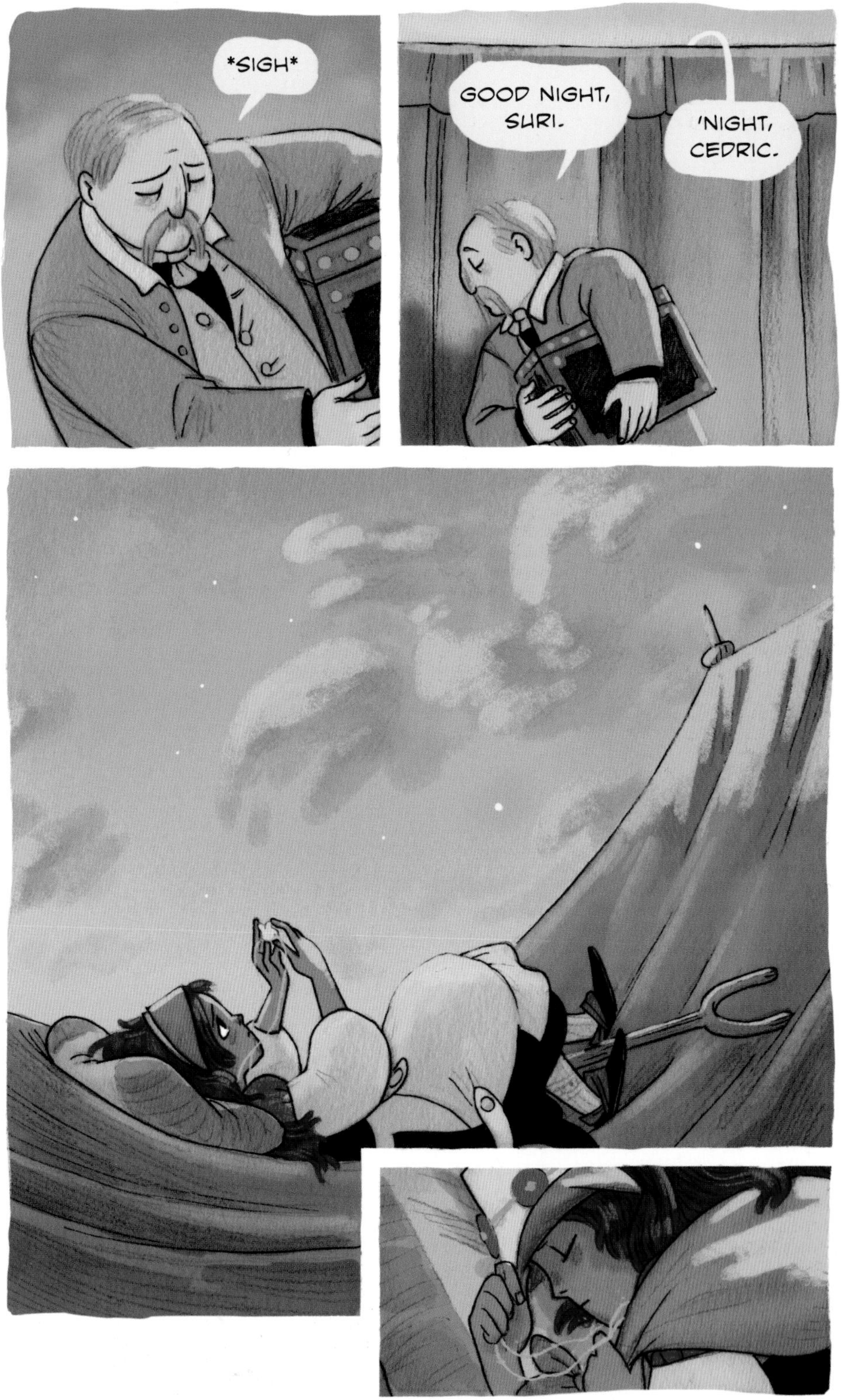
SIGH
GOOD NIGHT, SURI.
'NIGHT, CEDRIC.

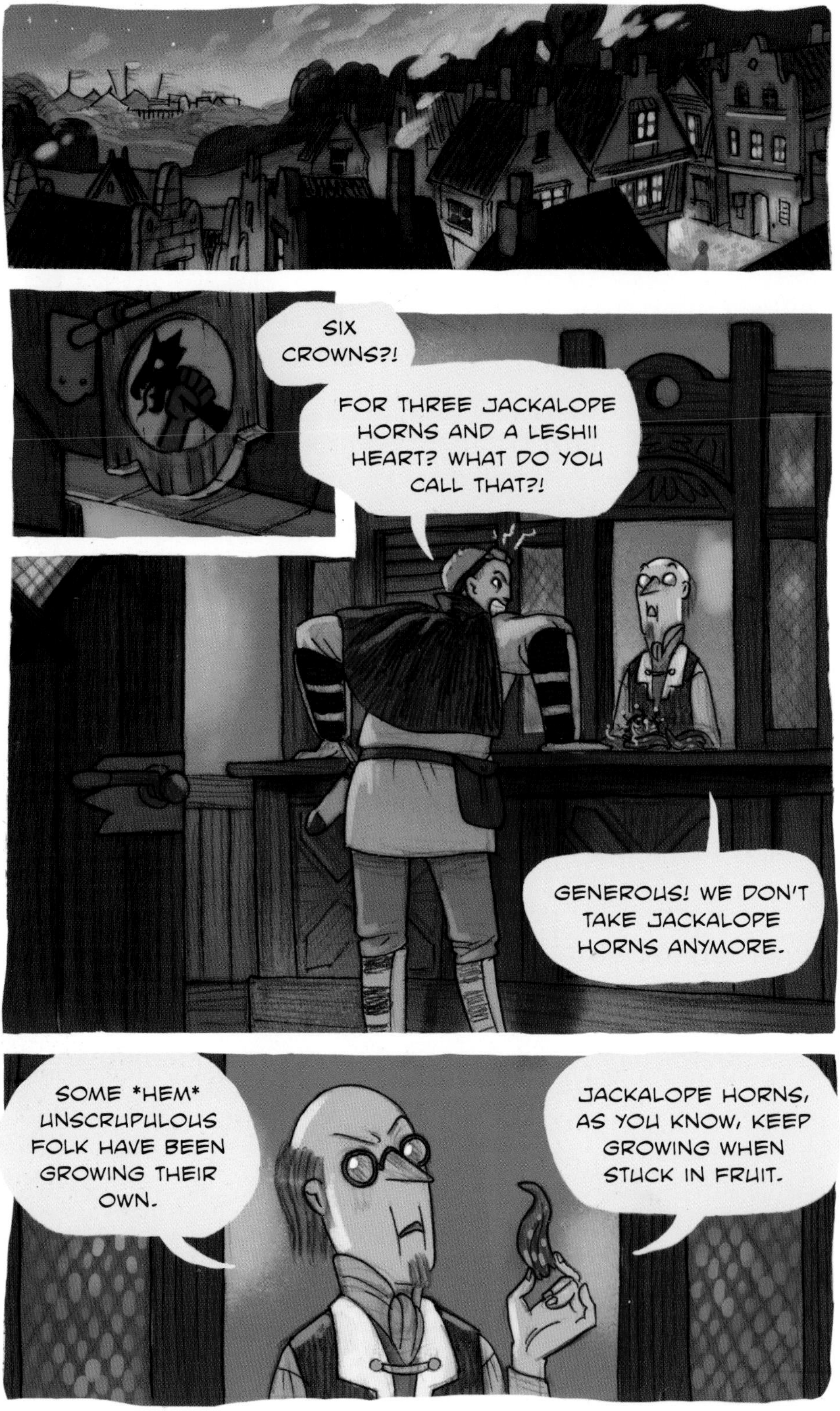
SIX CROWNS?!
FOR THREE JACKALOPE HORNS AND A LESHII HEART? WHAT DO YOU CALL THAT?!
GENEROUS! WE DON'T TAKE JACKALOPE HORNS ANYMORE.
JACKALOPE HORNS, AS YOU KNOW, KEEP GROWING WHEN STUCK IN FRUIT.
SOME *HEM* UNSCRUPULOUS FOLK HAVE BEEN GROWING THEIR OWN.

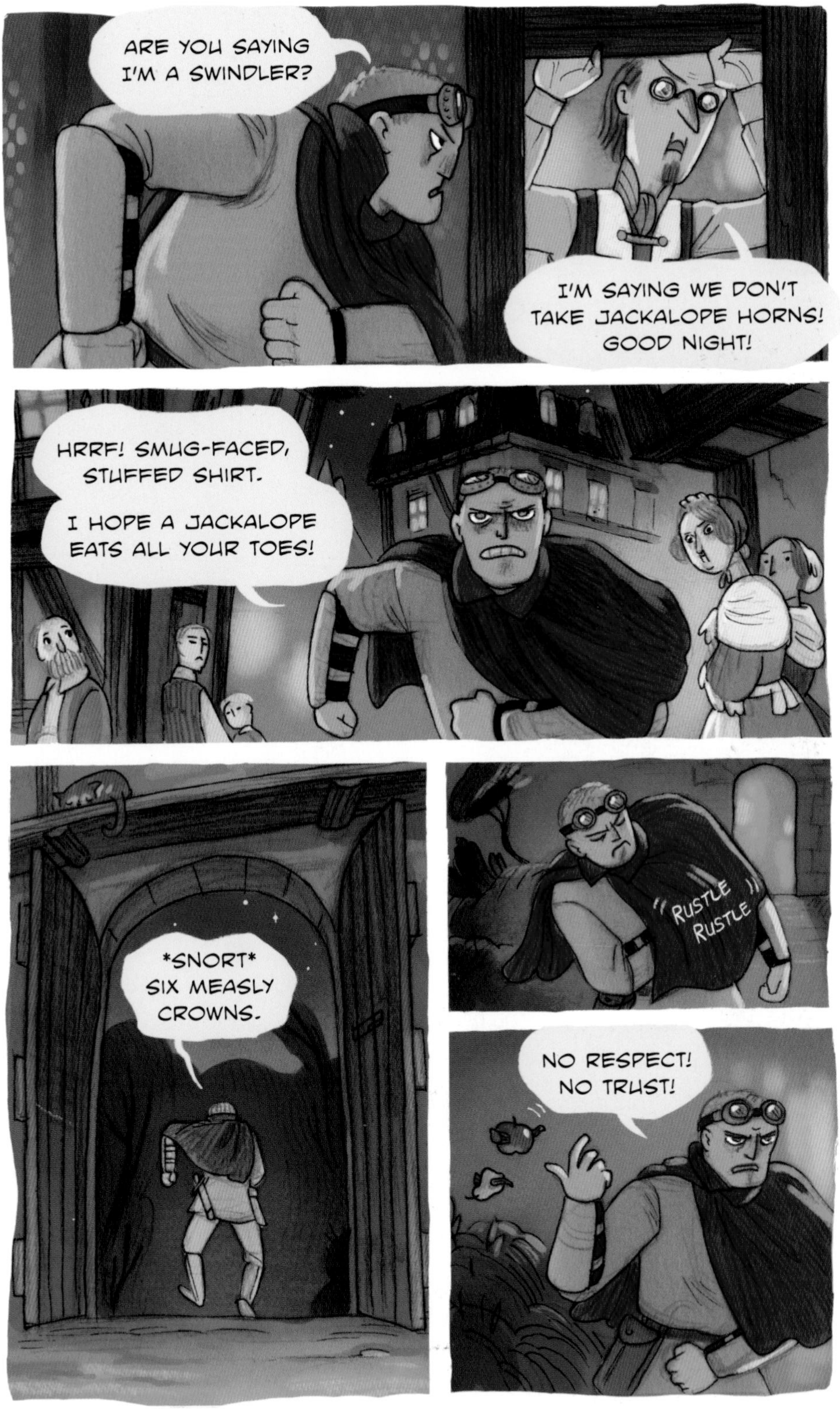
ARE YOU SAYING I'M A SWINDLER?
I'M SAYING WE DON'T TAKE JACKALOPE HORNS! GOOD NIGHT!
HRRF! SMUG-FACED, STUFFED SHIRT.
I HOPE A JACKALOPE EATS ALL YOUR TOES!
SNORT SIX MEASLY CROWNS.
RUSTLE RUSTLE
NO RESPECT! NO TRUST!

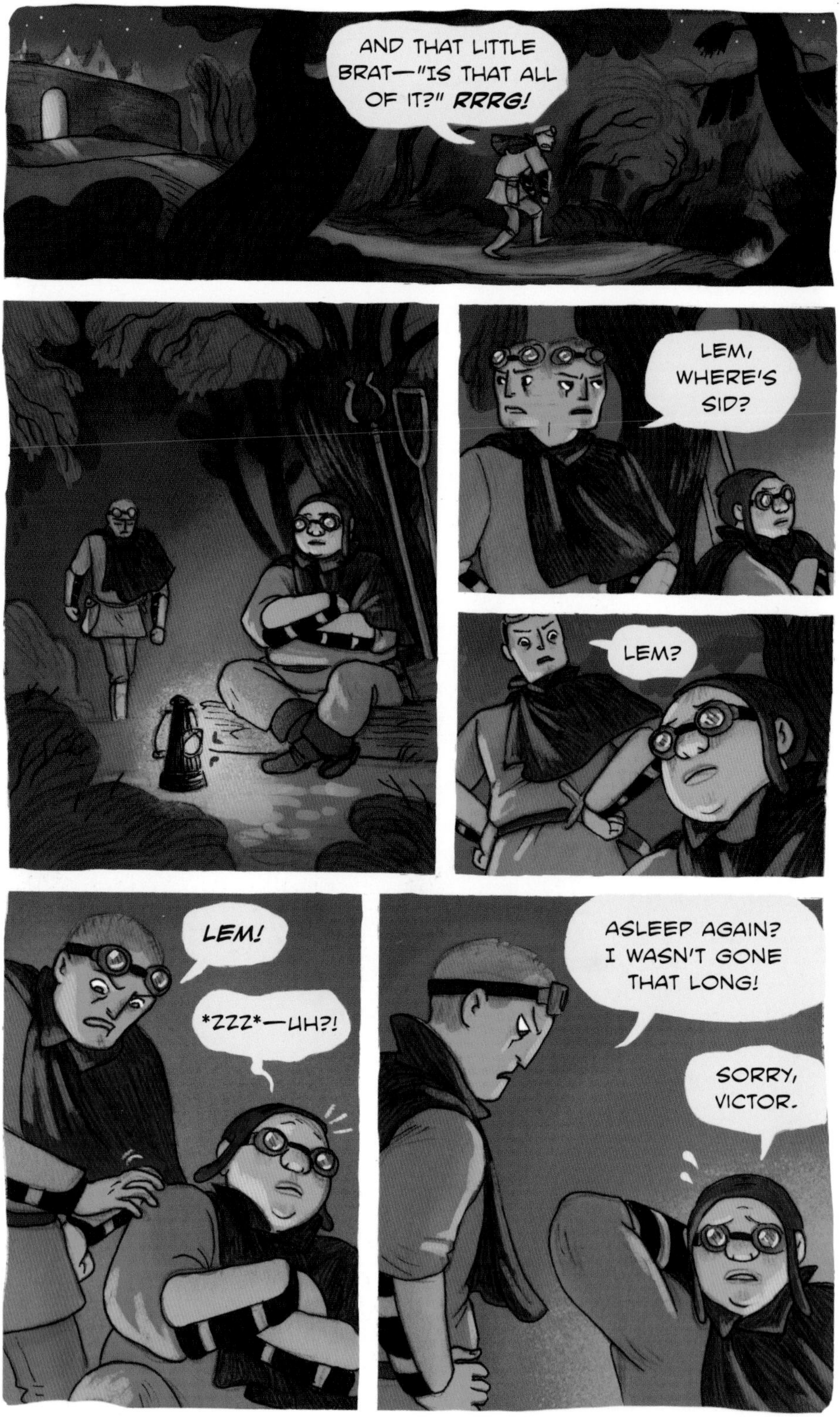

AND THAT LITTLE BRAT—"IS THAT ALL OF IT?" *RRRG!*
LEM, WHERE'S SID?
LEM?
LEM!
ZZZ—UH?!
ASLEEP AGAIN? I WASN'T GONE THAT LONG!
SORRY, VICTOR.

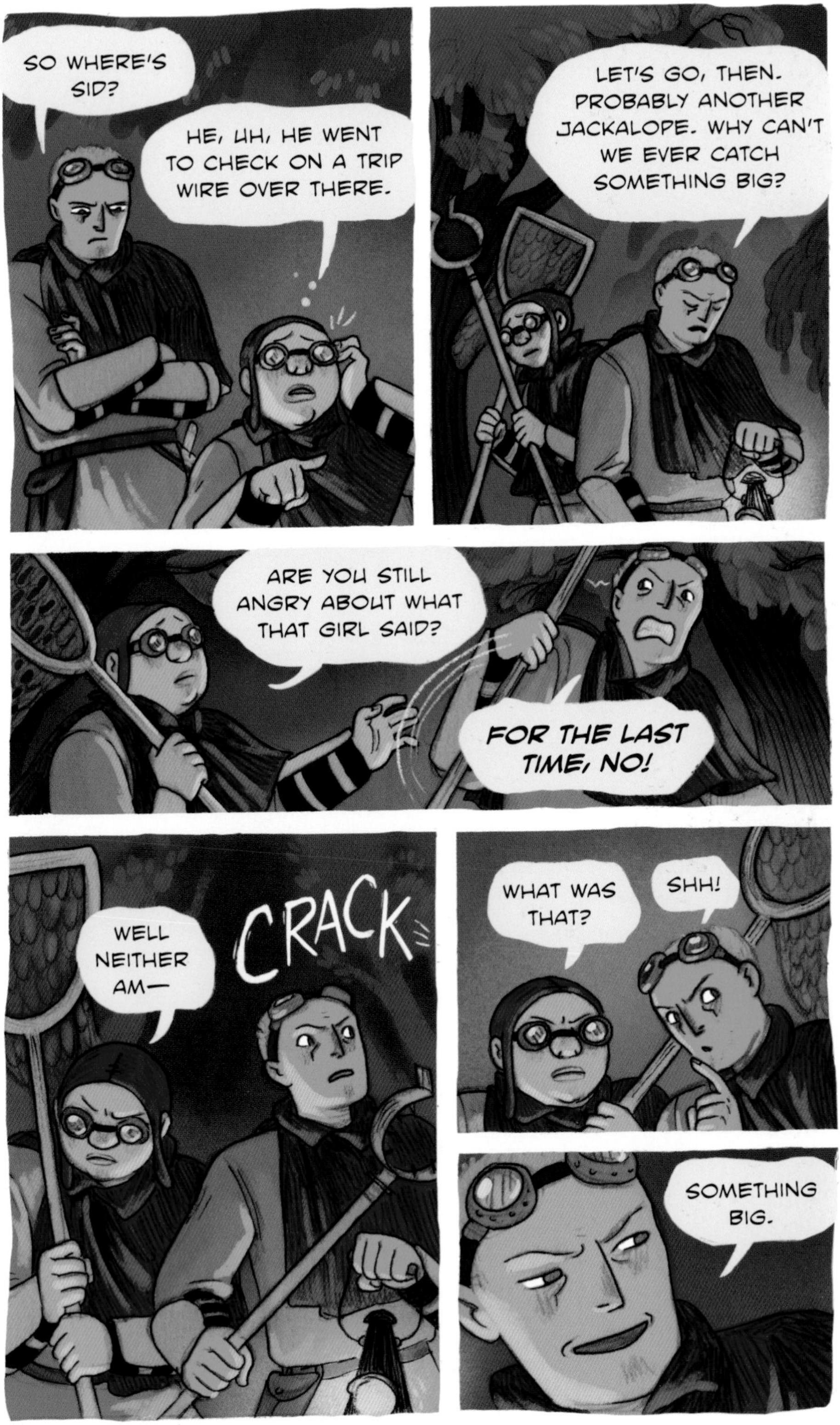
SO WHERE'S SID?
HE, UH, HE WENT TO CHECK ON A TRIP WIRE OVER THERE.
LET'S GO, THEN. PROBABLY ANOTHER JACKALOPE. WHY CAN'T WE EVER CATCH SOMETHING BIG?
ARE YOU STILL ANGRY ABOUT WHAT THAT GIRL SAID?
FOR THE LAST TIME, NO!
WELL NEITHER AM—
CRACK
WHAT WAS THAT?
SHH!
SOMETHING BIG.

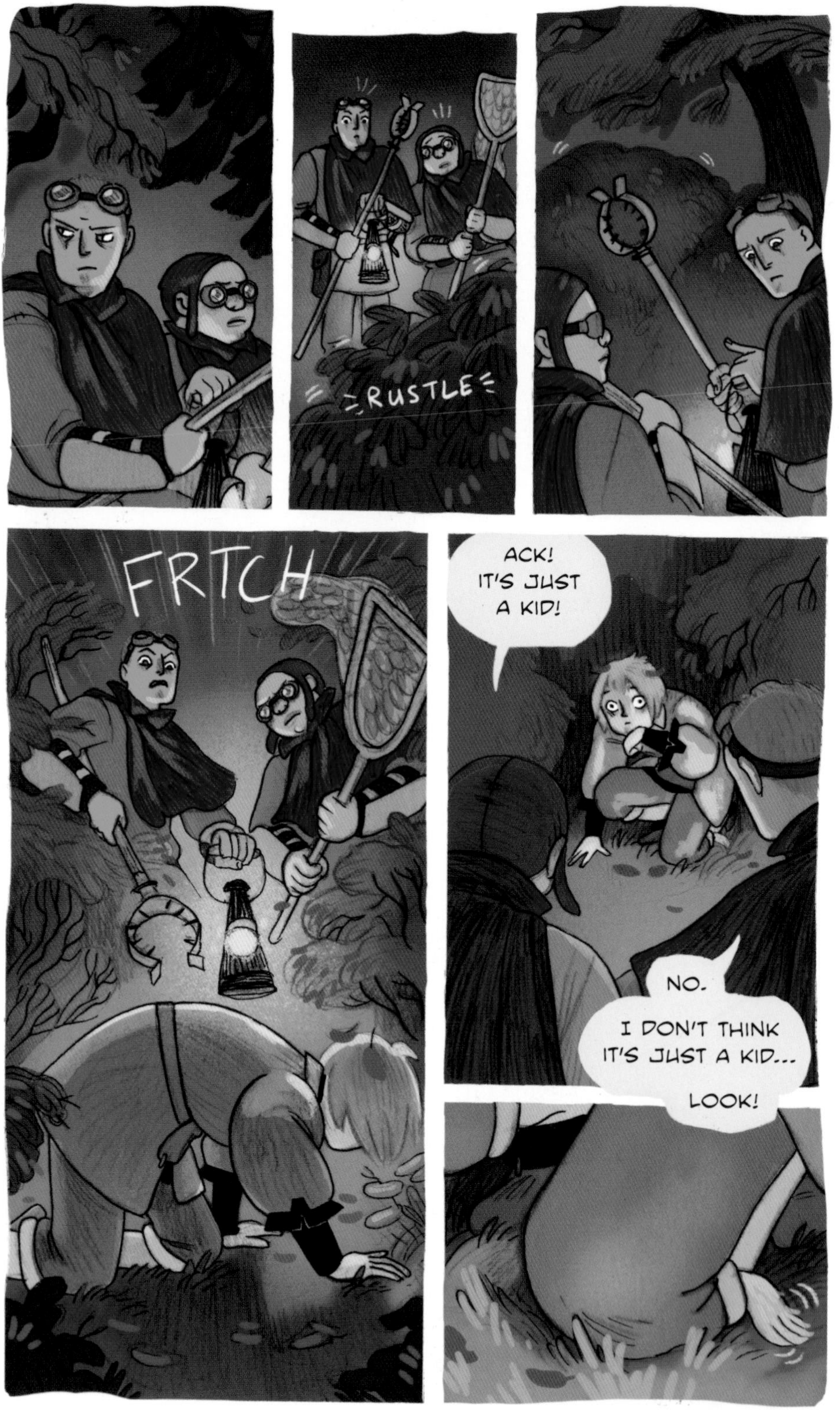
RUSTLE
FRTCH
ACK! IT'S JUST A KID!
NO.
I DON'T THINK IT'S JUST A KID...
LOOK!

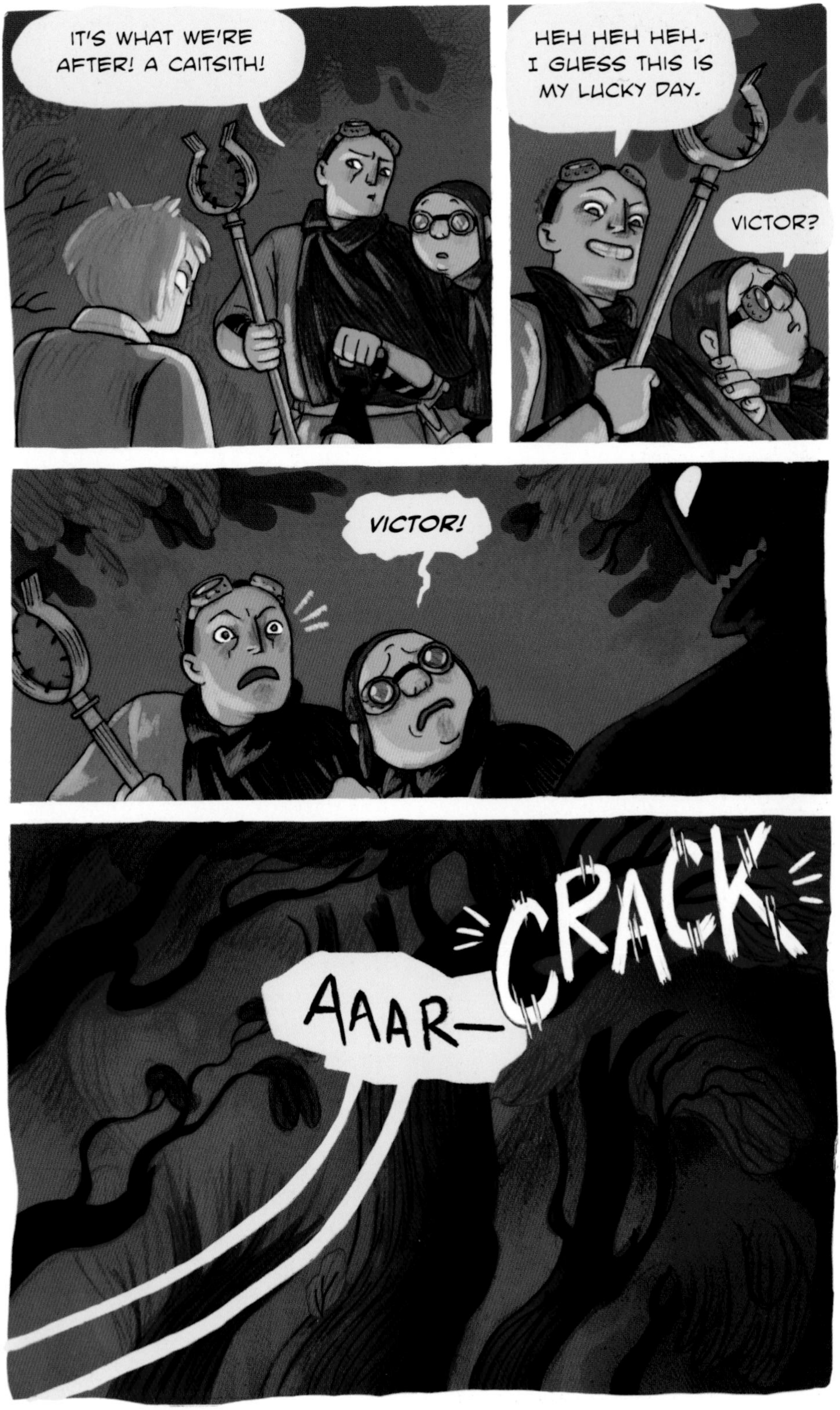
IT'S WHAT WE'RE AFTER! A CAITSITH!
HEH HEH HEH. I GUESS THIS IS MY LUCKY DAY.
VICTOR?
VICTOR!
AAAR—
CRACK

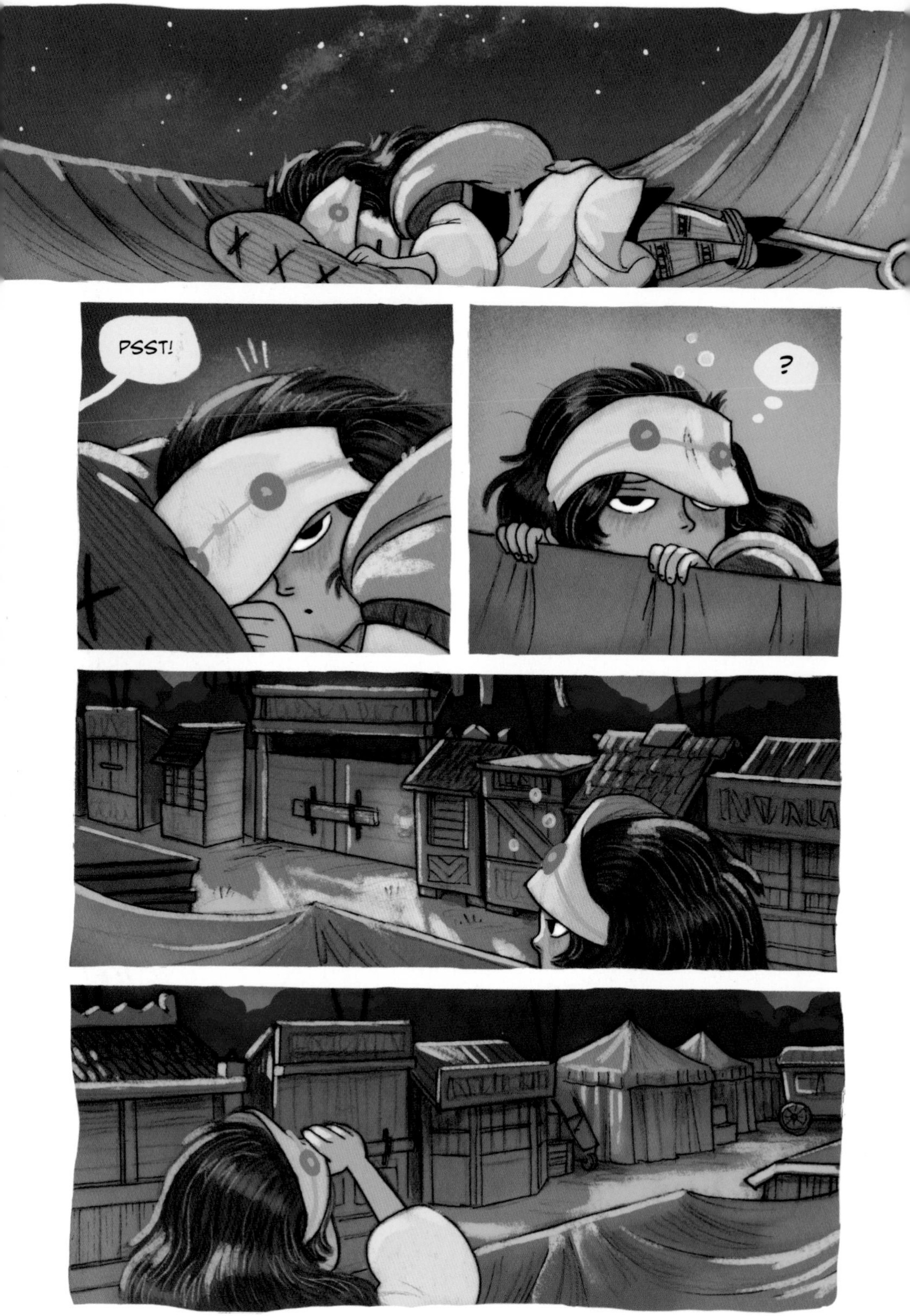
PSST!
?

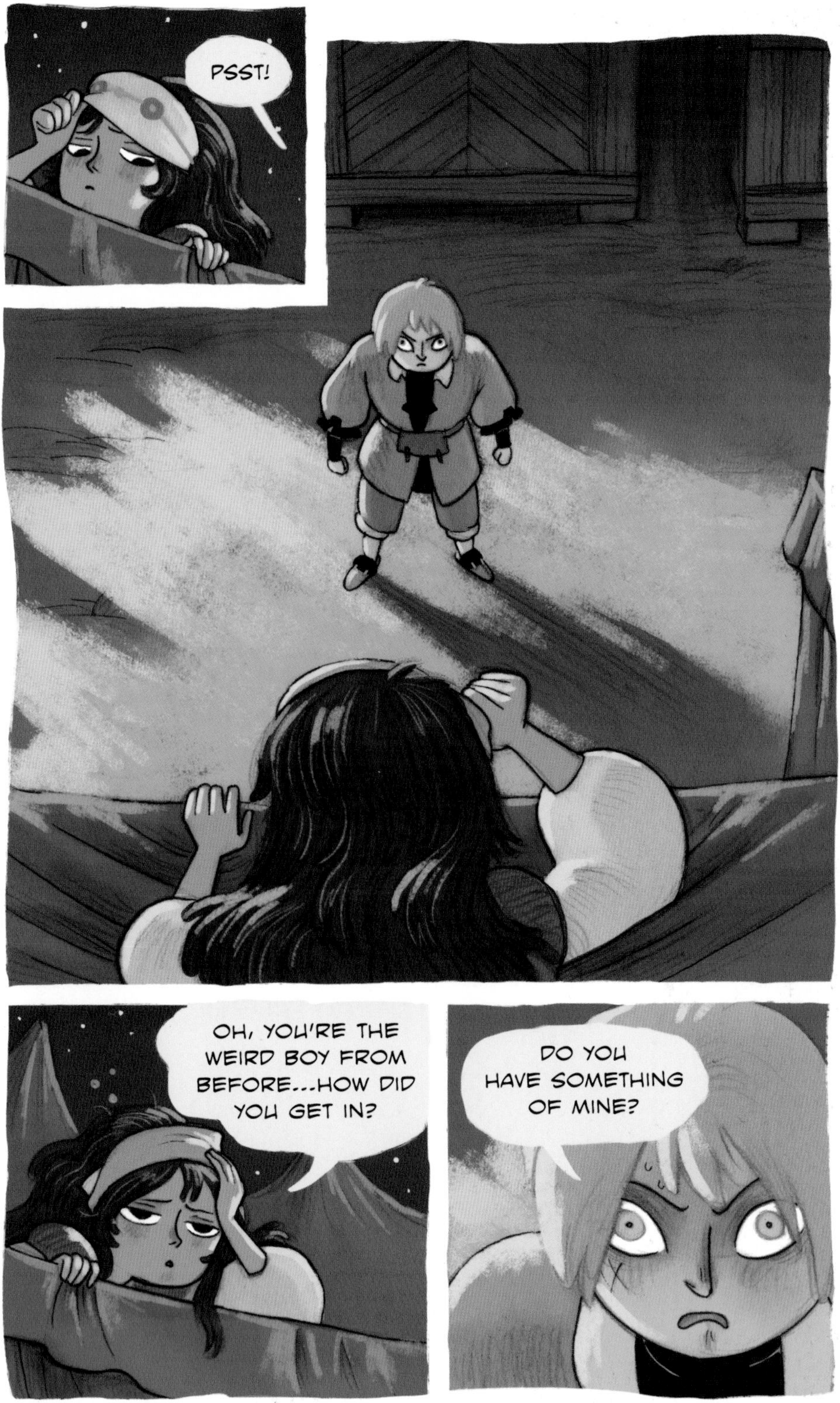
PSST!
OH, YOU'RE THE WEIRD BOY FROM BEFORE...HOW DID YOU GET IN?
DO YOU HAVE SOMETHING OF MINE?

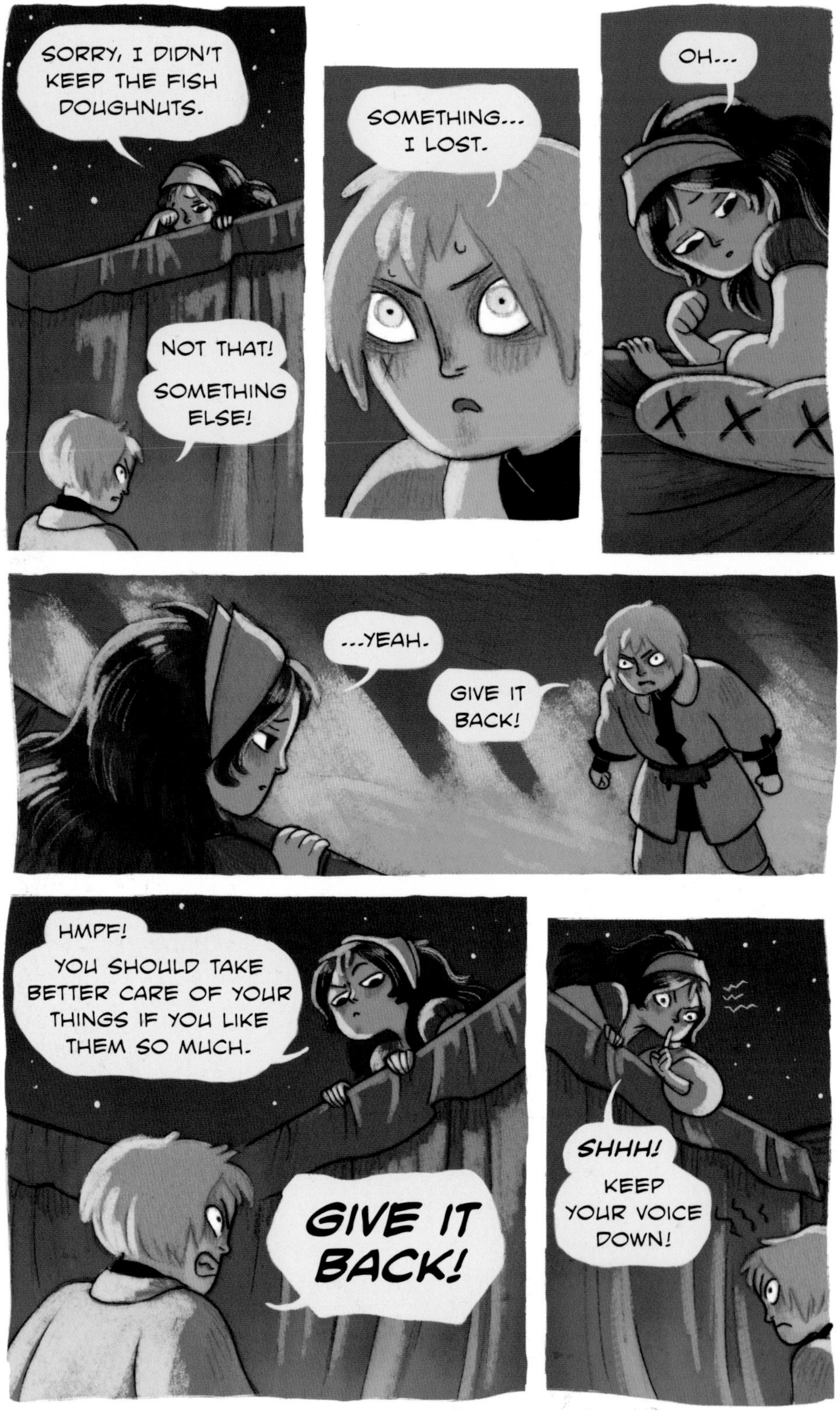
SORRY, I DIDN'T KEEP THE FISH DOUGHNUTS.
NOT THAT! SOMETHING ELSE!
SOMETHING... I LOST.
OH...
...YEAH.
GIVE IT BACK!
HMPF!
YOU SHOULD TAKE BETTER CARE OF YOUR THINGS IF YOU LIKE THEM SO MUCH.
GIVE IT BACK!
SHHH!
KEEP YOUR VOICE DOWN!

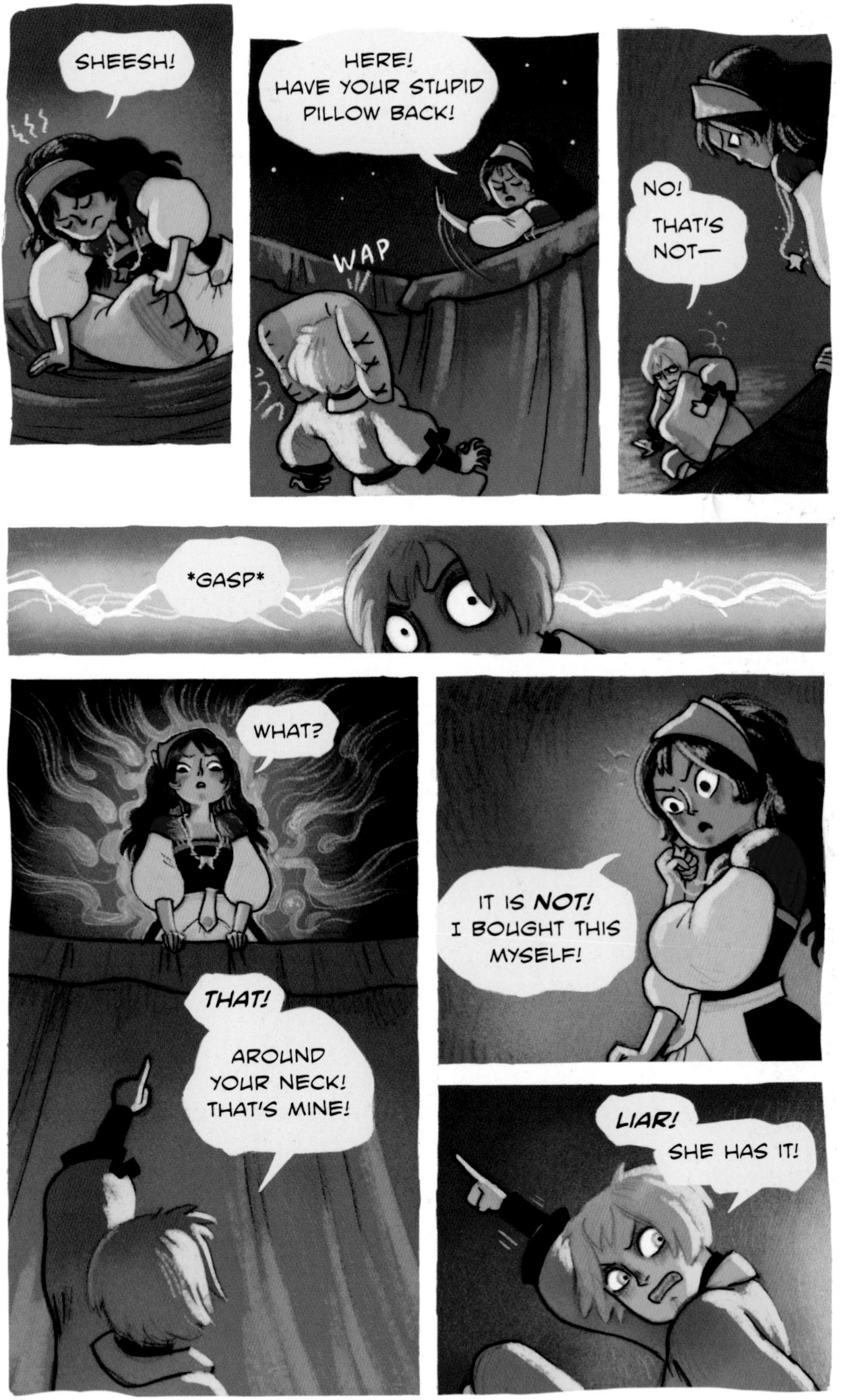
SHEESH!
HERE! HAVE YOUR STUPID PILLOW BACK!
WAP
NO!
THAT'S NOT—
GASP
WHAT?
THAT!
AROUND YOUR NECK! THAT'S MINE!
IT IS **NOT!** I BOUGHT THIS MYSELF!
LIAR!
SHE HAS IT!

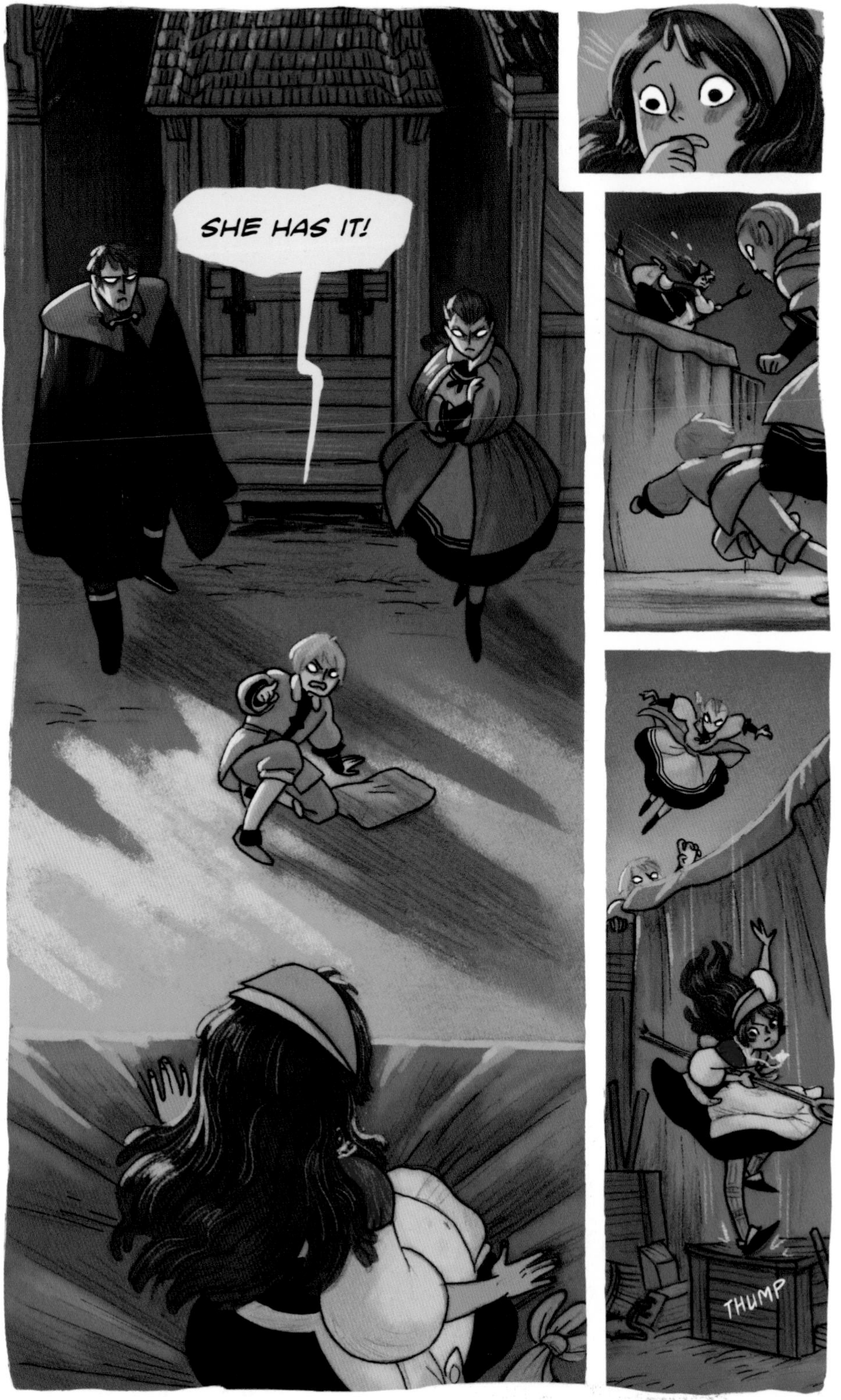
SHE HAS IT!
THUMP

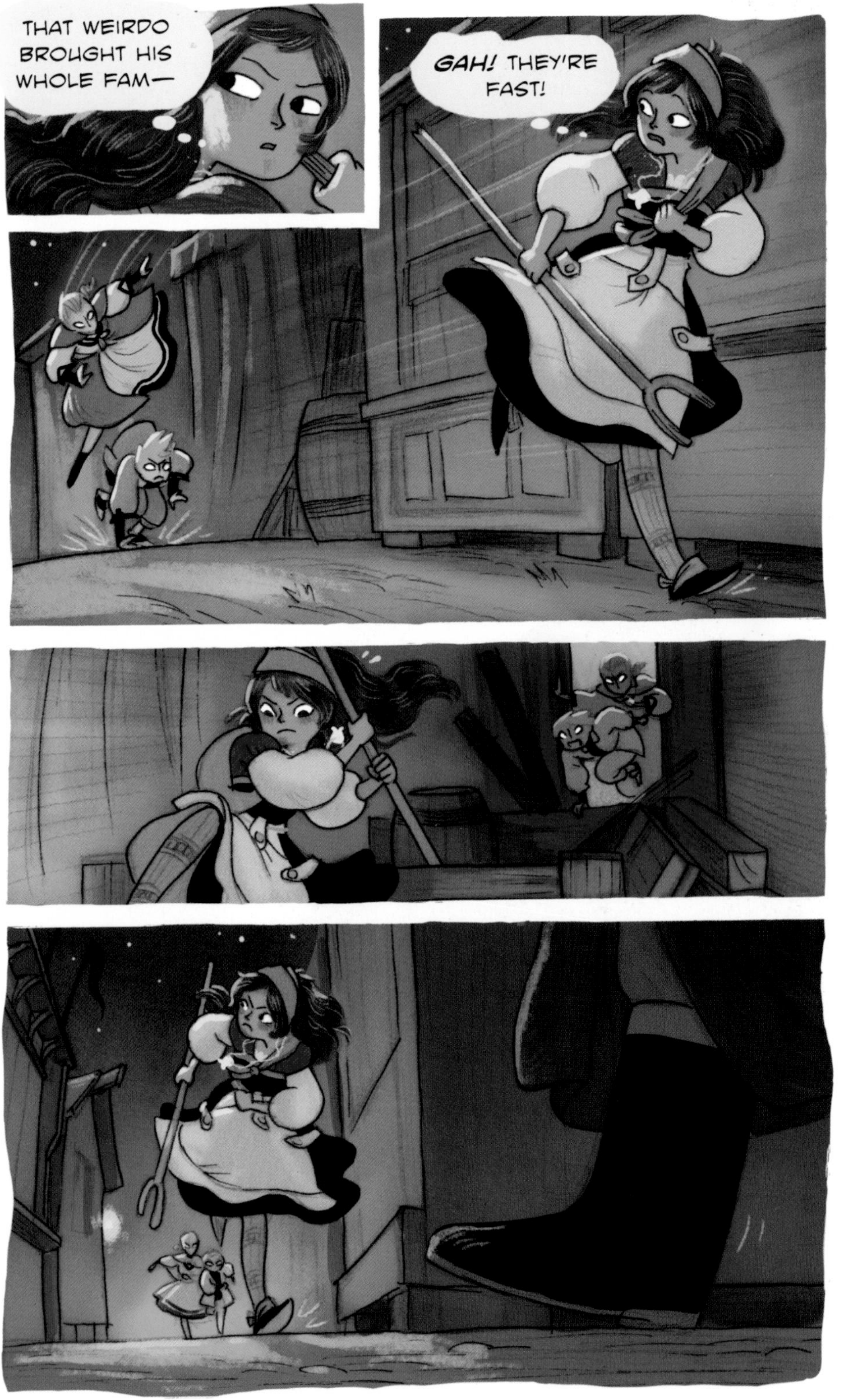
THAT WEIRDO BROUGHT HIS WHOLE FAM—
GAH! THEY'RE FAST!

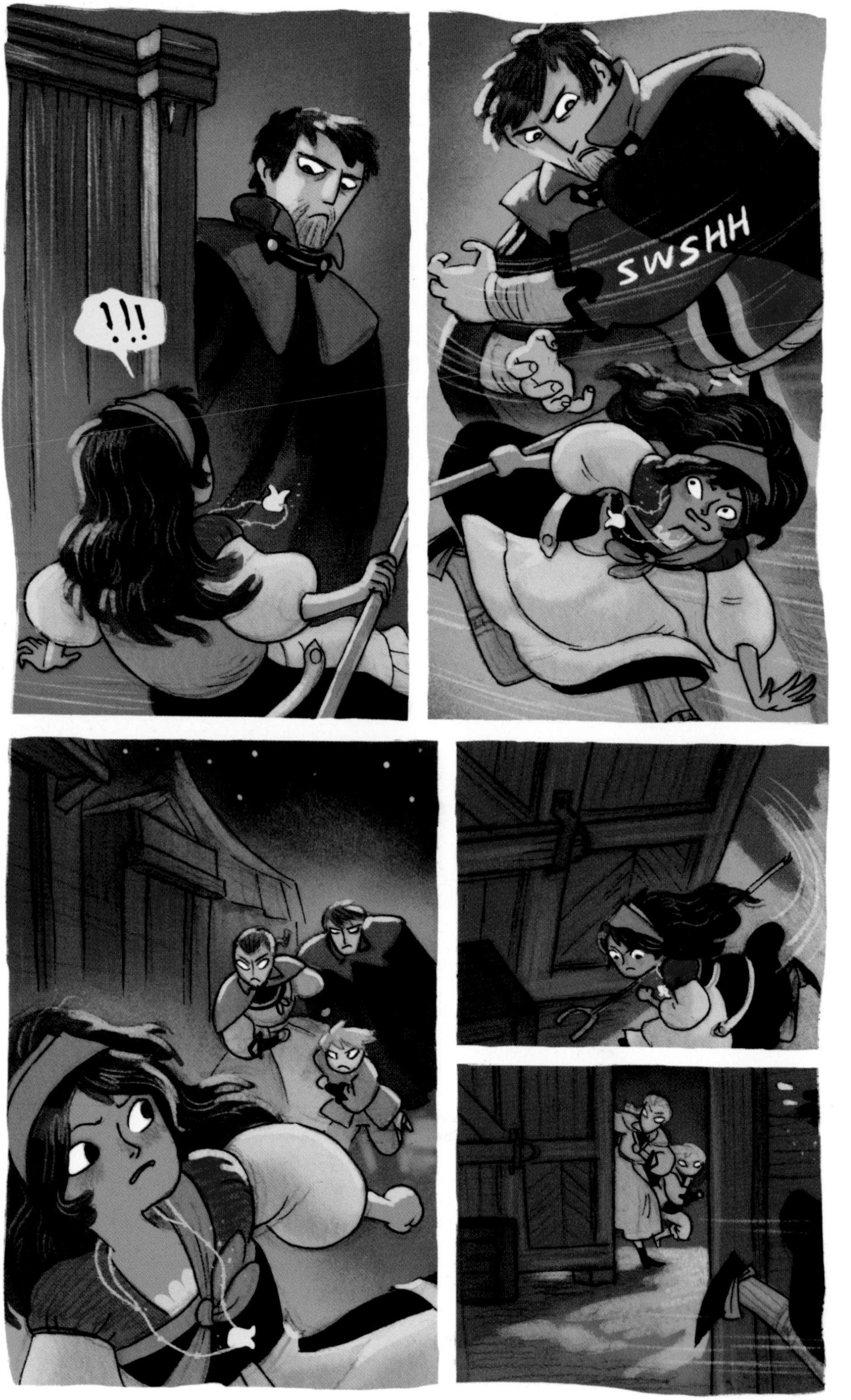
!!!
SWSHH

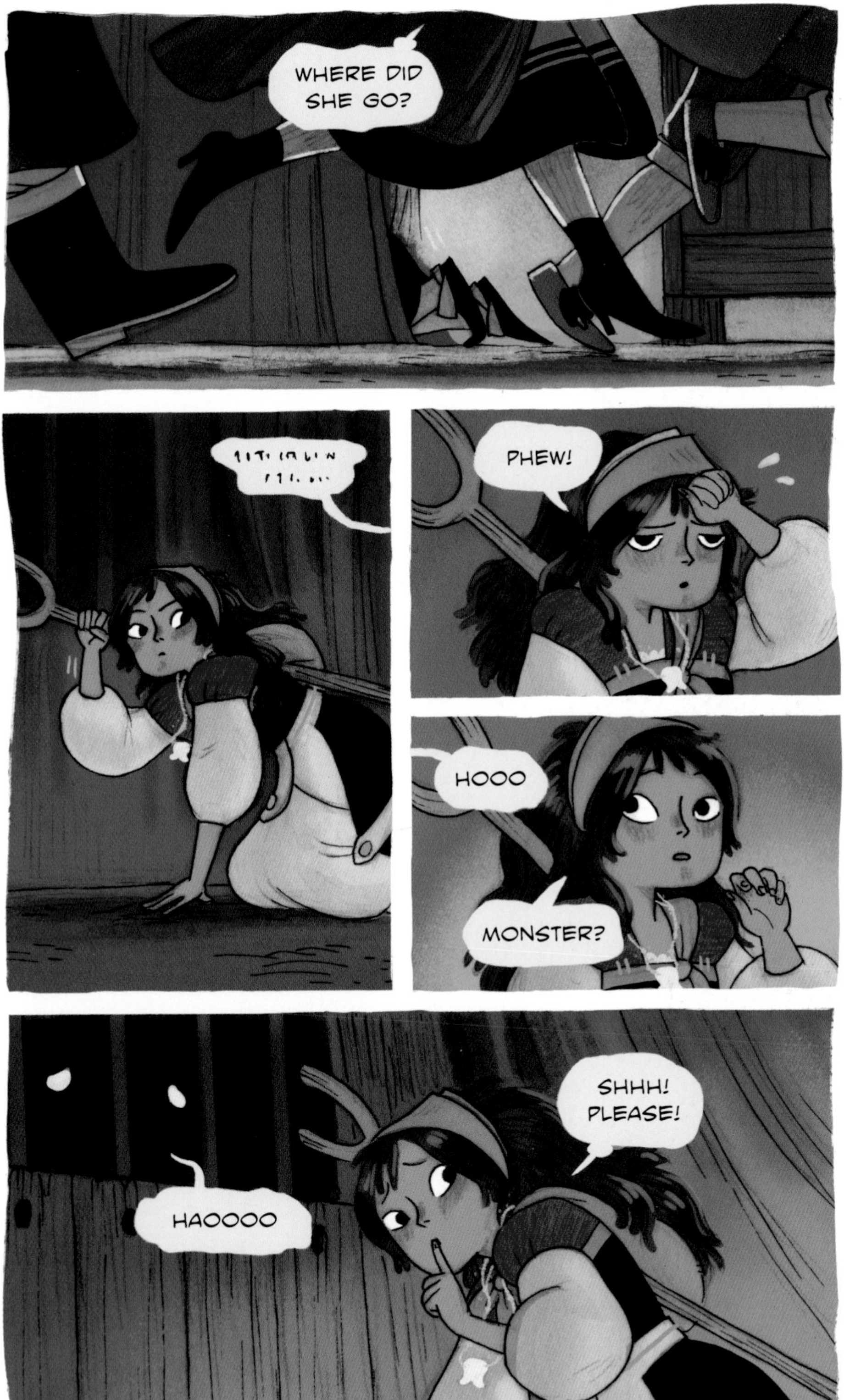
WHERE DID SHE GO?
PHEW!
HOOO
MONSTER?
HAOOOO
SHHH! PLEASE!

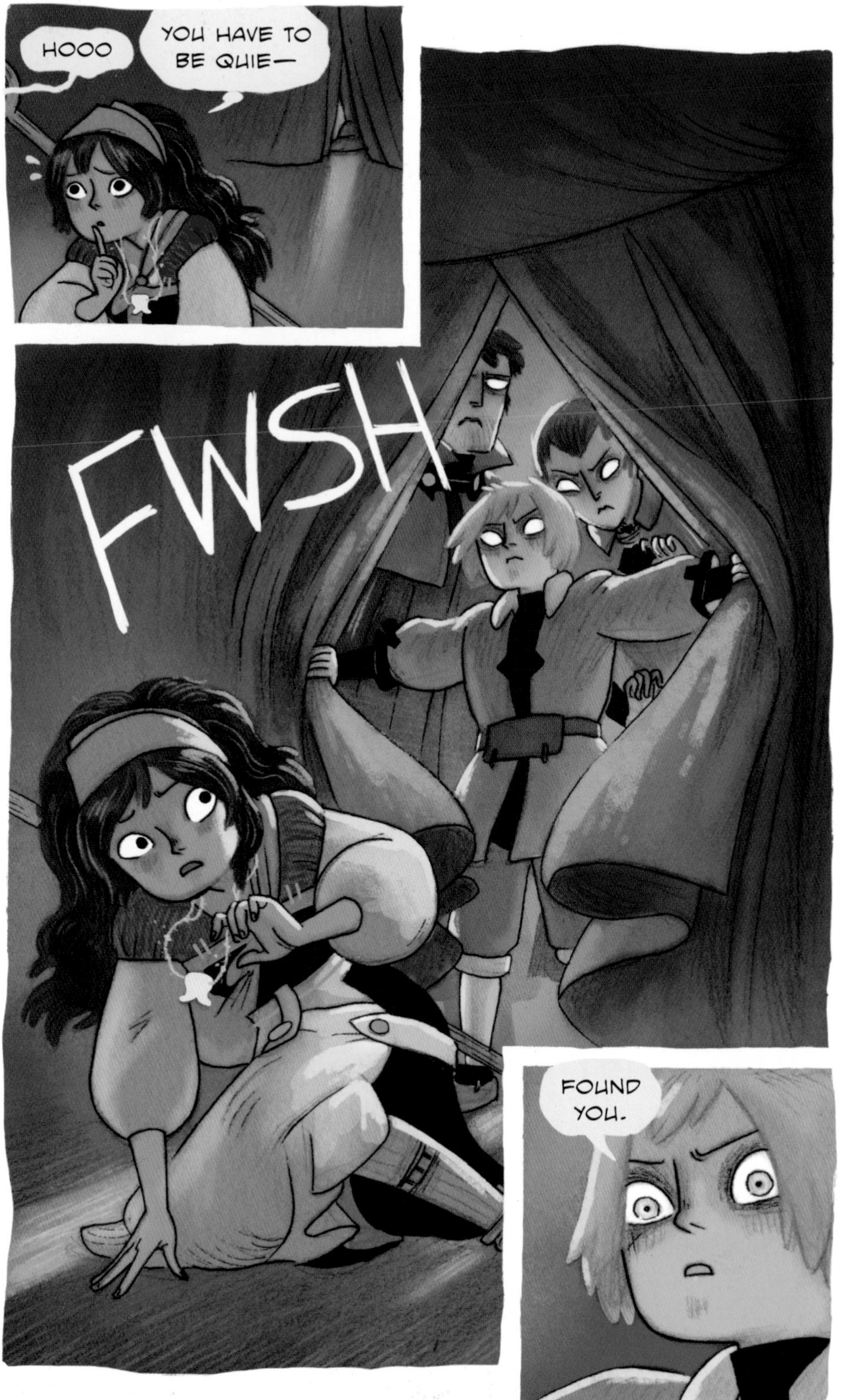
HOOO
YOU HAVE TO BE QUIE—
FWSH
FOUND YOU.

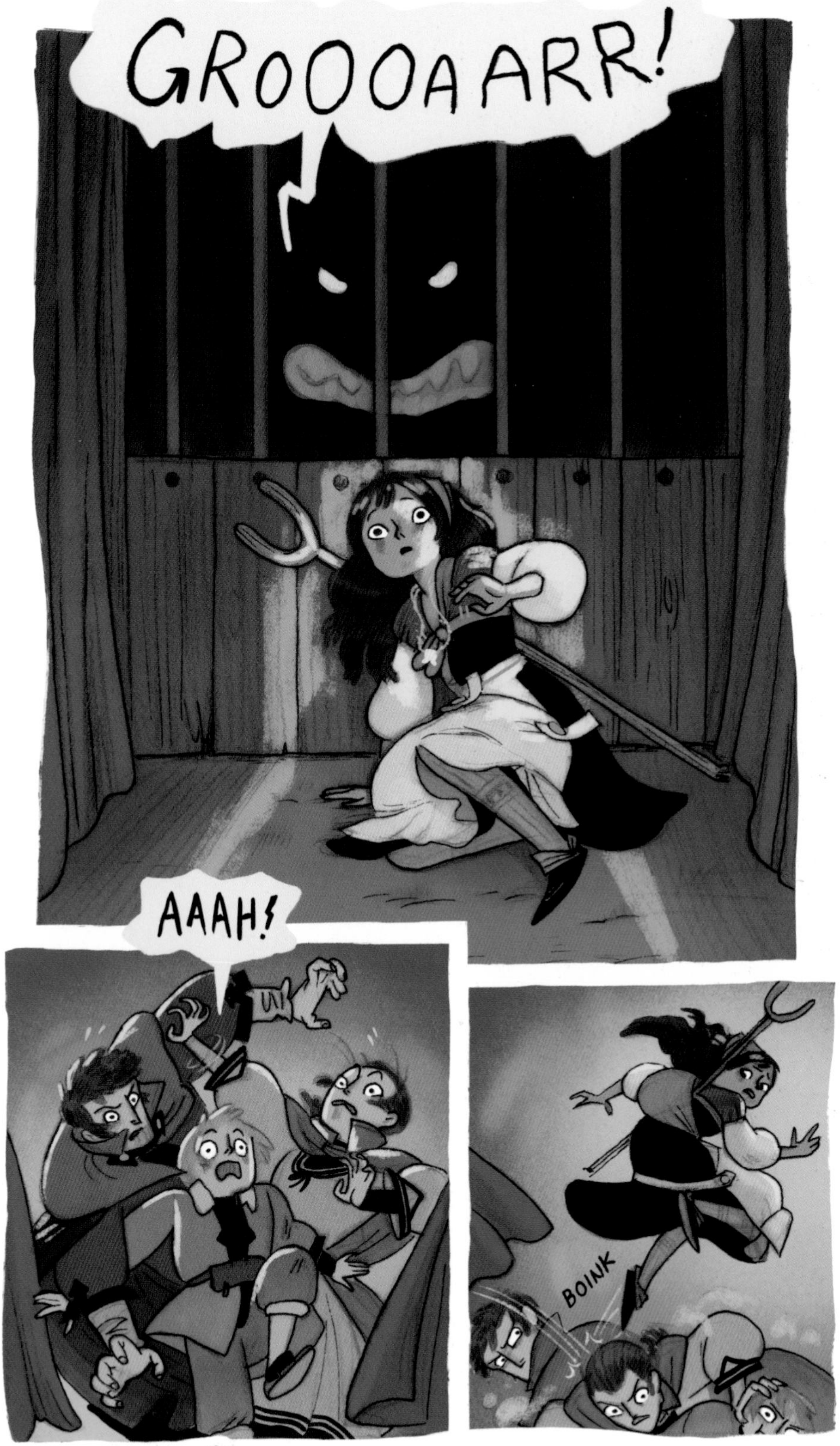
GROOOAARR!
AAAH!
BOINK

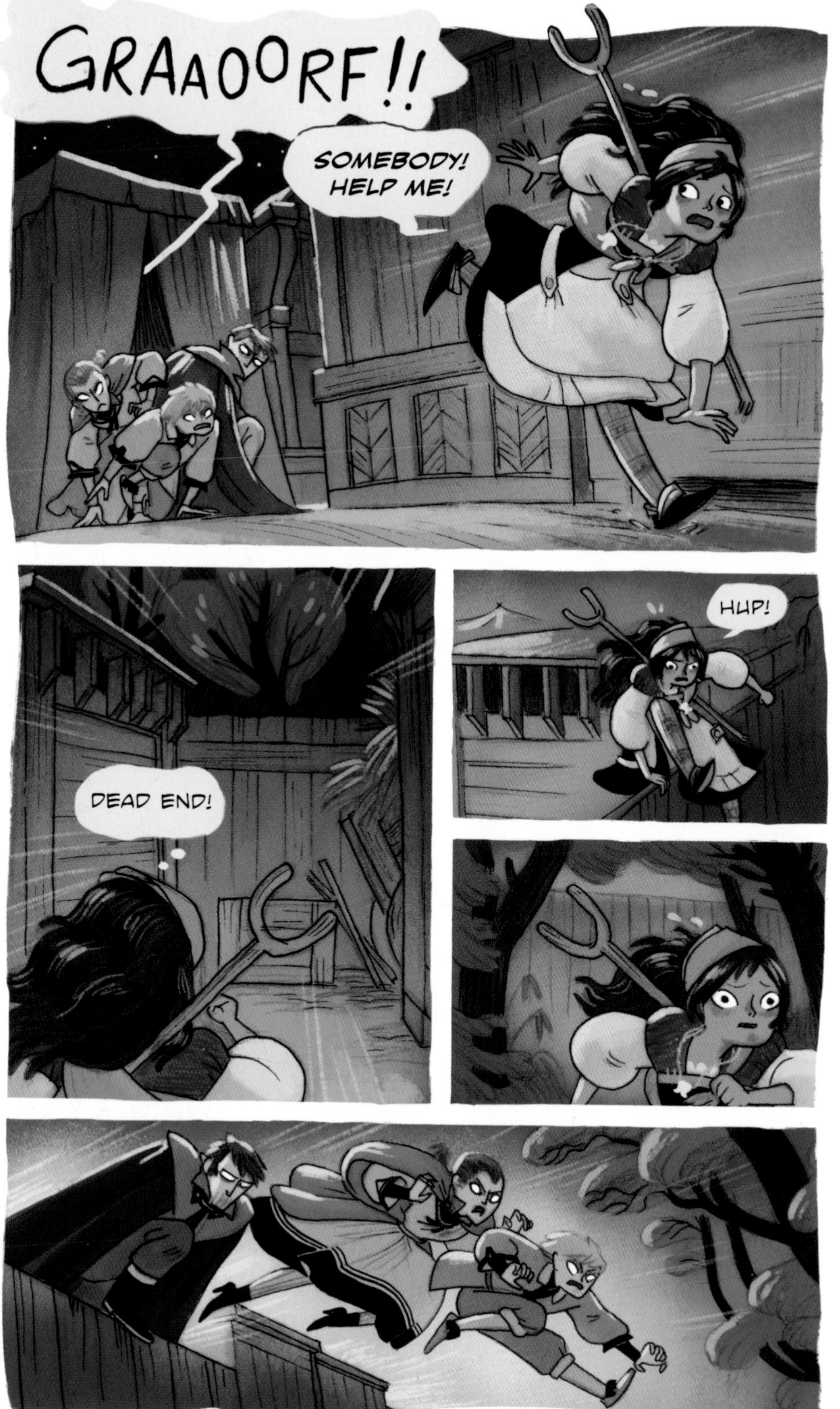
GRAAOORF!!
SOMEBODY! HELP ME!
DEAD END!
HUP!

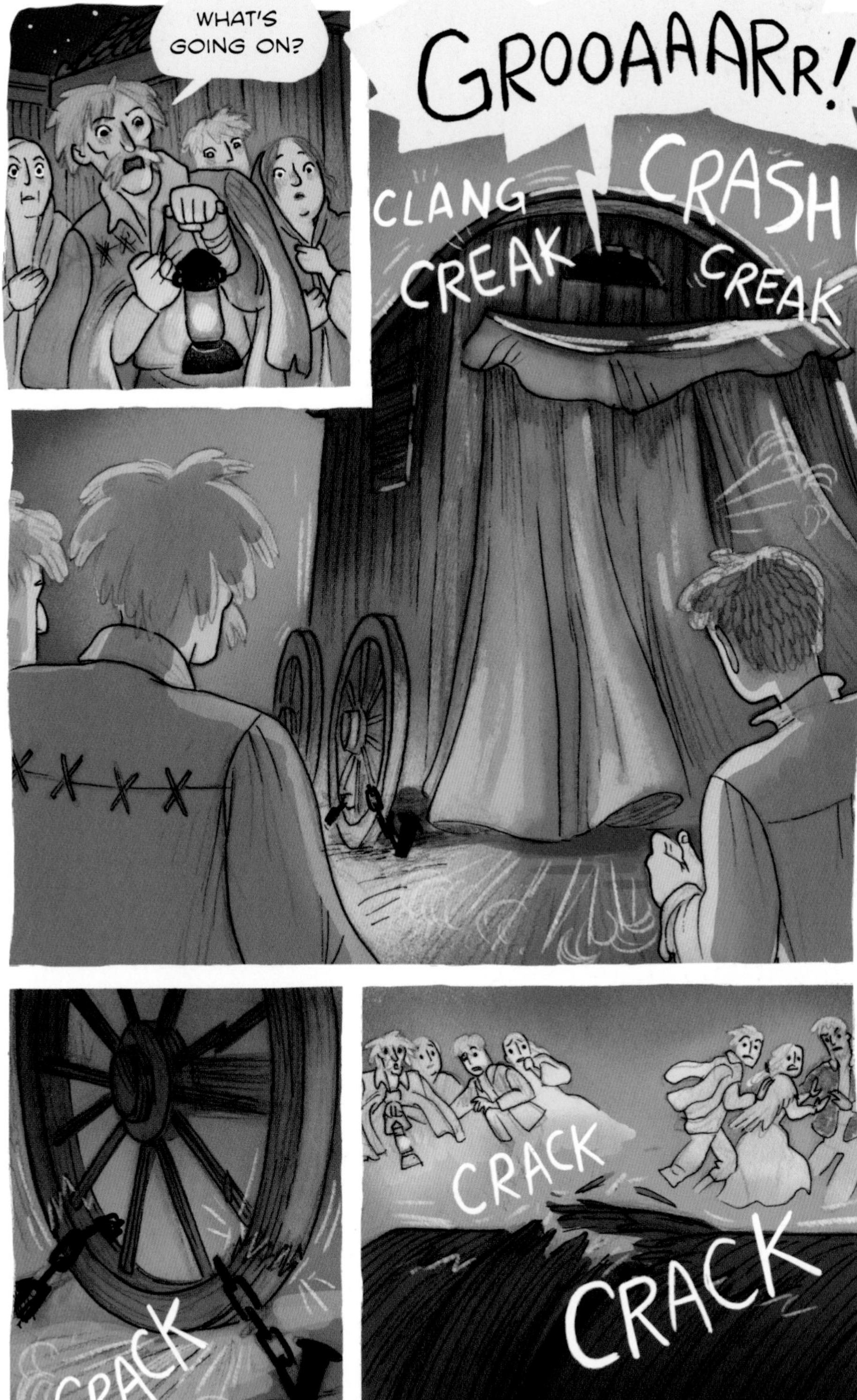
WHAT'S GOING ON?
GROOAAARR!
CLANG
CREAK
CRASH
CREAK
CRACK
CRACK
CRACK

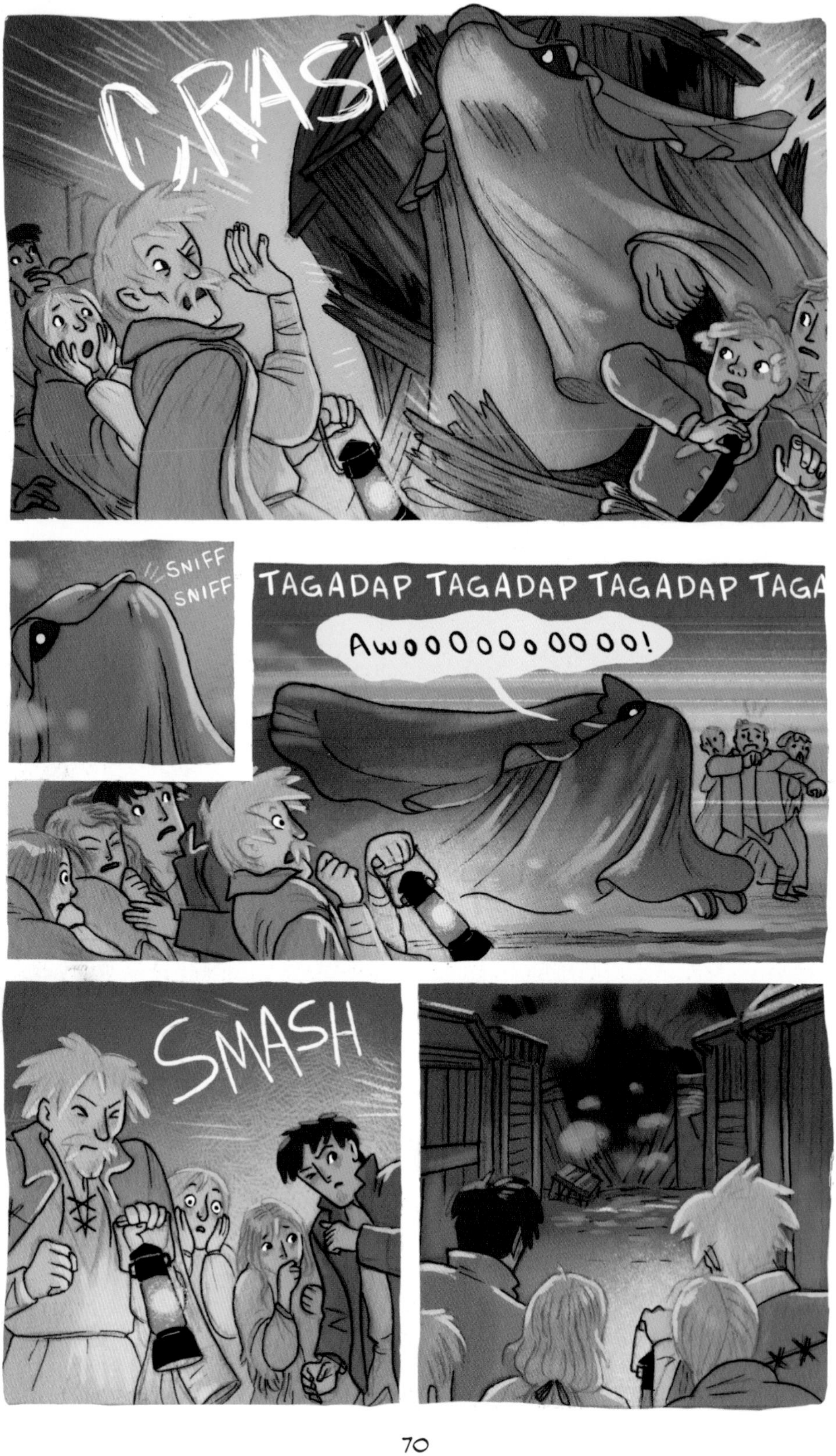
CRASH
SNIFF
SNIFF
TAGADAP TAGADAP TAGADAP TAGA
AwoOOoOoOOOO!
SMASH

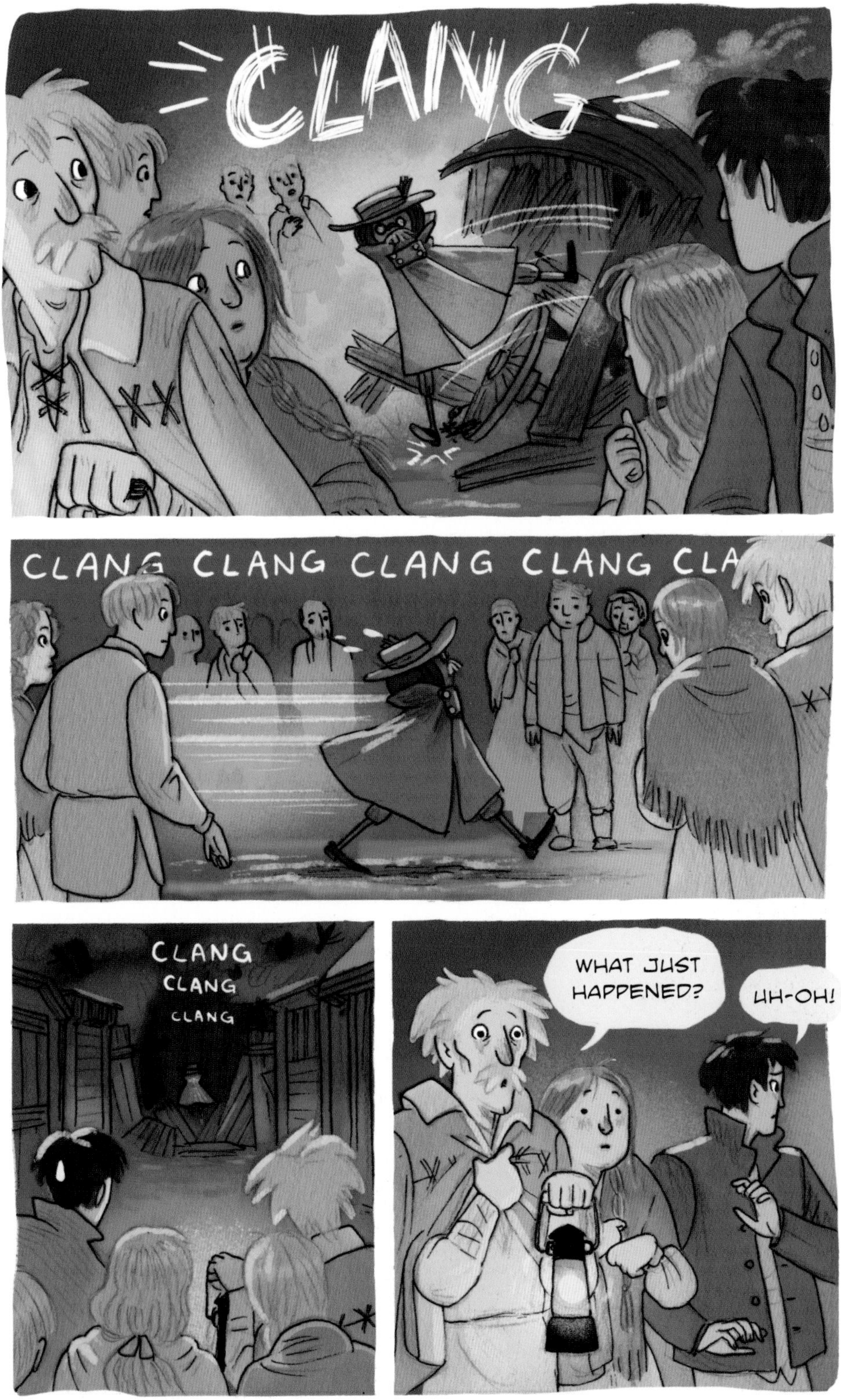
CLANG
CLANG CLANG CLANG CLANG CLA
CLANG
CLANG
CLANG
WHAT JUST HAPPENED?
UH-OH!

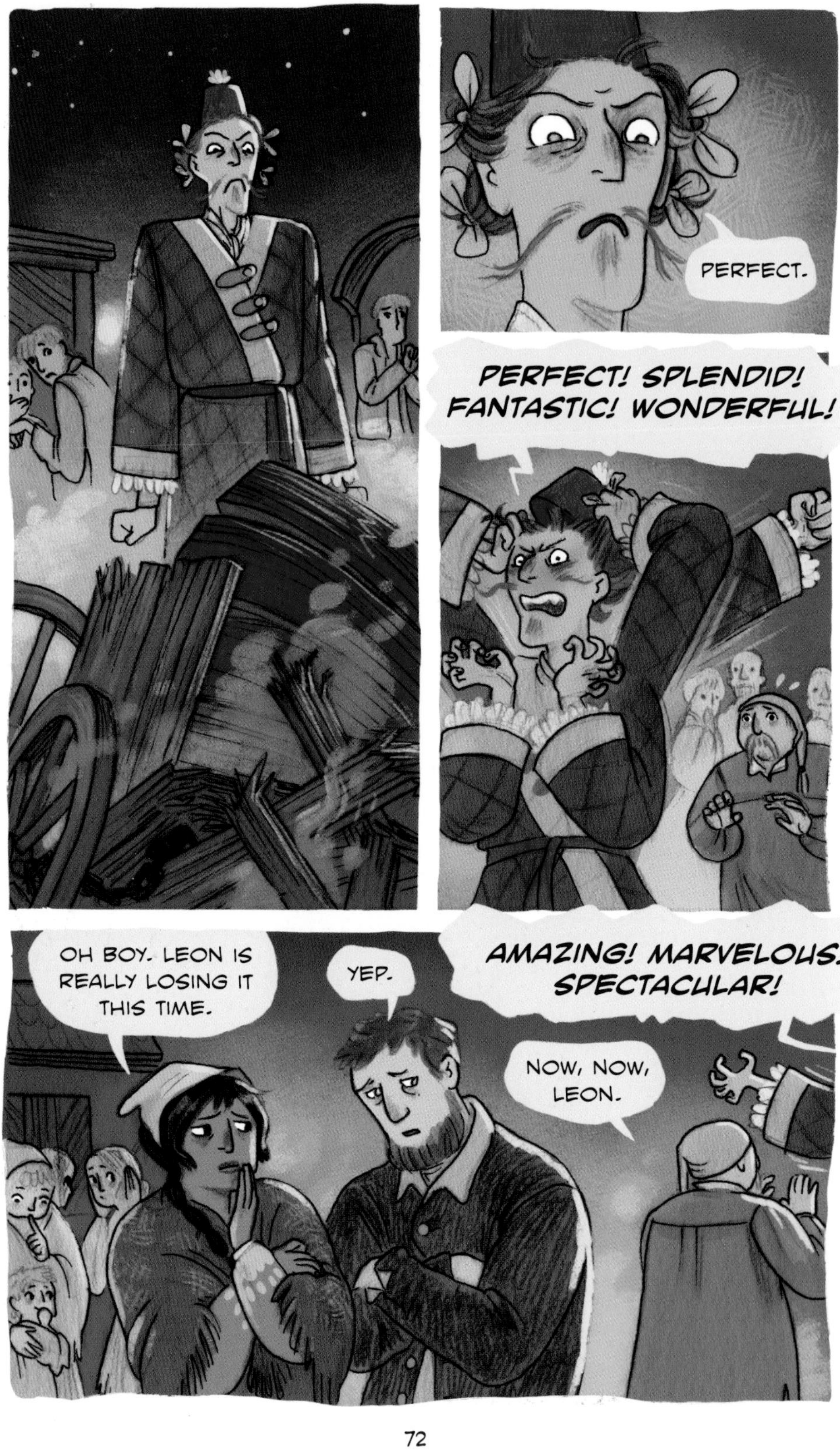
PERFECT.
PERFECT! SPLENDID! FANTASTIC! WONDERFUL!
OH BOY. LEON IS REALLY LOSING IT THIS TIME.
YEP.
AMAZING! MARVELOUS! SPECTACULAR!
NOW, NOW, LEON.

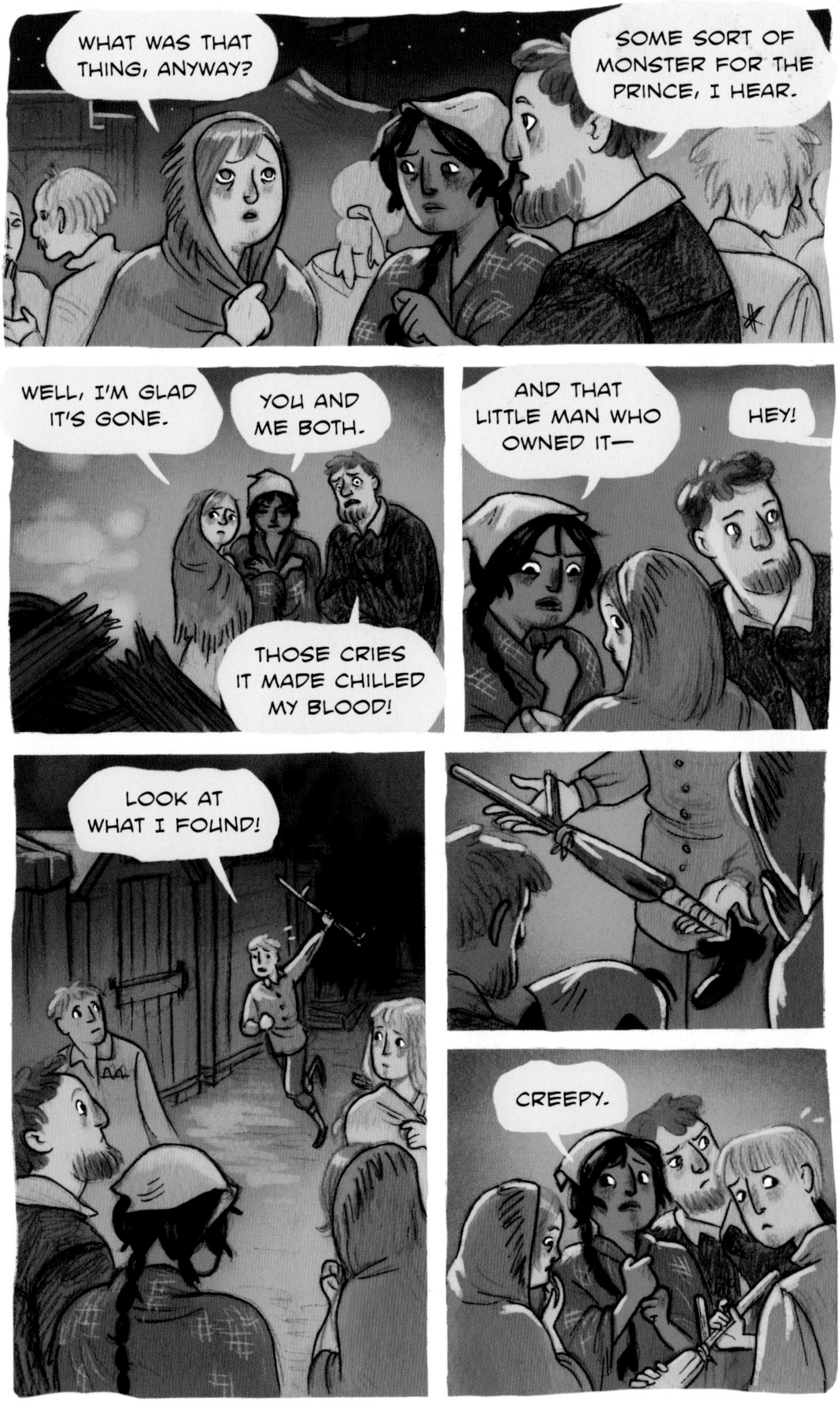
WHAT WAS THAT THING, ANYWAY?
SOME SORT OF MONSTER FOR THE PRINCE, I HEAR.
WELL, I'M GLAD IT'S GONE.
YOU AND ME BOTH.
THOSE CRIES IT MADE CHILLED MY BLOOD!
AND THAT LITTLE MAN WHO OWNED IT—
HEY!
LOOK AT WHAT I FOUND!
CREEPY.

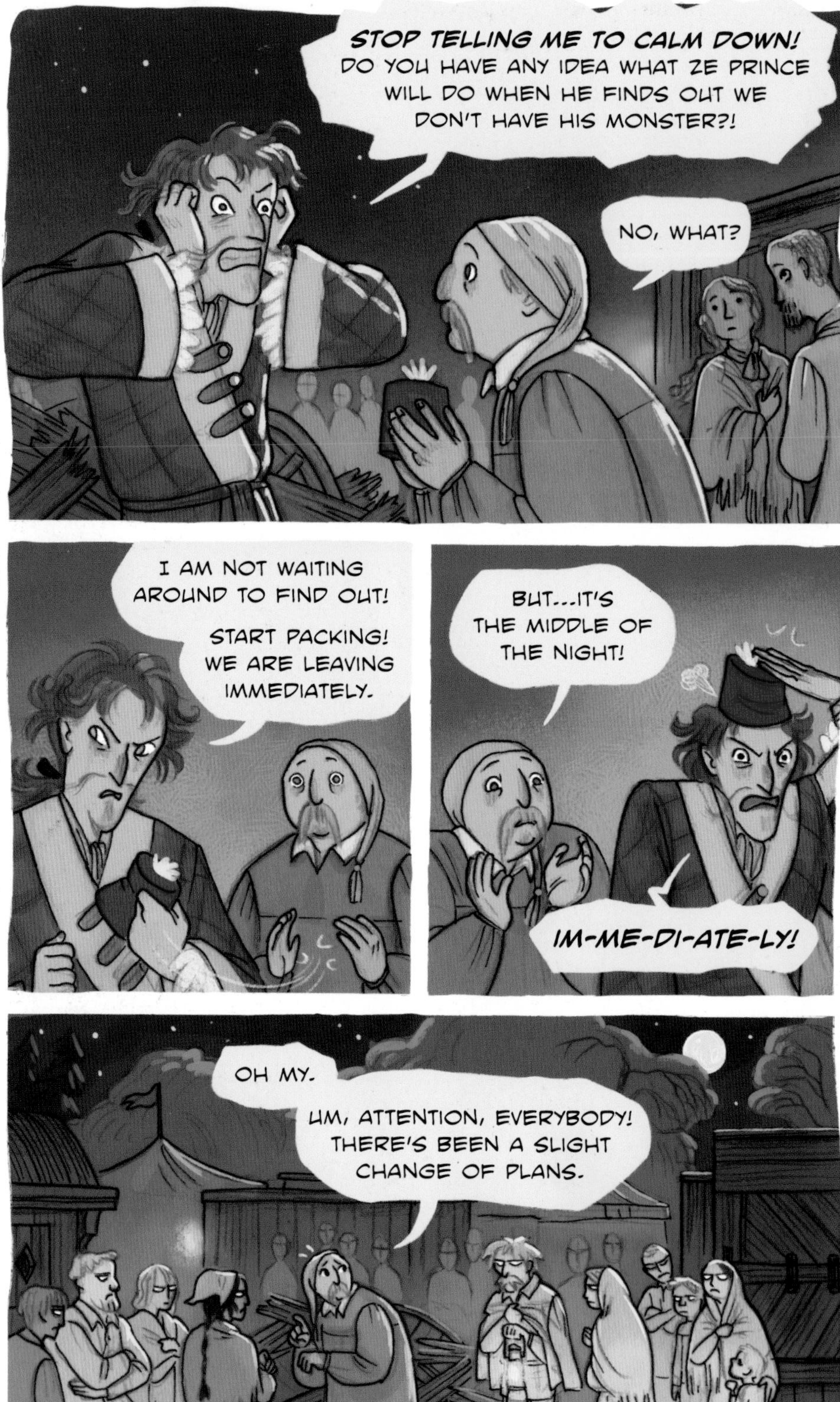

STOP TELLING ME TO CALM DOWN! DO YOU HAVE ANY IDEA WHAT ZE PRINCE WILL DO WHEN HE FINDS OUT WE DON'T HAVE HIS MONSTER?!
NO, WHAT?
I AM NOT WAITING AROUND TO FIND OUT!
START PACKING! WE ARE LEAVING IMMEDIATELY.
BUT...IT'S THE MIDDLE OF THE NIGHT!
IM-ME-DI-ATE-LY!
OH MY.
UM, ATTENTION, EVERYBODY! THERE'S BEEN A SLIGHT CHANGE OF PLANS.

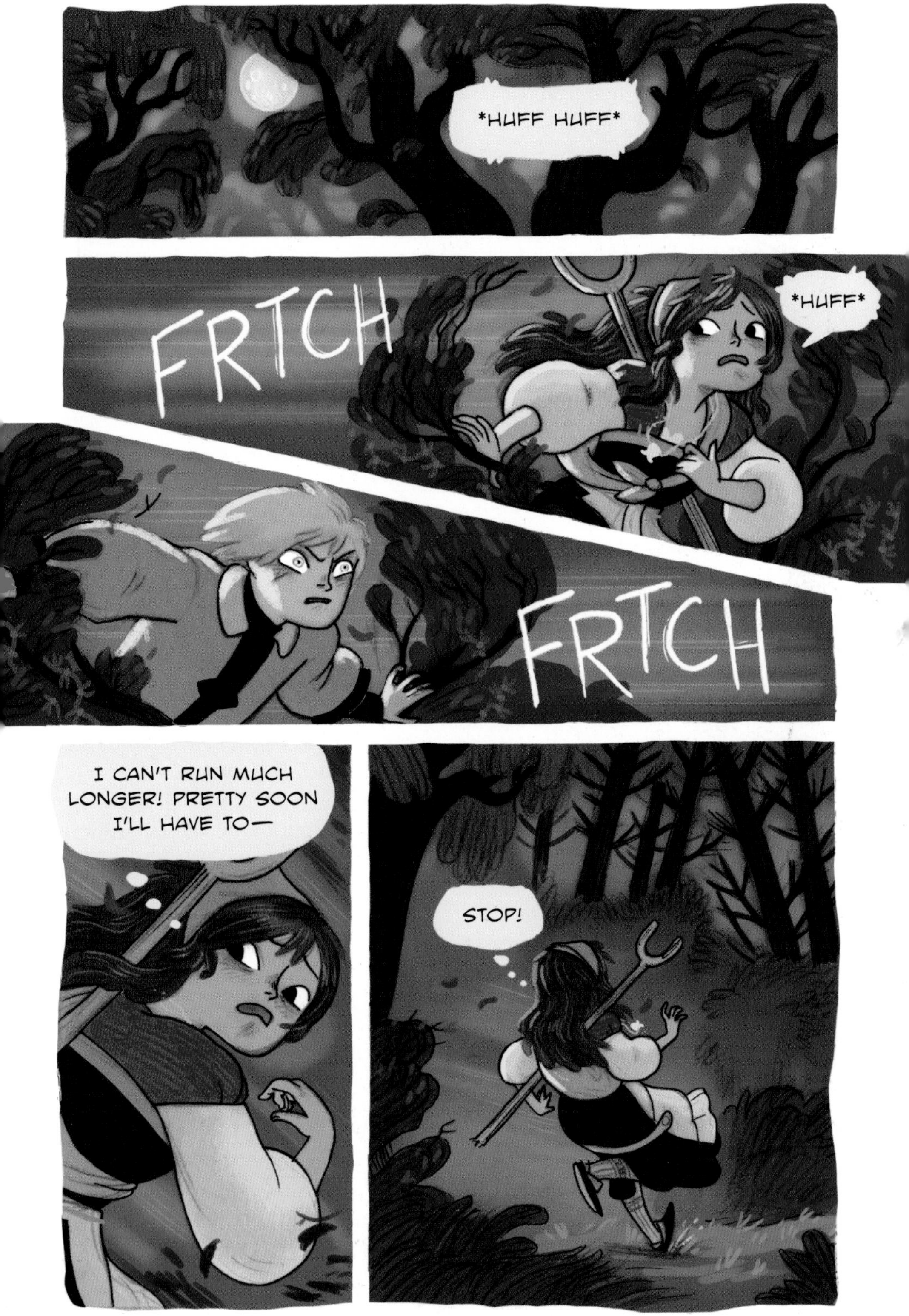
HUFF HUFF
FRTCH
HUFF
FRTCH
I CAN'T RUN MUCH LONGER! PRETTY SOON I'LL HAVE TO—
STOP!

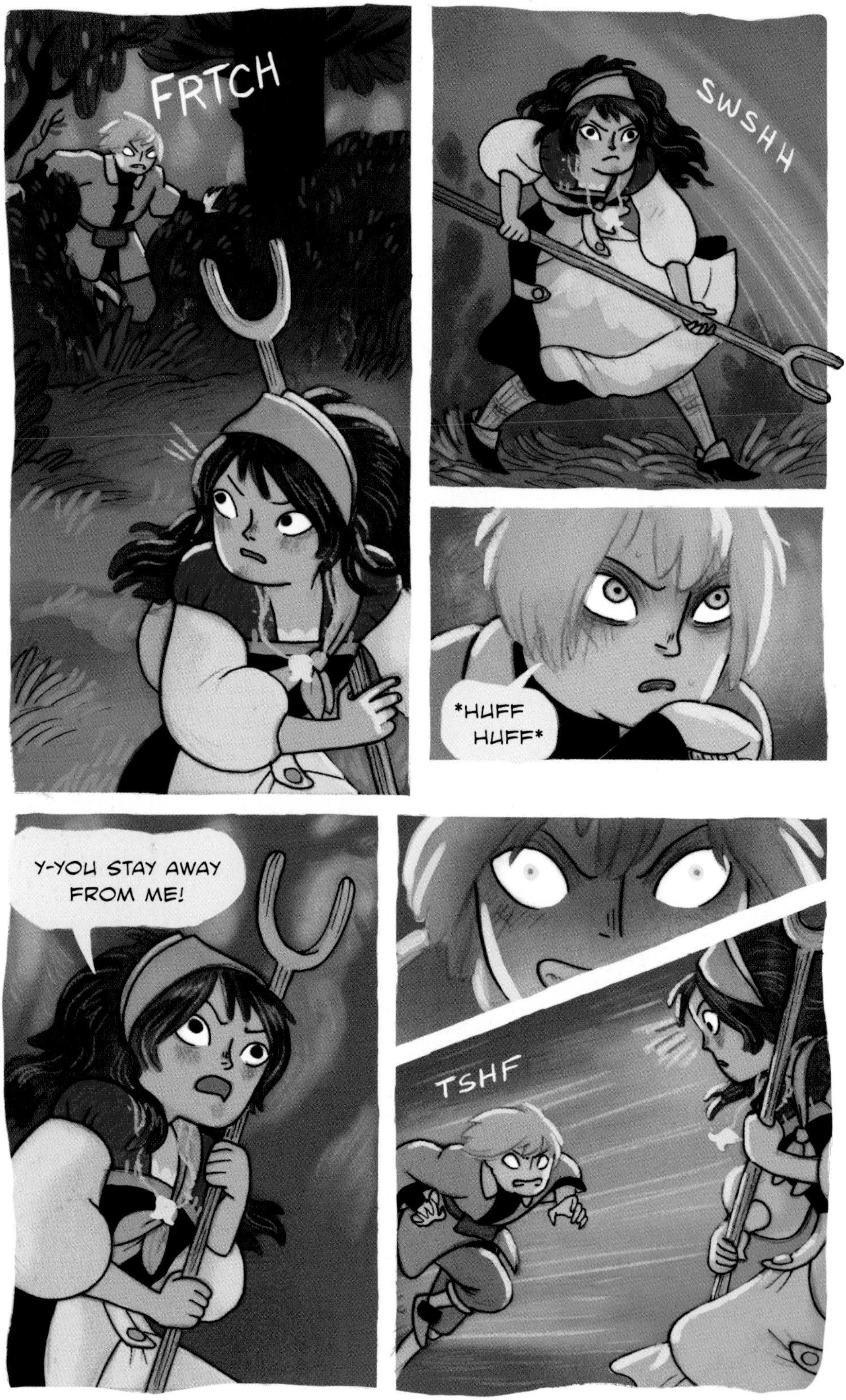
FRTCH
SWSHH
HUFF HUFF
Y-YOU STAY AWAY FROM ME!
TSHF

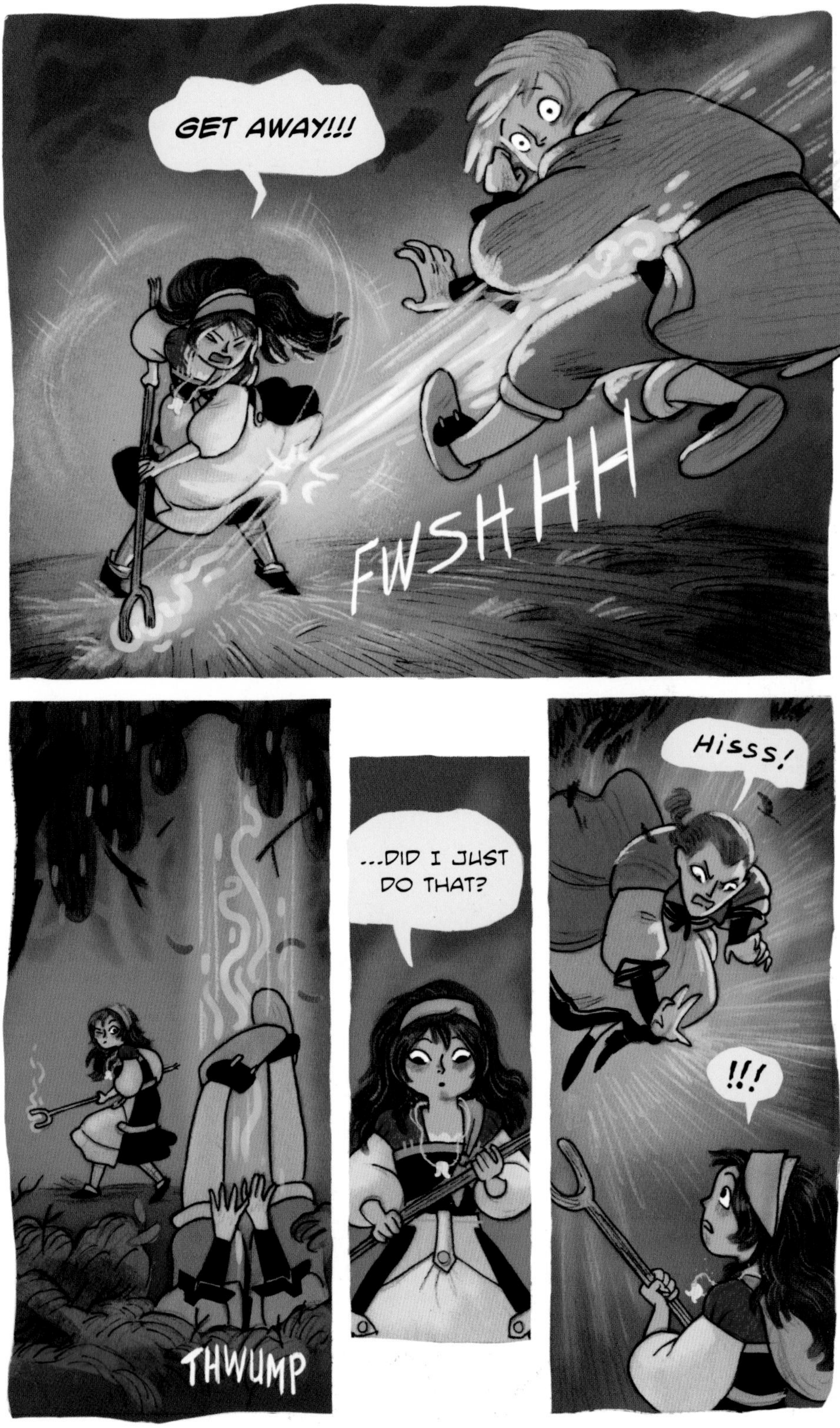
GET AWAY!!!
FWSHHH
THWUMP
...DID I JUST DO THAT?
Hisss!
!!!

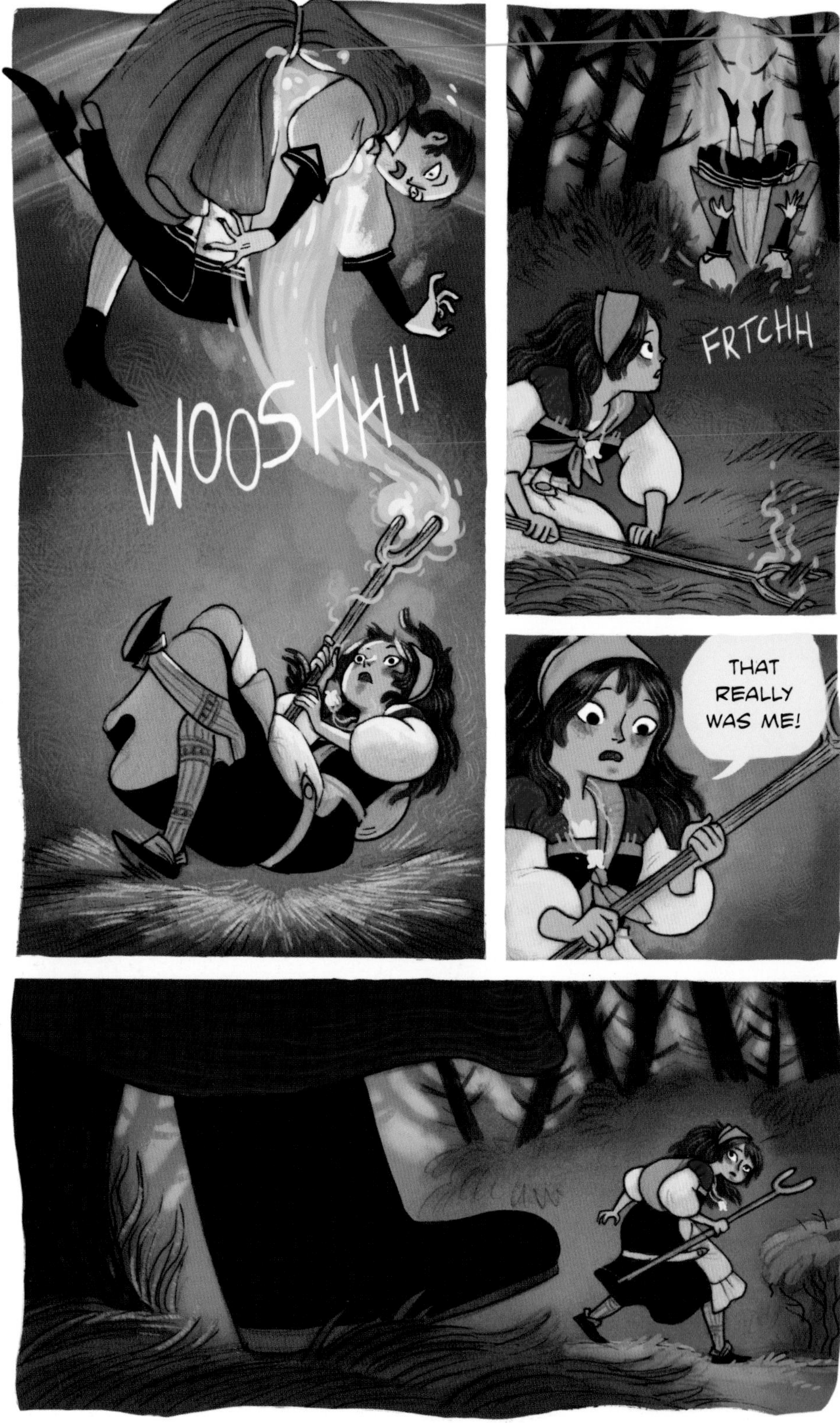
WOOSHHH
FRTCHH
THAT REALLY WAS ME!

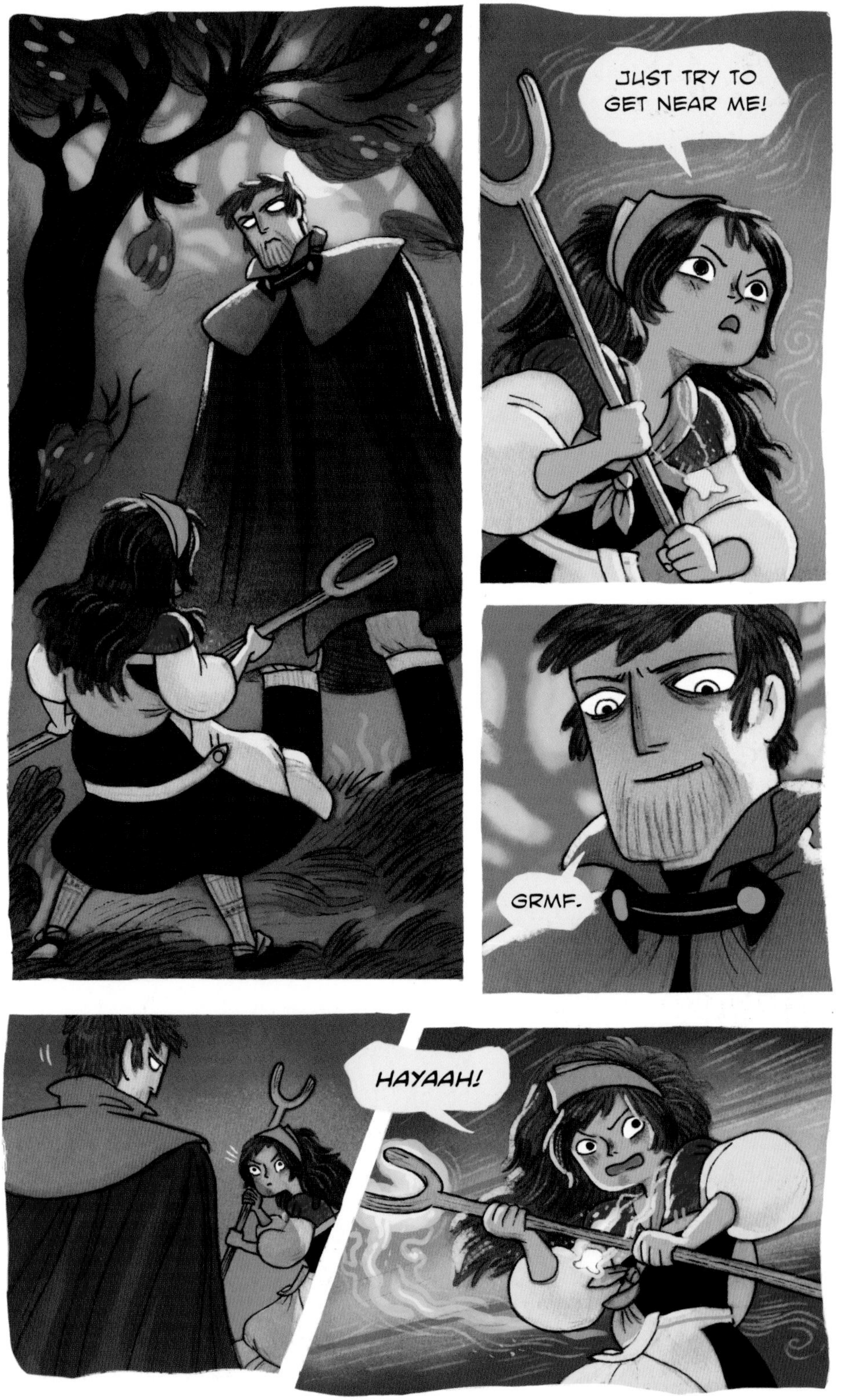
JUST TRY TO GET NEAR ME!
GRMF.
HAYAAH!

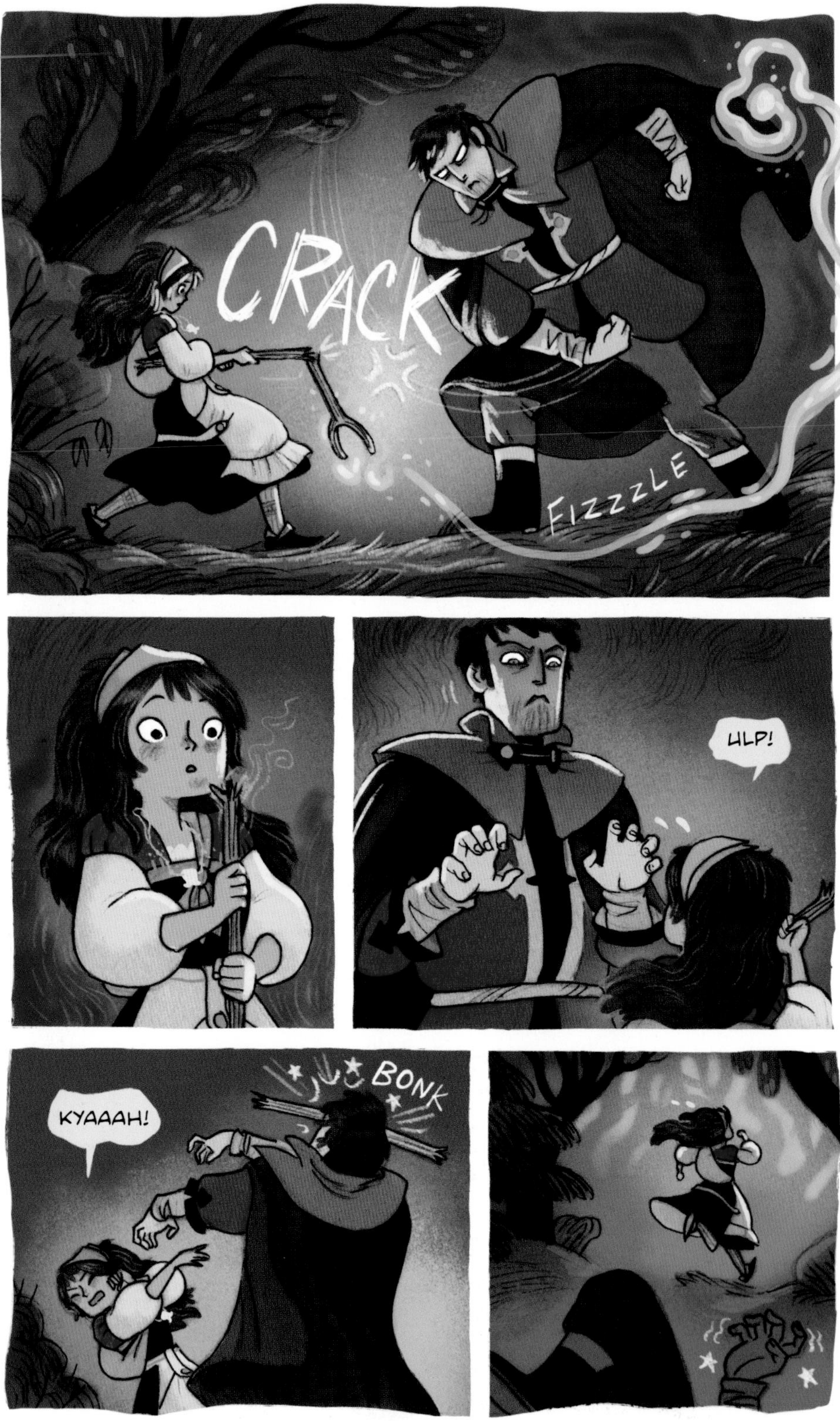
CRACK
FIZZZLE
ULP!
KYAAAH!
BONK

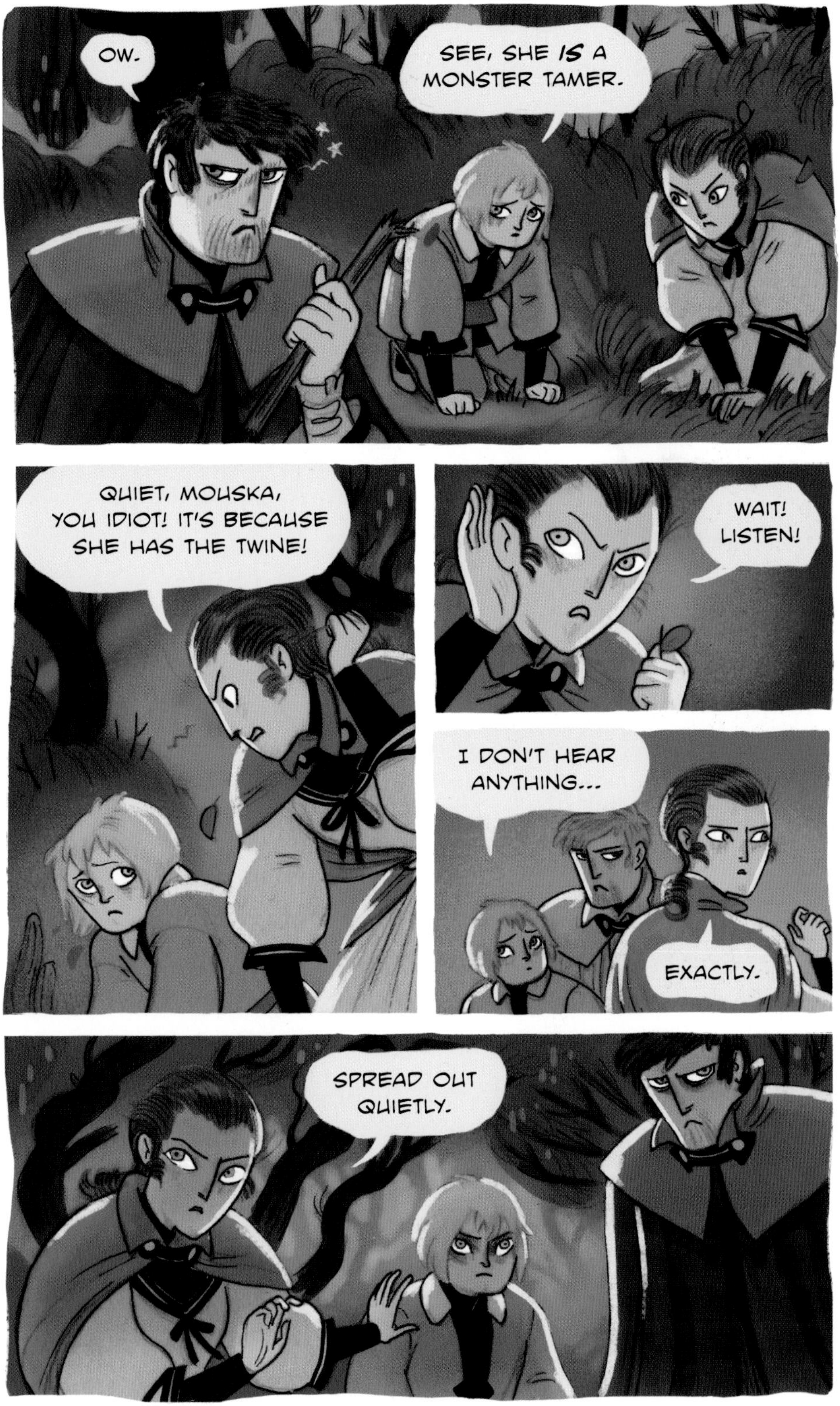
OW.
SEE, SHE IS A MONSTER TAMER.
QUIET, MOUSKA, YOU IDIOT! IT'S BECAUSE SHE HAS THE TWINE!
WAIT! LISTEN!
I DON'T HEAR ANYTHING...
EXACTLY.
SPREAD OUT QUIETLY.

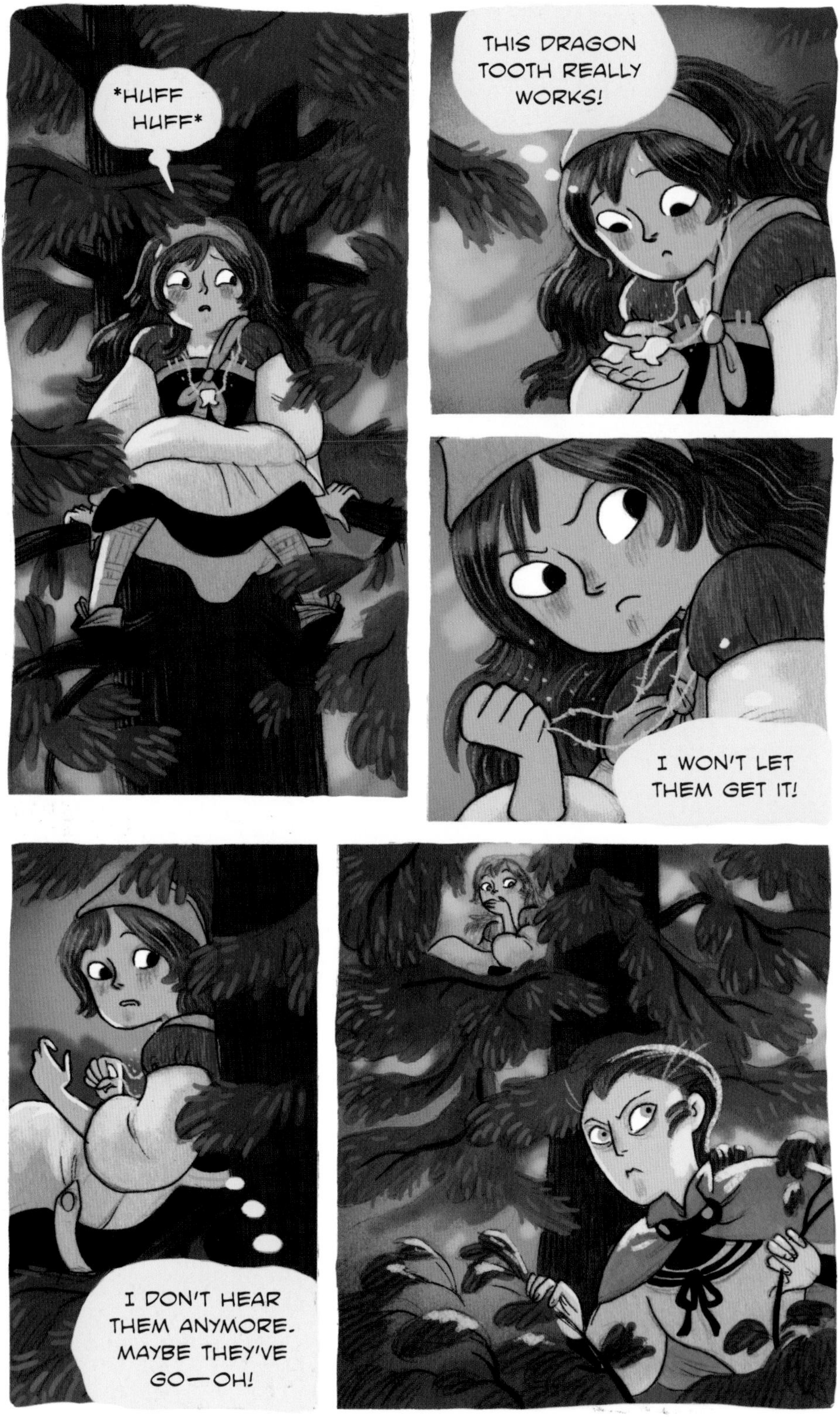
*HUFF
HUFF*
THIS DRAGON TOOTH REALLY WORKS!
I WON'T LET THEM GET IT!
I DON'T HEAR THEM ANYMORE. MAYBE THEY'VE GO—OH!

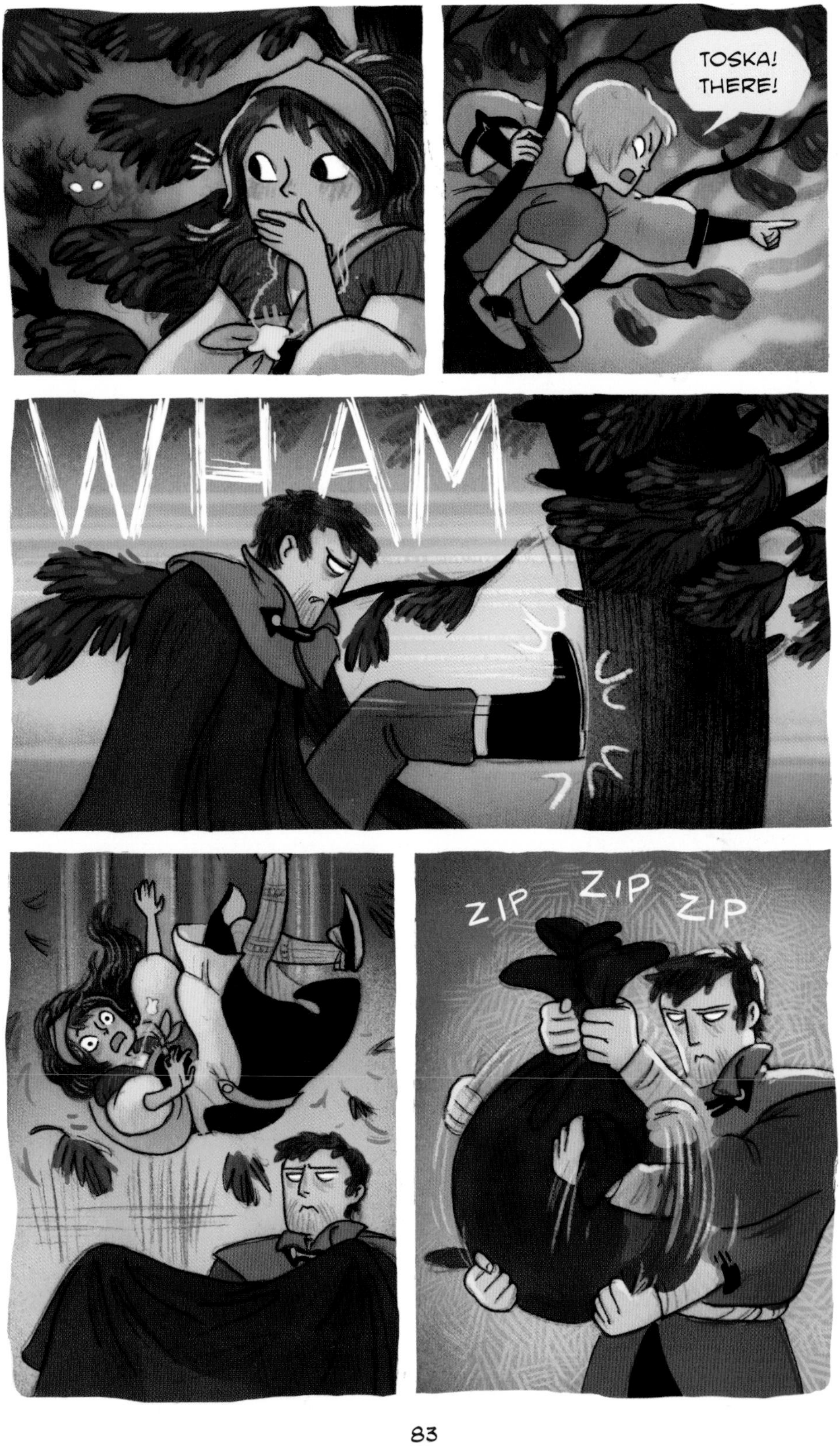
TOSKA! THERE!
WHAM
ZIP ZIP ZIP

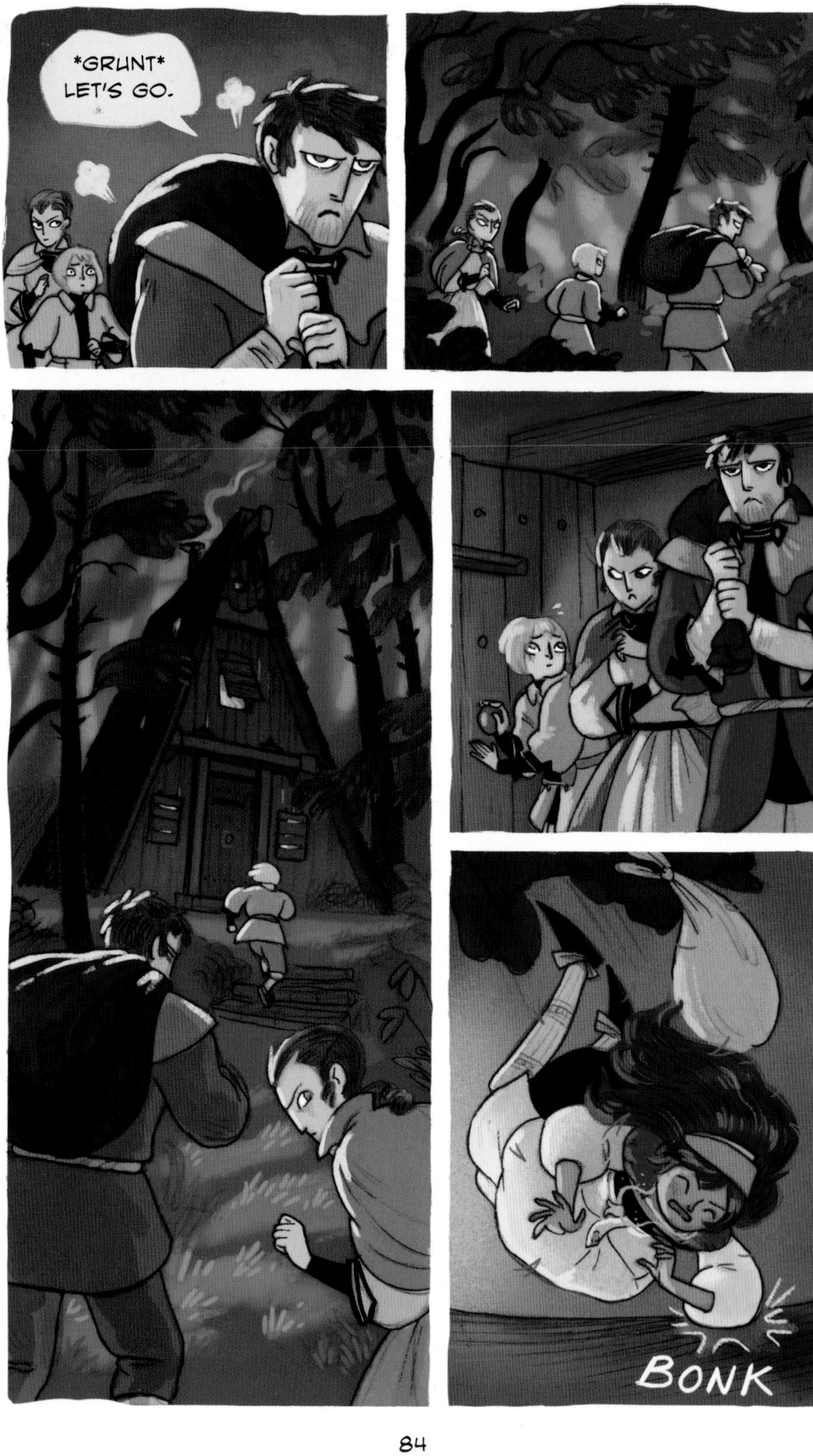
GRUNT
LET'S GO.
BONK

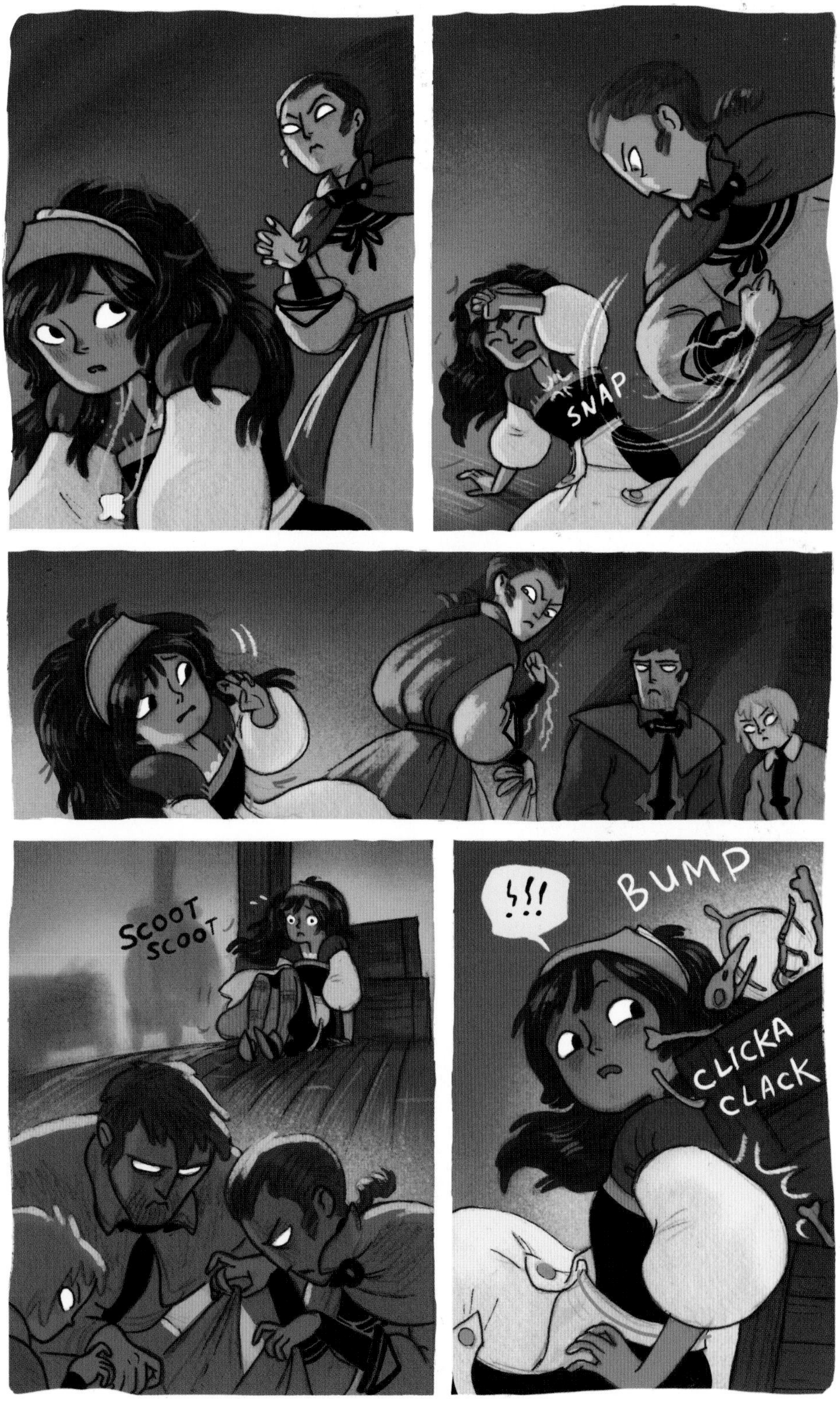
SNAP
SCOOT
SCOOT
!!!
BUMP
CLICKA
CLACK

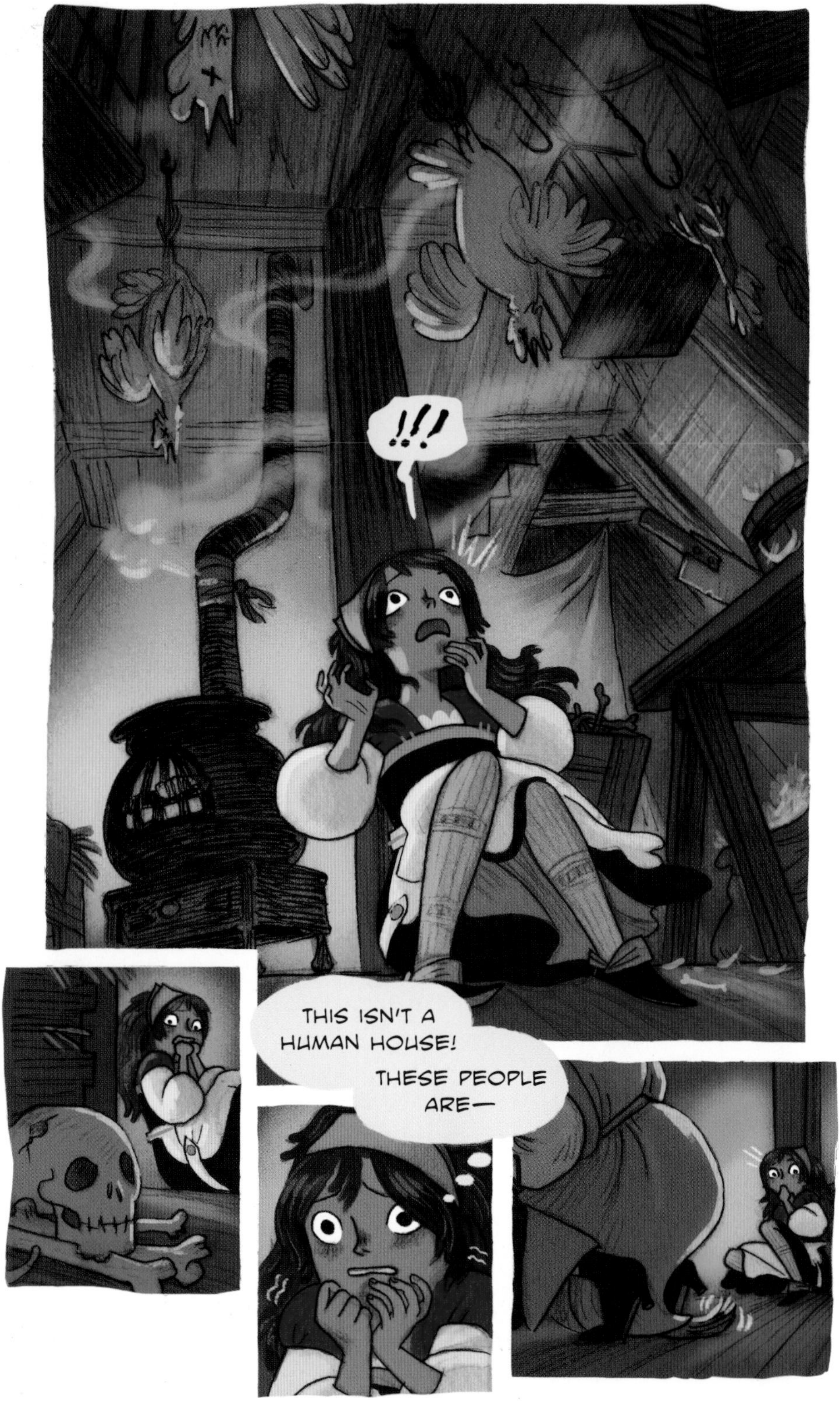
!!!
THIS ISN'T A HUMAN HOUSE!
THESE PEOPLE ARE—

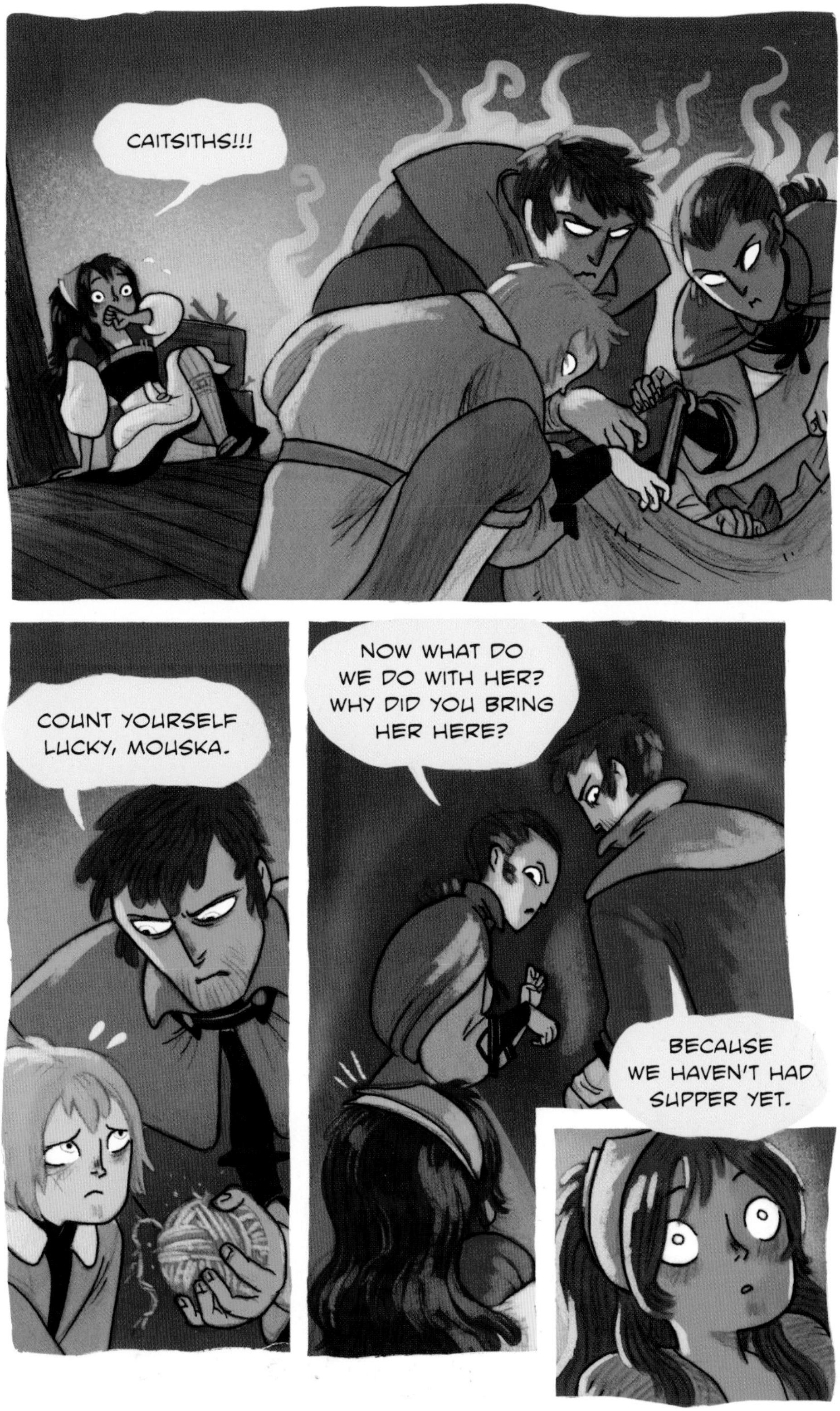
CAITSITHS!!!
COUNT YOURSELF LUCKY, MOUSKA.
NOW WHAT DO WE DO WITH HER? WHY DID YOU BRING HER HERE?
BECAUSE WE HAVEN'T HAD SUPPER YET.

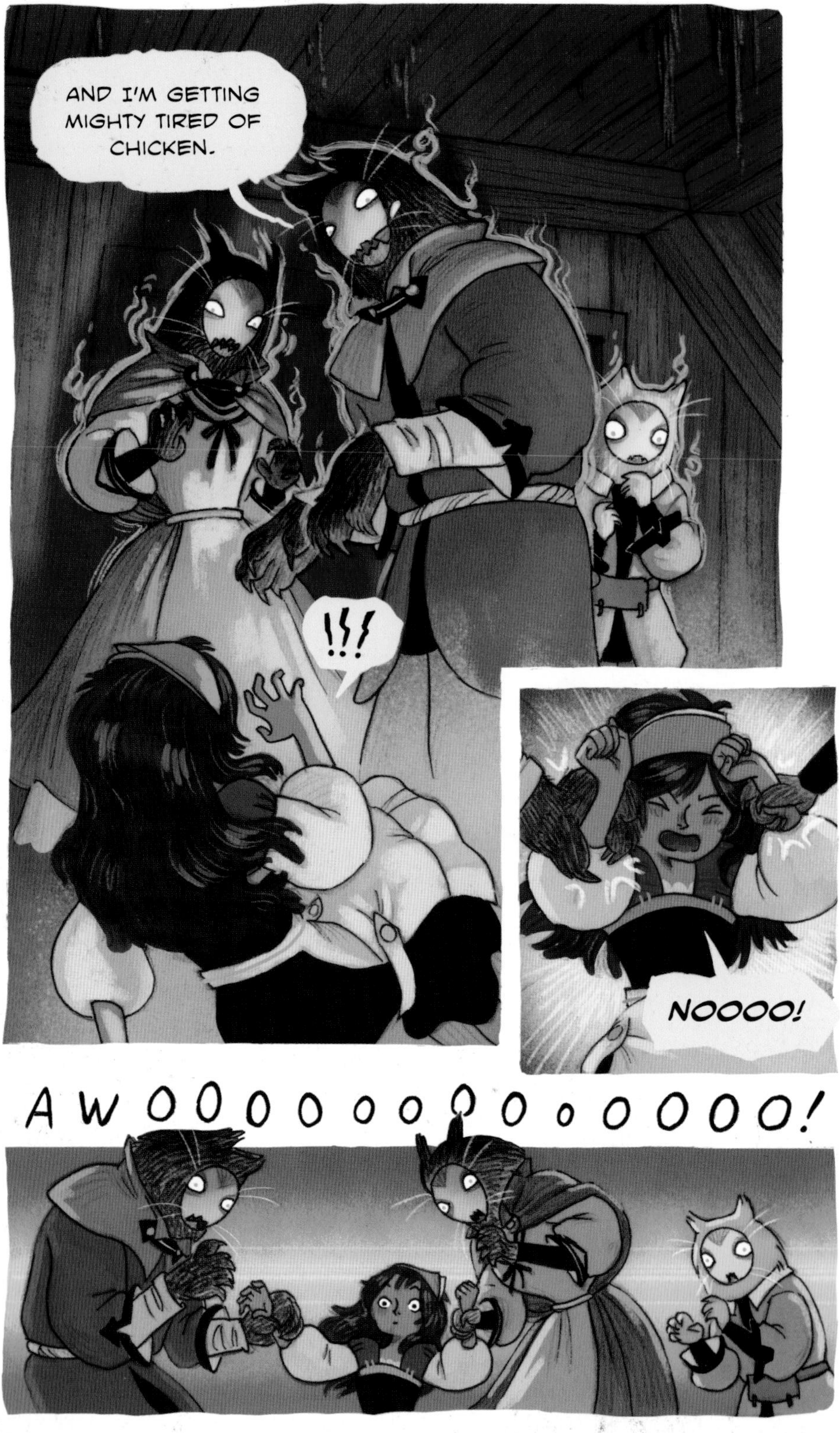
AND I'M GETTING MIGHTY TIRED OF CHICKEN.
!?!
NOOOO!
AWOOOOOOOOOOOOO!

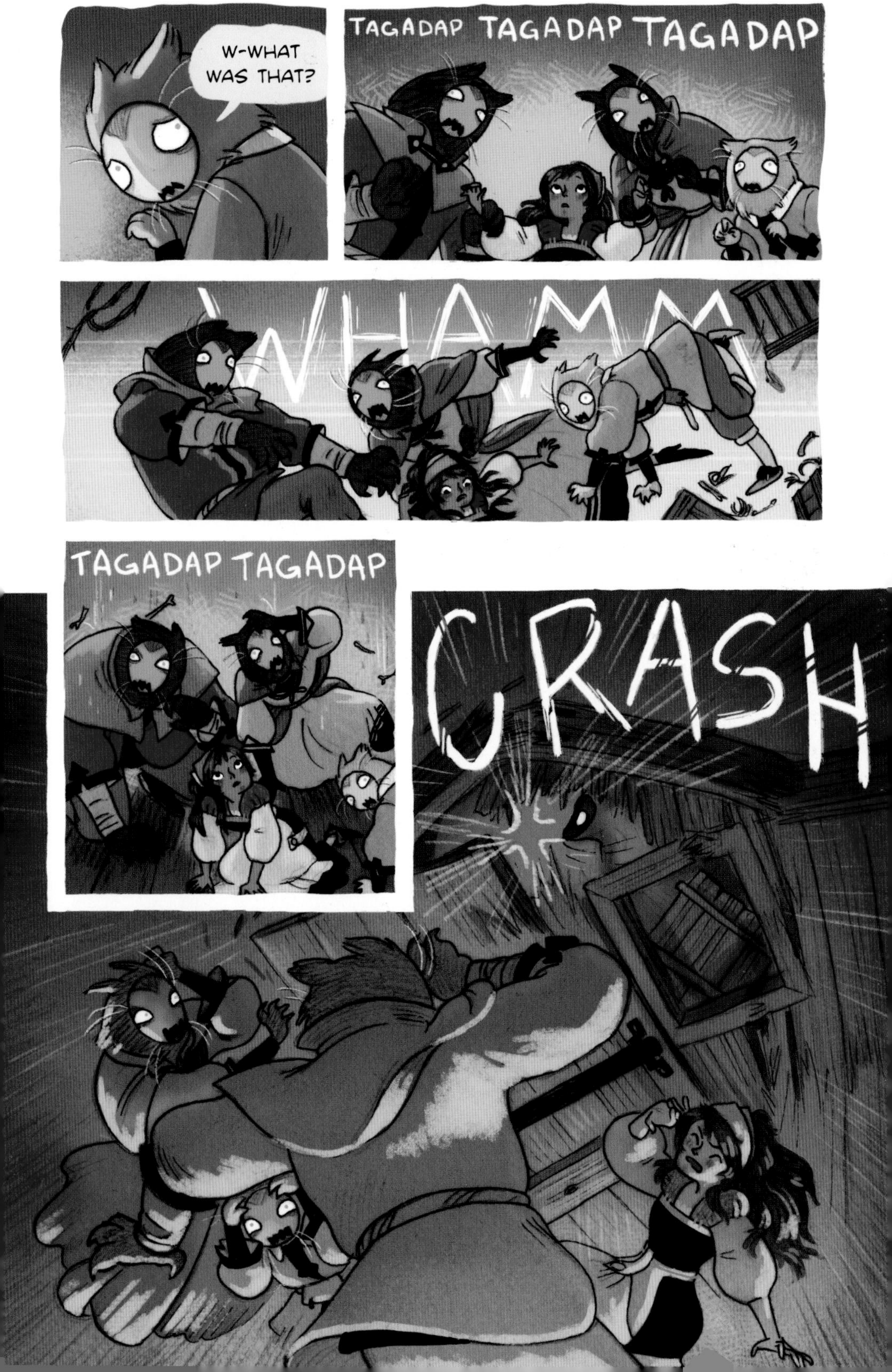
W-WHAT WAS THAT?
TAGADAP TAGADAP TAGADAP
WHAMM
TAGADAP TAGADAP
CRASH

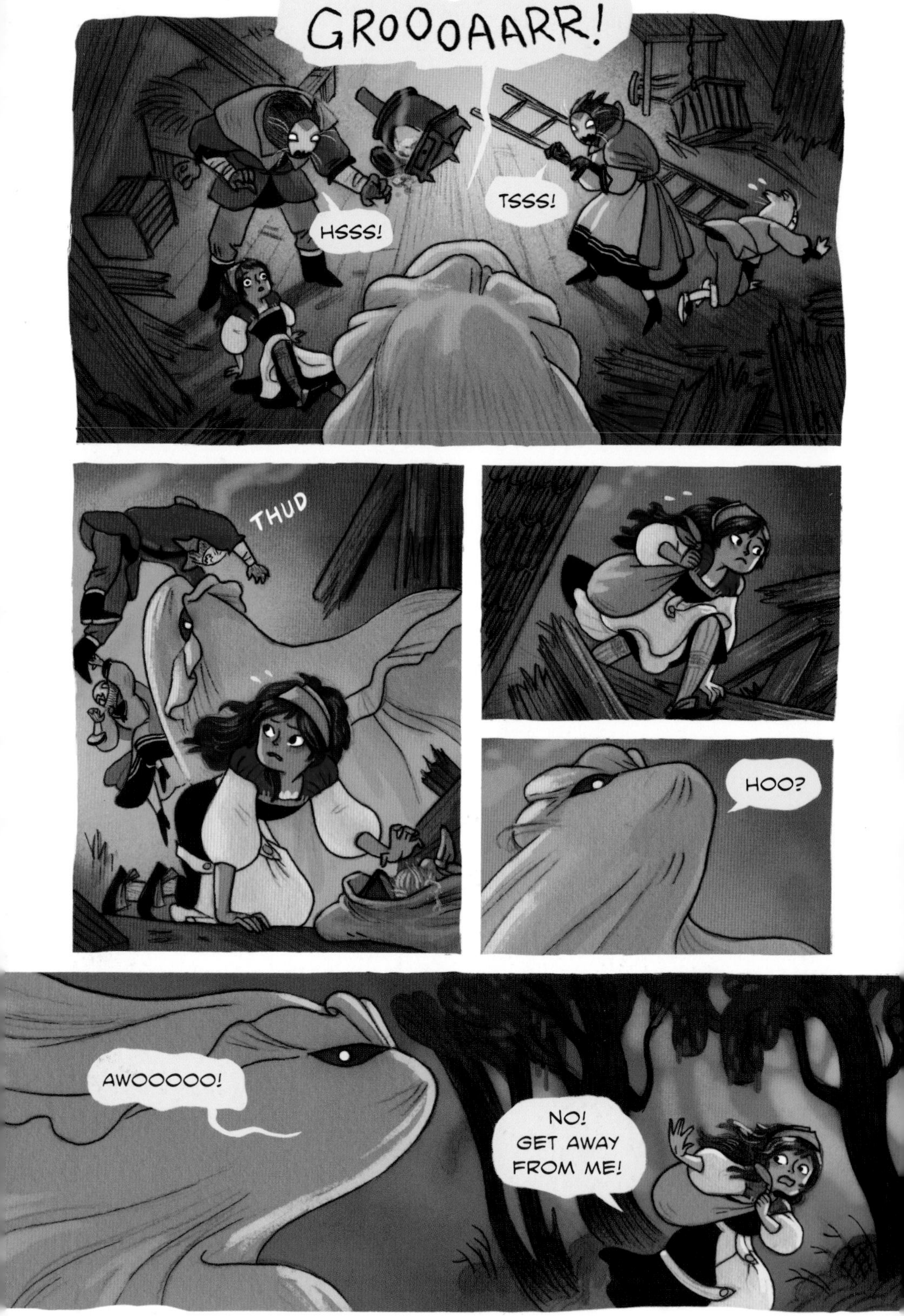
GROOOAARR!
HSSS!
TSSS!
THUD
HOO?
AWOOOOO!
NO! GET AWAY FROM ME!

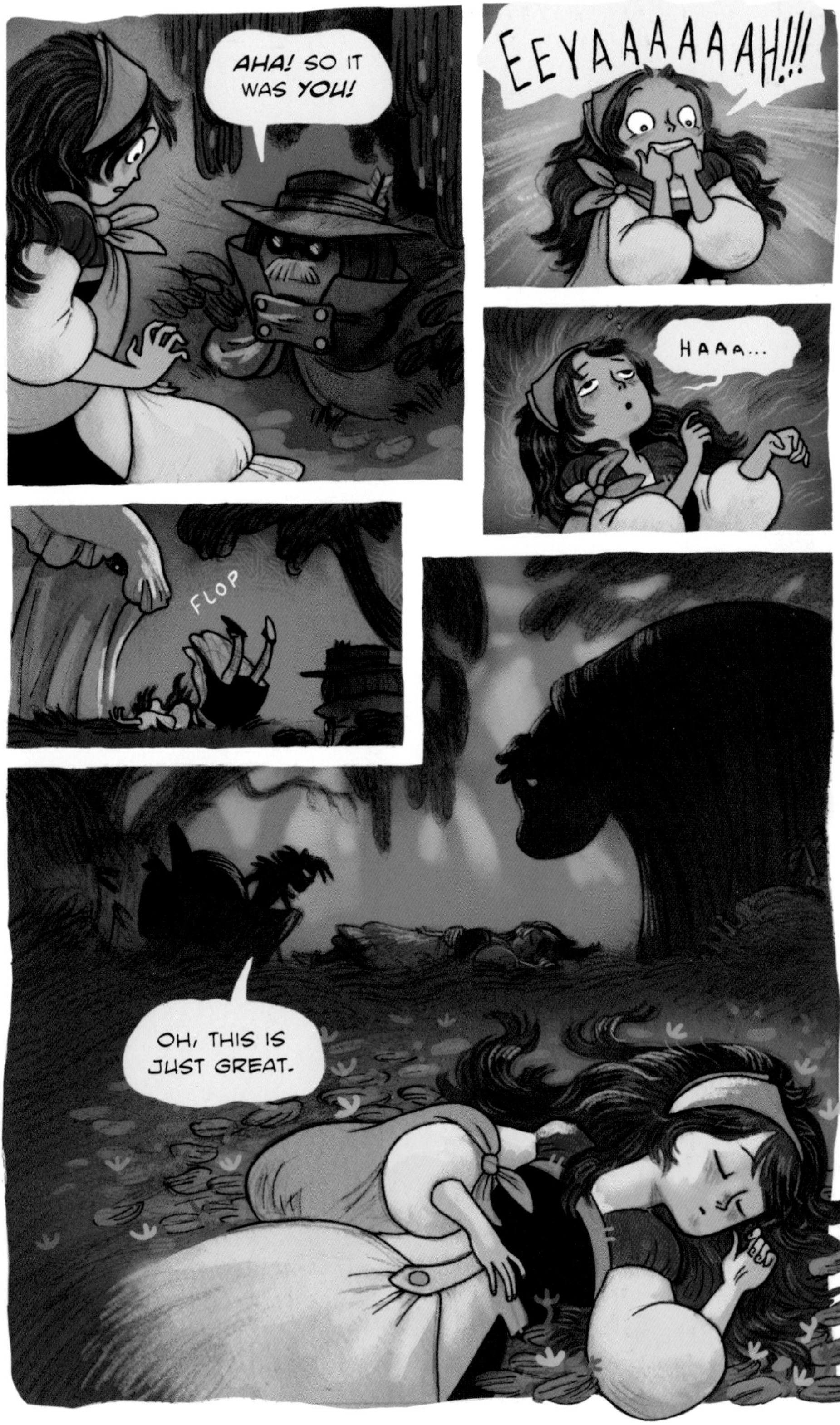
AHA! SO IT WAS YOU!
EEYAAAAAAH!!!
HAAA...
FLOP
OH, THIS IS JUST GREAT.

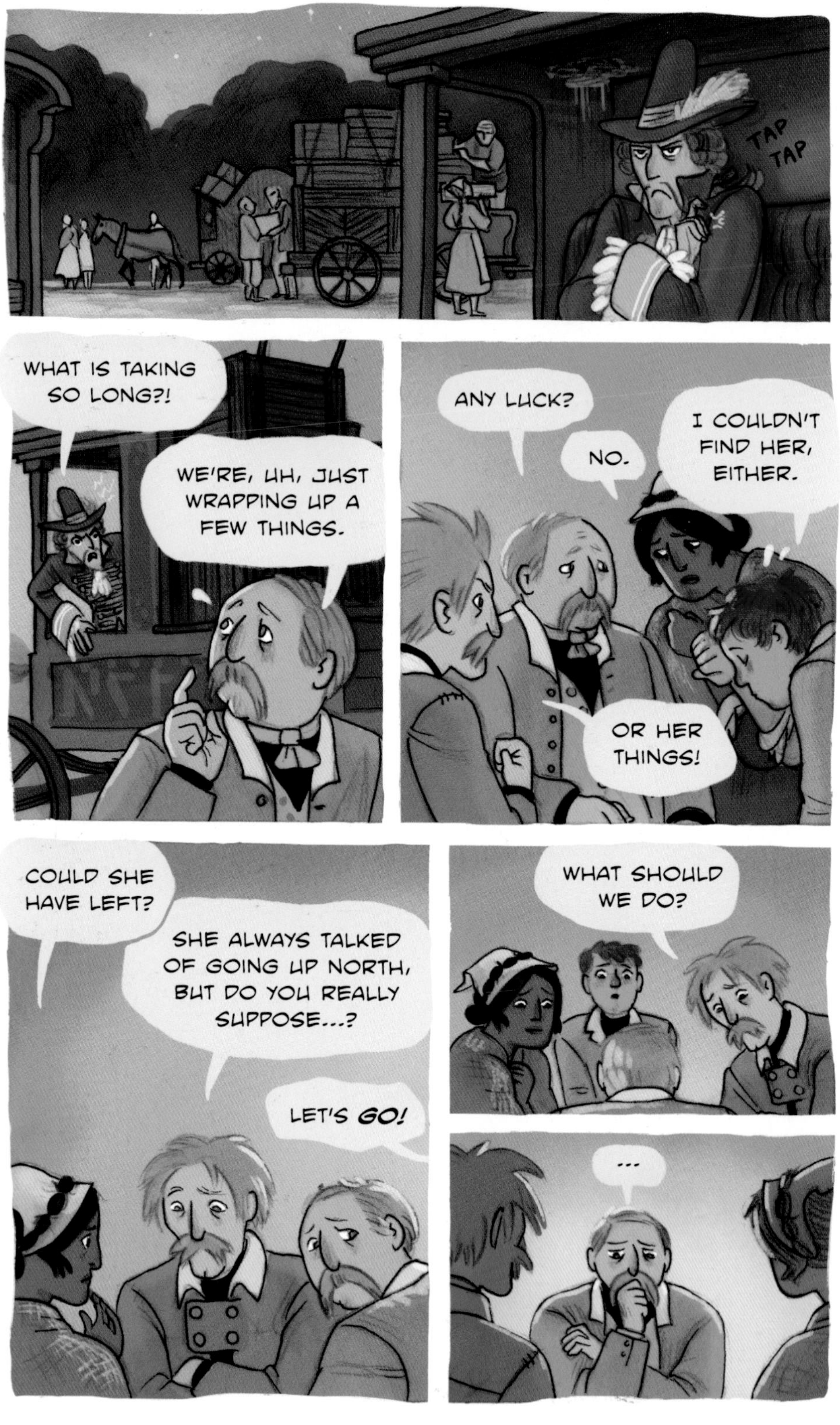
TAP TAP
WHAT IS TAKING SO LONG?!
WE'RE, UH, JUST WRAPPING UP A FEW THINGS.
ANY LUCK?
NO.
I COULDN'T FIND HER, EITHER.
OR HER THINGS!
COULD SHE HAVE LEFT?
SHE ALWAYS TALKED OF GOING UP NORTH, BUT DO YOU REALLY SUPPOSE...?
LET'S GO!
WHAT SHOULD WE DO?
...

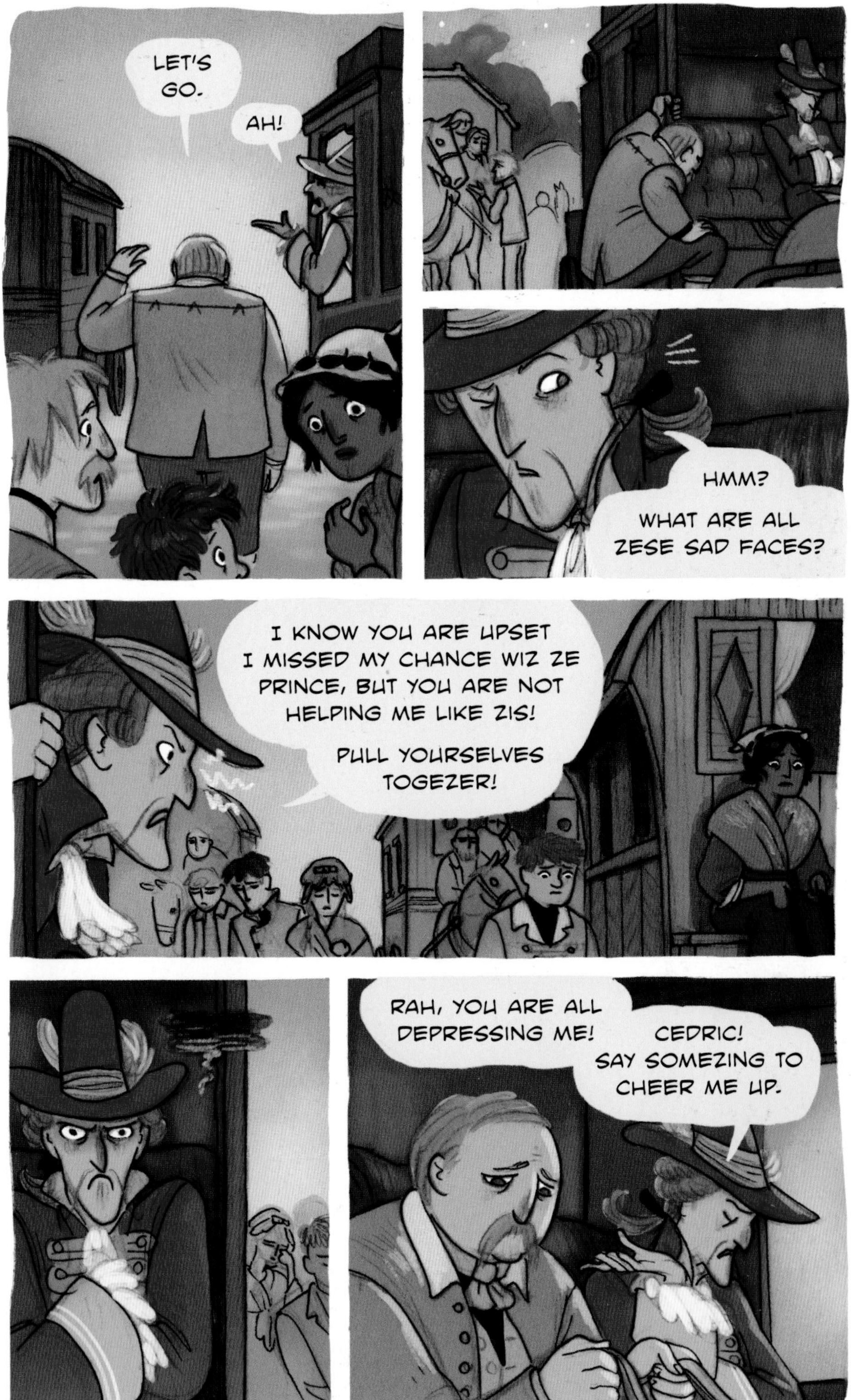
LET'S GO.
AH!
HMM?
WHAT ARE ALL ZESE SAD FACES?
I KNOW YOU ARE UPSET I MISSED MY CHANCE WIZ ZE PRINCE, BUT YOU ARE NOT HELPING ME LIKE ZIS!
PULL YOURSELVES TOGEZER!
RAH, YOU ARE ALL DEPRESSING ME!
CEDRIC! SAY SOMEZING TO CHEER ME UP.

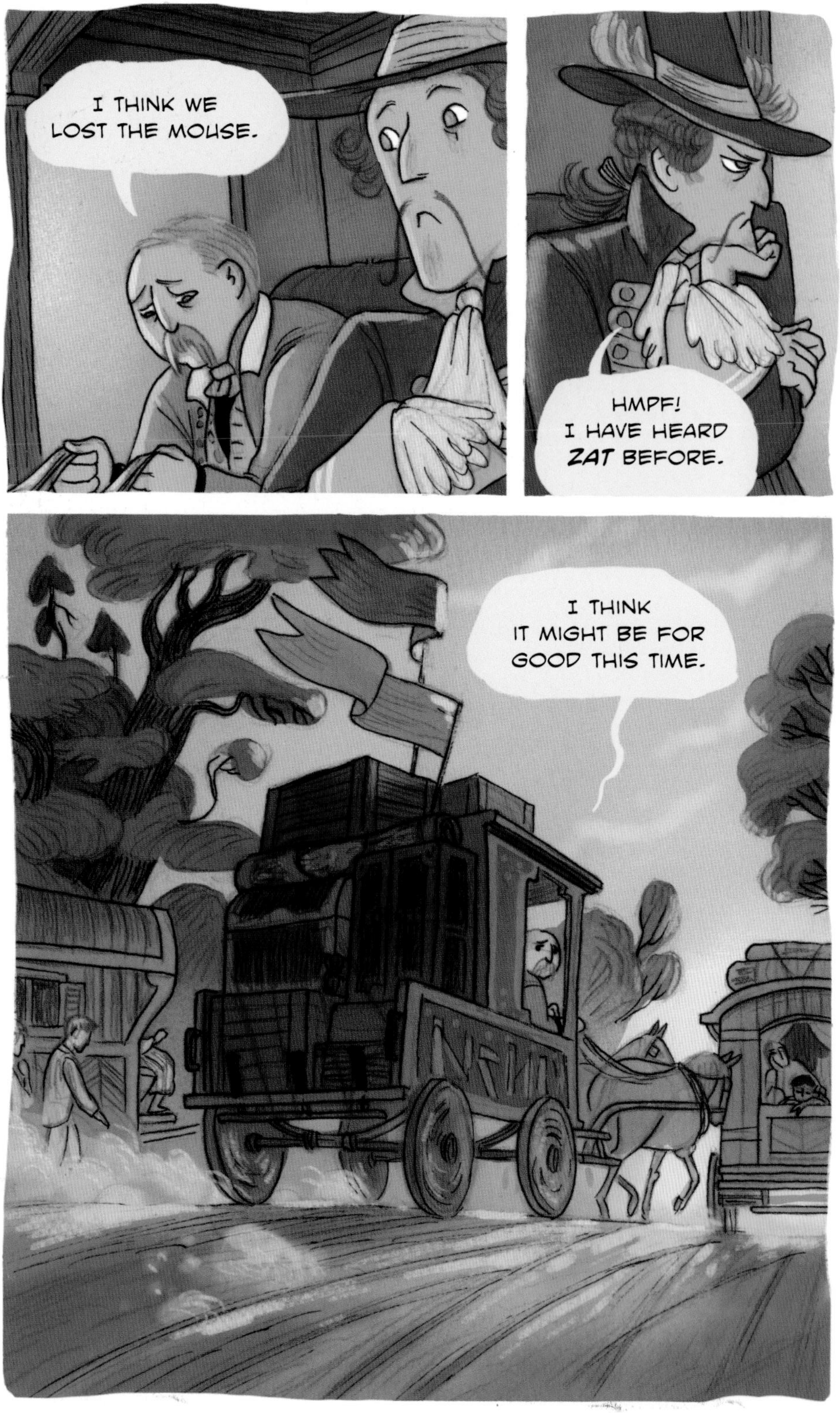
I THINK WE LOST THE MOUSE.
HMPF! I HAVE HEARD ZAT BEFORE.
I THINK IT MIGHT BE FOR GOOD THIS TIME.

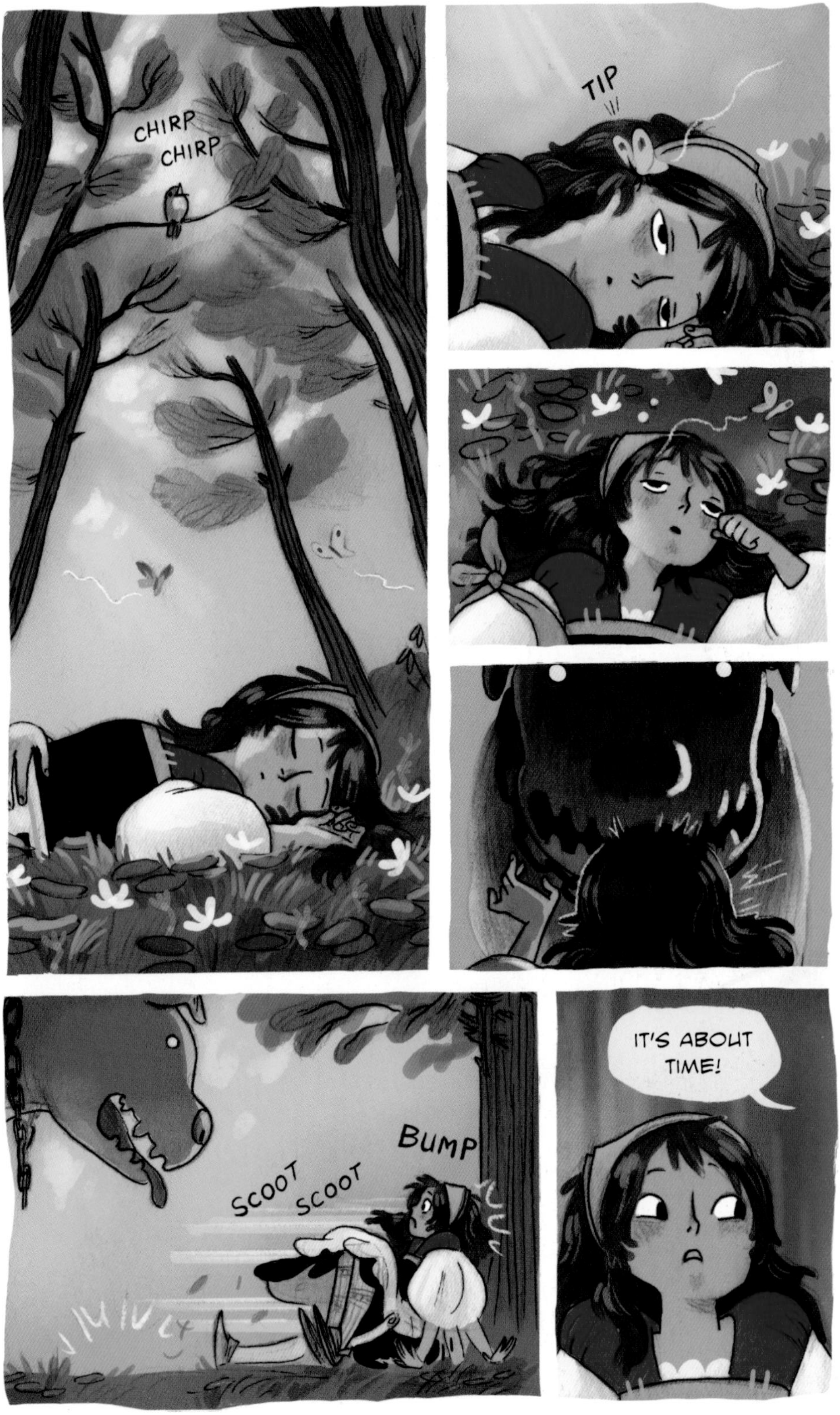
CHIRP
CHIRP
TIP
BUMP
SCOOT
SCOOT
IT'S ABOUT TIME!

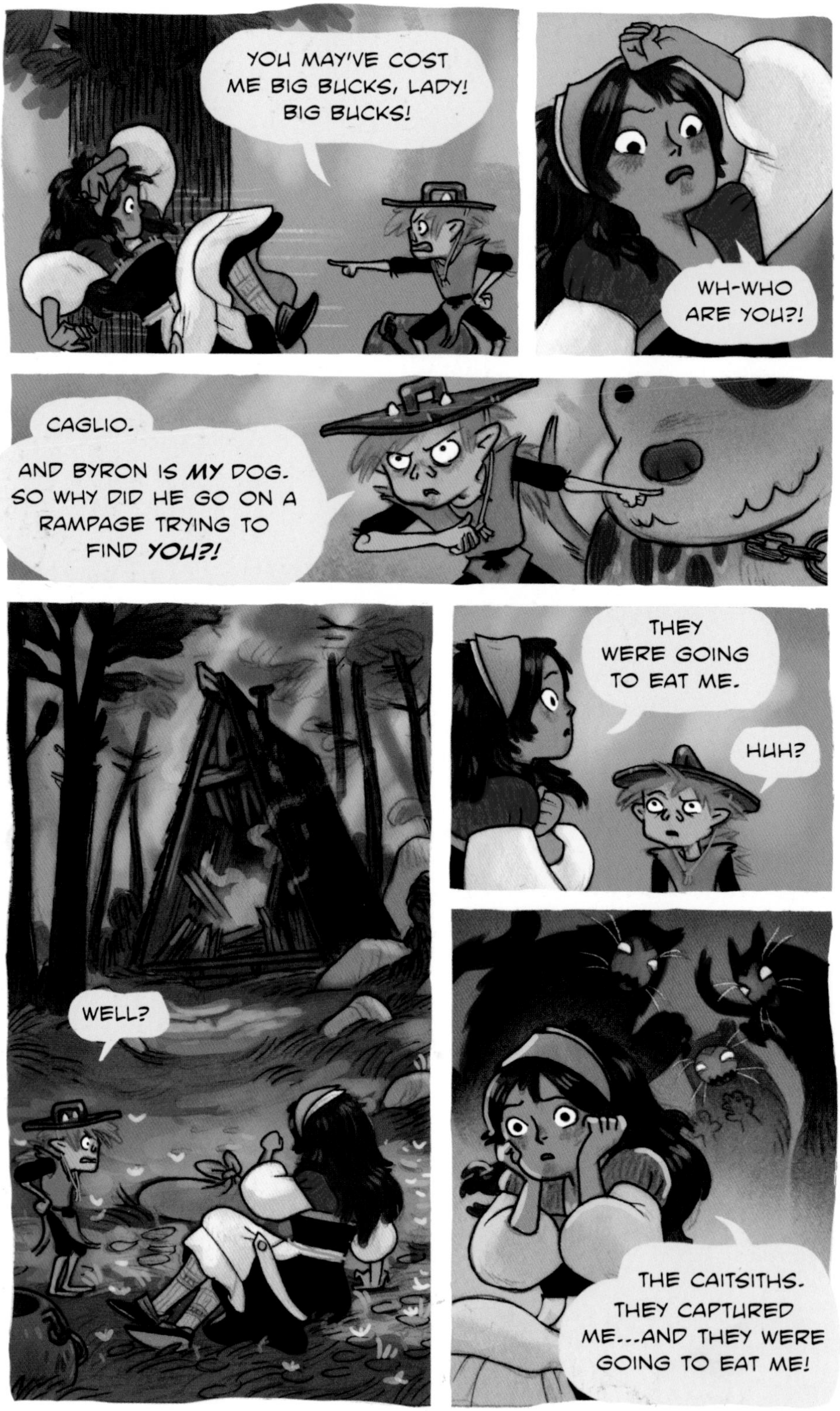
YOU MAY'VE COST ME BIG BUCKS, LADY! BIG BUCKS!
WH-WHO ARE YOU?!
CAGLIO.
AND BYRON IS *MY* DOG. SO WHY DID HE GO ON A RAMPAGE TRYING TO FIND *YOU?!*
WELL?
THEY WERE GOING TO EAT ME.
HUH?
THE CAITSITHS. THEY CAPTURED ME...AND THEY WERE GOING TO EAT ME!

YOUR DOG SAVED ME.

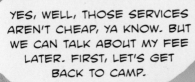

YES, WELL, THOSE SERVICES AREN'T CHEAP, YA KNOW. BUT WE CAN TALK ABOUT MY FEE LATER. FIRST, LET'S GET BACK TO CAMP.

OH!

SNAP

HEY! THE CAMP IS THAT WAY!

IT SHOULD BE HERE SOMEWHERE!

AHA!

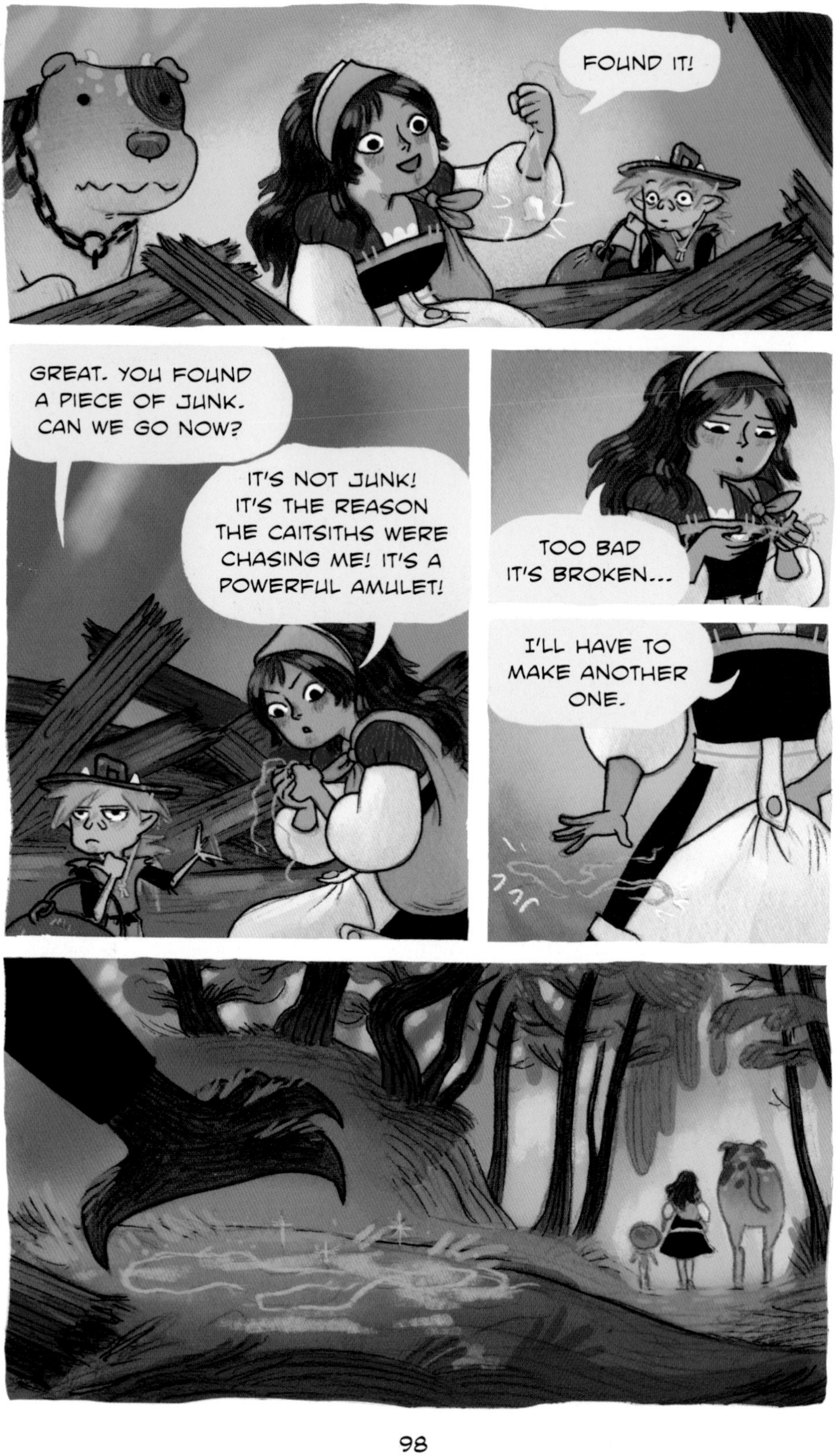
FOUND IT!
GREAT. YOU FOUND A PIECE OF JUNK. CAN WE GO NOW?
IT'S NOT JUNK! IT'S THE REASON THE CAITSITHS WERE CHASING ME! IT'S A POWERFUL AMULET!
TOO BAD IT'S BROKEN...
I'LL HAVE TO MAKE ANOTHER ONE.

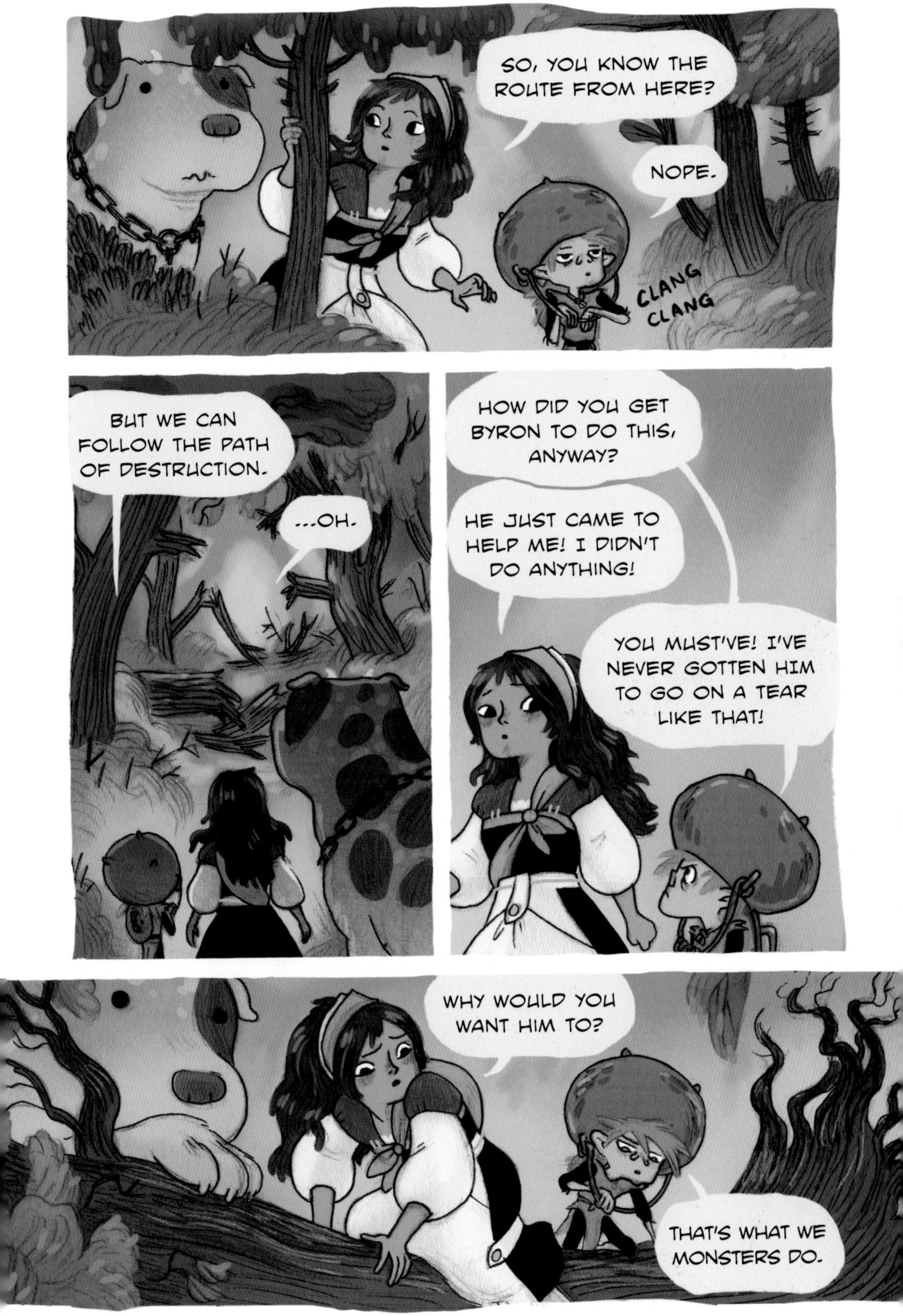
SO, YOU KNOW THE ROUTE FROM HERE?
NOPE.
CLANG CLANG
BUT WE CAN FOLLOW THE PATH OF DESTRUCTION.
...OH.
HOW DID YOU GET BYRON TO DO THIS, ANYWAY?
HE JUST CAME TO HELP ME! I DIDN'T DO ANYTHING!
YOU MUST'VE! I'VE NEVER GOTTEN HIM TO GO ON A TEAR LIKE THAT!
WHY WOULD YOU WANT HIM TO?
THAT'S WHAT WE MONSTERS DO.

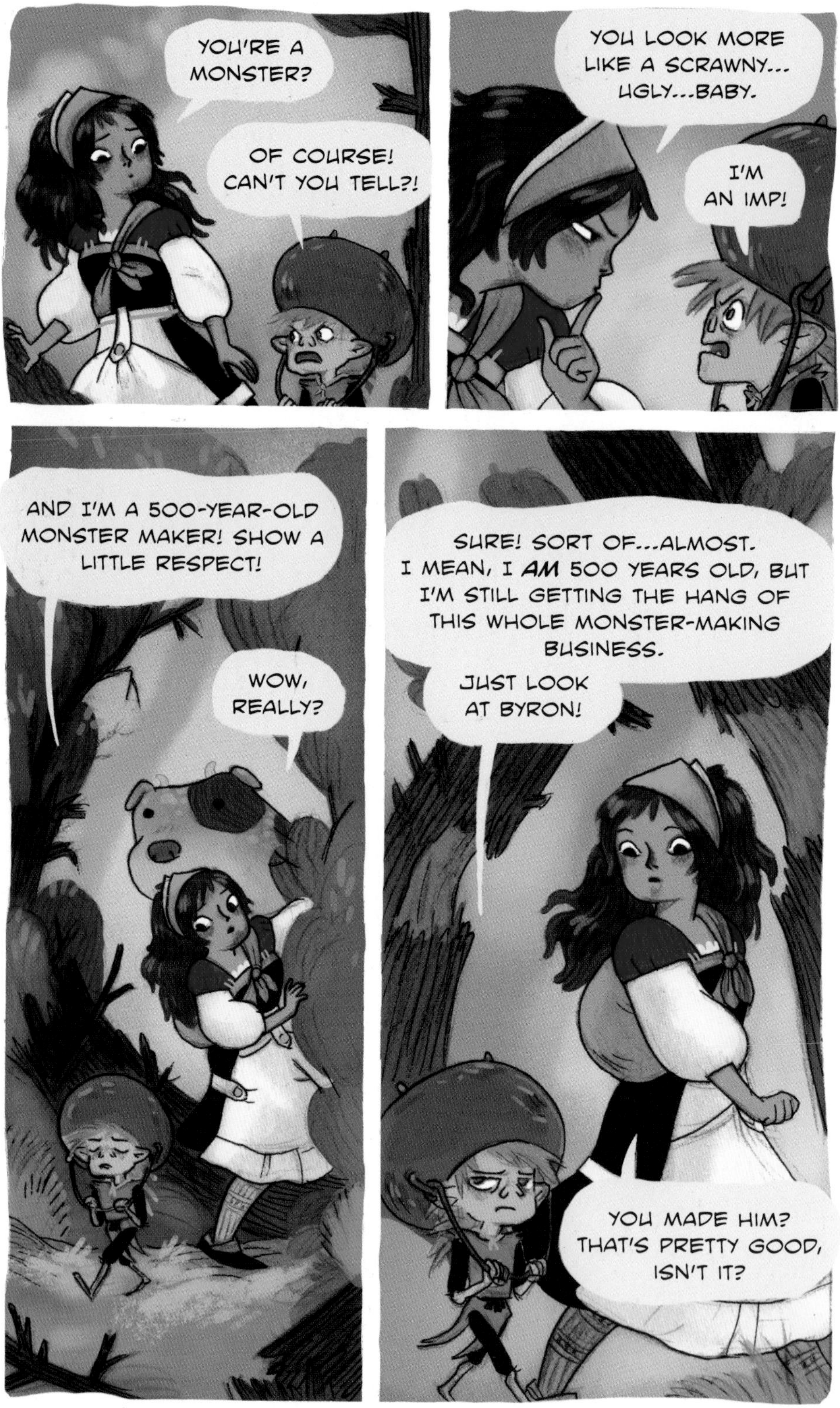
YOU'RE A MONSTER?
OF COURSE! CAN'T YOU TELL?!
YOU LOOK MORE LIKE A SCRAWNY... UGLY...BABY.
I'M AN IMP!
AND I'M A 500-YEAR-OLD MONSTER MAKER! SHOW A LITTLE RESPECT!
WOW, REALLY?
SURE! SORT OF...ALMOST. I MEAN, I **AM** 500 YEARS OLD, BUT I'M STILL GETTING THE HANG OF THIS WHOLE MONSTER-MAKING BUSINESS.
JUST LOOK AT BYRON!
YOU MADE HIM? THAT'S PRETTY GOOD, ISN'T IT?

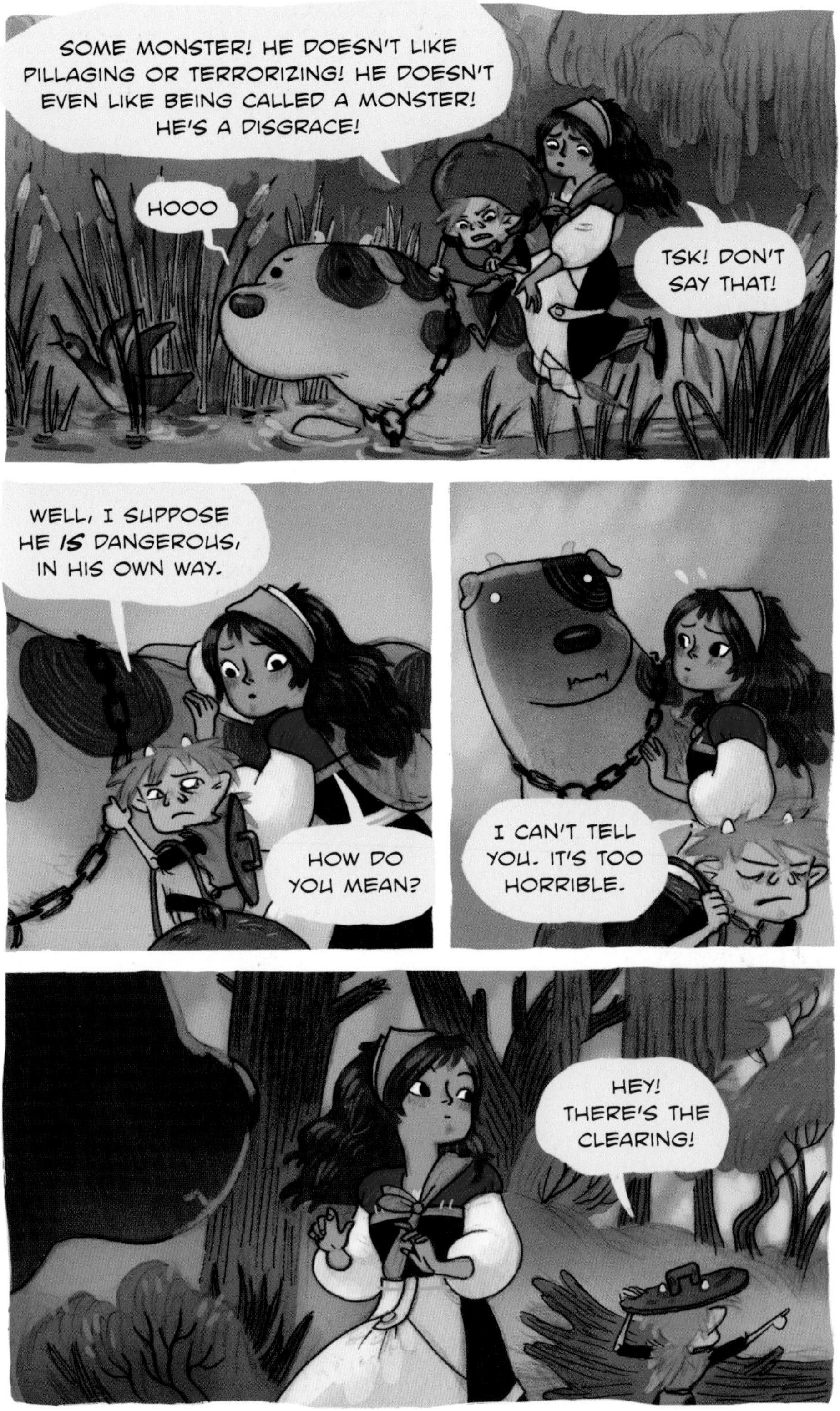
SOME MONSTER! HE DOESN'T LIKE PILLAGING OR TERRORIZING! HE DOESN'T EVEN LIKE BEING CALLED A MONSTER! HE'S A DISGRACE!
HOOO
TSK! DON'T SAY THAT!
WELL, I SUPPOSE HE *IS* DANGEROUS, IN HIS OWN WAY.
HOW DO YOU MEAN?
I CAN'T TELL YOU. IT'S TOO HORRIBLE.
HEY! THERE'S THE CLEARING!

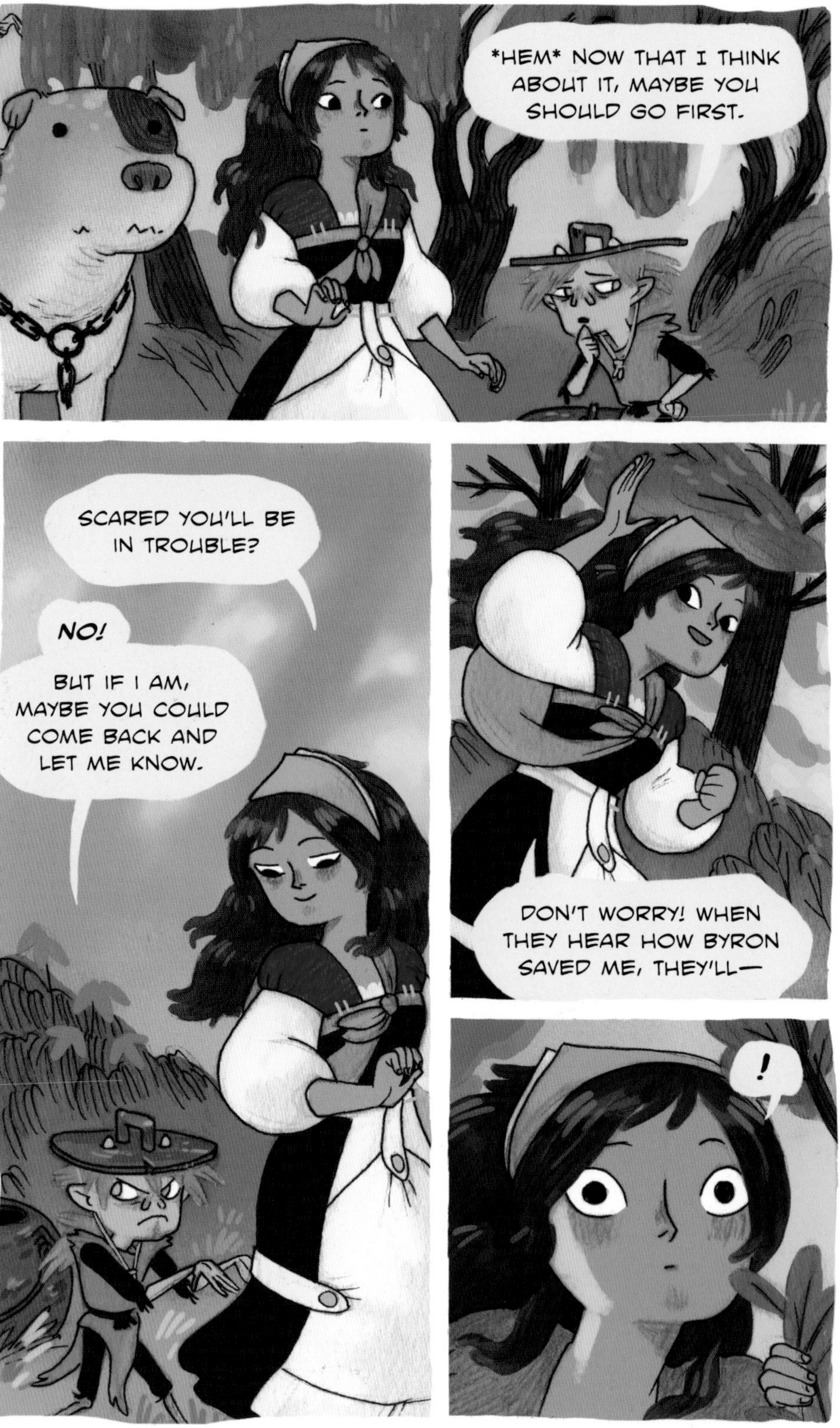
HEM NOW THAT I THINK ABOUT IT, MAYBE YOU SHOULD GO FIRST.
SCARED YOU'LL BE IN TROUBLE?
NO!
BUT IF I AM, MAYBE YOU COULD COME BACK AND LET ME KNOW.
DON'T WORRY! WHEN THEY HEAR HOW BYRON SAVED ME, THEY'LL—
!

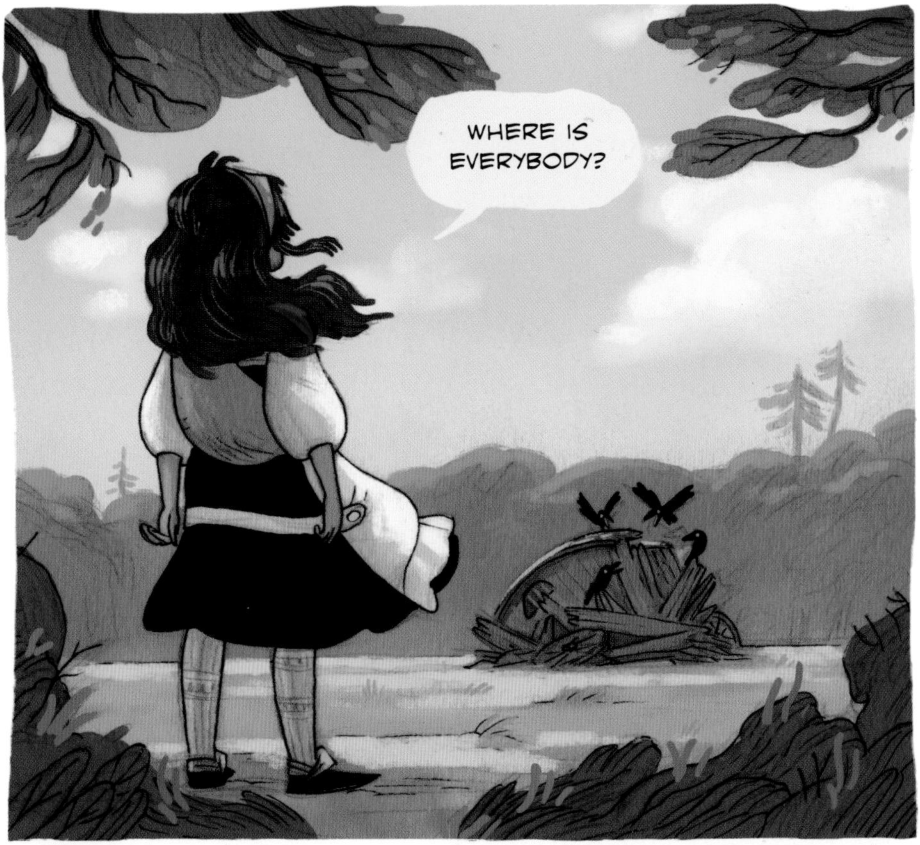
WHERE IS
EVERYBODY?

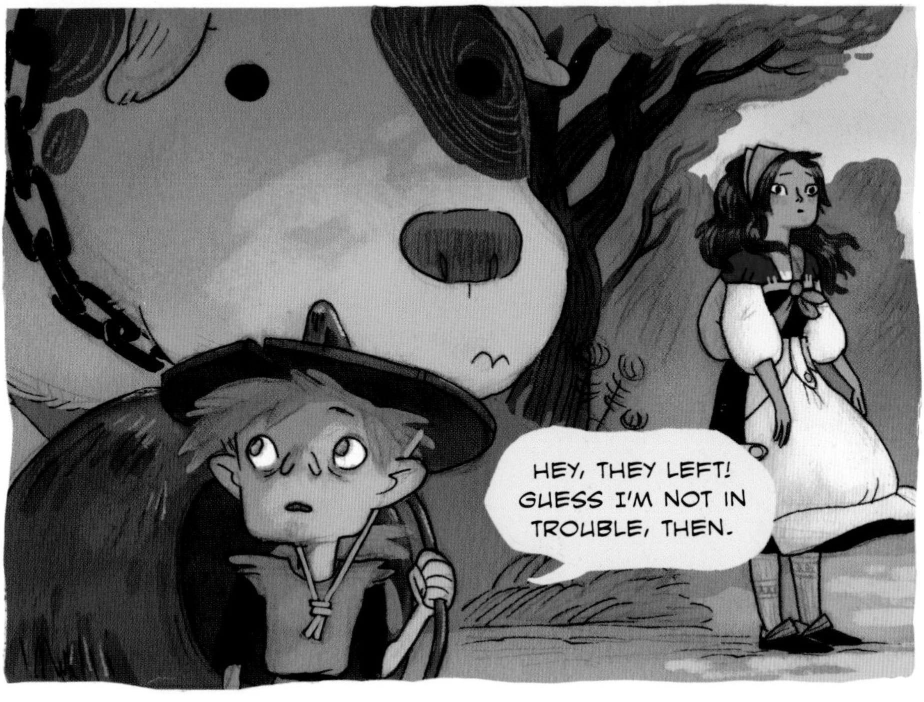
HEY, THEY LEFT!
GUESS I'M NOT IN
TROUBLE, THEN.

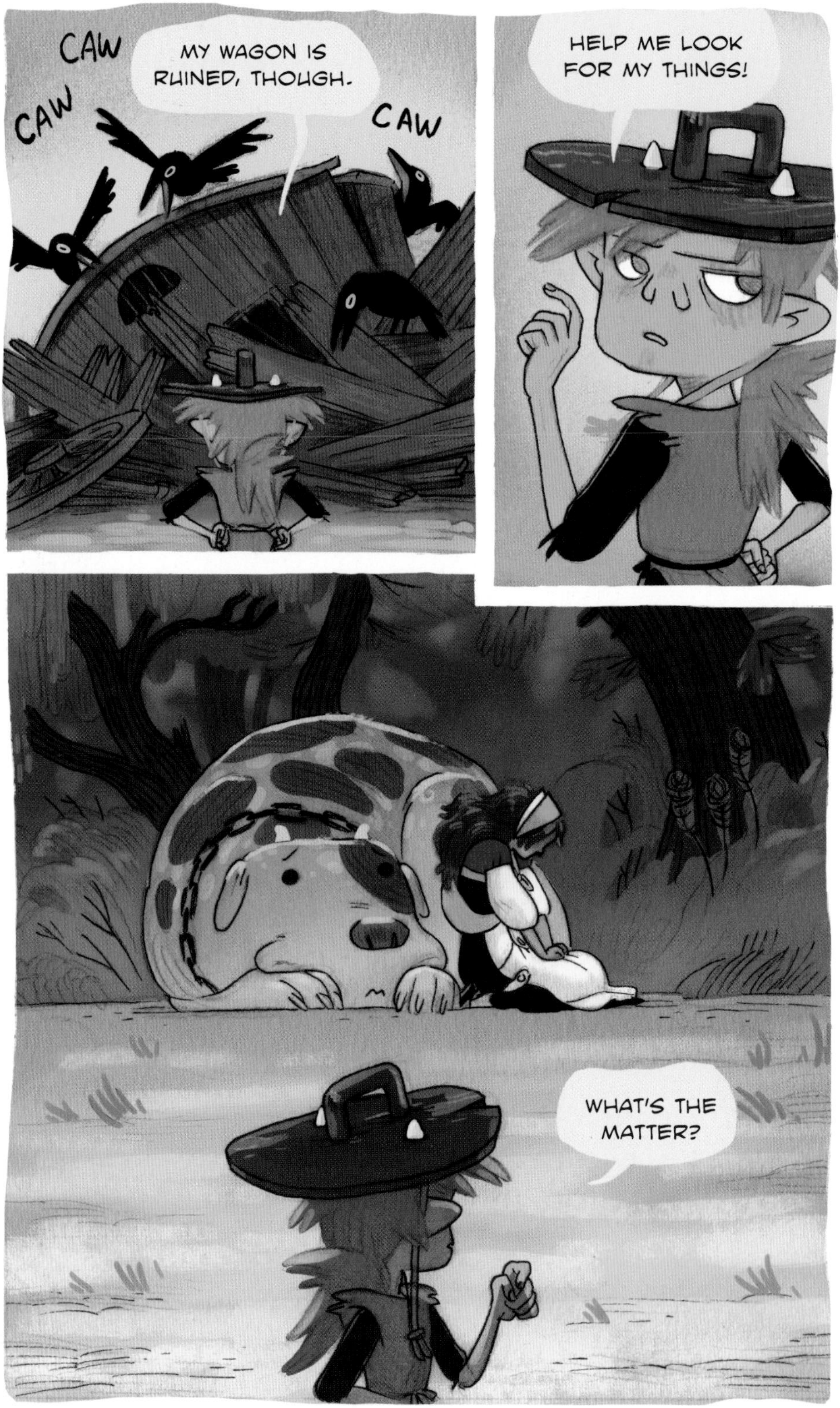
CAW
CAW
MY WAGON IS RUINED, THOUGH.
CAW
HELP ME LOOK FOR MY THINGS!
WHAT'S THE MATTER?

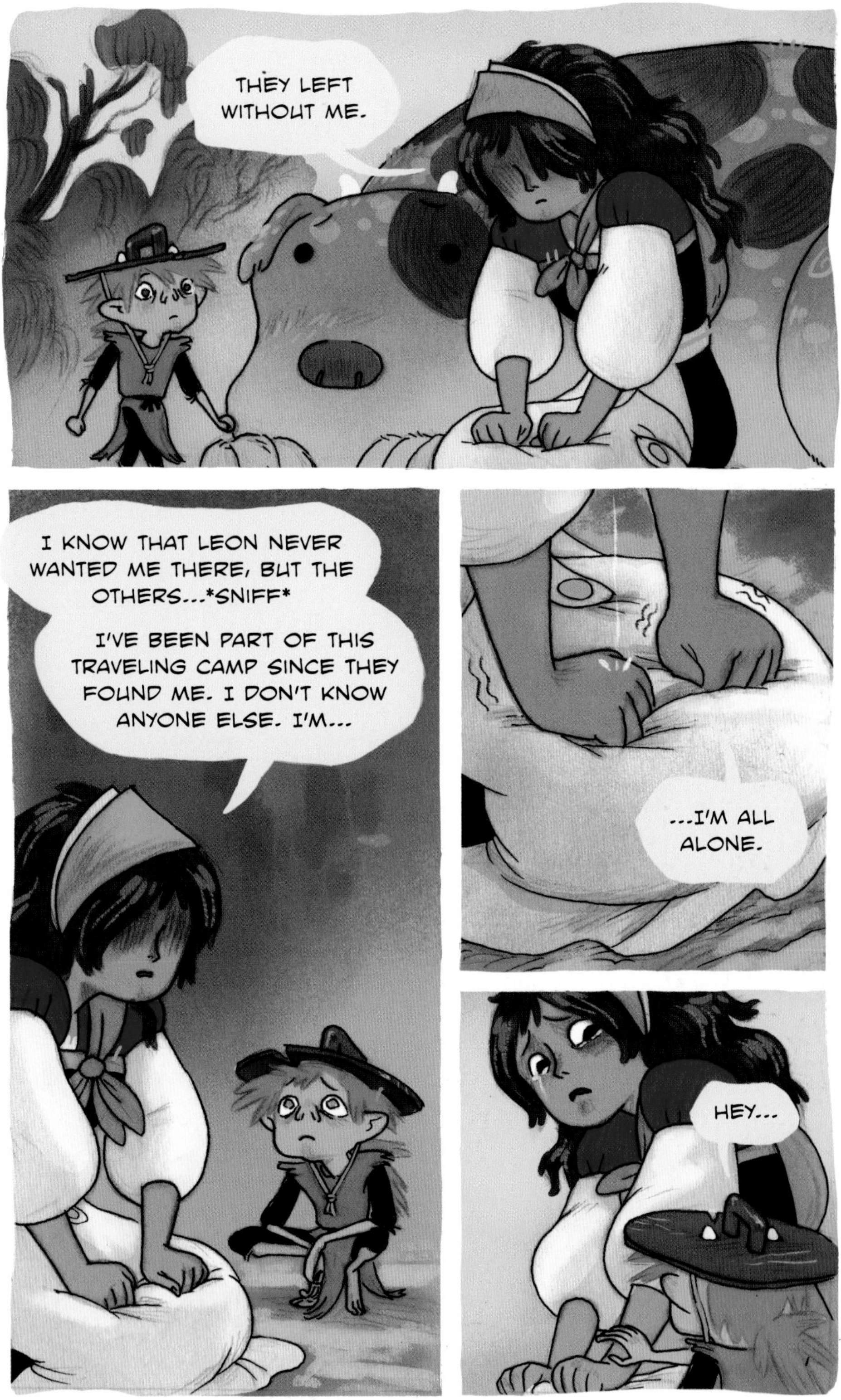
THEY LEFT WITHOUT ME.
I KNOW THAT LEON NEVER WANTED ME THERE, BUT THE OTHERS...*SNIFF*
I'VE BEEN PART OF THIS TRAVELING CAMP SINCE THEY FOUND ME. I DON'T KNOW ANYONE ELSE. I'M...
...I'M ALL ALONE.
HEY...

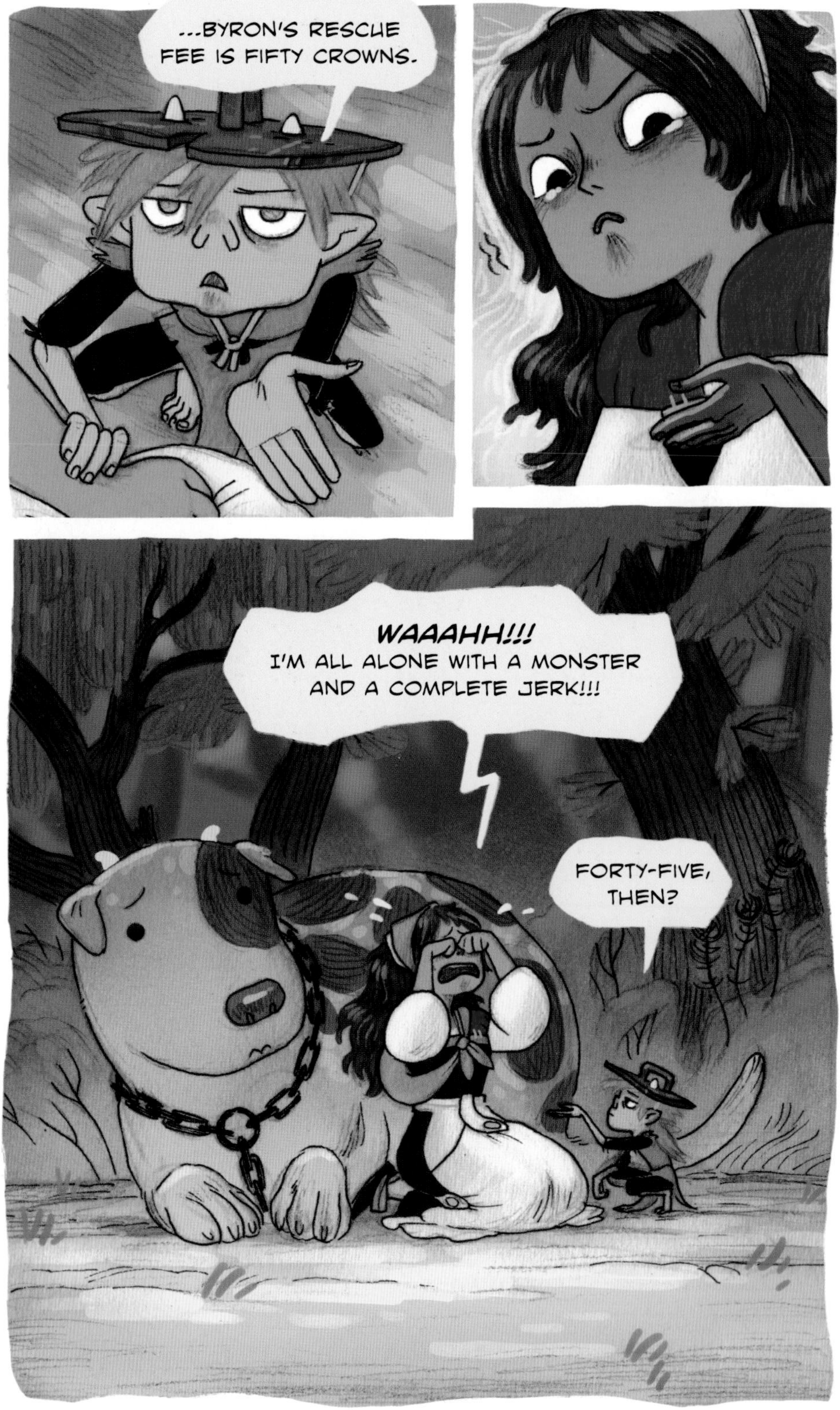
...BYRON'S RESCUE FEE IS FIFTY CROWNS.
WAAAHH!!! I'M ALL ALONE WITH A MONSTER AND A COMPLETE JERK!!!
FORTY-FIVE, THEN?

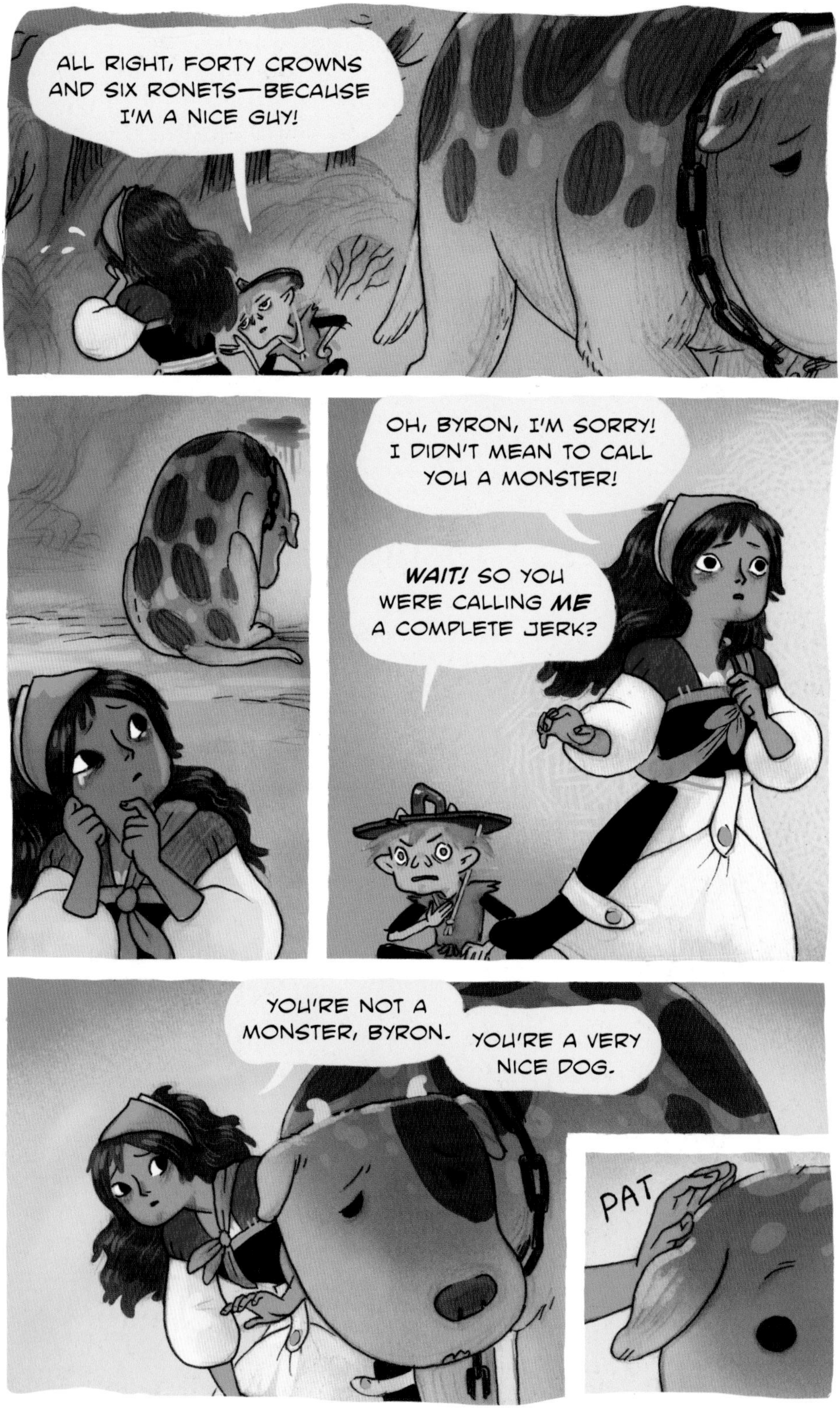
ALL RIGHT, FORTY CROWNS AND SIX RONETS—BECAUSE I'M A NICE GUY!
OH, BYRON, I'M SORRY! I DIDN'T MEAN TO CALL YOU A MONSTER!
WAIT! SO YOU WERE CALLING ME A COMPLETE JERK?
YOU'RE NOT A MONSTER, BYRON.
YOU'RE A VERY NICE DOG.
PAT

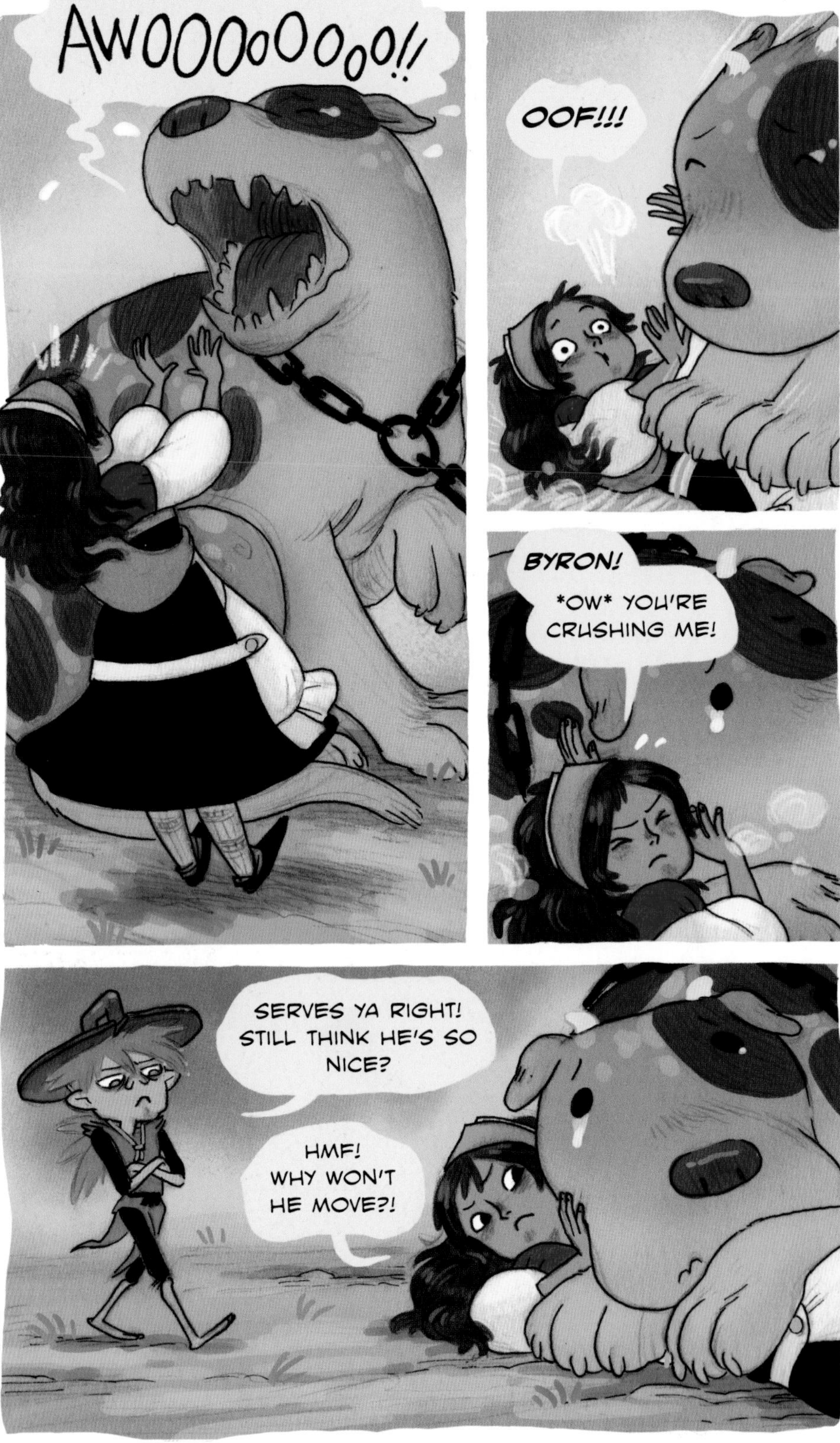
AWOOOOOOOO!!
OOF!!!
BYRON!
OW YOU'RE CRUSHING ME!
SERVES YA RIGHT! STILL THINK HE'S SO NICE?
HMF! WHY WON'T HE MOVE?!

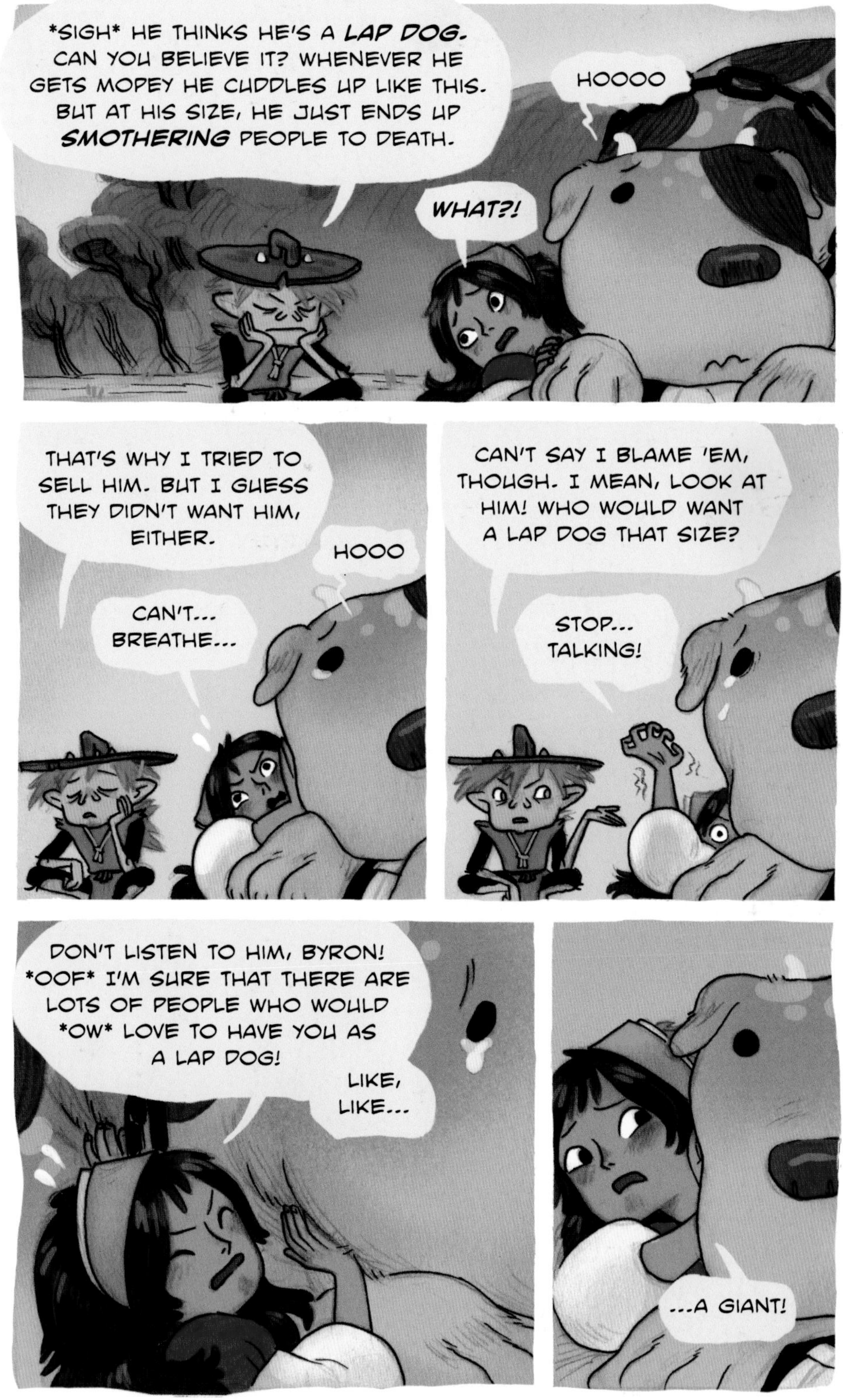
SIGH HE THINKS HE'S A LAP DOG. CAN YOU BELIEVE IT? WHENEVER HE GETS MOPEY HE CUDDLES UP LIKE THIS. BUT AT HIS SIZE, HE JUST ENDS UP SMOTHERING PEOPLE TO DEATH.
HOOOO
WHAT?!
THAT'S WHY I TRIED TO SELL HIM. BUT I GUESS THEY DIDN'T WANT HIM, EITHER.
HOOO
CAN'T... BREATHE...
CAN'T SAY I BLAME 'EM, THOUGH. I MEAN, LOOK AT HIM! WHO WOULD WANT A LAP DOG THAT SIZE?
STOP... TALKING!
DON'T LISTEN TO HIM, BYRON! *OOF* I'M SURE THAT THERE ARE LOTS OF PEOPLE WHO WOULD *OW* LOVE TO HAVE YOU AS A LAP DOG!
LIKE, LIKE...
...A GIANT!

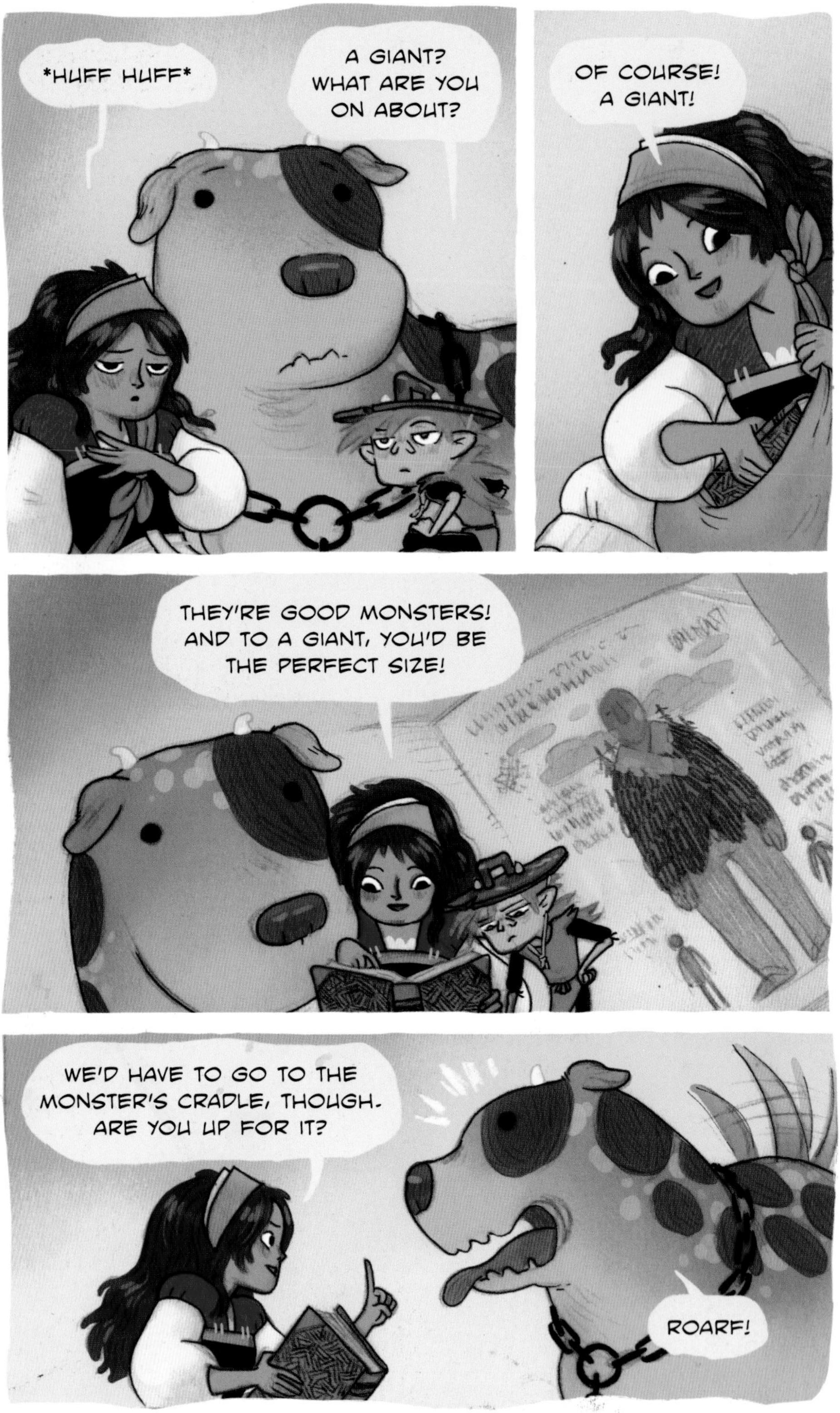
HUFF HUFF
A GIANT? WHAT ARE YOU ON ABOUT?
OF COURSE! A GIANT!
THEY'RE GOOD MONSTERS! AND TO A GIANT, YOU'D BE THE PERFECT SIZE!
WE'D HAVE TO GO TO THE MONSTER'S CRADLE, THOUGH. ARE YOU UP FOR IT?
ROARF!

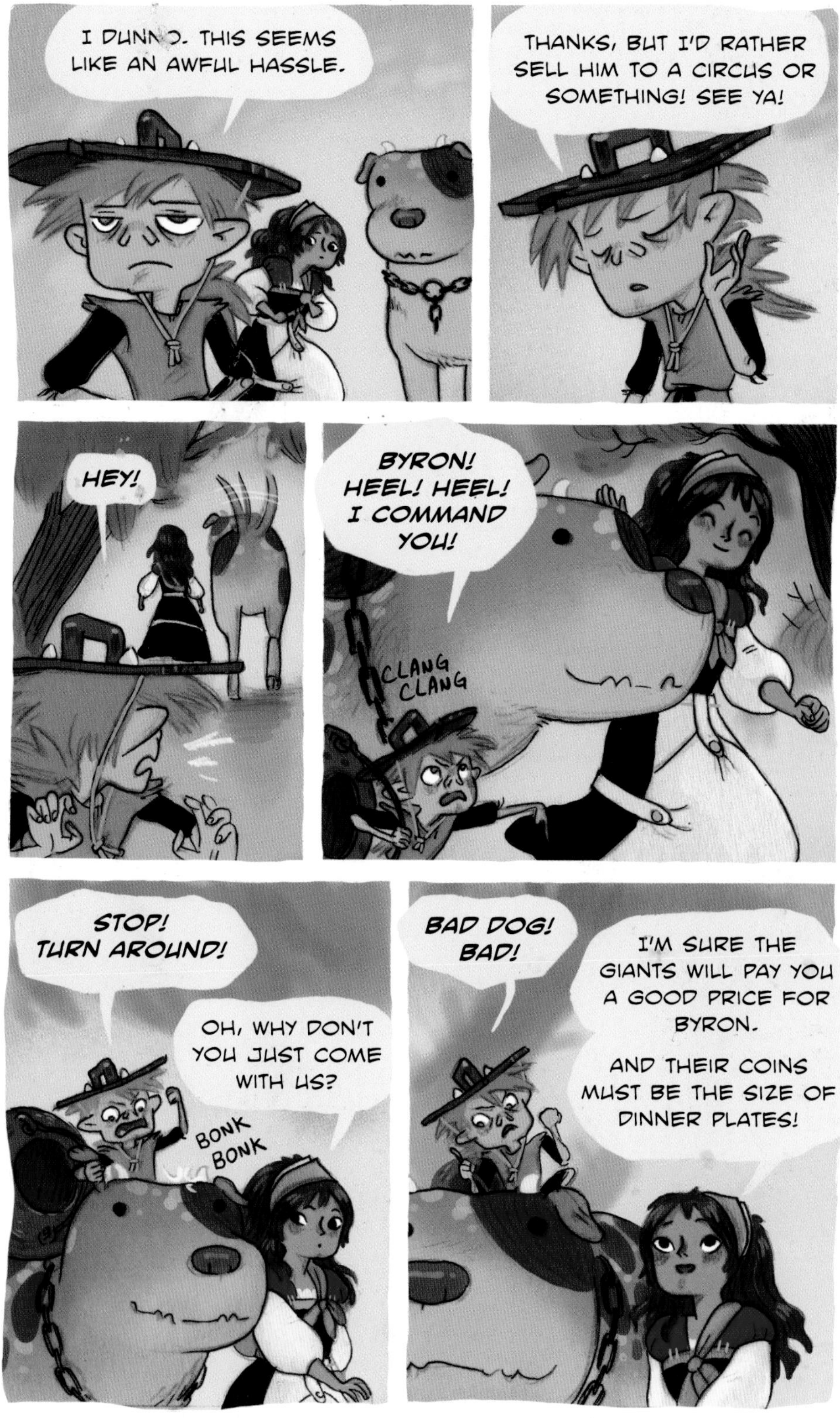

I DUNNO. THIS SEEMS LIKE AN AWFUL HASSLE.
THANKS, BUT I'D RATHER SELL HIM TO A CIRCUS OR SOMETHING! SEE YA!
HEY!
BYRON! HEEL! HEEL! I COMMAND YOU!
CLANG CLANG
STOP! TURN AROUND!
OH, WHY DON'T YOU JUST COME WITH US?
BONK BONK
BAD DOG! BAD!
I'M SURE THE GIANTS WILL PAY YOU A GOOD PRICE FOR BYRON.
AND THEIR COINS MUST BE THE SIZE OF DINNER PLATES!

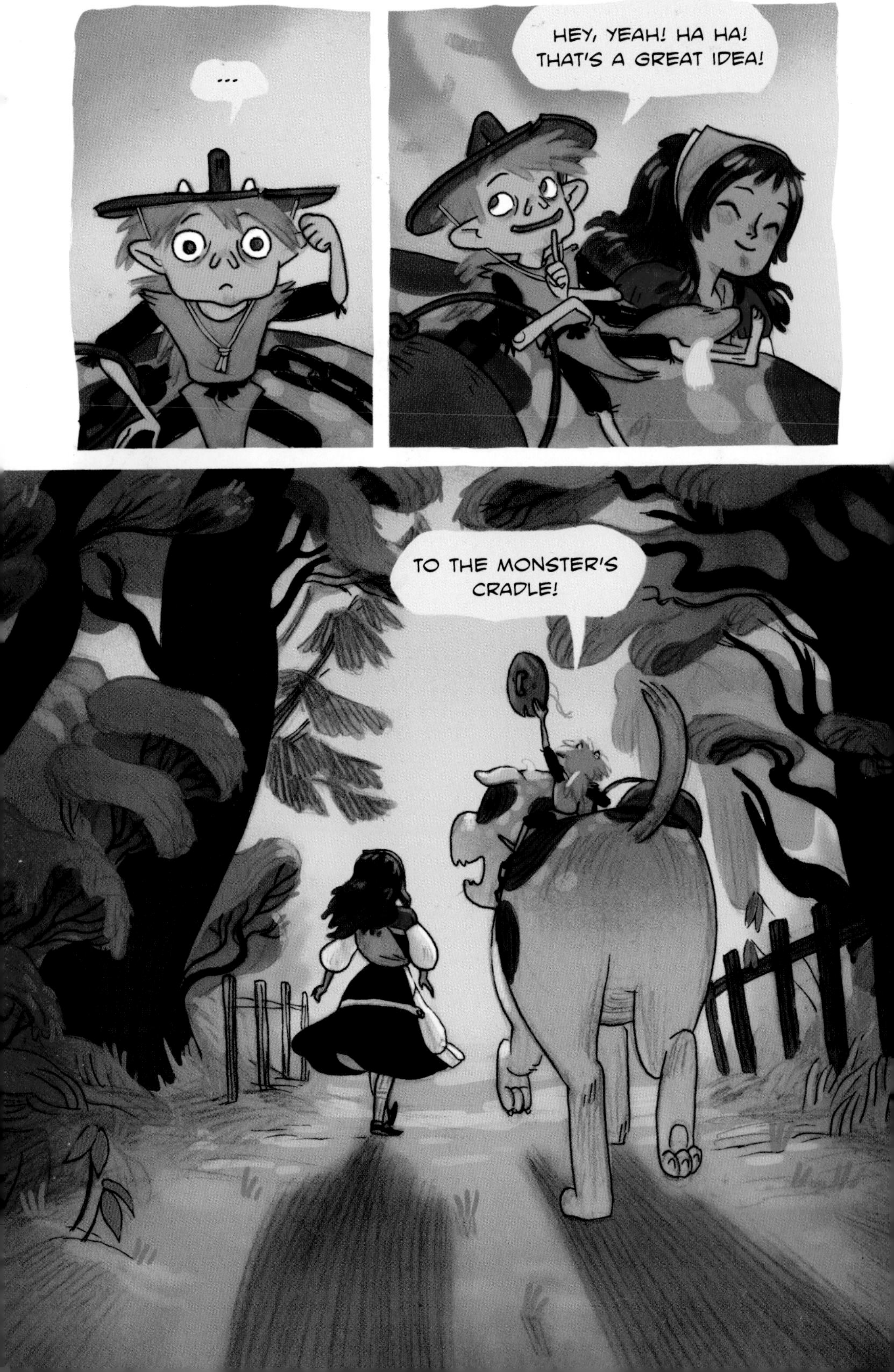
...
HEY, YEAH! HA HA! THAT'S A GREAT IDEA!
TO THE MONSTER'S CRADLE!

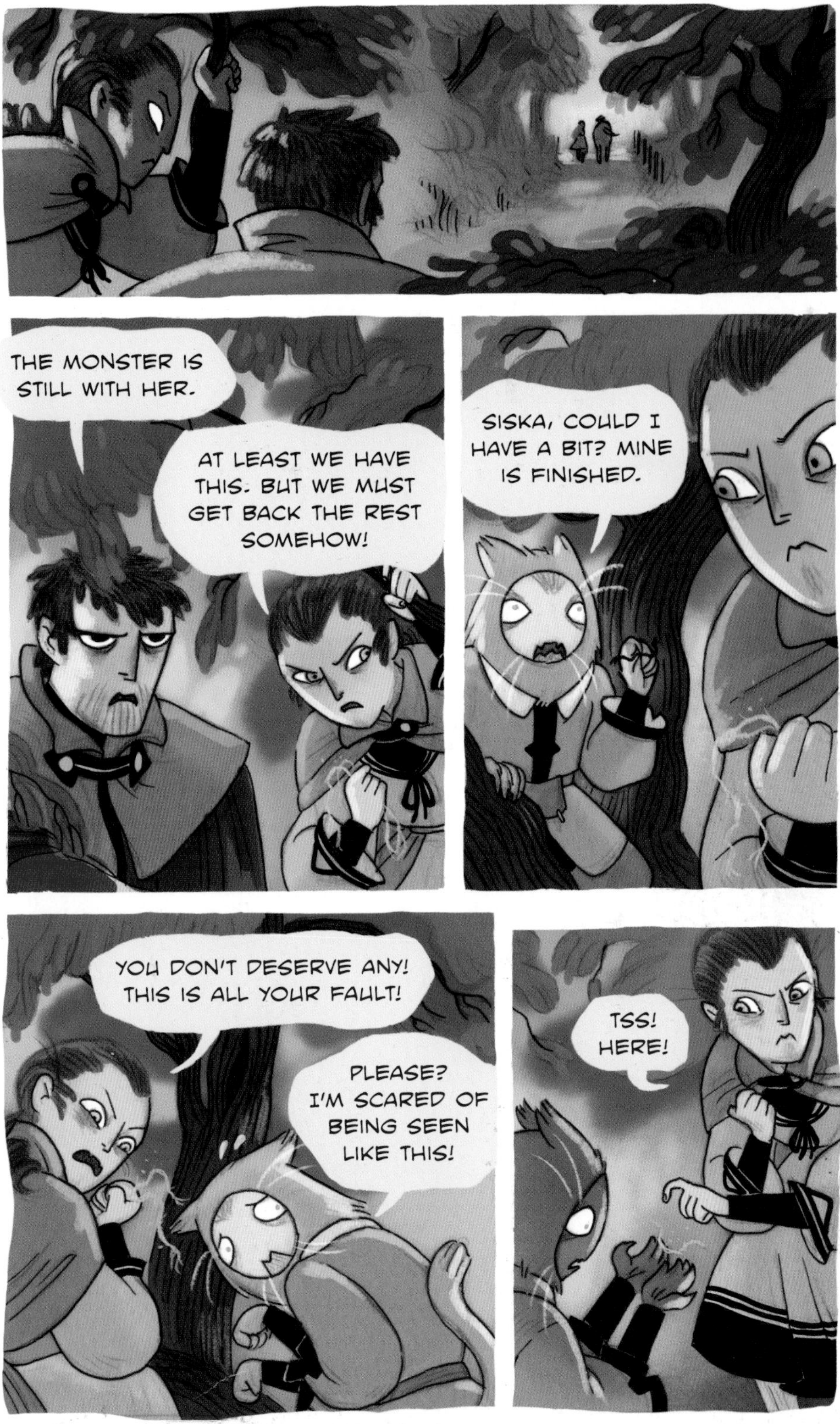
THE MONSTER IS STILL WITH HER.
AT LEAST WE HAVE THIS. BUT WE MUST GET BACK THE REST SOMEHOW!
SISKA, COULD I HAVE A BIT? MINE IS FINISHED.
YOU DON'T DESERVE ANY! THIS IS ALL YOUR FAULT!
PLEASE? I'M SCARED OF BEING SEEN LIKE THIS!
TSS! HERE!

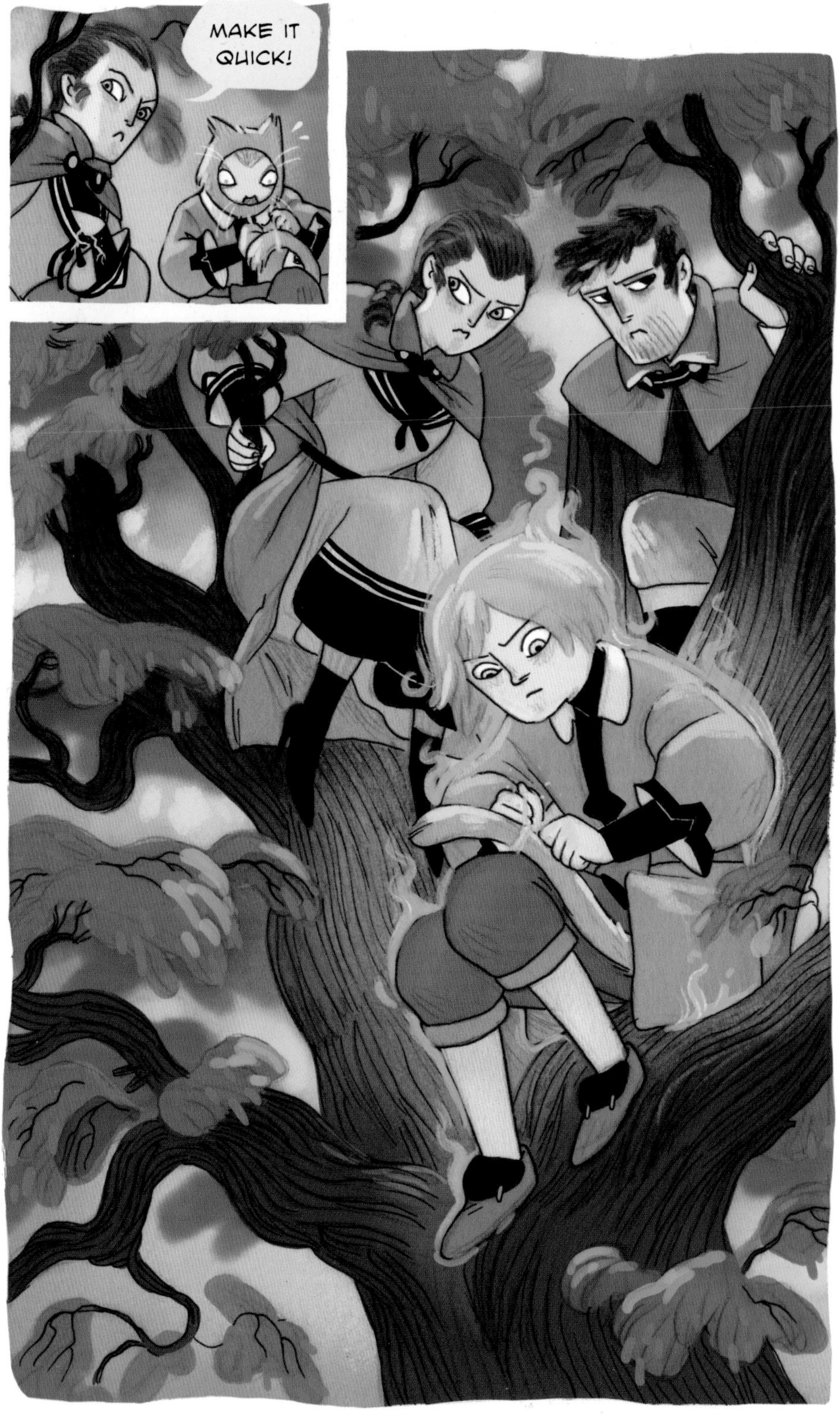
MAKE IT QUICK!

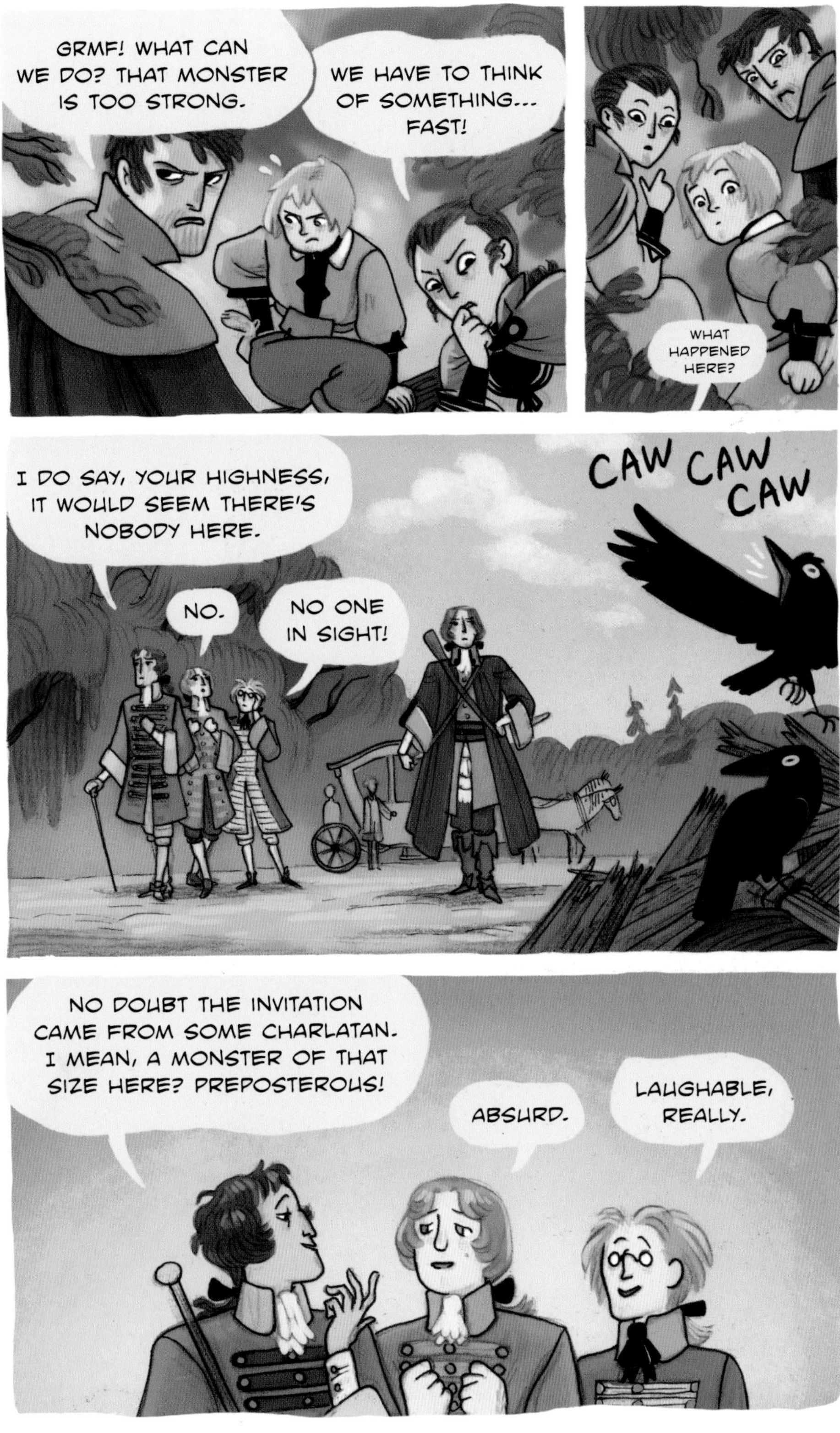
GRMF! WHAT CAN WE DO? THAT MONSTER IS TOO STRONG.
WE HAVE TO THINK OF SOMETHING... FAST!
WHAT HAPPENED HERE?
I DO SAY, YOUR HIGHNESS, IT WOULD SEEM THERE'S NOBODY HERE.
NO.
NO ONE IN SIGHT!
CAW CAW CAW CAW
NO DOUBT THE INVITATION CAME FROM SOME CHARLATAN. I MEAN, A MONSTER OF THAT SIZE HERE? PREPOSTEROUS!
ABSURD.
LAUGHABLE, REALLY.

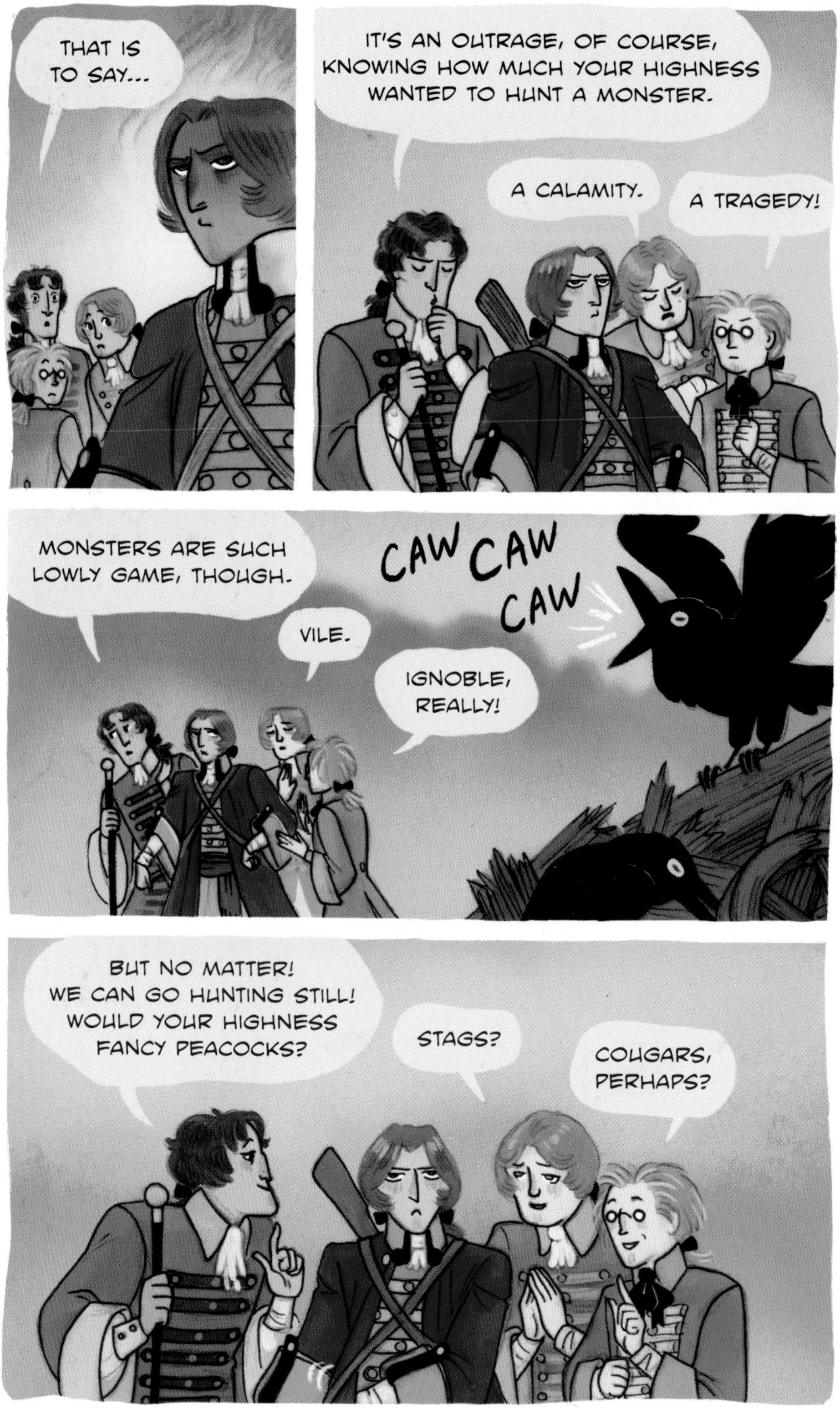
THAT IS TO SAY...
IT'S AN OUTRAGE, OF COURSE, KNOWING HOW MUCH YOUR HIGHNESS WANTED TO HUNT A MONSTER.
A CALAMITY.
A TRAGEDY!
MONSTERS ARE SUCH LOWLY GAME, THOUGH.
VILE.
IGNOBLE, REALLY!
CAW CAW CAW
BUT NO MATTER! WE CAN GO HUNTING STILL! WOULD YOUR HIGHNESS FANCY PEACOCKS?
STAGS?
COUGARS, PERHAPS?

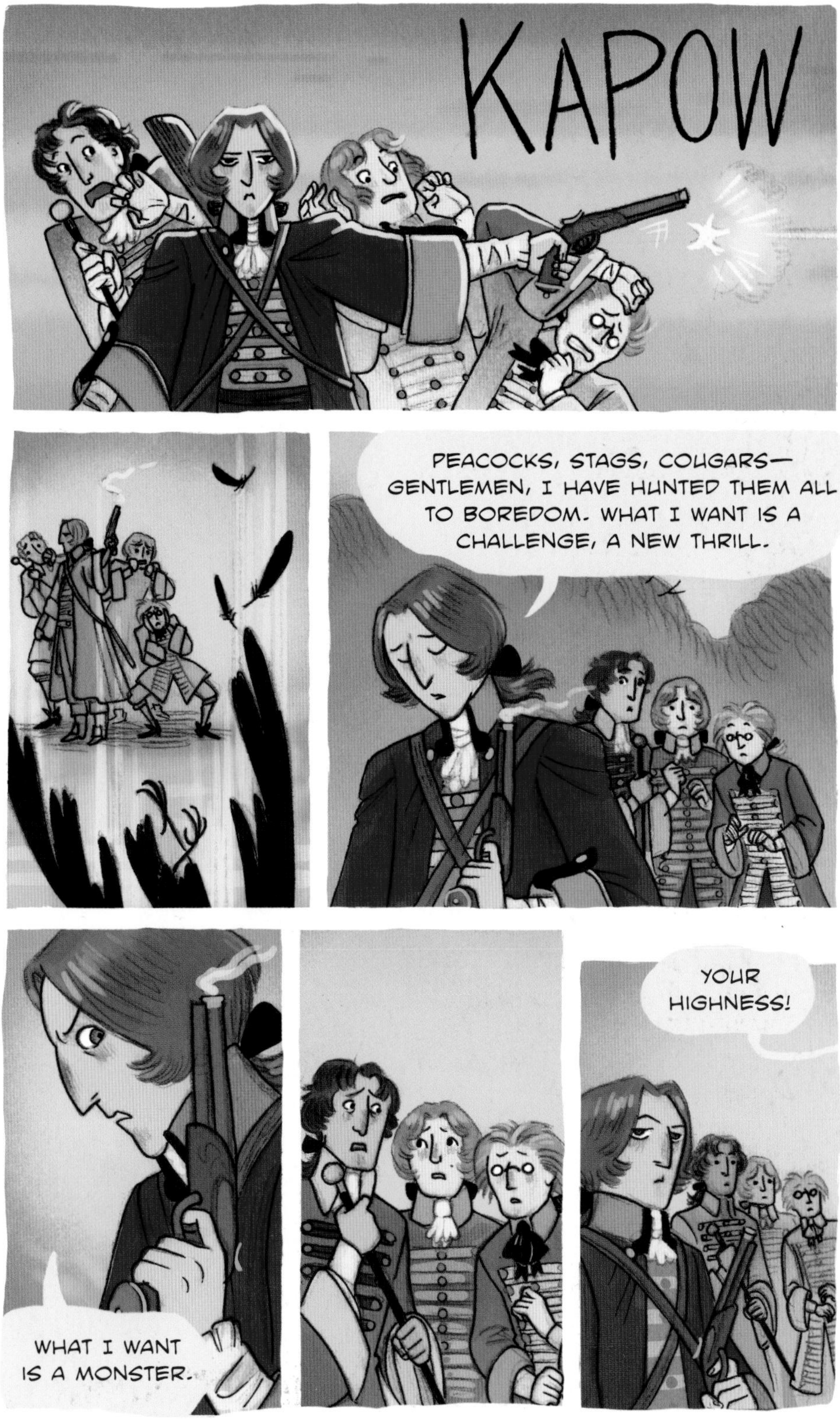
KAPOW
PEACOCKS, STAGS, COUGARS—GENTLEMEN, I HAVE HUNTED THEM ALL TO BOREDOM. WHAT I WANT IS A CHALLENGE, A NEW THRILL.
WHAT I WANT IS A MONSTER.
YOUR HIGHNESS!

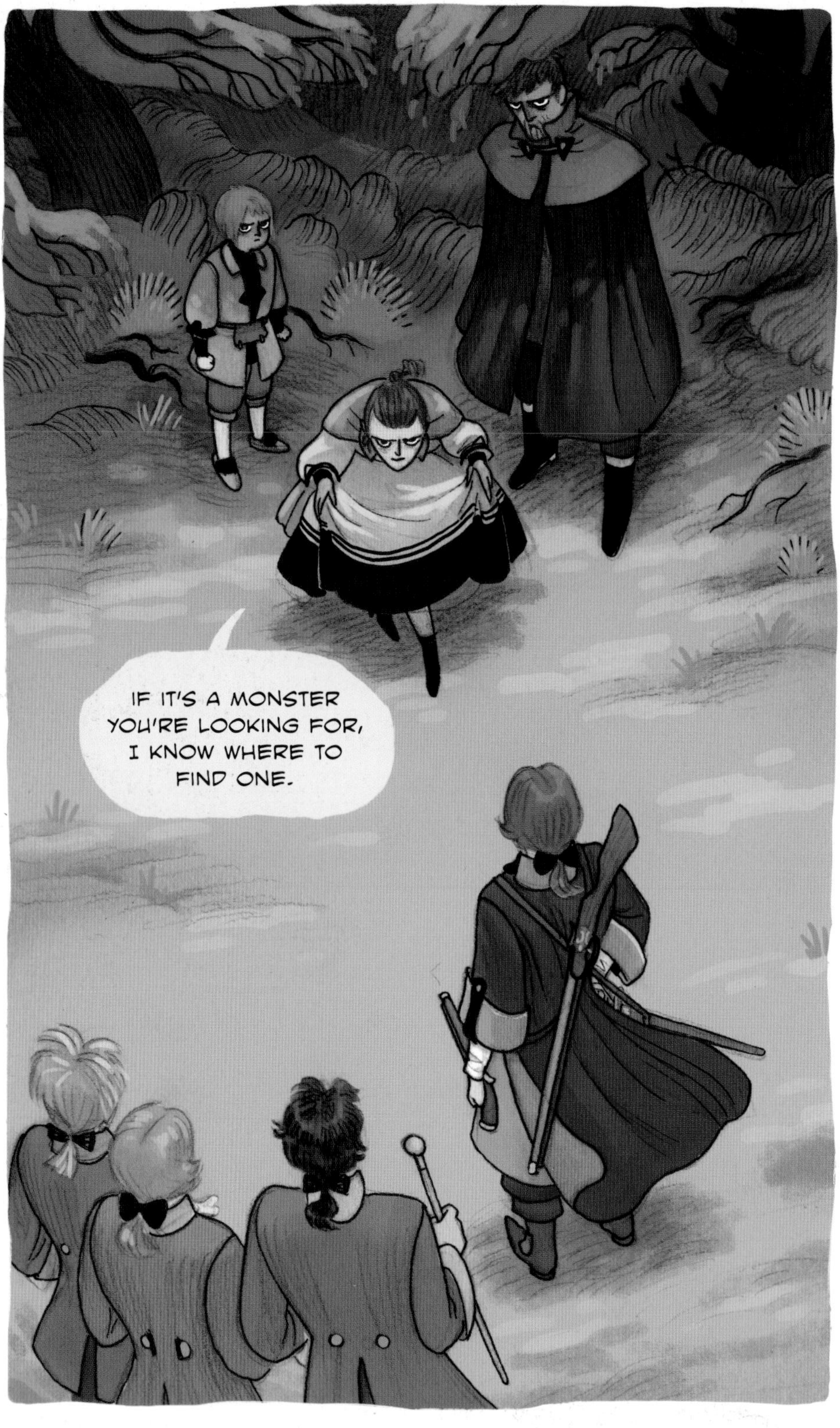
IF IT'S A MONSTER YOU'RE LOOKING FOR, I KNOW WHERE TO FIND ONE.

Suri's story contines in

CAT'S CRADLE
THE MOLE KING'S LAIR
JO RIOUX

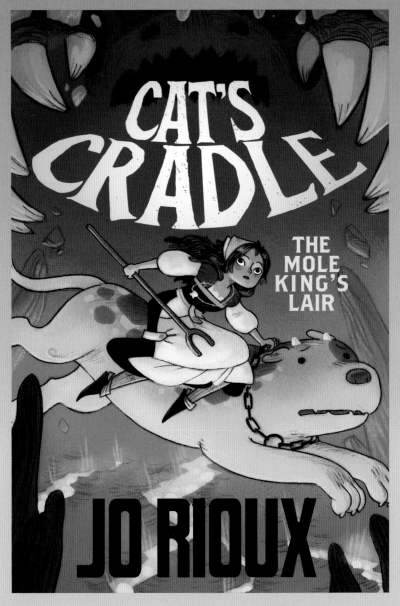

EXCERPTS FROM SURI'S JOURNAL

JACKALOPE

TYPE: PLANT MONSTER
DOMAIN: GARDENS, ORCHARDS
NATURE: BOTHERSOME

THEY USE THEIR HORNS TO FEED AND THEIR GIANT MOUTHS TO BITE UNSUSPECTING TOES.

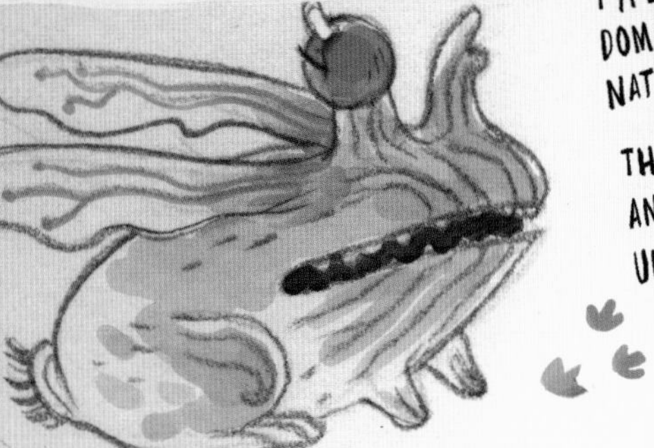

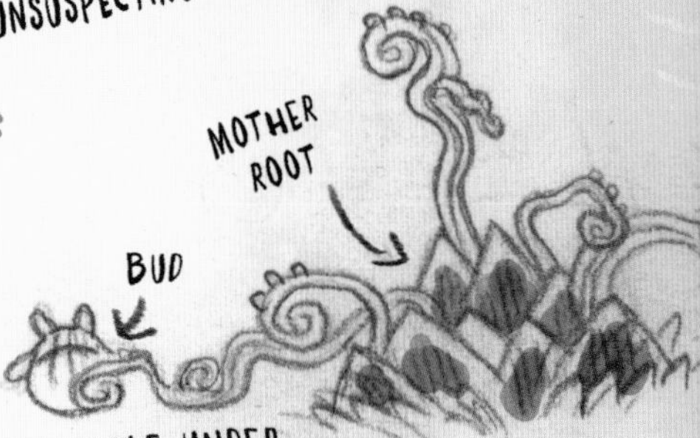
MOTHER ROOT
BUD

JACKALOPES BUD UNDERGROUND FROM A MOTHER ROOT.

TO FIND THE MOTHER ROOT, LEAVE A WINTER APPLE UNDER A BUCKET ON THE GROUND. WHEN THE BUDDING JACKALOPE SPEARS IT, FOLLOW THE ROOT AND DIG OUT THE MOTHER.

BASILISK

TYPE: ANIMAL MONSTER
DOMAIN: ROOFTOPS, SPIRES
NATURE: EVIL

FAIRLY COMMON, ESPECIALLY IN THE SOUTH OF SURN.

BASILISKS SEEK HIGH PLACES, WHERE THEY LIKE TO STARE AT THE SUN. THEY WILL PARALYZE YOU WITH A STARE AND CLIMB ON YOUR HEAD IF YOU'RE THE HIGHEST THING AROUND!

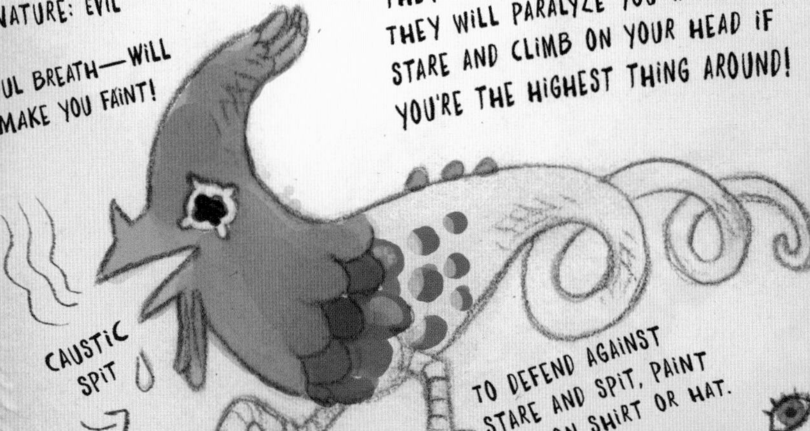
AWFUL BREATH—WILL MAKE YOU FAINT!
CAUSTIC SPIT

TO DEFEND AGAINST STARE AND SPIT, PAINT EYES ON SHIRT OR HAT.

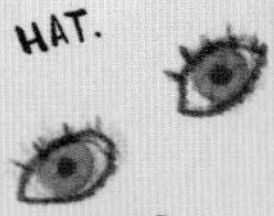

CAN LIVE A HUNDRED YEARS AND A DAY, AFTER WHICH THEY LOSE THEIR WATTLE AND TURN TO STONE.

JACKALOPE JAM

- 2 POUNDS OF JACKALOPE EARS ✱
- 5 PINCHES OF ORANGE RIND
- 3 OZ OF ORANGE JUICE
- 14 OZ OF SUGAR
- 4 OZ OF WATER

BOIL EVERYTHING OVER A LOW FIRE UNTIL THICK

✱ USE RHUBARB IF JACKALOPE ISN'T IN SEASON.

REMOVE VEINS ↘

CAITSITH (PRONOUNCED KATE-SITH OR KET-SHEE)

TYPE: SHAPESHIFTER
DOMAIN: AMONG HUMANS
NATURE: EVIL

RARE, THOUGH NO ONE KNOWS THEIR TRUE NUMBERS. MORE COMMON UP NORTH, NEAR THE MONSTER'S CRADLE. THEY CAN APPEAR PERFECTLY HUMAN EXCEPT FOR THEIR TAILS.

THEY LIKE THE NIGHT.

VERY DECEITFUL. THEY LIKE TO STEAL FROM AND TRICK HUMANS. IT'S SAID THEY EVEN LIKE TO EAT HUMAN FLESH!

I COPIED THIS FROM AN OLD WOODCUT. THE PANTS ARE KIND OF FUNNY!

LESHii

TYPE: PLANT MONSTER
DOMAIN: GARDENS, FIELDS
NATURE: BOTHERSOME/BENIGN

VERY COMMON. THEIR STICKY TENDRILS CAN CHOKE PLANTS AND JAM FARM EQUIPMENT.

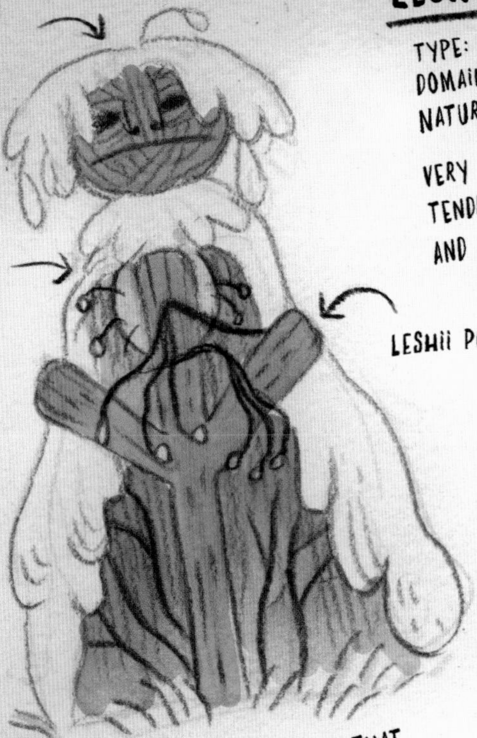
FALSE HEAD
LESHii HEART
LESHii POST

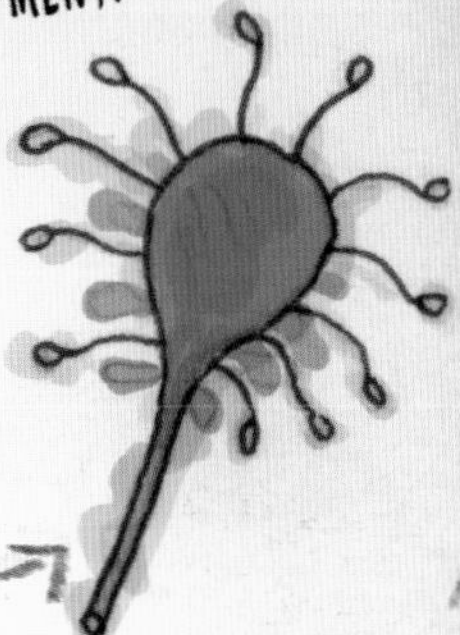
LESHii LEAF
STICKY SAP SMUDGE!

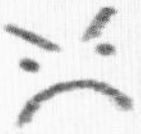

THEY GROW A FALSE "HEAD" THAT OFTEN RESEMBLES THE OWNER OF THE GARDEN THEY OCCUPY.

TO DESTROY, CUT OFF ALL TENDRILS UNTIL YOU REACH THE HEART. ALTERNATIVELY, WILL STOP SPREADING IF THE FALSE HEAD IS CUT OFF EVERY YEAR.

BETTER IDEA!

LESHii CAN EVEN BE HELPFUL! SOME FARMERS PLANT SPECIAL POSTS JUST FOR LESHii, AS THEY HELP TO KEEP JACKALOPES AWAY.

LESHii ANTI-ITCH SALVE

SCRAPE THE SAP OFF THE LESHii LEAVES AND MIX WITH A FEW DROPS OF WALNUT OIL. GOOD FOR JACKALOPE BITES!

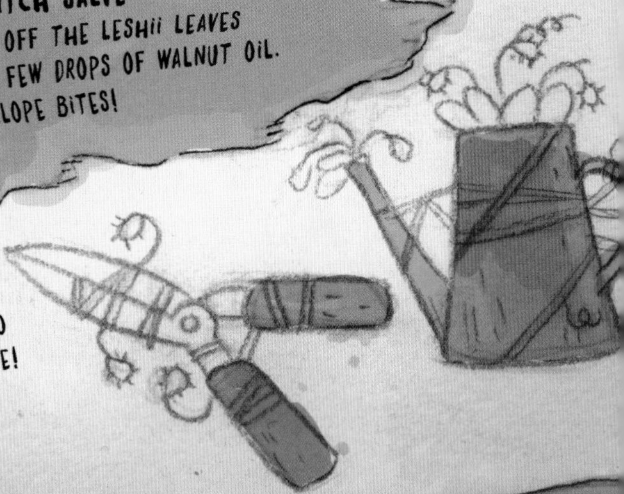
HARD TO DETANGLE!

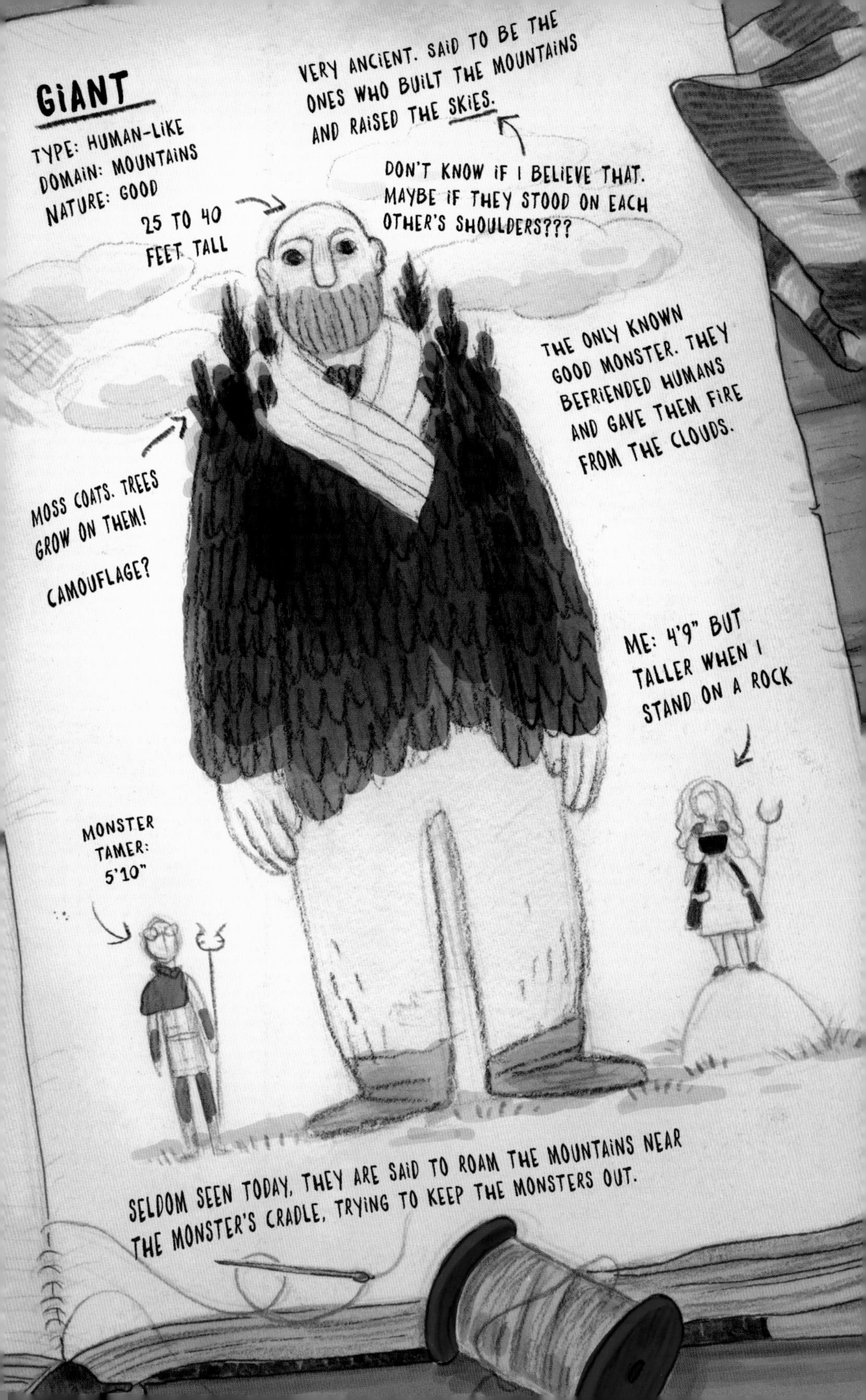
GIANT
TYPE: HUMAN-LIKE
DOMAIN: MOUNTAINS
NATURE: GOOD
VERY ANCIENT. SAID TO BE THE ONES WHO BUILT THE MOUNTAINS AND RAISED THE SKIES.
DON'T KNOW IF I BELIEVE THAT. MAYBE IF THEY STOOD ON EACH OTHER'S SHOULDERS???
25 TO 40 FEET TALL
THE ONLY KNOWN GOOD MONSTER. THEY BEFRIENDED HUMANS AND GAVE THEM FIRE FROM THE CLOUDS.
MOSS COATS. TREES GROW ON THEM!
CAMOUFLAGE?
ME: 4'9" BUT TALLER WHEN I STAND ON A ROCK
MONSTER TAMER: 5'10"
SELDOM SEEN TODAY, THEY ARE SAID TO ROAM THE MOUNTAINS NEAR THE MONSTER'S CRADLE, TRYING TO KEEP THE MONSTERS OUT.

First Second

Published by First Second
First Second is an imprint of Roaring Brook Press,
a division of Holtzbrinck Publishing Holdings Limited Partnership
120 Broadway, New York, NY 10271
firstsecondbooks.com
mackids.com

Library of Congress Control Number: 2021923932

A previous version of *Cat's Cradle: The Golden Twine* was published in 2012 by Kids Can Press.
This new edition from First Second was reimagined and completely redrawn by the author.

Our books may be purchased in bulk for promotional, educational, or business use.
Please contact your local bookseller or the Macmillan Corporate and Premium Sales Department
at (800) 221-7945 ext. 5442 or by email at MacmillanSpecialMarkets@macmillan.com.

First edition, 2022
Edited by Mark Siegel with help from Robyn Chapman
Cover design by Kirk Benshoff
Interior book design by Molly Johanson

Penciled with Prismacolor Col-Erase in terra cotta and black.
Inked with Prismacolor Premier fine line marker in black.
Colored digitally with Photoshop.

Printed in June 2022 in China by 1010 Printing
International Limited, Kwun Tong, Hong Kong

ISBN 978-1-250-62536-6 (paperback)
10 9 8 7 6 5 4 3 2 1

ISBN 978-1-250-62535-9 (hardcover)
10 9 8 7 6 5 4 3 2 1

Don't miss your next favorite
book from First Second!
For the latest updates go to
firstsecondnewsletter.com and
sign up for our enewsletter.